DELIVERY

PETER JONES

Crown Publishers, Inc.
New York

Grateful acknowledgment is made to Random House, Inc., and Heinemann Educational for permission to reprint an excerpt from *A Man for All Seasons* by Robert Bolt. Copyright © 1960, 1962 by Robert Bolt.

Published by Crown Publishers, Inc., 201 East 50th Street, New York, New York 10022. Member of the Crown Publishing Group.

Manufactured in the United States of America

Book design by Nancy Kenmore

Library of Congress Cataloging-in-Publication Data

Jones, Peter (Peter W. J.)
Delivery / Peter Jones.
I. Title.
PS3560.05242D45 1990 90-2189
813′.54—dc20 CIP

ISBN 0-517-57780-1

10 9 8 7 6 5 4 3 2 1

First Edition

To all my friends
for their help and encouragement,
but especially to
Geoff for his knowledge and
Rodney for his safe haven for the rewrites

FOR ALISON

I

VERRE

It was a quiet house on a quiet street in a small town in Germany: two stories with gabled ends, cream trim, and thick, brick walls. The yard was neatly kept in an unfocused way: weedy marigolds around the foundation and slightly patchy grass. It was September and there was a tinge of yellow in the leaves of the two linden trees flanking the entrance gate. The wall surrounding the property was eight feet high, topped by sharp slate shards.

An ordinary sort of couple lived upstairs: she, a brown-haired housewife; he, a blond tradesman who, it was said, worked the night shift. They seemed a quiet pair, but perhaps it was just the thick, brick walls.

The keepers of this ordinary house called it a Revolutionary Training Complex, but Flight Officer Lieutenant John Tyson Verre would have thought that a grand name for what seemed to be a frightening interrogation center. His opinion had some weight; he had been here for three weeks, starting four days after his plane was shot down over the Lebanese city of Tyre.

He'd been flying strike-assessment missions off the USS *John F. Kennedy,* following up A-6 fighter-bombers after they'd made their runs over Lebanon. It was loiter, wait till the strike had cleared, and then make a quick pass with the cameras in the recon pod. There was no credible opposition, and it was as close to a nine-to-five job as you could get in an F-14 at five hundred knots; Verre had been here just over a month.

The President had warned that the next terrorist attack on the United States would bring swift retaliation to "those who had not heard God's call for peace among men." Perhaps no one in this part of the world had listened; maybe they didn't know the President had built a political career on doing just what he said he was going to do. Who knows? But in Washington at the end of July, a passing mother and child had been killed by a bomb planted at a State Department gate. The Islamic Action League had claimed responsibility; following the call of God, they said.

The CIA had identified the League as a Lebanon-based group, and two weeks later Verre and his fellow pilots had been shipped down the Med to pound the living shit out of any village that might house IAL supporters. Jack had seen this as something more neutral: a chance to finally do what he had been trained for.

He was a handsome guy: six feet tall with a wide-shouldered, athlete's build, sandy brown hair, and eyes of the same color. But it wasn't his good looks that had brought him here to Lebanon; rather, his truly great hand-eye coordination. It was this gift that had made him the hero of his Ohio high-school baseball team, made him an all-American college shortstop, gotten him into the Naval Aviation School at Pensacola; he had always been the star.

At the fighter school, he had discovered there were others in this world even more gifted than he. That's why he was flying the post-strike assessment rather than the strikes themselves. Though he had never been one to join the crowd, the experience had made him a bit more standoffish. He still had his midwestern good looks, which gave him his pilot's nickname.

It was quiet in the corridors far below the flight deck. Jack leaned against the wall, waiting for the fighter briefing to let out, the white metal chilly under his back; the air-conditioning was set to take care of the fierce heat that would come later in the day.

A muted burst of laughter came from the briefing room; the

fighter-bomber pilots were sitting around joking with each other before their flight was called. Jack liked to get away by himself before a mission; the briefing had been routine, and he thought he knew what to expect. It had been the same before baseball games in college: listen to the coach's pep talk, then find a quiet corner for a few minutes before the contest started. Just the unobtrusive sounds from the briefing room and his own thoughts: go over in your mind what you plan to do; be clear on your goals.

He looked up as someone stepped into the corridor. "Hey, White Bread, make sure my boys look good this time!" Caesar "Slugger" Alvarez stood framed by the door of the briefing room. Short for a Navy pilot, his waist was small, his shoulders huge.

"Slugger, you do your job, and the pictures will take care of themselves."

"Hey, *we're* not the tourist; we shoot *real* bullets." There was a laugh from one of the pilots behind him. "Don't be afraid to get too close . . . You made us look bad on the last sortie."

"You want to be a film star, Slugger, you're going to need a better makeup artist."

A buzzer sounded in the briefing room. "Gentlemen," said a voice, "report to your aircraft."

Alvarez looked at Jack, then turned to his group. "Okay, you lame buzzards, let's be sharp on this one. Remember what I said . . ."

It was just after seven-thirty in the morning; the sky was clear except for a slight haze blowing in from the area burning near the city of Tyre. The A-6's had made a beautiful approach, feinting an attack on a warehouse complex by following a shallow valley that led down from the coast and then popping up over the top of the valley to hit the bunker.

The fighter-bombers were already just small gray-white dots heading back for the *J.F.K.* when Jack left his loitering circle and started his recon run. Go in fast and low, he thought, pop up, hit the cameras, and then get my ass out of here.

Alvarez had been the A-6's flight leader. He'd told his men, "Never, ever go straight in. Never even seem to *look* at your real target. My guide for these things is José Torres, one great fighter, smarter even than Ali in his prime. He said the best boxer is the best liar. My man was right: you lie to your opponent about where you're going, what you're going to do, and how you're going to do it. This is just like boxing, except in boxing the game is not about killing. This is about killing, and not getting killed yourself. I'm not going to have any of my guys get his ass whacked. You do this right, or you answer to me!"

Jack didn't like Alvarez, but couldn't fault his flying or group tactics. Slugger had been a junior Golden Gloves champ as a kid . . . never knocked down, he claimed. So, always lie about where you are going, Jack thought. Great for his guys, but it's real obvious to those geeks down there where I'm going.

Jack kept his plane below the ridge line, jinking side to side to throw off any ground fire. The bunkers looked as if they had sustained a direct hit; soft towers of dust and smoke hung like banners over the top of the ridge. He pulled the stick gently to the left and back, paused, then reversed the motion. It brought him a bit higher than the ridge and about three hundred yards out to the side.

Two thousand yards from his target, he started his recon pod rolling, then cut hard to the right, slashing across on a diagonal over the edges of the target. "Hope those bastards still have their heads down," he mumbled.

So far, surface-to-air missiles hadn't been a problem; the *J.F.K.*'s pilots had seen only infrared-guided SA9's in this area. The briefing officer had said there were the radar-guided—and thus more deadly—SA6's in the Bekaa Valley, controlled by the Syrians. The Syrians had been warned to keep those missiles out of the coastal area . . . so as he finished his recon run, it didn't worry Jack when he saw the exhaust plume of a SAM start up after him from the back side of the ridge.

Be cool, he thought. It looks like a 9. Cut right hard; make the missile turn with you to gain a bit of time. Drop the parachute flares—one, two, three—then turn left again and get out of here while the SAM is delayed by the flares. By the numbers.

And that was the way it went down, except that he only felt one little bump of a flare popping out instead of three. "Oh, shit, that flare chute's stuck again!" He hit his afterburners.

Jack pushed the stick forward again to get a bit more speed and looked back over his shoulder to try to pick up the SAM. He couldn't see it, which he knew was bad news: "Oh fuck, it's getting inside my turning radius!" Whip back left again, tight circle. Still no SAM in sight.

Now here was the choice: Keep turning and diving, trying to keep your speed up and turn inside the SAM. You might lose it, but if you didn't, then you might be too low for a good eject. Or pull higher and turn, lose speed, and make it more likely you'll be hit.

Jack decided to try both: a tight outside loop with a roll halfway through, which would bring him right side up at the bottom of the loop. Then he could look up to see if the SAM was following him around. If it was, then it was time to go straight up and eject before the SAM hit his pipe. If the SAM wasn't tight on him, he could turn again and get back toward the coast.

Jack squeezed his eyes shut for a half-second, gathering himself, then pushed the stick forward. As the nose of the plane went down, he pushed the stick hard to the right. He gave a bit of balancing right rudder pedal, and as the plane started to roll on its axis, eased off and brought the stick back so that the jet continued its loop as the roll progressed around.

It was a pas de deux on a blue-and-tan stage; gray fighter and brown missile. As the jet rolled out at the bottom of the loop, Jack looked up, blinking hard to fight the G-induced blackout. "Rat Fuck!" The SAM was following him around the loop, and closing. Be cool, be cool, he thought. Time to leave.

Jack pulled up again on the stick and then punched his radio button. "Red Bird, Red Bird. I've caught a SAM, got to leave. Ahh, one klick seaward of the target ridge. Come get me! Out." He reached between his legs to grab the eject-sequence handle. Settling his shoulders, he pulled the striped loop; the canopy blew off and his seat fired to throw him out of the plane. The jolt from the seat was echoed by a heavier shock as the SAM entered the tail pipe and exploded. This second blast pounded Jack's head back into his seat, and he was unconscious when his chute opened.

The white circle drifted down toward the smoky tan hill below.

Little figures jumped out of a line of trenches and ran to meet him. Flight Officer Lieutenant John Tyson Verre was on his way to becoming a headline.

Afterward, he could only remember two events in his next voyage. He had come half-awake to find himself lying on a dirty woolen blanket inside the back of what he guessed was a small truck, his hands tied in front of him. Jack tried the wrist bonds and then looked up at the small man with blue jeans and an ugly assault rifle who sat in the corner. "Who are you?" Jack asked.

The man grinned and aimed his barrel at the center of Jack's chest, then put one finger to his lips and made a shushing sound. "*Pas un bruit*—not a sound," he said. Jack faded out of consciousness.

The next time he awoke, it was to a vague awareness of being put in a large box, shown a water bottle, and having the top nailed shut. He hadn't objected, and the solemnness with which he greeted his treatment made Jack sure later that he had been drugged.

Finally, he awoke, clearheaded, in a single bed in a small room; he sat up and looked around him.

The room was about twelve by fifteen feet, and contained the bed, a battered, three-drawer wooden dresser, a straight-backed chair with its seat covered in worn gray velveteen, and a small bedside table. The walls were papered with a fine floral print in mustard yellow and peach. Two small gray rag rugs lay on the floor.

On the wall over the bed was a framed print of a mountain scene. The table was covered with a lace cloth. There was a sweet mustiness to the air, as if something had spoiled, but the smell was quite faint, almost not there. The single light was a dim bulb in a paper shade mounted on the ceiling. There was no switch.

He had had his flight suit taken away, and was now dressed in a comfortable pair of tan wool slacks, a green, long-sleeved shirt, and a gray wool sweater. He still had his watch.

It was all very quaint, all very homey looking, but there was no window and no handle on the inside of the door. That worried

Jack. When the screaming started in the next room, he began to feel fear for the first time since Tyre.

That first night, it seemed to be coming from the room to his right. It began with a long shriek. There was a pause, then rhythmic cries timed as if someone were kicking or punching the victim. It went on for perhaps five minutes, and then stopped. Jack got up to listen, and heard low voices pass outside his door.

I don't like this, he thought. His chest hurt and he realized that he had stopped breathing. He forced a deep breath. Be cool, be cool. He moved back from the door and sat on the edge of the bed.

Forcing another deep breath, he again surveyed the room; there was no way out besides the door. "I don't like this at all."

The door was unvarnished and looked fairly new. It seemed to be made of vertical boards, probably laminated to another layer on the other side, for the whole surface was studded with nail heads. The hinge pins were hidden, there was no sign that there had ever been a door handle, and at head height there was a small glass peephole. A wide brown stain started a third of the way up the door and trailed down to the floor line. Jack got up slowly and went to examine it. "Oh shit . . . blood."

For the rest of the night, there were no further sounds from the next door, no sounds from anywhere. In spite of himself, he fell asleep sitting on the bed and was awakened by the noise of a lock being undone.

The door opened slowly outward and bright lights from the corridor flooded into the room. A figure was silhouetted in the entrance. As his eyes adjusted to the glare, Jack saw that it was a young man about five foot six, dressed in blue jeans and a short black leather coat over a crewneck sweater. He had white-blond hair cut in a spiky, somewhat punk style. Jack was startled—the man looked European, rather than Arabic. "Why am I here?" Jack asked.

The man said nothing and stood looking at him. The silence stretched on.

Now that he had a person in front of him instead of just sound, Jack's fear strangely disappeared and was replaced by anger: at being shot down, at his strange treatment, at this young punk who wouldn't answer his questions. "Hey, what's going on?" he shouted.

The man continued to stare at him, then reached out of sight around the door and brought a bucket and a paper bag into view. He placed both on the floor inside the room, looked at Jack again, and then turned and left. The door closed behind him. There was the click of the lock. Jack advanced and checked the bag. It contained a meat sandwich, a piece of yellow cheese, a pear, and a bottle of water. He assumed the bucket was for his wastes. He put both the bag and the bucket to use.

"Where the hell am I?" It looked like some damned tourist hotel, not anything in Tyre. That was what worried him. Nothing was as expected, nothing was like what he had been taught in Escape and Evasion. He had clothes, he had his watch, he was in a pleasant enough room. There was no blindfold, no sensory deprivation, no shouting Lebanese or Iranians. His keeper looked European, not Arab. In spite of the treatment others seemed to be getting, he had not been beaten. In fact, even the food was pretty good. It all disoriented him.

He sat in the chair and thought of his family. His wife, Judy, was tough: a very perky, redheaded Navy brat he'd met while at fighter school in Pensacola. Most of the young fighter jocks, full of themselves and their newfound power, had made passes at her: they all took the attitude that she was oh, so lucky to meet them—just lie back and spread your legs.

Jack had been different. Not shy—no fighter jock is shy—but quieter, a bit more reflective. After the others had flamed out, he moved in and asked if she'd like to go to a baseball game with him. A *college* baseball game, for Christ's sake, she'd told her friends, but the move had been so different, she'd accepted. The two had fallen completely, totally in love. They married as soon as he graduated from the school, and their son, Bo, had been born ten months later.

Some of his flight mates told him he was crazy to marry, to tie himself to a wife and child when they were about to go out and knock the world around. But Jack knew he needed a base, a foundation; in spite of their crazy courtship, that's what Judy gave him.

So now he worried. She was tough, she knew the risks, but right now he was sure she didn't know if he was dead or alive. He had to get word to her. He felt that more strongly than he felt the need to get word to his commander.

This was to be the way the next few days passed. Only next door, the screaming started again and got worse. At first, the cries were in Arabic. At least he thought it was Arabic. It sounded like the language the announcers had used on the stations he had picked up on his bunk radio in the Med: wavering women's voices singing incomprehensible things interspersed by rapid-fire announcers that reminded him of the fast talker on the Federal Express ads at home.

The screams would start in the morning. They would go on for a half hour, and then stop for an hour, then start up again. The morning of the fifth day, they went on for longer than usual. For the first time, Jack thought he could hear someone shouting in a manner that suggested commands. The screaming continued, and then was abruptly cut off by a gunshot. Jack did not touch his next meal.

The seventh day, the screaming started again. Now it seemed to be coming from both rooms on either side. And one of the voices seemed to be crying out in English. Jack listened closely and once thought he could make out the words, "Oh, please God! Not that again! Please, I can't take it! No!" but he wasn't sure.

When the young man next came with his bucket and meal bag, Jack asked him a question. "Who is that speaking in English?" The young man stared at Jack, and then, surprisingly, answered. "We now have one of your friends."

It became worse. Jack thought that it might be the voice of another pilot. He started standing near the door, trying to recognize the voice of one of his flight mates in the piercing cries. It was high-pitched, but he thought that the things they were doing to the man might be the cause of that.

One night, the screams went on for hours, and became high, gasping, wheezing. Then there had been silence, and the light-haired guard had opened Jack's door. "I have something to show you," he had said. His face was calm, but his voice held a tone of gloating. The guard walked up to Jack and thrust something under his nose. Jack pulled back and looked. It was some kind of red, bloody meat. "Your friend will not have to shave anymore."

The screaming continued the next day; Jack listened. There was nothing else to do, he could only listen.

Late in the afternoon, one voice seemed familiar. He got up and pressed his ear to the wall. It did seem to be in English. He stilled his breath and tried to make out the phrases. There was a moment of silence, and then he heard it again. "Oh, please God! Not that again! Please, I can't take it! No!"

Jack went back and sat on the bed. He'd heard that same phrase before. He sat there stunned . . . head games! So this had all been head games; someone must have screwed up and run the same tape twice. He was here all alone; there were no other prisoners, just tapes and sound effects.

It didn't make him any less afraid.

At the beginning of the third week, at ten in the morning, the door opened. It was the light-haired man, but this time he carried a gun, a short Uzi with a folding stock and shoulder sling.

"Please stand." Jack got up off the bed. As he stood there, he noticed that his left knee was starting to shake. He tensed and released his stomach muscles to try to force himself to relax, to be calm.

"Move away from the bed." Jack did as he was ordered and the man circled behind him.

"Please take the chair and place it in the center of the room facing the door. Sit."

Jack picked up the chair. Should I try to take him? Jack thought. But the man seemed to know his business: he had stayed behind and at least four feet away while Jack had moved. "Don't try to take out a pro," his Escape and Evasion trainer had said. "They practice. They are as good at what they do as you are at flying. Unless it is clear that they are going to kill you right then, bide your time. Pick someone else. Wait to see if a nonpro makes a mistake, then make your move." Jack decided to wait. He put the chair down in the center of the room and sat.

"Now, I am going to tie your hands. Do not try anything funny

. . . you will die if you do, and then I will have my boss angry at me. He would like to talk to you." He came up behind Jack. "Put your hands behind you." With a small cord, the man fastened Jack's hands tightly together behind the chair back. "Now, don't move."

Jack heard a group of footsteps and looked up. Three men entered the room. The first was an Arab-looking man dressed in a conservative blue suit. About sixty with gray hair, he looked like a banker. The second man also looked vaguely Arab; he was younger, perhaps thirty, dressed in jeans and a turtleneck. He seemed a bit nervous, as if he was not sure of the role he should play. The third was Asian, perhaps fifty, powerfully built. The cut of his impeccable gray suit deemphasized his strength, but did not diminish the feel of menace he carried about him, nor his military air.

The three stood just inside the door, looking at Jack. The older man gestured with his hand and the German guard left the room. The Asian man stepped against the wall next to the door and stood there, very straight. The older man walked over until he was in front of the chair. He had a slight limp: his left foot seemed stiff and turned out a bit at the toe. He was obviously in charge.

No one said anything for a minute more. All three stared at him; the room seemed very quiet. Be cool, wait them out, Jack thought.

Finally the leader spoke, "So . . . we have here the captive . . . our lesson for today." The young man behind him nervously cleared his throat. The Asian did not stir.

"Your name and rank?"

"Lt. John Tyson Verre, USN."

"I am Hussein Baalbek. You fly F-14's, no?"

Jack did not think it was a question.

"The Tomcat is a very nice weapon, Lieutenant Verre. Very fast, very capable. Usually very hard to bring down, but . . . we seem to have been lucky. Do you like flying it?"

Jack thought. His E and E trainers had told him not to try to restrict himself to just name, rank, and serial number. That didn't work under very tough questioning. It gave you no room to give, and made you brittle, easier to break. But they had also said don't start talking too soon. Make them work, give yourself some space. He decided not to respond.

Baalbek waited, then said, "You don't have to answer; I know. You love flying it. It makes you feel good, powerful, bold." He turned for a moment to the Asian man. "The power of a weapon . . . a real weapon."

He turned back to Jack. "The F-14 implies much. My young friend here does not yet understand that. He thinks fervor is enough. He has not been wounded as I have; he still has his family.

"Tell me, Lieutenant Verre, do you know how many people were killed by the Islamic Action League bomb that brought you and your fellow fliers here?" It was like a college lecture hall—the professor calling out a question to a student he thought ill-prepared. Jack did not answer.

"You don't remember?" He leaned close to Jack and stared into his eyes. "But you should know this!" He straightened again and went on with his lecturing tone. "Two: a mother and one child. Innocent victims, I believe you call them. The Islamic Action League has a talent for bad publicity—they were trying for the Assistant Secretary of State; they killed two 'innocents.' But it was only two. They may be fervent, but they are not very powerful. It is the same for all the groups fighting for our cause.

"Do you know how many women and children have been killed in our villages since your strikes began?"

Jack was sure he should be silent now.

"Probably not. Three hundred and forty 'innocents.' That is the power of your weapons, the weapons of a major power. Those weapons also get you better press. When you use them you are, of course, not terrorists, you are just good people *punishing* terrorists." He leaned close again and put his face close to Jack's. Jack forced himself not to draw back, not to avert his gaze from the other man's. "*Our* innocents still die." His voice was very low.

The older man walked away a few paces and then turned to face Jack again. He folded his arms on his chest. "Two of yours, hundreds of ours . . . such an imbalance. Because we have only little weapons, insignificant ones. A bomb, a mortar, perhaps a few hand-held SAMs . . . the weapons of a people without a real country.

"People who are not stateless—who have real countries with names like the United States, Israel, France, Great Britain—they have real weapons, formidable weapons: planes, tanks, ships, napalm, even nuclear bombs. And when they use some against us with such terrible effect, the rest of the world does *not* call them terrorists. We don't have the power of real weapons . . . yet. We shall see."

He dropped his arms and his tone became brisker, almost friendly. "But I ramble. That is not the issue before us now. You are here, alive and, it seems, well. Do you have any questions?"

Jack decided on a gamble. "Does my family think I'm dead?"

"An interesting question, that. We all die." He paused.

Jack was silent.

"Now, my young friend, Dari. Did you know today is a test?" Baalbek turned and stared at the young man behind him, who returned his gaze with a slightly confused look. "Yes, a test. We have here a man who has killed our people very efficiently—his side has weapons that we do not. Perhaps I can change that soon, but I will need men I can trust."

The older man put his hand into a side pocket of his jacket, pulled it out, and held up a knife. Its blade was long and thin, a stiletto with no finger guard. "So come, take this," he said. "Prove yourself."

The young man stared at the knife, then the older man, and then down at Jack in the chair. He stood where he was.

"Take it."

The young man shivered and then moved forward to take the knife.

Baalbek walked around behind Jack and put his hand gently on Jack's shoulder.

"Here is an enemy. Look into his eyes, kill him."

The airman's eyes darted to the side, trying to see the man behind him, and then down to the knife. He looked up into Dari's face and saw no reaction. Just like the tapes, he thought. They're playing with my head again: another interrogation game. He let his shoulders relax.

Baalbek said quietly, "This is your test. Slit his throat."

Dari's hand raised the knife toward Jack's throat and paused again. Suddenly his hand began to shake. He lowered his eyes and moved the knife closer.

Jack, suddenly worried, tried to move back, but Baalbek grabbed Jack's forearm with one hand and lifted his thumb hard with the other. The airman gave a little cry and tried to twist, but the pain kept him from rising to his feet. He grew still. Be cool, he thought. This is just another head trip. They wouldn't have gone through all this if they planned to kill me.

Baalbek spoke again quietly. "Look into his eyes and do it."

Dari looked at the older man and then closed his eyes for a second. He tried to see the larger issues, to see again the deaths he had witnessed in his own village. It would not come. He opened his eyes again and looked at the coldness in Baalbek's face. He realized suddenly that this was truly a test, and to fail here was to confirm suspicions. It would mean his own death. This was only one American; Dari tried to think of the bigger plan and started to shake. He pressed the knife to the side of Jack's neck, and surprisingly, it entered. The airman screamed and jerked his head back. The knife continued its path and the scream turned into a bubbling gurgle. Jack struggled violently for a few moments, and then a look of puzzlement came over him, his eyes went blank, and his head rolled forward.

"So," the older man whispered.

Dari stood frozen, his knife hand now poised over the airman's lolling head as if in benediction. He slowly focused on the older man.

"See, your hand no longer shakes," Hussein Baalbek said.

Dari examined his own hand as if it were another's. It was still, its fingers red.

"So, now you can be used." Baalbek motioned to the Asian man. "Let us eat and discuss our plans for a real weapon, one that will give us true power." He walked toward the door, and as he got to the threshold, turned to Dari for a moment. "Please change your clothes." The Asian man, as impassive as ever, followed him out.

Dari's hand went to his breast. It felt warm. He looked down and saw that the warmth was that of the airman: his front was soaked with the dead man's blood. How could he report this? Dari suddenly vomited.

THOMAS

The long car sped through the predawn darkness. Its tinted windows made an even darker pool where the two men sat in the back, insulated from the driver by a glass panel.

"How is he physically?"

"He's fine, Chris, there was never any question of physical damage."

"Yes."

"You're going to call him back?"

"Simpson, he's the best I have for the job."

"You mean 'was.' "

The car swayed slightly as it took the entrance to the parkway. The engine's note surged as they accelerated up the slope, then dropped back. The double beat of tires on the road's tar strips slowly increased its tempo.

He sighed. "No, I think I mean *is*. He sees things others don't; he's not afraid of individual action, but he's not a loose cannon—in that I can trust him as I would myself. I need him on the team."

"But what about that last screwup?"

"He didn't screw up anything *we* asked him to do . . . he just failed his own goals."

"Does he blame us?"

"No, Simpson, he still blames himself."

"That can ruin a man."

"But I don't think it ruined him."

They rode in silence for a while until the car slowed to exit for the bridge that would take them into the city.

"No, I don't think it ruined him," he repeated. "He's had a lot of shocks in his life—parents killed when he was in his late teens, only brother died when he was twenty-one. He weathered those; he's solid, good education—"

"He never married," said Simpson.

"No, never."

"That's something I look for in an asset."

"Perhaps . . . the way you mean it; but I think it's just he's afraid of losing it all again, like he lost his family. I only hope it's not too soon." He shifted in his seat. "You recruited him, what do you think?"

Simpson had been his personnel aide before going to NSA, one who still kept tabs on his old finds.

"My new bosses have taught me something, Chris: if you have an asset, use it."

The car came off the bridge into the city. The older man straightened. "I want him . . . working again. Find him. Get him back."

2

HITCH

The sleet slashed his face as he towed the boat along the shore in the darkness. A gun rested in the crook of his arm. It had been raining when he started out this morning, but now the temperature had begun a plunge he knew would bring a couple of hours of snow before the front blew through.

On the shore to his right there was a roaring sound from the wall of cedars: the wind was still rising. It would really hit him when he passed the shelter of the trees and headed down toward the ocean. It must be blowing thirty knots. He turned and called to his dog, who was heading off into the trees. "Come on, George! Get over here; we've got a great day ahead of us!"

It was a glorious day to be on the marsh. A cold storm like this only happened once or twice in the early part of the duck season, and William Hitch was happy to be out in it. He had awakened a little before five—just before his alarm had rung—dressed, and had a quick cup of coffee. He had put on waders and his old olive drab parka, and because it was going to be a cold morning, had fed his retriever an oily snack to help keep her warm. Before she would eat it, he had to convince her that no, he was not going to leave her, and yes, she could come. She had gulped it down and then bounced back to the door where she sat and stared at him, mumbling low whines of excitement. He swallowed down the rest of his coffee. "Okay, fur face, let's go!"

He had gathered his shotgun and then set off down the pond, towing a small punt loaded with his decoys and gear. He thought he would hunt from the small blind at Deer Cove, that hollow in the shore named after a doe that had startled him while he fished for perch there, long ago when he was eight. The good eating ducks—the blacks, mallards, and widgeon—were too wary to set into the cove on calmer days, but they loved its shelter when there was a northeast blow on. And this was making up to be a short, vicious storm.

As he passed out of the shelter of the trees, the wind took on the metallic whistling that announced gusts of over thirty-five. He had taken this route many times over the years, and with his eyes adjusted to the darkness, the very faint glimmer of the shoreline sand was enough to guide him. He veered to pass a small spit of sand that extended from the shore, and suddenly there was a flash of movement four feet in front of him. A defensive crouch and roll was stopped by the sound of a harsh *"Quark!"* Bill straightened, took a deep breath, and laughed—a night heron taking shelter along the shore had flapped into startled flight. "God, I'm still wired!" He laughed again: he wasn't sure who had been more startled, the heron or himself.

The night herons fished here, gathering along the edge of the pond each evening, looking like slightly nerdy young punks hanging out—shoulders hunched, eyes downcast as though unsure if they looked tough enough. If you came across them in the darkness, they took alarm and flew off, croaking, *"Quark, Quark!"* It had happened often enough in the past—practically every time he walked along the shore in the darkness. But the last few years had, for good reason, made him a much jumpier man.

As he got to Deer Cove, Bill started to whistle a tune that was torn away from his lips by the wind. He pulled the punt up onto the shore, propped his gun up on the bow rail, and started to set up his rig for the morning's hunt. It had been four years since he had been able to get out to the Vineyard for duck season. It was a good morning to be back here and out on the marsh—alone and without fear.

Bill whistled for the dog, who splashed out of the darkness and stood looking at him. "You stay around here, George Bird, you old fool. Don't want you getting acquainted with any skunks this morning." The dog sat. Bill had spent an amazing morning in the blind with George when she was a puppy. She had tangled with a skunk in the darkness, and even downwind, she had been too powerful to bear. "I'm going to set out the decoys. You stay."

George Bird was a ten-year-old golden retriever, still goofy as a puppy in spite of her stiffening hips. Bill's friends, knowing his literary bent, assumed he had named her after George Eliot. But she was named after George Bird Evans, whose lyric writings on dogs and bird hunting with wife Kay had given a teenage Bill his first sense of the greater ceremonies of the hunt.

Bill picked up two decoys from the bottom of the punt: a battered, oversized, black duck decoy, and a fat sea gull, carved from a chunk of cedar post. The black duck was set out ten yards from the shore and perhaps five yards upwind from the blind. He then turned and waded downwind, counting his paces from in front of the blind until he was forty-seven steps away. That put it at forty yards from the blind, a marker for the limit of sure kill range with number four steel shot.

The sea gull was a confidence decoy, not meant to attract sea gulls—though immature ones sometimes flew over to squall at it—but to convince ducks that this was a real scene, not a dangerous trap. When he was young, an old island gunner had told him, "Well, you always see gulls setting with ducks, hoping to pick off something they bring up. You never see a gull setting with decoys. What you want to do is make everything look nice and cozy. If you do, the ducks might come in."

Bill splashed back to the blind and George came out to meet him. He rubbed the dog's head and then bent to take the rest of his gear out of the punt. He carried it over and placed it in the blind—a small *V* of old fence boards, two feet high and covered with marsh grass. There was a shallow pit for his feet and he could lean back against a cedar tree to break up his outline. He took the punt, towed it two hundred feet up the pond, pulled it up on the bank, and tucked it behind some low bayberry bushes.

He walked the shoreline back to the blind and stood there. It was now forty-five minutes before sunrise, fifteen minutes before legal shooting time. The day was slowly gathering itself, and there was now enough gray light to make out the rows of waves angling away from him. The far shore of the pond was still a black line, separating the water from the sky, each of the same gray color. He looked at his decoys. The black duck rode calmly, its heavy cork body smoothing the effects of the gusts. Bill had made that decoy when he was eleven, under the stern, watchful eye of his father. It was his first decoy, and still his favorite. His father had shown him how to use it. "Don't get too fancy when ducking in a blow," he had said. "The more you try, the more chance you have to make a mistake. When it blows up, the ducks don't need much of an invitation; a single big decoy will do. If you put up a big spread, all those blocks bouncing around can look too lively. You just make it simple and elegant." If ducks came in, they would set in behind the decoy, and just in front of his hide. It all looked right. He turned and climbed into the blind, settled himself, and called in the dog.

So here he was, alone as always, but sheltered from the gusts. It hadn't been that way the past few years . . .

He had been busy in Washington, Europe, the Mideast, and recently Asia, helping to put out fires started by incompetent politicians or bumbling businessmen; running high-stakes, high-danger missions for the Admiral, who through some fluke in an administration populated by simpletons and seers, was National Security Advisor. It had been crisis following crisis like a looping tape—the same mistakes and screwups repeated again and again. It reminded him too much of fourteenth-century France in Barbara Tuchman's *A Distant Mirror:* incompetent egomaniacs causing great death and desolation while never seeing beyond their uncomprehending vanities.

But that had been the job, hadn't it, Bill thought. That was what he had been hired to do: deal with it, handle it, move on. But he hadn't, had he? Not on the last one.

Bill tightened his right hand into a fist, squeezing until his fingers hurt. He held the fist tight, then relaxed.

Handle it, then move on; remember what the game is.

That was how the Admiral had put it when he first took Bill on. "This is a tough game we're playing," he'd said. "You're not always going to be sure what the rules are; even if you know the rules, not everyone is going to play by them. The point is, it's a game we've got to win; if we don't, we could forfeit everything. Never forget that."

Maybe the Admiral did see it as a game and the lives he wagered as simple ivory pieces. Maybe that helped explain it; maybe it was just the kind of man the Admiral was, the kind he thought Bill could become.

Admirals, generals, CEOs—that clan of men who, for two percent gain on the bottom line, could close a factory, then go home, have a drink, and go to bed. It was not that they would relish it, but the parts of their minds that would empathize with the workers had been shut off. Not just for business, but for much of their lives.

Put fifteen hundred men who supported their families out of work forever; or abandon a gentle man whom everyone knew had been falsely accused. "He was endangering the President" —or endangering the next quarter's results. That was it; that was all.

In certain situations, they could be good companions: on fishing trips, the golf course, at big football games or dinner parties. What they had given up they saw as something gained, and like a secret signal, it allowed them to recognize others of their clan and be comfortable with one another. The larger issues were most important. And those who thought they had given loyalty for loyalty in return found themselves left behind, doing what wounded soldiers had done for thousands of years: watch the baggage train move on down the road, leaving them behind to their fate. Not because they weren't valued, but because the greater good demanded it.

In going after Sutan, he had failed a test. "Don't get involved, Bill, this is business," the Admiral had said. "That's not the way to do it." But he *had* done it, and in doing so had stepped outside the circle, failed a subtle test.

The Admiral had been his mentor—using him, testing him, guiding him. Giving Bill the little bits of insight that could help him grow in the right way—but their relationship had changed. The Admiral wasn't cold to him, and Bill sensed that he was still valued, but now as a staff person; valued, but no longer in the circle of those who were, or would become, the leaders.

I made a mistake, Bill thought. I tried to go back for one of the wounded, tried to go back for a man who was going to die anyway.

"Shit!" he cried out. His dog turned and stared at him. "Nothing, girl," he whispered, answering her questioning look. "It's nothing at all."

Nothing, he thought, just the life of a good friend, a life that should not have been lost, except that a certain senator had made a much-publicized defense of a local strongman as "a true friend of democracy, a man like we need more of in our own country." That statement had emboldened that "friend of democracy" to have an opposition leader "die tragically of injuries received while resisting legitimate questioning on matters of national security."

And the mistake I made was to go after him, to try to save Sutan from his fate in that dirty little police station. Got emotional; got involved; got noticed. Bad form.

All that and he hadn't saved Sutan anyway, had he? So just take the news to your friend's wife and children, and then go and be abused by that same senator in a hearing . . .

So what did it mean? Who had been right? . . . *Was* the game more important than the lives involved? Bill only knew that he wanted to get out. A deadness had overcome him, and he realized that if he didn't get some better sense of who he was, and What It All Meant, he might very well end up walking in front of a truck, literally, or figuratively—which in his line of work was just as fatal.

Bill had walked into his boss's office on a July afternoon after the Senate hearings and told him he wanted to sign off.

The Admiral had been standing by his window which overlooked the back White House lawn. "Don't make it formal yet," he'd said. "You've learned some hard lessons in a tough situation. A lot of people in this business find themselves where you are now. Some leave in anger, some just drift away, some make mistakes that get them killed. But some, Bill, some decide that all in all it's still a job worth doing. You find your own way.

"I value your help." Your help, not you, thought Bill. "I'd like you back, but if you don't want to be here, you won't do either of us any good." He walked back to his desk which always seemed paved with a layer of pink "Immediate Action" folders. "You've got two months coming to you, and I can get you one or two months more. The job's here if you want it." He started to say more, then closed his mouth and sat down. He picked up one of his folders and started to study it. Bill waited a moment longer, then spun on his heel and walked out.

So that had been the way they'd left it: the job was there if he wanted it. A week later, he'd picked up his old dog from a friend who'd been caring for her and seen to turning on the water and fixing the screens at his old family place on Martha's Vineyard. He'd put in a late garden, started fishing, and tried to settle into another rhythm of life; something different from the past four years.

So, who was he, and what did he want to do? The job was there if he wanted it, and he was very good at the job. Was that enough?

He could find something else to do, another line of work where the pressure was less and the stakes lower. But was that enough? What you are is what you do, he thought. And you had been doing some good. So even if you've lost your relationship with the Admiral, that wasn't why you were doing that job anyway, was it? Figure it out. Figure yourself out. Could you ever be happy doing something that doesn't test you to your limits?

You lost Sutan, but he knew the risks, too. *He* decided to stay, even knowing what was probably coming. Don't flatter yourself that you could have made that decision for him. So the Admiral hurt you, he thought. Leave it at that. The job you were doing did some good. Maybe that was all you could ask for in life.

■

Bill leaned back into the shelter of the cedar tree. George sat by his left side, and started intently scanning the sky—she often saw, or heard, the ducks before he did.

He looked around. The land was starting to get some color as the light got brighter, the very special red-tan of a Vineyard fall, paler from the sleet, bracketed by the still-dull gray of the sky and water; more beautiful in a sleet storm than on a pretty summer day.

When he was a kid, he had found arrowheads in the mud here. Arrowheads from people who had hunted here long ago. Being here helped connect him with the natural world, a world that had been there for thousands of years—a world that had no reality in Washington—and duck hunting was a wonderful excuse to be out in it.

He always thought that if you told someone, "You know, a front's coming through, and it's supposed to be really cold and sleeting tomorrow. I think I'll get up before dawn, go lie on my back on the marsh, and just watch for a couple of hours," they could probably get you committed. Ah, but if you said, "There's a big blow coming. I think I'll go out for a spot of duck hunting," well then, you were considered a fine and noble fellow. So even on the days that the ducks or his aim didn't cooperate, it was a gain. He got to be outside and see and smell and feel things he didn't get to experience any other way. And if the ducks did cooperate, well, then he had gathered some of the best tasting things that it had been his pleasure to eat. That was the way his father had taught him.

George stirred, and Bill looked up to see a pair of black dots across the pond, racing downwind just above the gray water. He checked his watch: shooting time. He pulled his hood tighter around his pain-cold ears. The sleet had turned to snow. "Okay, fur face, let's see what we can do."

Four eyes started scanning the sky and water, trying to pick up the form of ducks through the snow. The wind was blowing left to right, quartering slightly off the shore. If birds were going to come into the decoys from the left, they would tend to first circle wide to his right to land into the wind. If they were heading east to other ponds, they would often come in just over his head and be gone over the pond and out of range before he could react.

George looked right, gave a little shiver, and then froze in concentration. "Okay, I see them," Bill said. Two ducks were slowly beating their way upwind from over the rise of dunes at the ocean. They tracked from side to side as they came closer to the lee shore. They were too far away to pick up their color, but the fact that their silhouettes were dark but not black, and the pattern of their wing beats were clues. They started to rise higher as they approached, and Bill saw a flash of gray-white from their wings. "Mallards."

They were going to pass too far to his right. Bill pulled out his call and gave a loud hail call: a series of seven quacks, the first one long and each succeeding one shorter in length—the "come over here and join me, you guys" call of a hen black duck or mallard. The path of the two ducks jumped as they heard the call; they slowly turned and headed toward the decoys.

Eighty, seventy, sixty yards; they came, losing altitude. Bill bent his neck to hide his face under the brim of his hood. "Keep coming," he whispered. They were two mallard drakes. His hand slowly crept to the stock of his gun.

At forty-five yards, the ducks gained altitude and started to veer to their right. Something might be spooking them.

Here was the perennial question: take them now, not a sure shot, but perhaps the only chance he would get. Or wait, and see if they would come around again to set into the decoys. Have faith, he thought, let's give the setup a try.

The ducks swung around to the right and headed back downwind. The lead duck seemed intent on leaving, but the second started to swing back and hung there to see if the other followed. "Come on, come on back, you guys," Bill hissed. "Don't prove me wrong."

The lead duck hesitated, and then turned too. "Ah . . ." They swung back into the wind and swiftly lowered down toward the water. They were committing.

Bill eased the shotgun back toward him. George started to shiver in anticipation. "Easy, girl."

Sixty yards, fifty yards, forty yards: they were over the sea gull decoy and starting to cup their wings as they flared to set in behind the black duck decoy.

Okay, now. Bill sat upright, drawing the gun toward him until he could grasp the forestock with his left hand. He concentrated on the rear duck and brought the gun up. He hardly felt the shock of recoil. The water just behind the duck turned to spray: a stronger crosswind than he thought.

He swung again on the duck as it climbed, holding a bit more lead, and squeezed off his second barrel. It was a solid hit, and the duck folded in the air and crashed to the water. The other duck put on its afterburners and arced up and away.

George had leapt up and had her front paws braced on the front of the blind. "Okay, girl . . . back!"

George leaped over the blind, landed on the sand in front, and took another leap into the water, crashing the surface apart with her chest. Bill stood, opened the action of his gun, and stepped out of the blind.

The duck lay on its back, orange feet pointing into the sky. It had been a clean kill. A few feathers blew quickly downwind.

George swam strongly toward the duck, adjusting her path for the wind drift, her wake swirling from the churning of her feet. As she neared the duck, she rose a little out of the water, gave a lunge, and grabbed it in her mouth. She turned and started back to the shore at a more leisurely pace. "Good girl," Bill called.

George slowly swam up to where Bill was waiting and came up on the shore. She walked slowly around him and sat at his side.

"Good, good girl. Give." She dropped the duck into his hand. Bill held it up to examine it. George gave a shake, covering him with spray, and went off to sniff at a bunch of marsh grass.

It was a beautiful duck, water drops beaded on the glossy feathers, a few flakes of snow joining them. "You're a fat one," Bill said. He went back and stepped into the blind. The duck was placed carefully belly down in the grass next to the tree.

The dog was snuffling at the base of a hummock. "George, get over here. Leave those mice alone; kennel up!" She gave a snort and jumped back into the blind. She nosed the duck and then looked at Bill.

"Nice job, girl. It's a pleasure to work with you." He scratched her under her wet chin. "Now back to work." He put two new shells into the chambers and closed the gun. Propping the gun up on the edge of the blind, he settled back against the cedar.

The next two hours passed quietly. The snow started to taper off and two flights of common mergansers came in. The first flock had just circled the decoys and flown on, but a second group of four set their wings and came in.

Mergansers are fish-eating ducks. Bill's brother had said that rather than considering them fishy-tasting ducks, he thought of them as ducky-tasting fish, and therefore quite palatable. Bill didn't agree and never shot them.

He let them splash to a landing unmolested. Swimming in circles, they flapped their wings, preened to get pinions into neat array, and then started to feed. The mergansers started swimming in larger circles, dipping their heads underwater and looking from side to side as they searched for minnows. With their long, wet head feathers, they looked like someone who had just used a discount coupon for a hairdo at a failing, new-wave hair salon. Finally, they spied their prey. One by one, they executed neat little dives and disappeared beneath the surface chasing their meals.

Through all this, George was getting more and more excited, watching the ducks splash twenty yards away. She gave a yelp and stared at Bill as if to say, "What's wrong with you? Those are ducks, D-U-C-K-S! Shoot them!"

Bill just gave a little laugh. "No, girl. Those guys are not headed for our dinner table. Let 'em be."

George kept staring at Bill, then gave up with a sigh and flopped down to the bottom of the blind, where she found a piece of root and determinedly began to rip it to pieces. The mergansers continued fishing and slowly drifted down the pond.

The snow finally stopped around nine-thirty, and from time to time small rents appeared in the clouds through which bits of blue sky could be seen. As the blind was bathed for a minute in a yellow shaft of light through one of these holes, Bill picked up flashes of gray from across the pond. "Heads up, fur face. Looks like something more interesting's on the way." George popped her head up to look.

Six or so widgeon were coming across the water in a tight group. They swung around to the south of the blind and started to make their way toward the decoys. They passed into one of the patches of light and, lit with its gold, stretched out into a line. It reminded Bill of the Frank Benson oil of incoming ducks that had once hung in the members' room of Boston's Museum of Fine Arts.

The widgeon started dropping in for a landing just ahead of the black duck decoy, and then suddenly rallied and tried to gain altitude. Something has really spooked them, Bill thought. Take them now.

He grabbed up his gun and swung through the rearmost bird as he pulled the trigger. The duck folded and he continued his swing, picking up another in his sight picture. Swing through it and squeeze again. The second duck folded. It fell with a splash and pumped its wings for a second before it lay still. "Back, girl," and George hit the water.

What had spooked those ducks? A movement to his left caught his attention. Up at the next point, a man in an olive green duffle coat came into view, walking quickly toward him along the edge of the pond. Bill scanned slowly around himself . . . no one else in sight. Opening the gun, he stepped from the blind.

As the man came closer, Bill recognized the seamed face of Burt Eccles, assistant clam warden and an old shooting friend of his father's. "Burt," he called out, "what in the devil could get you out at this time of the morning? Think I'm down here shooting flying—" The look on the older man's face stopped him. "What's wrong?"

"Bill, they got a message for you up at the emergency center. Called me; I said I thought I knew where I could find you."

Bill felt an emptiness. "Who was it?" As if I don't know, he thought; there is really no one else.

"Don't know exactly. Someone from Washington. Said it was a code blue."

"Shit." I'm not ready for this. I'm supposed to be off the list. "Anything else?"

"They're sending a plane. Said it would be here a little over an hour from now."

They both watched George coming in with the first duck. The old man kicked at a clump of weeds at the water's edge. "This big trouble?"

Burt was an old Yankee, and Bill knew how much it had cost him to ask. He lowered his voice and intoned, "The good Lord knows."

Burt laughed. "Don't mock the President, son, he's your boss."

"Don't I know it. And this is probably just a little job, but they want me back, and fast."

"Well, I guess it's nice to be needed."

"Yeah . . . if that's what it is." Bill took a deep breath of the cold air; he was calm. He realized the four months had done a lot to heal him. He looked out at the waves, the pond now all in sun. "I'd better pull the decoys."

George came up on the shore with the duck and released it into Bill's hand. She gave a quick nosing of hello to Burt, and then plunged back in for the second bird.

"Burt, I think you're going to have to look after my dog for a while."

3

The Sabreliner lifted into the tendrils of the upper storm clouds and sunlight burst into the cabin. Bill frowned. He had been staring from the window with unseeing eyes as the plane climbed from the Vineyard airport. Now the sudden light dazzled and woke him from his thoughts. He lowered the window shade halfway, then sat back, staring at the ceiling. You're going back in, he thought. What's the crisis this time? If it's a real one, who's there to deal with it?

The Admiral . . . the Admiral was good. But what about his boss, the President? That's a serious matter.

George Tipple Western had been President of the United States for eighteen months now. An historic figure: America's first religious-fanatic president. This past summer he had come out of his closet to proclaim on the Fourth of July that it was time for this country to become the true Christian nation it was destined to be. Some commentators said this was just his way of talking, just the President's way of expressing his conservative ideals. Bill thought he had been serious and was starting to go off the deep end of religious dementia.

In the primaries, George Western had come on as a staunch and somewhat quaint conservative. "The Christian way of life as a model for a troubled world" and "the importance of applying the moral lessons of the Bible as a guide in a world without a moral rudder" had been interpreted as colorful but useful bits of rhetoric. Besides, he had finished no higher than second in any primary. The week of the convention, the front-runner had been caught in a hotel room with the leader of his campus organization, and George Tipple Western had found himself with the nomination.

He had won the election paired with Frank Bass, a black vice-presidential candidate who brought together the conservative and black vote. Bass had been a formidable legal scholar at Georgetown, a man so strict on constitutional interpretation that he and Western were called the "Two Fundamentalists"—one legal, the other religious.

U.S. News and World Report said Bass got the nomination because of his strict constructionist view of the Constitution. *Newsweek* said it was to keep him from getting to the Supreme Court. *Time* said it was to get George Western elected. Bill agreed with *Time*.

So, Bill thought, we have a crazy for President, whose latest project is replaying the Crusades in Lebanon: throwing the U.S. military behind the Christian minority, trying to defeat the Muslims . . . losing us our former Arab friends and isolating us from our European allies who have interests in the region. If the Admiral is calling me back, then there's a major crisis. If there's a major crisis with Western as President, then we may have major troubles.

He shifted uncomfortably in his seat, then reached behind his back and adjusted a strap on his shoulder holster. He supposed that he'd lost some callus in his time off—he'd have to get used to wearing it again. Right now it was a bit like carrying a wallet in the wrong rear pocket, but he knew in a day or so he wouldn't feel it; in fact, he'd feel wrong without it . . . just like old times.

Some men Bill had worked with liked tricky ankle holsters, or to carry the gun in the small of their back. Fine without a jacket, but pretty impractical if you had to get at your gun fast while sitting in a car or chair. He tensioned his left lapel and then made a fast draw with his gun. Too slow . . . something he should have practiced more in his time off. But he'd needed to forget more than to practice.

He looked at the gun: a Smith and Wesson Airweight: .38 caliber, two-inch barrel, bluing scuffed and worn from the holster; a very familiar feel in his hand. Most of the Secret Service and the other plainclothes Feds carried Model 66's: .357 magnums in stainless steel polished to look like chrome, two-inch barrel, and rounded butt. Cult items for most of those guys because you couldn't buy them—the only way to get one was by being a Fed or Secret Service plainclothes. They had become the services' version of a designer logo: "See, I've arrived." He preferred his old Airweight: a .38 was enough firepower.

There was an FBI guy who used to kid him about carrying a "lady's gun"; Bill'd told him that if the stuff really hit the fan, you'd be going against people with AK-47's or Uzis, and a .357—even if it looked chrome plated—was just not going to do that much to impress the bad guys. He preferred the speed and concealability of the old Airweight, and the blued finish caught less attention. True, with p+ loads you could shoot the light alloy frame out of alignment with 1,000 rounds, but Bill did his range work with a Chief Special, exactly the same gun with a steel frame.

He'd had to use a gun only twice in his career; the Airweight had been enough. The Admiral had taught him that going to the guns was the first step of fools.

So what was he going to find in Washington? Bill sighed. He'd find whatever was waiting for him, and he would just have to deal with it. Just like old times. Speculating was not going to give him any answers; he'd been up before five this morning and had better get some sleep while he could. If this deal was going to be like any of the other code blues, sleep was going to be an infrequent visitor. He pulled the window shade all the way down, closed his eyes, and went to sleep.

The turbulence from the flaps extending woke him on the plane's descent into Washington National. He opened the shade and looked out. They were coming down the river toward the airport. The city lay ahead; the wind must be out of the east, he thought—rain again.

The jet, getting priority clearance, made a straight-in approach and settled onto the runway. The cabin shook as the engines reversed thrust, and then became quiet as the craft turned off onto the taxiway. So here we are, he thought.

The engine's note whined upward again as the plane swung toward the general aviation terminal. He was glad they had gone into National. One man he'd worked for had always routed his flights into Andrews Air Force Base on trips to D.C., then taken a helicopter into the city. After all, that's how the President and cabinet officers did it. Bill stretched. Sure, but that was for security; this way was at least a half hour faster.

The plane gave a final creak as they came to rest, and for the first time since the Vineyard, a member of the flight crew appeared in the cabin. "I'll get the door, sir." The man pulled a lever and the door swung downward with a hiss, deploying the stairs. They had come to rest close to the front of the terminal, so he didn't have to take one of the white vans that ferried corporate jet passengers around the crowded apron.

Bill took his coat from the locker and slipped it on. It was chilly outside—the result of the same cold front that had brought snow to the island. He picked up his small suitcase and swung his garment bag over his shoulder. "Good flight. Nice landing."

"Thank you, sir. Have a good day."

Bill went down the stairs and through the gap in the low concrete-block wall that surrounded the entrance. Inside the first set of glass doors a small group of businessmen laughed and talked among themselves around a luggage trolley piled high with suitcases and golf bags.

To the left inside the second set of doors, a young man in a blue suit stood in front of the flight operations counter, holding a sign that said HITCH. As far as Bill was concerned, that was a security lapse. He would have to mention it to the duty officer.

Bill nodded and the man stepped forward. "Welcome to Washington, sir."

"Where's the car?"

"This way, just outside the door." Bill followed him out to an undistinguished-looking blue Ford LTD. It had government plates. The driver got into the front and started the engine. Bill got into the back.

"Where's the meeting?"

"I'm to take you to the White House, sir."

"Okay." Ah, the White House and not the Old Executive Office Building next door. That meant whatever was going on was getting high-level attention.

The trip through the midday traffic was fast, and they soon were at the west entrance. The guard at the first post waved them through and they stopped at the gate house. A guard approached the car. "Identification, please."

Bill handed his ID to the driver, who handed it and his own to the guard. The guard bent down and looked through the window at Bill, then the driver, and then the floor behind the front seat. He turned, went back to the gate house, and handed the cards through the window. Bill knew they would be checking the cards against the daily duty orders, which listed expected arrivals.

The guard walked back to the car and handed back the ID cards. "Thank you, gentlemen," he said. "Could you please open the trunk?" The driver reached into the glove compartment and activated the trunk release. A second guard came out of the shack with a German shepherd on a leash. He walked the dog around the back of the car to sniff in the trunk, then came around to Bill's door and opened it. The dog stuck his nose in and sniffed, then abruptly sat and stared at Bill. "I'm carrying," Bill told the guard.

There was a moment of tension and the first guard said, "He's okay—he has LX clearance." The driver straightened in his seat.

"Very good, sir," the dog handler said. "Please leave your weapon with the lock officer at your entrance." He bent his head and spoke quietly into a radio microphone clipped to his lapel. "Have a pleasant afternoon."

The gate opened and the driver took the car up the roadway that ran between the EOB and the White House. He jumped out, opened Bill's door, and tried to carry his bags. Bill kept them to himself as he stepped out, went through the gateway and into the staff entrance. Inside the door was a simple mahogany desk where a woman sat with a very erect carriage, apparently checking various lists on a stack of paper in front of her.

She looked slightly taller than average, early thirties, brown hair with just a few streaks of gray. He watched her, the way her lithe body, wrapped in a standard blue Secret Service blazer and skirt, moved as she sorted through her work. The way the soft fabric of her blouse pulled across her breast as she reached for another paper. A blue bruise peeked out from under the cuff on one of her wrists.

She glanced up at him, then lifted her face and looked him in the eyes. "Bill Hitch, I thought I overheard someone using your name this morning, and I thought, 'No, it can't be.' But then your name shows up on the noon list, and here you are! Memories of old times." She gave him a little grin. He had not seen her for four years now; there was that delicate tension of meeting an old lover.

They had once run a watch-and-grab together in a nasty little Mexican town. Afterward, Bill wondered if it had been the fear they might not get out alive, or maybe just the mix of boredom and anxiety that a watch can have, but lovers they had become. Incorrect procedure . . . but there it was.

The watch had gone well; they had gotten their man. Again, perhaps it was just the coming violence, the fear of death, but in those few short weeks, their lovemaking had held a rare intensity: joining with someone who also knew the edges of life, who had seen enough violence to know how far was the fall. The affair might have gone on, for they were good together, but the pressures of their work had gradually pried them apart.

"Hello, Karen. It's been a while."

"Yes, and I've heard you've been up to some interesting things in the meantime. It's good to see you, Bill."

He smiled back at her. "Good to see you again, too. Things just as humdrum in your life?"

"Sure . . . nine to five, go home, watch TV, veg out, sleep all weekend."

"Ah, then what's the bruise from?"

She shook her head and pulled down her cuff. "Bill, you always saw too much."

"Just playing?"

"No, a tournament." She grinned. "I won." Karen Hobbs was a *sandan*—a third-degree black belt in judo. She worked out practically every night. Like most *judoka,* she called sparring in the training center "playing." That was her attitude to physical violence: it could be a wonderful game.

"Well, O keeper of the sacred doorway, here is my sword." He pulled out his gun and opened the action. She put out her hand and he placed the gun in it. She turned and put it into a locking cubby to her left, then handed him a plastic disk with a number on it.

"Don't lose that."

"Nope."

"I hear something's up; you could be a busy guy."

"Maybe I'll have time to take you to lunch or something . . ."

"Why, Bill, is this a date? From Mr. Self-sufficient?"

"Don't make it hard."

She hushed him with a smile. "I'm just teasing. We're still good friends; that's why it's always good to see you." She sat back and looked at him. "I'm glad you're back."

"Sure, boss. And where do I go now?"

She glanced at a small ship's clock mounted on the wall. "The meeting is called for ten minutes from now, in the back conference room. The National Security Advisor asked that you go down to see him as soon as you get in. He's in Sid Mole's old office. Leave your bags here; I'll have a porter store them for you. Take care."

He placed the bags in the corner, then clicked his heels together and touched his forehead with one finger. He went off down the corridor. Karen smiled fondly at his back, then shifted in her seat and went back to her paperwork.

Bill threaded his way down the corridors and then up a half set of stairs and into the anteroom outside the Admiral's office. He stopped in front of the secretary's desk, which was occupied by a male B school type in shirtsleeves.

"William Hitch to see Admiral Thomas."

The secretary checked the lights on his phone and then looked up. "He's on his phone at the moment. Please have a seat. When he's finished, I'll tell him you've arrived."

Bill went over to a grouping of blue leather-upholstered chairs. When he had been with the Admiral, the offices had been in the Executive Office Building. This setup was new, and Bill wondered why Chris had moved into the White House. The new location carried much more prestige, and possibly a bit better access to the President, but the security needs of the building that housed the President would make it much more difficult to run a day-to-day operation. Bill knew that the Admiral valued efficient operations above practically anything else.

There was a quiet phone conversation at the secretary's desk, and then he called to Bill. "Mr. Hitch, Admiral Thomas will see you now." He gestured to the closed door next to his desk. "Please go in."

Bill walked over and paused with his hand on the knob. So the game begins, he thought, and opened the door.

The Admiral sat on the opposite side of the room behind his large desk that was, as always, covered with an organized clutter. Bill was struck by how much Chris Thomas had aged in the few months he had been gone.

He looked up with a sudden smile that seemed to just as quickly be damped down. "Bill, very good to see you again." No other comment given, none expected.

"And you, too, sir. How have things been?"

He stared at Bill. "Close the door, son."

Bill closed the door and walked over to the desk.

"Haven't much time before the meeting; we'll let the reason I asked you back wait until then . . .

"Things have been a bit worse here." He leaned forward and rested his forearms on the desk. "The President is not doing very well. He may be falling apart on us. The somewhat strange statements you may have heard from him in the press these past few months are nothing compared to what we've been hearing from him here in the White House. We've been doing some fearsome damage control—that's one of the reasons that I moved my offices here . . . to be near him, to work with the others around the man to help keep things controlled.

"As you'll be briefed in the meeting, we have a potential problem on our hands . . . and the President wants to start up a small response team—an inquiry/action type of organization. He wants Charles Fonsgraf to lead it."

Bill started. "Fearless Fosdick?"

"That's right."

"But the man is a total incompetent!"

"True enough: a man who has the ability to take a difficult situation and turn it into an impossible one. But the Colonel is now fondly thought of. He told the President that he has become born-again."

"Colonel Fonsgraf born-again? That man would claim to believe in Aztec ritual sacrifice if that was what was in the wind. His only talent's bootlicking! How can he run a team?"

"Charles has always understood the value of managing his boss; it's taken him very far up the ladder. But the fact is, the President has asked him to lead the team. That's why I need you to ride herd on Fonsgraf and be my voice of reason, as it were, in this operation."

Bill stifled an outburst; he looked at the floor, then up again at his old boss. "You know he cost me a couple of good men."

"Yes, I know that, but it's just another condition we have to deal with. Bill, the stakes are higher here. He's in a position to screw up on things that could do real damage to the country. I want you to be my man on his team . . . to keep an eye on things, add your operations talent, keep me informed. I have to stay here close to the President."

"Who else is on the team?"

"The usual technical staff, but I think I'm going to lose the battle on the selection of the action forces: they are going to be Fonsgraf's people. I did pull in Tina Lucia from Langley. She will give you the informational support you need."

"Well, that's a plus at least. I've worked with her a couple of times; there's no one better."

The intercom on the desk gave a discreet buzz. The Admiral glanced at his watch. "Let's get going. I think Tina should be in my waiting area."

He got up from his desk, and grabbing his jacket from a hook near the door, led the way out into the outer office. A tall woman stood waiting for them. She had dark, short hair and was dressed in a simple gray suit that seemed to sum up her whole style: practical, neat, clean, and unconcerned with any sense of fashion.

"Hello, Tina," the Admiral said. "You two follow me," and like an imperious heavy cruiser, he steamed out of the office and down the hall. Bill and Tina looked at each other and trailed in his wake.

4

A nerd—pale skin and collar-length, black, stringy hair; dressed in stained denims and a plaid short-sleeved shirt; five feet eight inches, with the indeterminate weight and muscle tone that comes only from a total absence of interest in things physical. He lacked only a plastic pocket protector: it had been accidentally thrown out with his last set of clothes. Kevin Cox had calculated that it took too much time to do laundry, so he bought his clothes in sets of twelve, wearing each set for a month and then throwing it out. He was only ten days into this cycle, so the smell in the studio apartment had not reached its periodic height.

Rap music pummeled the room from a pair of four-foot-high speakers topped with a pile of empty pizza boxes. It was eleven A.M. and sunny out, but none of that reality trespassed here. The shades were drawn and then taped to the window casings. The only light came from one corner, where a collection of blue-white screens and a small desk lamp lit a table piled with computer equipment. The rest of the room was a chaos of cardboard boxes, dirty clothes, comic books, wires, manuals, phone books, and papers.

Kevin had twenty-nine years and had been living in the silicon world for seventeen of them. By its rules he was ancient.

Sittin' by the pool with all our toys, we rule . . . we rule
All the girls . . . tain't nothin' but toys, das right . . . fool
By the pool, right, our daddies' pool, das right . . . you drool
we cool, fool, we cool; not some urban tools, some drool
Cut it, Cut it! Hung! Cut it, Cut it!

We got it all. We set, take a bet.
We got it all. We set, got no debt. . . . Get wet. . . .

Fat Brat was a recent addition to his life. The rap music was better white noise than the Grateful Dead he used to listen to. He sat in front of one of the monitors. Its screen was covered with row upon row of figures:

```
40750      ADD   DX,1
40760      SHR   DX,1
40763      AGAIN:     OR     DW,2
40770      INC   AK,[BX]
40780      DB     00001101
40790      CMP   BL,'M'
40800      PUSH     DX,0
```

He was programming directly in assembly language, for Kevin disdained the use of higher-level languages. "Compilers don't produce tight code."

The CD paused between bands, and he heard a buzzing. It was a sound he did not remember hearing before. Looking around, he checked the other monitors to see if some alarm had been set off, but all seemed normal. The sound from the stereo started up again, and Kevin silenced it with a preoccupied flip of a switch. The buzzing was gone. What the hell was that? he thought.

Kevin knew his electronic world here, had constructed over half of the computers himself, but he couldn't imagine what had made that noise. Well, he thought, I'll finish this section of code and then go debugging.

As he reached to turn the music back on, the buzzing started again. This time he localized it as coming from near the door to the apartment. Really strange, he thought. It's the doorbell.

He picked his way through the debris to the door and pushed the intercom button. "Who's there?"

"Open the door, please, Mr. Cox. I have come to see you."

Kevin reached for the door button, then stopped. "Who is this?"

"Mr. Cox, open the door. I have been pushing this bell for five minutes, now."

Oh bug, Kevin thought. The music must have been drowning him out. He pushed the button that unlocked the outside door. Who would be coming to see him? It must be the landlord . . . No, he'd paid this month's rent when he'd changed his clothes. Kevin opened the apartment door a crack. He stood there a moment, looking out in the hall, and then remembered a pivotal point in a subroutine he was working on. Leaving the door ajar, he went back to his equipment and looked at the monitor. A thin band of light from the hall lay across the room.

Scratching his chin, he tried to recapture his train of thought. Line 40810 AND LX,2 . . . no that would loop when . . . got it! He sat, turned the music back on, and commenced typing.

```
40810   JNZ    AGAIN
40820   MOV    DX,814
```

A shadow covered the light coming from the door.

```
40830   REP   MOVDB
```

The door swung slowly open. A large figure stood there, a silhouette with its hand on the knob.

```
40840   ADD   DI,2
40850   DB    10100010
```

"Now where's that code list?"

The door closed and the figure advanced toward Kevin as he searched the desktop for the missing code book.

"Damn, it must in a box . . ." Kevin stood, turned, and ran into the figure now standing behind his chair. A large and silent Asian man looked down at him in the dim light.

"Hey, who are you?"

"Turn off the stereo, please."

"Well, look. Who are you, sneaking up on me like . . . ?" Kevin's voice trailed off, stopped by the man's quiet stare. He didn't look evil, exactly, but implacable, powerful. "Sure." He turned off the speakers. "But who are you?" Kevin thought his voice sounded unnaturally high-pitched in the now-quiet room.

"I am Mr. Onryo. You are Kevin Allen Cox."

Kevin edged away from the man to give himself some room. "That's right. What do you want?"

"Mr. Cox, I may have a project for you." His gaze had not left Kevin's face. "If you can do the work."

Kevin felt as if he were being examined by a very big—and perhaps hungry—cat. A cat whose nose twitched as it sniffed the air. The man standing before him looked fifty, large chested but not fat. Onryo sounded like a Japanese name, Kevin thought. He had oiled hair, combed straight back, and stood very erect with his hands hanging by his sides. His calmness gave him a slight sense of menace. It made Kevin uneasy. He reminded Kevin of someone. Perhaps it was the gray suit. He decided that the man reminded him of his old lab director. And that made him angry. "Well, I don't do work for suits."

"I do not believe you have done any meaningful work for anyone the past few years. For people with suits or people without suits. No one out there knows who you are anymore."

"What do you mean? I've done a lot of famous things!" Kevin started to sweat; he was getting angry. "Do you know who I am?"

"I know who you are, Mr. Cox—that's my business. *You* are 'The Greek.' Very few know that. But the point is that no one talks of The Greek anymore. Not in California, not in Japan, and certainly not in Israel."

"Well, what do they know, anyway?"

"Please sit down, Mr. Cox. We should talk." Onryo gestured to the chair.

"Listen, I don't—"

"Sit down! I can offer you a path to fame again."

Kevin slowly sat. The Asian man pulled out another chair and sat facing him, four feet away.

"What do you mean, fame? And how do you know I'm The Greek?"

"As I said, it is my business to know such things. I even know how you got that name. You were very famous, fifteen years ago. You wrote an innocuous-looking program that got past the security systems of a certain large, corporate mainframe. It destroyed that mainframe from the inside—a Trojan horse; it was the talk of all the computer bulletin boards.

"Thus your *nom de guerre:* The Greek. It was on the lips of all the young hackers. You were their hero. You defined a style: The Greek, who perfected the Trojan horse. But now they have all forgotten you."

"That's not true!"

"Yes, Mr. Cox. It is true. You know that the center of hacking is no longer here in the eastern United States. It is in California, Germany, Israel. And the new, young hackers have not heard of you. I have asked them. They don't even dream of doing your specialty Trojan horses anymore; they want to do 'viruses.' And what does a 'Greek' have to do with a virus? Perhaps you should change your name to 'The Doctor.' "

"Look, I'm as good as I ever was. I've done lots of things since that feeble kludge."

"Perhaps. But no one knows who you are anymore. And you are no longer a fourteen-year-old kid. And you are living like this"—one hand swept to include the room as his nose wrinkled—"not in your parents' house."

Kevin stared at the man. "How do you know all this?"

"That is not important, Mr. Cox. And that is why you find yourself in this condition: you have forgotten to look at what *is* important. Think back on what I said. I can offer you a path to fame again. This time the fame should be more permanent."

"Well, look. I don't do charity cases."

"No one said that. You will be able to earn a very good living from what I propose." Onryo gestured at the room. "But that is not why you do what you do. Not for the money. You do what you do because you must. That is part of what makes you the best. I think you should be acclaimed for your talent. That is what I meant by offering you fame."

The whole time Onryo had been in the room, his gaze had not left Kevin. Kevin kept shifting his eyes away, but every time he would look back, Onryo's eyes would be locked on his. Kevin could not stand it. He turned his back to the man and started to fiddle with some wiring that lay in a heap on the tabletop.

"Look, I don't even know who you are . . . and I'm not sure I even care. This is all too fast. I've got work to do. Why don't you come back?"

"I won't come back because I offer a project like this only once. If you are not interested, then perhaps you can't do it. I will go someplace else and find someone who can do it . . . perhaps in Israel."

Kevin spun around. "I tell you, they know nothing there! There's no elegance. Everything they write has loose code! That's because they're just . . . wet children!" He wiped the sweat from his forehead.

Onryo smiled. "If you are better, then why not prove it?"

"I am better."

"In that case, I have a trial."

"I don't do tests. That's why I left school."

"This is not a test, Mr. Cox; I came to you, remember? This is a real project, but possibly only the first step in our relationship. There is a very large corporate computer. On a day that I will specify, I want all data about a certain event destroyed."

"Whose system is it?"

"Let's keep that aside for the moment: I have my own security commitments to protect, and you might not take the project."

"Is it a single-site computer, or is it networked?"

"Oh, a very large network."

"And how is it accessed?"

"By hard-line terminals and microwave links."

"Then it can't be done."

Onryo folded his hands on his abdomen, and his face got very calm. "What do you mean?" he asked quietly.

"Times have changed since my Trojan horse. Any intelligently networked system has data security caches now. You can't destroy all records, because they would be doing real-time archiving of their data onto a WORM."

"Ah . . ."

"A write-once-read-many disk, right?" He picked up one of his Fat Brat CDs. "An optical disk that looks like one of these CDs, only bigger. A laser would write the information onto the disk just like they do in the factory to make these. It can't be erased, but you can store so much information on each disk—a couple of gigabytes—that you don't need to reuse them. You just do your backups one track after another. I archive every version of my working code on a unit that's over there on the end of the table. It takes a five-and-a-quarter-inch, four-hundred-megabyte optical disk. A big network would use nineteen-inch disks; then they'd only need to change disks every other day or so.

"Since they're archiving so often and you can't write over the tracks already laid down, you can't call for a disk data painter to destroy all the data. You've got to blow up the building where the backups are done. And they're probably archiving at multiple sites in case *that* happens."

"This is not good news . . . if what you say is true. We cannot have them reading certain records." He started to rise.

"Wait. Do you want to destroy data or keep someone from reading data?"

Onryo leaned forward toward Kevin. "That is the same thing."

"No it isn't. You were giving me an imprecise instruction set: garbage in, garbage out. Tell me exactly what you want to do. Be precise."

"I need to prevent them from accessing certain records."

"Why didn't you say so? For how long?"

"A few days. Perhaps a week."

Kevin stared off into space. He reached over and turned on the stereo.

Onryo got up and put his hand on Kevin's shoulder at the base of his neck. His fingers tightened.

Kevin focused his eyes and looked at the man. "Don't interrupt me while I'm thinking."

Onryo released his grip and sat again. Kevin's eyes lost their focus and he started to hum along with the music.

Five minutes passed. Kevin reached over and turned off the speakers. "There is a way."

Onryo nodded. "Yes?"

"I'll make this real simple. See, the thing is, you can't destroy the records: they reside in the read-only optical disks. But you can't see the records directly, they're just data in binary code. If you want the records in a form you can see and understand, then you have the computer display it alphanumerically on a terminal. But . . . if the program calls a routine that throws up a dummy display when someone tries to read those records, then they can't see the data. The effect is the same as destroying the data."

Onryo nodded. "Your renown is justified, Mr. Cox. Would you like to do this project for me?"

"What do I get for it?"

"You tell me, Mr. Cox."

"Well, first I need some new iron; this stuff I'm working on is pretty good, but there's a new machine out with CMOS SIMMs and brutal-fast clock speed. And, ah . . . and I'm going to need certain information on the target system—how it's accessed, address methods, bus protocol . . ."

Onryo reached inside his jacket. He removed a notebook and pen. "Tell me what you will need. And please be precise." He smiled.

5

HITCH

The uniform's creases looked sharp enough to cut. It was a conceit of Col. Charles Fonsgraf—thinking it added to his command presence. He had the looks of a past American hero, though well under six feet tall: barrel chested, with rough, red cheeks and short, thinning, grayish blond hair. He looked up from his seat at the end of the table as Admiral Thomas, Bill, and Tina entered the small conference room.

"Charles," the Admiral said, "this is Tina Lucia. You know Bill."

"Well, Bill and Tina, coming by for a visit to see how the big boys work?"

There was a pause. "No, Charles," said the Admiral, "they're on the team."

Fonsgraf sat up straighter. "What is this, the VP's idea? Equal opportunity day? Look, I'm running a very important operation here, and I want the best people for the team." He glanced at Bill and then looked at Tina. "No offense meant, of course, but facts are facts."

The Admiral stared at him for a moment. "No, the fact is that this isn't your men's club . . . and these people are on the team.

Bill is to be my man and contact here. You know his skills; I've trained him, and he has a good working relationship with the technical and operational support groups you'll need at Langley and NSA. Tina is the best information/assessment person I have."

"Well, you may be fond of her, but I hope you realize that the President feels very strongly about his July directive on women in the military: 'the country's honor cannot allow any woman to be placed in a situation where she might be subjected to combat.' I'm just quoting, of course." He smiled. "Bill is welcome, but I'm sure that the President feels that the combat military should be handling this, and that means Tina is out."

The two men stared at each other, then Chris Thomas smiled. When he spoke, his North Carolina accent was suddenly broader. "Charles, I know you're just having fun here: we're old-time kidders, the two of us. But I wouldn't want these two to get the idea that you're doing anything but make a little joke. I am the National Security Advisor, and the President has given me oversight on this issue. Everything that I am doing is with his full consent."

"Now, Chris . . ."

"Let's just call the President and check this out. There's the phone. If you don't have the direct-access extension number with you, well, I can give it to you." Again a smile on his lips, but his eyes were granite hard and cold.

Fonsgraf met his gaze, then slowly let his eyes drop. He rearranged some papers on the desk in front of him. "Oh, I was just joking, Chris. And anyway, we both know the President is a very busy man."

The smile now reached Chris's eyes. "I know that, Charles. That's why he wanted you to lead the team, to take some of the burden off his shoulders. Now let's bring the rest of the team in here and get them briefed." He took the seat at the other end of the table. Bill walked around the table and sat so that he was facing the door. Tina sat across from him.

Fonsgraf spoke into an intercom in front of him, "Okay, let's get everyone in here. Chop, chop!"

There was the sound of feet from the corridor and six men filed into the room—five in suits, and a major in a uniform that, if anything, was more sharply pressed than the Colonel's. Fonsgraf did the introductions. "Admiral Thomas, you know Tom Wald from State and Jack Phillips from Secret Service. This is Peter Hanson from FBI and Dale Kuhn from CIA, who's brought along, ah . . ." Fonsgraf consulted a paper in front of him, "Steve Long, who I assume is going to tell us a story. And Maj. Bunk Cole, here, who will be my action force leader. He served with me in Nam; a good fighting man.

"Gentlemen, this is Admiral Thomas, the National Security Advisor, and two of his people whom he wants to work with us: Bill Hitch, and the lovely lady is Tina Lucia."

Bill looked at Tina; she raised an eyebrow.

"Hello, Dale," said the Admiral.

"Good afternoon, sir. Very good to see you again."

This drew a glance from Fonsgraf, who cleared his throat and said, "Let's be seated. And Dale, have your young man tell us what he has to say. Jack, be a good man and close the door." The CIA men joined Bill on the side of the table facing the door.

Steve Long was a young-looking thirty-two, but his dark brown eyes held a field man's intensity that was not common in the White House. He looked around the table and then started his narrative. "I'm involved in West German liaisons for the Agency. I have some troubling events to relate.

"Two nights ago, I got a call from my German counterpart in the Bundeskriminalamt, the BKA—that's their internal security agency. He asked me to come to a house in Leer—a small town near the coast, about ten kilometers from the Netherlands border.

"On a tip that it was an Ost-Sturm hideout, the BKA raided this house, and found two bodies. They wanted me to help with an ID on one of them."

"Why you, and who is or are the Ost-Sturm?" Peter Hanson asked.

"Ost-Sturm means east storm. It's an ex–Red Brigade outfit. It's thought they've been free-lancing out, recently to some Shiite factions, I believe," Tina said. "They—"

Fonsgraf cut her off. "Why don't we just let young Steve tell his story? Go on, son."

"Yes, sir. We've made the ID on the body; it was John Verre." There was a rising level of murmurs around the table. "His throat had been cut."

"What!" the State Department man barked. He rose from his seat. "I've got to report this." There was a general rumble of conversation.

Bill sat very still, watching the others. This was bad news, he thought, but he noticed that Charles Fonsgraf and Bunk Cole hadn't seemed surprised. He also noticed Fonsgraf had a small smile on his lips.

"Sit down, Tom," Fonsgraf said. "The *senior* people have already been informed. Let's let Steve tell the story to the rest of you who haven't been briefed."

Tom Wald returned to his seat with a slightly sheepish look.

"The other man had been garroted. He had a note in his shoe, which we found. In it, he said the Ost-Sturm people were on to him and that he was going to be killed. He claimed to be an agent of Israeli intelligence—Mossad—and asked that some code scrap be passed on to them for a big reward. The identification methods used in the note conform to what we know of Mossad tradecraft."

"What does Mossad say?" asked Tom Wald.

"Well, there's a problem. The man had a knife in his pocket that matched the wounds on Verre's throat. On analysis, the blood on the blade and under his nails matched Verre's."

"What are you saying?" demanded Phillips, the Secret Service man.

"It appears that for some reason, perhaps in an attempt to maintain cover, the Mossad agent killed Verre."

There was a stunned silence in the room, except for Peter Hanson, who growled, "I never thought we could trust those bastards!"

"Is there any hint yet that Mossad knows anything about this?" the Admiral asked quietly.

"No, although we can assume they know the house where they'd placed their agent has been shut down. They have been making discreet inquiries with the BKA, but they can't push it. They hadn't cleared the agent placement with the Germans, and in any case, the two services haven't really gotten along since the Olympic thing years ago."

"The consensus in the Agency," said Kuhn, the senior CIA man, "is not to deal with Mossad on this until we develop some information on our own. We don't like their keeping quiet when they had an agent in place where Verre was being held. We know from past experience that we need to get our position clarified before we confront them." Kuhn looked around the table. "But as bad as this information is, we have something from this Mossad agent that may worry us a bit more.

"We have methods of dealing with Mossad's field ciphers. In the code scrap that we got from the agent's shoe, he says that Ost-Sturm and someone allied with them have firm plans to hijack nuclear weapons in the U.S. at some point after Christmas. They plan on using them."

"Come on," said Peter Hanson. "You can't be serious. What terrorist group is going to go up against an armed forces base in the U.S. and snatch nukes?"

"We should take anything that Ost-Sturm is involved with seriously," said Kuhn. "As Tina mentioned, they're an offshoot, originally formed by some ex–Red Brigade members. They have a reputation for good technical-operational expertise. Terrorism is becoming more high-tech, just like everything else—look at the bomb that took down the Pan Am flight over Scotland. Other groups have felt the need for help in this area, and Ost-Sturm has evidently been ready to step in. They seem to have some of the best people on the other side.

"Over the past few years, we've heard some stuff, specifically that Ost-Sturm has been operating on a free-lance basis, supporting other groups in technical matters. We think they've done two recent operations in Germany: both showed a high level of technical sophistication and good knowledge of security weaknesses.

"Their recent communiqués have been talking up the Middle East conflict. With what we've been doing recently in Lebanon, I'm surprised that they've not targeted the U.S. before."

"But I don't see what the problem is," said Tom Wald from State. "As Peter said, what terrorist group is going to go up against a U.S. armed forces base? If the weapons stay on the bases and on the Navy ships, what's the real risk?"

"Not great . . . that is, if the weapons stayed on the bases," replied Dale Kuhn. "The problem is that they don't. Our past analyses have shown a measurable threat because of a pretty constant flow of nuclear weapons around the U.S. in highway convoys."

"You've got to be kidding! Why are they shipping them around?"

"There are three main reasons, Tom: force modernization, changes in deployment strategies, and reconditioning of the weapons themselves. The last is the most common."

Colonel Fonsgraf broke in, "This is not a serious issue. Let's go on to one that is: the death of our missing airman. In the meantime, if you think this little group of Germans and Arabs is a threat, then the answer is obvious to me at least: just stop the refurbishing and highway transportation of weapons for a while."

"That can't be done," said Tina in a quiet voice.

Fonsgraf jumped at this contradiction and leaned forward to stare at her. "Look, young lady, when I want to hear from you, I'll ask your opinion on something I think you know about. Let the experts discuss this."

"Ah, Colonel," said Kuhn. "She's right. The transportation convoys can't be stopped." Bill noticed that the Admiral was nodding his head in agreement.

The Colonel turned an angry glare at him. "And why not?" he demanded.

"Because nuclear weapons, especially hydrogen ones, deteriorate over time. The key problem is the heavy hydrogen—the tritium—that provides the fusion energy in the explosion. The main plant DOE has to do the refurbishing is in Amarillo, Texas. Truck convoys deliver the weapons from the various bases to Amarillo, and take the rebuilt weapons back out to the bases. If we stop that process, our weapons start to lose effectiveness over time. We could stop for a week, or perhaps two or three, but longer than that and we'd start to back up with scheduling problems."

Tom Wald spoke up. "I can't believe that the public highways are being used for this! Why aren't they flown?"

The Admiral gave a small cough. "Tina, I believe that this was something you briefed me about a year ago. Please explain it to these gentlemen."

"Yes, sir. As Dale explained, from time to time nuclear weapons have to be moved from one base to another or to the Pantex plant in Amarillo. Originally, we used to fly them, until the incident in 1958, when a B-47 accidentally dropped a nuke in South Carolina.

"The chemical explosive trigger demolished a farmhouse and vaporized a chicken coop. No fatalities, just some children with cuts and bruises. There was no nuclear explosion since the bomb wasn't armed. The government claimed all the plutonium was cleaned up without a problem, but the event got people thinking: even if a nuke doesn't go off, if you crash one you've got a lot of environmental problems.

"This accident happened on a regular Air Force training flight, but here we were flying bombs from all over the country to Amarillo. Someone thought to calculate the mean time to failure for airplane versus truck convoy delivery, and came up with some scary numbers. Also, if you crash a plane, you've got an impact speed of, say, four hundred knots. If you crash a truck, you're doing it at sixty miles an hour. The total energy in a crash goes up with the square of the speed—which means not six, but over forty times the destructive energy in a plane crash. That makes for quite a difference in cleanup: you can hope to maintain the integrity of the shipping container in a sixty-mile-per-hour crash, but not at four hundred knots.

"We could do another analysis, but my gut feeling is that the safety differential between air and road paths remains the same. The other issue is that a mature security system has been built up around the convoy method. You would have to develop one for air transport. I would think that—"

Fonsgraf interrupted her. "I think security issues are the domain of my people, thank you. Jack, Bunk, what do you two think of the issue of security for our nukes? Do we worry about these German terrorists getting at one of our bombs? It seems pretty farfetched to me."

Bunk Cole straightened his shoulders and spoke in a deep, resonant voice. "I think I agree with you, Colonel. I know the boys at DOE; they're a good bunch when it comes to security. That's not to say that that bunch of Reds may not try, but I don't think there could be anything that security can't handle."

"Jack?"

"Yes, Colonel. I go along with Bunk. And I agree with you, it seems to me the main issue here is that of our flyer, and his death."

"Well, if no one else has any objections, I'd like to move on to what I see as the central issue here: how we are going to deal with the death of our boy, and what we're going to do about Mossad."

Before Fonsgraf could continue, Bill looked quickly around the table. It appeared no one was going to speak up. The Admiral was examining the opened folder on the desk in front of him, but Bill knew the reason he had been put on the committee was to help counterbalance the Colonel. So . . . I've got to deal with the idiot, he thought. "Colonel, I'd like to make a few points."

Fonsgraf took a deep breath as if he was going to chew Bill out, and then glanced at the Admiral. He rolled his eyes upward. "Sure, sure, Bill. Why don't you enlighten us."

Be diplomatic, Bill thought. There's an important point to be made here. "This issue of Jack Verre is very important—what he was doing in Germany, why he was killed, how and what we are going to tell his family and the rest of the country, and how we are going to deal with Mossad on this . . . all of that. But I'm also concerned about the tip about the bomb.

"Ost-Sturm may have sounded a little wacky recently, but they're not a group without a record. They have produced some sophisticated events in the past and have a reputation for taking over badly run operations where they've been sort of consultants, and making those operations run well. And think about this: Lieutenant Verre showed up in Germany. We had a lot of assets looking for him in Lebanon; they got him past everyone and into Germany. That shows some organizational ability.

"When you're talking about nuclear weapons, you're talking about an area where the stakes are the highest. We might consider looking at the current security arrangements and perhaps adding on some security forces from the military to back up the DOE team."

Bunk Cole spoke up. "Hey, I know the fellows at DOE. Some of them are ex–Army Special Forces. The top man there is Edgar Platt. I served with him; we go way back. He can handle this, and I wouldn't want to step on his toes by trying to bring in forces from the services, even if they are Army. DOE's never had a problem on their transport runs."

"And perhaps that's a reason to be a little concerned," Bill replied. "They may never have had a real threat; they may be complacent. The issue is important enough that I think we should increase the security on the truck runs until we get some understanding as to whether or not the tip was a credible one, or find out more about Ost-Sturm and what they're up to."

"You may not understand how things work here between the services," Fonsgraf said. "We can't just plunk down a group of Army or Marine people into an operation that's run by another department. That's the sort of thing I'd expect you'd've learned in Organizational Procedures 101."

"I think I agree with Bill," said the Admiral. "The stakes are high enough that something should be done."

Fonsgraf looked disconcerted for a moment, and glanced at Major Cole. He doesn't want to lose control of this, thought Bill. That's really his only concern.

"Well, Bill," said the Colonel. "I'll tell you what. I'll have Bunk talk to his friend at DOE and tell him we want them to increase their security training, shake up their teams a bit. Remember, we have until Christmastime to get them into top form. Bunk, handle that for me, will you?

"Now let's talk about what we are going to do about Lieutenant Verre. We should be thinking about who we're going to hit in Lebanon."

6

BAALBEK

"You must be working for the Americans!" she hissed. "How could you let them know? How could you do anything like that without consulting me?"

The lamp cast a small, yellow pool of light on the table in the center of the room. Two figures sat there. One was a brown-haired woman in her thirties, dressed in black jeans and turtle-neck top. The other was Hussein Baalbek.

"Your partner was there. He agreed to the plan."

"Don't mock me, Baalbek. What Rudi agrees to means shit. It's what I agree to that matters: I run Ost-Sturm."

"Yes, but you have partners now, and this operation is run by the group. If you had been in Germany, you would have taken part in the decision, but you were here in the United States. We had to act quickly when we found out that our young friend was a Mossad agent. Would you have had us wait two weeks to discuss it when you got back? In this business there are times to act quickly. We made the correct decision."

"But think of the asset you wasted! We had an important hostage. My people would have broken him in two more weeks. He would have said *anything* we wanted!"

"You want us to have waited two weeks for you to break Verre? Two weeks after we found out who Dari really was? . . . And what is Dari doing during these two weeks, reporting to his controller, perhaps? And then one fine morning we are driving down the road and, poof, a bomb in a parked car goes off!"

"Don't talk down to me, Baalbek."

"No, Uli, my friend, I'm not talking down to you, I'm talking facts. I've kept most of my poor body away from the Mossad. They know their business, and they fight as everyone who fights for religion does—mercilessly. Every day my leg reminds me to be cautious with the Israelis.

"We needed to act quickly, and we did. Your 'asset' had no great value. There are many hostages in my country, and I don't seem to remember that any have done any good for our side. We now have a chance to get a *real* weapon, and for that I will spend any assets we have."

The woman pulled out a cigarette and lit it. She sat there taking hard drags and staring at Baalbek. She thought it would unsettle him. Baalbek was not unsettled.

The silence stretched between them until she finished the cigarette and dropped it into a small water glass she held in her hand.

Baalbek spoke. "I want to bring Kakimoto in for the rest of this conversation."

"Kakimoto, Kakimoto. Why are you trusting him with this?" She slammed the glass down on the table. "He is a rightist, a member of the ruling class. He should be our enemy, not our ally."

"And why would a right-wing fanatic join us leftists? Your skepticism comes from a mistake in definition. You see the political spectrum as a line, with leftists at one end and rightists at the other. It's not. It is a circle, and what separates us, the right from the left, is only a step. What unites us is a belief in the power of violence."

"So, I'm your student now, and you're back at the university?" She stared past him at the wall.

Baalbek ignored her and continued in his dry tone. "Kakimoto, you, and I all believe the same thing: that only violence gives the power, the right to rule. So it doesn't take much for a man to switch from right to left; you Germans should know that. Right and left, we are really quite close. And what you call the center is actually the other side of the circle, occupied by those who are afraid of violence—the meek who accept their condition."

He put his arms on the table and enclosed his right fist with his other hand. "Kakimoto sees himself a warrior, a warrior avenging a great outrage—the death of his parents. They were killed at Nagasaki while he was out of the city on some school trip. More than that . . . his grandparents were killed there, too.

"That loss, and being raised an orphan, not the proud firstborn of an old samurai family, that is something he will never forgive, never forget. A whole life waiting to strike a blow at those responsible—the Americans. That anger lets him join us . . . and lets us use him.

"He is a very valuable addition, Uli. His cover as a Japanese businessman—a Mr. Onryo—is perfect. He can travel, consult, and recruit for us here in the United States without raising the suspicions that an Arab would."

"I don't like it."

"I don't think we have a real choice. We need his talents." Baalbek got up, walked over to the door, and opened it. "Please come in, Yataro." The Japanese man's form appeared in the doorway. As always, there was a sense of stillness and strength about him that implied a coming blow. "Please join us," Baalbek said.

Kakimoto brought over a chair, and the two men joined the woman at the table.

"Yataro, Uli has found us a good location, don't you think? But she is very angry about our hinting to the Americans about our plans to get bombs. That is what we are discussing now."

"We are not discussing anything, you are explaining!"

"Uli," said Baalbek, "I have dreamed for many years about a chance to get a real weapon like this. And through great fortune, I have found an agent to get me that dream.

"Select good people and then give them their head. The man I have in place knows his business. He told me that for us to have the best chance of achieving our goal, things had to be stirred up a bit with our target."

"Come now, since when is it a good idea to tell your victim that you are coming after him?"

"Perhaps Yataro can explain this to you."

"What, another lecturer?"

"Uli, I studied kendo for many years as a young man . . ."

"Not karate?"

"Karate is for farmers; kendo is for samurai. Its lessons are much more powerful. I remember one very well from the training floor. An opponent in a stable defense is very difficult to attack. The trick is to draw him into movement. When he moves, he must create an opening for you; *then* you attack suddenly, strongly."

"But this is life, not some arcane sport," Uli scoffed.

"The lessons are the same. Mushashi also taught this in the 'Fire Book' of *A Book of Five Rings;* a good guide to strategy; a good book to take to heart. As Hussein has said, his agent asked that we do something to draw an unbalanced movement in the bomb security forces: we left our note in Dari's shoe."

"But why should they believe that note?"

"Ah," said Baalbek, "as much as I distrust the Islamic Action League, they do have some solid connections to the Syrian intelligence services. It was through them that I learned the correct Mossad tradecraft. The note will pass as genuine."

"There is a real elegance to this," continued Kakimoto. "This simple maneuver has two effects. First, it gets the information to the Americans in a believable manner, information that will cause them to open up their security training. Second, forcing Dari to kill the pilot drives a wedge between the Americans and the Israelis, so that their security forces will not be so eager to cooperate in the near future."

"If we can get a weapon," Baalbek said quietly, "then many things will change, Uli. We can force the Americans to reunite Lebanon under the Muslim majority. My country has suffered too long as a pawn of the superpowers. With those weapons, we can end that."

His voice grew quieter still. "I also will be able to avenge my village's deaths—there are well over four hundred now. In this I am very much like my brothers in the Islamic Action League. Revenge is very important to me. I have found a small American

Army base; it houses just over four hundred men. About the same as my people's losses. That will be where we will use the first bomb. A nice symmetry, no?"

"Baalbek, you're a fool! If you do succeed in getting some bombs, how do you plan to deliver them to an Army base? With smiling Islamic Action League suicide squads? After losing a shipment of bombs, security will be tighter than a young boy's cheeks." She gave a crude laugh. "Or is your 'Japanese businessman' going to hand deliver them himself?"

"Oh no, Uli. We have a more elegant way, one that uses the efficiencies of the modern American business state. Yataro has even been recruiting someone to help us cover our tracks." He looked at Kakimoto. "How has your recruitment gone?" Baalbek asked.

"Very well. I think I have found our man."

"Baalbek, what's this about?" demanded Uli.

"We wouldn't want to have our trail backtracked, would we? Everything in this country seems to leave a computer trail, especially the way we will be delivering our package. Yataro has found a man who can cut that trail."

She slammed her fist on the table. "You're adding another member to our team without discussing it?"

"Oh, no," said Kakimoto. "He is not part of the team. He doesn't know anything about us; he knows me only as Mr. Onryo. He thinks I represent a Japanese shipping company that wants to expand into the United States, a quite ruthless company that wants to take action directly against its competition, and what I have asked him to do is simply a trial before he gets his real project."

"But what about our security? Surely when the first bomb goes off, he will connect your 'trial' with outside events?"

"That is one of his beauties: he never, ever watches television or reads papers. He has no interest at all in the outside world, only his internal one. He'll eventually hear about the bomb, of course, but he doesn't know enough about current events to make any connection with me. He is quite the virgin."

7

ROSS

A rusty Ford pickup sat on the road leading down to the highway. It was cold; the sky was white; the land was white. Below, Interstate 40 was streaked with pale ribbons where the wind had drifted snow across the pavement from the high banks left by the plows. Everything had the bleak lack of color of an early winter in the Texas panhandle.

A couple of cardboard boxes and an old suitcase were tied in the back of the pickup's bed. A thin dark-haired man sat in the cab. He was satisfied with the truck. It was rusty, but solid; a 4 × 4 Ford F-250, with a powerful engine and new tires. It was a good choice, one they'd not have seen before. He had placed a small red sticker at the lower left corner of the windshield.

He had been here since well before dawn; the spot was perfect for the stakeout: the pickup would be hidden from the convoy until they passed where the road joined the highway. They would have to pick him up in their rearview mirrors, and he did not think they would be alert enough to see him. They should have had no warning.

It wasn't his truck, and he didn't trust the exhaust system. He only ran the engine at five-minute intervals despite the cold. The cab couldn't stay warm that way, but Felix Ross was a very careful man. Pay attention to details, he thought. Better to be cold than to doze off from carbon monoxide. He had a large thermos of hot coffee on the seat next to him, but if things went well, he would need it later.

A few minutes past seven-thirty in the morning, a Chevy Suburban escort vehicle passed on the highway below. Felix started the engine and waited, and the gray tractor-trailer he had been looking for passed by seventy-five yards behind the EV. Another Suburban followed a hundred yards behind the truck. Both escort vehicles had the four-foot-long, white, cylindrical satellite antennae mounted on their left rear fenders. Felix waited until the convoy was a half mile away, headed up the next hill toward the New Mexico border.

There were only two EVs. He smiled grimly to himself. Two meant this was the trip he had been waiting for: the convoy was carrying small weapons—cruise-missile and artillery warheads. As the last truck dropped out of sight over the hill ahead, he put the transmission into drive and accelerated down toward the highway.

When he reached the roadway, he matched his speed to the last EV's, keeping back. There were two civilian cars between him and the convoy: a sedan and an old camper. Perfect. Felix started whistling a soft, happy tune. He hated waiting.

He was a man who had become hooked on action. It had been that way since his time in the military. Action like this seemed to be the only thing he could enjoy. Before the Marines, he had loved sports, but sports had been made too tame by the experiences Special Operations had given him: risks, movement, tension, and killing.

After leaving the service, he had joined a couple of security firms, but had learned that security life in the United States was not like on television. You didn't get to work, to use your skills. There wasn't that much action. Nothing happened, you just waited. He hated waiting . . . and he had languished.

So, he had signed on with an oil company, doing security and protective work in the Mideast. It had been enjoyable for a while. There had been some good times, and he had met some good people, men who had the same needs as he. But even there the work was too calm. When an old Marine buddy had written him about this job, Felix had talked it over with his new friends, said good-bye to the oil company, good-bye to the desert, and come back to the United States. Now Felix Ross was a field security trainer for the Department of Energy's nuclear weapons transportation teams. He tested for chinks in the protection, set up mock raids, and then debriefed the transport teams afterward. He had been doing it for two years. He had felt like he was trying to sweep back the tide with a broom.

The little red sticker he had put on the windshield was this week's code sign. It was supposed to let the transportation security team know he was a trainer doing a test, but not give him away until he got close enough to actually start his move. Well, he would see today if they were sharp enough to pick up a threat before they could see the sticker. He thought about last week. He had been able to cut the truck off before they had noticed him, let alone noticed the code sign. They never seemed to take this seriously.

Up ahead, the road leveled to a long, flat straight. He let the truck ease back so he was even farther behind the convoy. He knew where they were going, and it would be safer to stay back here until they got closer to the exit he had chosen for the attempt.

This was going to be too easy, and it offended him. He knew which were the escort vehicles, and could easily plan his attack. Early on, Felix had suggested they get some unmarked cars, like pickup trucks and older sedans, because the EVs were too easy to spot. He had been laughed down. Well, someday they'll learn, he'd thought.

Standard operating procedure was for the escort vehicles to box in a threat and force it to stay on the main road while the weapons truck took an exit and doubled back. The escort crews had been acting too much by the book, and in this case, that would be a mistake. The location he had chosen should allow him to pull a little surprise.

They were all sheep—the drivers, the other trainers, the higher-ups. At first, his work had been exciting, different. But then he had started to feel that the people he was working with did not deserve his respect. They had no pride in their work, they cut corners. Felix remembered one driver's retort to a tough critique early on: "What are you busting our butts for? We're not the Ruskies, you weasel-eyed turd. This is just a job, not some adventure show. Who the hell is going to try to steal warheads? Stop taking this cowboys-and-Indians stuff so seriously and ease up before you start to make some enemies."

That had made him angry, but worried, too. Was life becoming just playacting for him? Felix was very, very afraid of going soft. He clung to his memories of the action in Special Operations. His friends in the Mideast had told him, "You're a weapon, and a weapon wants to be used. You miss the killing. We all do."

They had said the killing made it real. Felix wasn't sure. What he did know was that he had to keep testing himself. Keep himself hard. The only thing that mattered was seeking perfection in his own actions. He had tried to train these people and they didn't seem to want to learn. So be it. "Let those soft clowns look out, here I come."

The isolated exit ramp was coming up. He pressed on the accelerator; the pickup downshifted, then surged forward.

He didn't want to make it too easy for them, so he kept his speed to just under sixty-five, and used the camper ahead of him as a screen. He pulled up on the convoy when the camper hid him from their sight, and eased up on the gas when the road curved and they could see him.

Slowly the distance closed up until he was thirty feet behind the camper and seventy-five yards from the rearmost Suburban.

Now here was the delicate part: how to close up the last two hundred yards to the truck and get in front of it. That was where Felix's choice of his own vehicle came in. The rust should do it, he thought. I'm just an Okie, passing through.

He took a red feed cap from over the visor and placed it on top of the dash behind the left corner of the windshield. These turkeys would never notice the red sticker. "All's fair in love and war."

He drifted out into the left lane, and as his speed increased, he felt the rusted right fender start to flap in the wind. Perfect. It's always the details that make an operation, he thought.

There was the sign ahead announcing the exit: three miles to go. Just less than three minutes. He had to move it. From scouting this morning, he knew there was black ice on the curve just ahead. The rear EV's driver would be concentrating on driving as he took the turn and not likely to glance out the window. That would be the best time to pass. He increased his speed and began to overtake the second Suburban.

Just stay in your left lane, he thought. Trust your camouflage. Stay in character. A guy who owned this truck would not be thinking about driving safely. He pulled up behind the lead guard truck and then passed it on the curve.

Now the next step was going to be a bit more difficult. They were approaching the exit. Felix had to get in front of the carrier, but his plan was dependent on the guard crews seeing a threat and boxing him once he got there. He thought he'd better make it showy to wake them up. Time to move. Blast off.

Felix stomped the gas pedal to the floor. The engine roared, and the truck's rear end fishtailed as he accelerated toward the carrier. That should get their attention, he thought. A glance in the rearview mirror told him that the guard truck had finally noticed him and started to accelerate, too, but not as quickly. They don't know if I'm a problem yet, he thought. Time to look like a bad guy.

Felix sped past the carrier, cut in front of it and stood on the brakes. As the big gray truck began to brake, too, he accelerated again and then weaved from side to side. This doesn't really make any sense as an attack mode, he thought, but that's not my game here. Felix kept up his weaving, but was careful to keep enough room between the carrier and his own truck to allow a Suburban to fit in.

"Come on, hurry up, you bastards," he mumbled. "Here comes the exit." The lead EV, alerted by radio, began to drop back.

When the exit was two hundred yards ahead, the rear EV finally caught up to him. The lead one dropped back more until its rear bumper was even with Felix's door, and the rear one swerved in behind him and pulled up close to his bumper.

Well, the guys in the front truck haven't learned anything, Felix thought. They're still in an easy field of fire from my cab.

Felix tried to slow a bit, but the guard truck behind him moved forward and gently tapped his bumper. Nice control, Felix thought. He tried to slow again and again was bumped.

They passed the exit, and Felix looked back to see the carrier start to bear off toward the exit ramp. Perfect. Felix slowed again, and this time the rear EV moved back to give him room. The truck on his left moved back, and the guard in the right seat craned his head forward to look into the cab. Felix watched his eyes take in the red code sticker, and then look up in surprise to Felix's face. The guard's face broke into a large smile. He was smoking a cigarette. He gave Felix the finger. Felix smiled back. "That's right, you bastard, be cocky."

The three trucks were now almost halfway between the exit and entrance ramps. Let's see if you can keep that smile, Felix thought. Action time!

He lowered his right hand and dropped the shift selector into neutral, then reached down to the floor and put the transfer case into four-wheel drive. Step on the brakes . . . the EV behind him braked, too, to keep from running into his rear. It gave him a bit of room. Great. Hand on the parking-brake release lever, stomp down on the parking brake, and put a little right lock on the steering wheel. The pickup started to slew sideways on the highway.

The rear guard truck, confused now, braked and swerved into the left lane.

Felix kept his eyes on the road side and his objective, a low spot in the bank of snow beside the road. Here it comes, ready . . . now!

Felix pulled up on the lever, releasing the parking brake. At the same time, he dropped the transmission back into gear and gently stepped on the gas. He had done half of a bootlegger turn. The pickup ended its skid and, powering forward, smashed through the snow wall and into the field beyond.

The pickup, now in soft snow only a foot and a half deep, churned down the slope toward the carrier truck. Up on the highway, the EVs went past the opening and started to brake to a halt.

Felix knew he had them beaten—they didn't have four-wheel

drive and couldn't follow him. It would be too slow for them to back up to the exit ramp. But if they continued on to where the entrance ramp joined the highway, the way the road was plowed would keep them from making a simple U-turn and coming down the ramp the wrong way to get him. "Yee-hah!"

Felix got down to the exit ramp, bumped through onto the pavement, and pulled up behind the carrier truck. He rolled down the window and began to sing, " 'Oh, I'm just an Okie from Muskogee.' " He stuck his arm out and gave the hand signal that would identify him as a trainer. The carrier pulled to the side of the road and stopped. "Hot damn!"

Felix stopped and got out. The cold wind cut through his jacket. He ran up to the tractor's cab. The driver rolled down his window. It was Fred Ash, actually one of the better men the teams had. "Well, I got you bastards again. Those turkeys let you down."

The driver shrugged. "Yeah, well, I guess if you get your rocks off that way . . ."

"Damn right. I love this. Look it's cold as a bitch out here. Keep on down the ramp, pull back on the highway going the same way. Stop in the rest area up ahead so I can debrief those bozos. You'd better get them on the radio and tell them what we're going to do. I don't want them to get their ugly selves killed up there trying to make the turn onto the ramp." Felix turned and ran back to his truck. Damn, it's cold, he thought. Just what I need.

Felix followed the carrier back up onto the highway. A mile ahead there was a rest area, just a pull-off with parking spaces and a few trash barrels overturned for the winter and sticking up through the snow. It was separated from the highway by a twenty-foot hill. The EVs were waiting as they pulled in. As the large truck parked at an angle to them, Felix pulled up next to the rear one and rolled down his window. The Suburban's window rolled down.

"Go back and put up the No Entrance sign, and then join us here." Standard operating procedure said block off the entrance to the rest area when stopping the convoy.

"Oh, fuck that. It's too cold to get out. Why bother?"

Felix's temper flared. "Damn it, I just rubbed your noses in shit, isolated your carrier, and you're telling me what to do? That's your problem, you do everything half-assed. Someday you're going to get caught. Get that sign up and get back here or I'm going to file a report on this fiasco!"

That got the guard's attention. For all his screaming, Felix had never filed a deficiency report that would bring other training cadres down here. And with all the increased training headquarters had ordered, a deficiency report could get a guard fired. "Yes, sir, yes, sir, three bags full, sir, Mr. Ross, sir." The guard rolled up the window and turned to the driver, who said, "Humor him."

Felix read his lips. It was a trick he had picked up in Special Operations, and it was often useful. He was very interested in what the crews were thinking about him, what they said when they thought he wasn't listening. It helped him learn where they were overconfident, where their vulnerabilities lay.

The Suburban backed toward the rest area entrance and Felix pulled up to the second EV. He got out and went up to the driver's window. "When they get back from putting up the sign, we'll have a postmortem. Roll down your rear window, I've got some stuff to put in the back."

"What's that?"

"Some laundry and books I want you to take back to Amarillo for me on your return trip. I have to leave this pickup with the rancher I rented it from in Clovis—I'll fly from Farwell back to base. You'd better take my gun, too." Standard operating procedure again: "All trainers are considered part of the protective force, and shall carry appropriate firearms."

Felix jogged to his pickup and untied the boxes in the bed. He carried them to the rear of the Suburban and started to pile them into the back.

"Hurry up, damn it. It's cold out there!"

"Cram it!" Felix put his things in the back of the Suburban, carefully placing the last box on top of the pile, bracing it against the radio cabinet that occupied the left rear corner. "That's it. Close 'er up." A thin coil of wire trailed out of the corner of the window and lay on the ground.

The other EV drove up. "Get into the other guard vehicle," Felix told them. "I want to talk this over."

He went back to his pickup. The cold wind cut his face. It really was desolate on this stretch of highway. The low hill cut off the view of the highway. Felix turned and looked the other way . . . empty desolation, no houses, no roads. "What a godforsaken place," and here he was, out here alone surrounded only by sheep. Very stupid, goddamned sheep.

He turned to the cab, reached in and got his M-16 and the thermos of coffee, and walked back to the EV. He opened the rear passenger door. The other guards were in the backseat. "Miller time. Here's some hot coffee; warm yourselves up."

They seemed surprised. "Hey, thanks!"

"I want to get Freddy; I'll be back."

"I'll be back," growled one of the guards in his best Arnold Schwarzenegger voice, and then laughed.

Felix walked around the back of the EV, and then around the big truck, trailing a wire behind him. It led into his pocket. He banged on the side of the cab and Freddy opened the door.

"I've got some hot coffee in the EV, come on and have some."

"No, I'm not leaving this truck: SOP. I don't ever forget you're a trainer."

"It won't matter." He shivered.

"What do you mean?"

"There'll be plenty of coffee left." Felix unslung his rifle and raised it.

"Hey, didn't they teach you anything in weapons school? Don't point that thing at anything you don't intend to shoot."

"You're right," Felix sighed, and pulled the trigger. A short burst tore into Freddy's chest. He bounced back into the steering wheel and fell headfirst out of the cab. His feet tangled in the pedals and hung him there, upside down. The back of his jacket was shredded.

Felix quickly pulled the wire from his pocket and pushed the button attached to the end. An explosion roared on the other side of the truck. A puff of snow filtered down on his head. He walked back around and took in the scene. The Claymore mine in the box placed on top of the pile had gone off. Four torsos were sitting in the truck, bloody stumps where the heads had been. The windows had blown out and a red and gray spray coated the frames. The cold wind blew the last of the smoke away. There was no fire.

Felix walked up to the driver's side and keyed the hidden button under the dash. The drivers called it "Mother." It sent an all-okay signal to the tracking satellite. Central's tracking discrimination was only a few miles, and as long as the okay button was hit every ten minutes they would be cool. They knew there was going to be a training test today and would expect a short stop, but Felix paid attention to details. He walked back to the carrier's cab and pulled the driver's body out onto the pavement. He reached in, got the radio mike, and keyed it. "Hello, Central, code gray shark, convoy West Five. This is trainer."

"Central here. Are you guys moving? Over."

"No, I just finished the training raid. We're having coffee while I do a postmortem. Tell Mother that we're going to take a break from her for a half hour or so while I talk to them. These guys are pretty levelheaded. I don't think I'm going to be able to teach them anything else."

"Good. Well, stay warm. Over."

"We should be on our way soon. Over and out." Felix reached up and changed the channel. He keyed the mike. "Done," he said. There was an answering beep.

Felix went back to the EV and got the thermos off the floor. He wiped off the cup and poured himself some coffee. He patted his jacket pockets, and then bent into the truck and took a pack of cigarettes from the shirt pocket of the torso in the right front seat, shook one out, and lit it.

He squinted into the blank, white northern sky. "Damn, it's cold." Felix went back to the carrier and started to disable its security systems. He shouldn't have long to wait . . . he hated waiting.

8

LIVINGSTON

An inside room, it had a large map of the United States on one of the long walls, blue carpeting on the floor, comfortable swivel chairs, recessed lighting, and muted tan walls. The desks faced the map and were equipped with a computer terminal, radio and phone links. The sibilant whoosh from the heating vents was a gentle white noise put there to mask the click of computer keyboards and murmured radio conversations. From this place the nuclear convoys and their security escorts were tracked and monitored on their many paths across the country. It was a calm and restful place to work.

Paul Livingston was the controller responsible for the West Texas–Arizona zone. He was calm and rested. He was also bored.

He stood and stretched. "Hey, Goose," he said to the man at the next terminal. "Cover convoy West Five for a few minutes for me, I've got to take a crap."

"What are they up to?"

"The trainer's just finished a mock raid. I've told him that they can leave Mother alone for a couple of cycles while he does his debriefing."

"Yo. I'll watch it. Bring me some coffee when you come back."

"Decaf?"

"You've got to be kidding. I can't keep my eyes open. Make it hightest. Black, sugar on the side . . . I swear, this job is like watching paint dry."

Paul went to the bathroom, bringing along the new issue of *Sports Afield* that had articles on ice fishing. He wanted to take his daughter for the first time this winter; she was six. He remembered the first time his father had taken him: the blue-bright sun, the gray ice, the little perch lying on the ice, frozen stiff as sticks.

The coffeepot was empty. "Damn it! Can't any of those lazy SOBs learn to make a new pot when they empty the old one?" He washed out the pot, dumped water in the hopper of the machine, and, tearing open the foil packet, dumped fresh grounds into the paper basket. He waited there at the machine while the coffee brewed.

"Did you have to go into town for it?" asked Goose as he stirred sugar into the cup of coffee Paul had handed him.

"No, an empty pot again. What time did my convoy say they left the rest area?"

"Huh? They haven't checked in yet."

"What do you mean?" Paul checked the clock on the wall. Forty-five minutes had passed since his last contact. "Lazy bastards, that trainer said he was just going to do a debrief, not retell the story of his life."

He sat down at his terminal. "Have they started keying Mother yet?"

Goose took a sip of coffee, and then spit it out. "Shit, I've burned my tongue!" He felt the tip with his fingers.

"Goose!"

"What?"

"Have they keyed Mother?"

"No, damn you. Why is this coffee so hot?"

Paul put on his headset and pushed the radio talk button.

"West Five, West Five, this is Control. Check in with me and get that convoy back on the road. Let's get a move on. I told you I made a fresh pot."

His earphones were silent. "West Five, West Five, this is Control, over."

"You could have told me. I really burned it."

"I did tell you. West Five, West Five. Goose, have you had any radio problems today?"

"Let's have a little sympathy about this tongue—I'm going out to dinner tonight. No, no radio trouble."

"Then I don't like this. Why don't they answer?"

"Maybe they stepped out to take a leak."

"All of them? I'm going to try the Satellite Two circuit." He keyed a change on his console. "West Five, come in, damn it."

The earphones were silent, and Paul felt something like a cold breeze at the back of his neck. "West Five, West Five."

"Check their carrier."

"Right." Paul's fingers flew on the keyboard as he told the computer to see if the convoy's radio links were still transmitting. "Ah . . . yes. Carrier's still there."

"Location?"

"I don't have a good satellite fix . . . Sat. Two is still pretty low on the horizon. It seems they're still in the general area of my last conversation. Locator's not on."

"Query it."

Paul hit more keys. "No response."

"What do you mean, no response."

"I said no response!" His neck felt tight, his shoulders cold. "What the hell is going on? Who's super today?"

"Kiley."

"Oh great. I'm going to be dog meat."

"Do you have any high cover in the area?"

"No, this convoy was just little stuff." Why did I say "was"? Paul thought. "They're only putting the planes on for the big toys, over ten kilotons. I want to send someone out to look." He looked up at the wall map. "Where they are, it would take just as long to send some EVs from Amarillo as it would to try and get choppers up from Cannon Air Force Base."

"That's Kiley's call."

"Tell me about it. Good-bye pension." Paul pushed a button on his phone dialer. There seemed to be a cold wind roaring through his chest. It was hard to catch his breath. "Livingston, West Tex–Arizona Control. Give me Kiley . . .

"Sir, I seem to have lost contact with my convoy. Something's happened to West Five."

9

ROSS

Sound came first: a faint drone that could be resolved out of the noise of the wind, a faint beat, growing louder. Only the whiteness of clouds lay on the horizon. The noise grew and then a dot appeared above the hills. They're here, he thought.

The pulse became the noise of helicopter blades. Felix left his post in the shelter of the trailer's open doors and walked to the edge of the pavement. The big Sikorsky helicopter settled in front of him, whipping up a circling cloud of snow. The engine roar dropped and became a whine, quieter than the beat of the rotor blades. A very pale-haired young man sat at the controls, watching Felix through the helicopter's windscreen. Felix returned his stare, then nodded and walked back to the trailer.

The pilot waited for the turbine temperature to settle and then got out and ran across the pavement. As the cold wind cut into him, he tugged his collar up, trying to protect his ears. He stopped next to Felix and looked beyond him to the damaged Suburban and opened trailer. "All right! I can't believe we've pulled this off!" He shuddered and hunched his shoulders. "*Gott,* it's cold out here! Do you have them ready?"

Felix gestured at the back of the trailer. "That's them."

The man looked surprised. "They don't look very impressive." Seven rounded metal boxes, painted olive drab, sat at the edge of the truck's gate. There were folding handles on the side panels.

"Tough. Let's get them loaded."

"Hey, sure, sure . . . this is great, but I don't know, I kind of expected something streamlined and silver, you know like—"

Felix cut him off. "These are just the shipping containers; now clam up! We're running an operation here, and in a little while, this place'll be crawling with angry guys with guns. You take any longer with your questions, they'll be here to answer you—now let's move them. I took one out of its case. Bring the empty case, too."

"Sure, sure."

"Where're the stand-in and the charge?"

"In the rear compartment of the chopper."

"Help me lift these down and then you use that hand truck to take them over to the chopper. I'll deal with cleaning the scene." They grasped the containers and lowered them to the ground.

While the other man got the hand truck, Felix went over to the helicopter and opened the rear door. On the floor in the back was a lumpy shape covered by a dark blanket. He grabbed a corner and threw it back. A hand flopped and grabbed at his throat. Felix started to jump and then smiled. It was a dead man's eyes that were staring at him, with a dark tongue that stuck out and a red ring around the neck. "Good," Felix said. "At least they got the hair color right."

The body in the helicopter was of around Felix's build, dressed vaguely like him in old blue jeans, plaid shirt, and insulated rancher's jacket. Felix dragged it out and onto his shoulders in a fireman's carry. He took the body around the truck and stuffed it into the front seat of the blown-out EV. He took his wallet and placed it in the body's back pocket, then went back to the trailer and grabbed another of the boxes.

The helicopter pilot was struggling with the hand truck on his second trip. "These are really awkward to carry alone."

"That's all right. Keep working that slowly and we can get help from the guard force when they get here." Why am I so edgy? he thought. Maybe because these people act like amateurs; they care more about politics and how they'll look than about discipline on an operation . . .

Felix returned to the helicopter and took the suitcase that had been with the body under the blanket. This he took back to the EV. Opening the suitcase, he set a dial, then connected a set of wires to a battery. He shut the suitcase again and set it on top of the front seat, wedging it against the body he had placed there. "Bye-bye, fellows." He gently closed the EV's door.

The pilot was carting the last of the boxes to the helicopter. Felix helped him store the cargo in the rear seat, then turned and studied the scene at the rest stop. A few bands of snow swirled across the pavement; one of the trailer's doors swung in the wind. It looked peaceful, calm. He was sure he'd thought of everything he needed to do here. The wind was cold again on his body after the exertion; he shivered. "Let's get out of here." He checked his watch. "We have six minutes."

Felix walked around to the right front seat and opened the door. He noticed deep scratches on the seat cushion and some smears of dried blood. "What's this?" he shouted to the pilot over the noise of the engine, gesturing at the seat.

"Oh, it was a little hard to convince the owner that I should take his toy."

Felix shrugged and got in. The pilot slammed his own door, then put on his headphones. He scanned the dials for a moment, and then slowly brought up the revs on the engine. The whine rose until it went out of hearing, replaced by a deeper roar. The helicopter lurched slightly as the weight came off the wheels. The pilot checked the dials again and increased the rotor pitch. Lifting, the helicopter spun to face the opposite direction, the thumping noise of the blades becoming smoother as they rose above the snowy ground. The helicopter headed north into the bare countryside. Behind it, an EV exploded in a hot, orange fireball. Looking backward from his seat, Felix saw the flash and smiled. "It's not often that you get to write your own demise."

They left the highway behind and the land became empty once more: white, barren, cold. The horizon was the faintest of separations between sky and ground. The helicopter slowly rose higher.

"Keep it low," Felix called out to the pilot. The pale-haired man tapped his ears and pointed to a second set of headphones and microphone that were hanging between the seats. Felix put them on. "Keep it low," he repeated. "I don't want to chance someone tracking us. Keep it to a hundred feet or less."

"Sure."

They rode on in silence for a while, the cabin surging from time to time in the wind gusts. The countryside slowly became more hilly; a few desolate farmhouses began to appear. The helicopter's track curved to keep a good distance from them.

"Where did you find the body?" Felix asked.

The pilot laughed, the headphones making it a whispery cackle. "Oh, it was love, don't you know. I picked him up in a bar, said I loved the country look . . . it must have been the music. I took him back to my place and had him dress in those lovely country clothes." Before or after? Felix thought. "Ah . . . then I made him dance." The whispery cackle came again. "What did you think of him?"

"A nice match. Will he be missed?"

"Not by me."

Felix decided to let it ride. He watched the pilot for a time. He seemed to be performing well. Felix had been up for twenty-four hours; this was going to be a long day. "Bring your height up to a normal cruise height as you cross I-70, okay? Wake me a little before we get to the unloading site." He lowered himself back in the seat and closed his eyes. He was quickly asleep.

The pilot's touch on his arm woke him. Felix shook his head and stretched his back. Straightening, he peered ahead: five miles away was the thin line of a highway. The snow was lighter here, the farmhouses closer together. "Do you know where we are?"

"Sure." The pilot pointed off to the right. "There's the truck stop on I-80. Three miles south and two miles west is the farm." He pointed left. "And there's the red flag—such a nice symbol."

Felix picked out the red flag attached to a tree up ahead. They drew closer, and he could see the shabby house and barn. They looked empty and deserted, but there were two vehicles in the yard—a sedan and a white van with panel sides. He checked his watch—2:15 . . . on schedule.

The pilot started to bring the helicopter down toward the yard. Felix looked at him. "What the hell are you doing? Where's the signal?"

"Look, there's the truck . . . I was here yesterday."

"I've seen a lot of things happen in a day. We'll do this the way I planned it—hover here." He picked up a large flashlight from the floor and pointed it at the trucks below. One long flash and then two short.

There was a pause. Nothing answered.

Felix tried again—one long flash and then two short.

Nothing.

The pilot glanced at Felix. "I wonder if . . ."

"There it is," Felix grunted. Below, there had been an answering three long red flashes from a spotlight inside the sedan.

"They sure took their time."

"Rudi, you guys may be what passes for hotshots in Germany, but your tradecraft sucks. Take us in."

"Go fuck yourself, cowboy. You're just playing games."

Right, you part-timer, Felix thought. I'll just remember what happened to the last guys who told me that.

The helicopter dropped in for a landing, and three figures left the vehicles below to meet them: a brown-haired woman dressed in black pants and leather coat, a heavily built blond man in a parka, and an older Arab-looking man dressed in a charcoal gray businessman's overcoat. They stood away from the helicopter until the rotors slowed and then the older man led the procession over to the right-hand door. "Rudi, Felix my good friend, where are they? Where are they?" he asked as the two men left the helicopter.

"They're in the back," said Felix. "Seven model W33, eight-inch, Nuclear Artillery Projectiles."

"Wonderful, wonderful!" He positively beamed, then he grabbed Felix's hand and pumped it up and down. "I can't tell you how happy you have made me, what this will mean for our cause!"

"Well, Baalbek," said Felix, "if we don't get hopping, get this stuff stowed, and the cover track laid, I can tell you what it's going to mean to me: I'm going to get my ass fried."

"Yes, yes. Let us get started." He turned and clasped the woman by her shoulders. "Uli, this is wonderful!" He gave her a little shake. "Just wonderful . . . well, let's get them in the truck!"

He moved in his quick limping stride over to open the truck's rear doors. Uli brushed off her shoulders where Baalbek had grabbed her and muttered, "Romantic idiot!" She turned to Felix and stared him up and down. "I haven't met you yet, our great hero. Are you a romantic, too?"

"And are all of you such dilettantes? Get this stuff out of the helicopter."

"Don't order me around. This end of the ground operation is mine."

"Then you're running it half-assed. Let's get some priorities straight. It's two hours to sunset. If we don't get this helicopter out of here and back to the phony drop site, then we're going to be pretty easy to find. Let's do our amateur theatricals later, all right?"

"They said you were an arrogant bastard."

"That may be, dearie, but I'm an alive arrogant bastard, and I plan to stay that way. If it's not too much to ask, why don't you help unload?" He and Rudi grabbed one of the bombs and carried it off to the panel truck. Uli stared after him, then smiled at the others. "At least he has spirit."

Baalbek held the van's door as they came up and dropped the case into the back. Baalbek leaped. "Careful!"

Felix straightened and looked at him. "These are Army munitions. They're made to take rough handling, and they're not armed yet. They'll be okay as long as you don't crash the van and burn it."

"What would happen then?"

"Not much. The trigger explosives might go off, but nothing nuclear . . . We'd just lose the weapons we made such an effort to get."

The group quickly unloaded the rest of the bombs from the helicopter, placed them in the van, and hid them under crates of fruits and lettuce. "My uncle used to be a merchant," Baalbek said. "I learned about vegetables from him. I thought that would be my best cover in case I was stopped."

That's what I remember about him, thought Felix, he can think things through.

Uli told the pilot and the sandy-haired man to refuel the helicopter and then came over to talk with Felix and Baalbek. "The truck is waiting at the other site. You should be able to get there before dark."

"Who are the guys who'll be at the decoy site?" Felix asked. "I've never met them."

Baalbek smiled. "There will be Hans Jüters, a weapons man from the Ost-Sturm group, and Yataro Kakimoto, a Japanese comrade who has been our main contact man here in the United States. Uli is not fond of him, but he is very, very efficient. You can trust him."

"I hope so. It would be sad to screw up at this point." He looked over at the helicopter. "Have Rudi and what's his name . . . Big Blondie . . . finished refueling?"

"Almost," said Uli. "Big Blondie's name is Dieter, please use it. He's a touchy guy and we want to be nice to him: he's good with his hands."

"Oh, I'm scared."

"Don't be a complete idiot, you're our fighting specialist. Dieter's our munitions and electronics expert. That's what I meant by 'good with his hands.' " She gestured at the van. "If we're going to get these things to work for us, we need Dieter in fine fettle; be good to him."

"Oh, I'm always good." He looked back toward the helicopter; the two men were walking back. "Looks like time to go."

Baalbek grabbed Felix by the hand and shook it again. "I want to thank you, thank you again for your sacrifice."

"Sacrifice? I'm having fun . . . more than I've had in years."

The helicopter was headed south, retracing its path with an offset of four miles to the west. Felix called to Rudi on the intercom. "People probably won't remember one helicopter going past in the course of a day, but the same chopper going north and then back south again an hour or two later has too great a chance of sticking out in someone's memory. Keep this offset, and keep it low."

"What happens when we get to I-70?"

"Then go west, keeping at least a mile north of it. There are no towns or truck stops between where we'll pick up 70 and our end point."

The sky still had its high overcast and the white-gray light was fading slowly into a deeper tone that augured the coming sunset. Felix wanted to be done with this last part of the operation before it became dark. They were keeping well to their schedule.

"There's the highway," Rudi said. "I'll start my turn west over that hollow up ahead." They banked over the small valley and then picked up the track of a partially drifted road below them. "I hope Hans and Kakimoto didn't have trouble with snow on their road up there."

"If they did, they have a backup location. Think out potential problems, make up contingency plans beforehand, and then relax while you're in the operation. That's how I plan things, Rudi," said Felix. He stretched. "I'm tired of sitting in this chopper. It will be good to walk around again." They rode in silence for a while.

"This looks like our place coming up." Felix pointed to a set of three silos up ahead, painted a faded silver-gray, with large red numerals and the legend MARTIN FAMILY'S FEED. "One and a quarter miles west of these silos, and a half mile north of the highway should be the abandoned grain depot we're looking for."

"Got it."

"Okay, now this time remember to wait for the password check."

"Sure."

Rudi slowed their speed as they approached a faded green clapboard warehouse with two concrete silos. It had a rutted parking lot that was shielded from the road by a screen of pines. Coming closer, they could see two vehicles—a small U-Haul van and a gray Olds 98. "Someone likes luxury."

Felix picked up the large flashlight. His code pattern this time was two short, two long, and two short again. The responding code flash from the car came quickly. "Take her in, Rudi. Place us around fifty feet from the van."

The helicopter flared as it approached the ground. Rudi swiveled it until it faced the car, and then set it down. He throttled the turbine back to idle.

A wiry, brown-haired man in a leather jacket got out of the Olds's driver's side and then went over to the van. An Asian man got out and stood by the car, regarding the helicopter. How quietly he stands, thought Felix. Who is this guy?

"Shut it down, Rudi."

"I've got to let the turbines cool for a couple of minutes before powering off."

"Rudi, she'll not be flying again." Felix opened his door and got out. As he walked over to the car, the helicopter whine started to fall.

The two men faced each other in silence for a moment. "It went well?" Kakimoto asked.

"Very smoothly."

"I am Yataro Kakimoto. I am pleased to meet you."

"Felix Ross." The helicopter had wound down to silence; the wind sighed through the pines in the gathering darkness.

Rudi came up to them. "Let's go," he said.

Felix turned to him. "Oh no, not yet. We've got a little more work to do. We need to make tracks from the helicopter to the van so it looks like we actually moved the bombs here."

"Baalbek said you were going to do that," Kakimoto said. "That is good planning, and I brought along something that might help." He gestured at the van. "In the back there I have a crate weighted with stones. If we carry that, it should make the footprints the correct depth."

I'm going to like working with this guy, Felix thought. He gave a smile and a little bow to Kakimoto. "Very nice move. Rudi, let's do it."

"No, have Hans help Rudi. How many trips?"

"Seven warheads."

"Fine. Rudi, please get Hans, he's with the van. Felix and I need to talk.

"And Rudi," said Felix, "leave that one empty case on the ground near the chopper."

Kakimoto turned to Felix. "There is a truck stop on the highway just west of here. I thought if we left the van there, it would imply we took a westward direction out of here. I have given one of the tires on the van a distinctive cut, which should make it easy for the police to identify it with this location."

"We should remember to ditch that crate of stones before we leave the van."

"Of course." Kakimoto looked around. "What have you planned for the helicopter?"

"There's a small satchel charge in the back. We can set it to go off in the dark after we've left. With the fuel left in the tanks, it should get attention. What time do you think?"

Kakimoto looked at his watch and then the sky. "Let us say one hour. Darkness has started to fall."

10

It came down like a hammer; the frigate was steaming quietly in the moonlight when the first blow struck. A bright flash, then yellow fire enveloped the bow and the alarm bell rang.

Bill was alone on the bridge, but not in combat dress. He ran to the door that led below to the companionway; it was jammed. He struggled there, pounding on the door but no one came; there was just the ringing of the bell.

He made it down the corridor to his room. "I've got to get Sutan out." He couldn't find his gun or the papers he needed. He was frantic. "They'll ask me about them. The Senator must have them. We have to stop the security police from taking Sutan!" The alarm bell was still ringing.

He ran up to the operations room. His bare feet felt cold on the deck. He tried the Senator's staff. They were working at their desks, ignoring the ringing, ignoring him. He couldn't get their attention. His chest felt as if it were going to burst. The ringing went on. "Look," Bill screamed, "he's going to die unless I get those papers!"

A young guard standing by the door turned to him. "If you don't like this scene, then just answer the phone."

■

He awoke in the dark . . . the phone ringing. He realized he was sitting on the edge of his bed and groped in the familiar place for the bedside lamp. It wasn't there.

He forced himself further awake, remembered more, and groped again. Locating the lamp, he switched it on. He wasn't home, he was in a hotel room. Where?

He looked around: beige, carpeted blandness, a quilted floral-patterned bedspread, color TV in the corner on a swivel stand, with a little tent card that advertised the pay movies. Heavy, beige drapes were drawn over unopenable windows. No smell or hint what lay outside, just the acrid tang of new carpeting; it could be anywhere.

He sat there dazed. The phone on the bedside table rang again. It brought him back a bit more. Washington, he was still in Washington.

The phone rang again. He looked at his watch which lay beside it . . . one A.M. He had been asleep for only forty minutes. "Why can't I wake up like the movie heroes?" He picked up the phone. "Hitch here."

"Sir, I'm calling for Mr. Brown. He'd like to see you."

Oh shit, he thought, and felt suddenly cold. "Mr. Brown" was the crisis code used for nonsecure lines. "Ah . . . ah, right. Shall I take a taxi?"

"No sir, he has a car en route."

Bill took a deep breath. "Okay, I'll be downstairs in less than five minutes." He rang off and sat staring at the wall, trying to sense if he was truly awake. "Let's see what's going on." He rose and dressed quickly.

The night air outside the hotel entrance was damp but bracing. It cleared the last of the mustiness from his brain.

A dark blue Ford sedan sat by the entrance, engine idling. The front door opened. The driver got out. He was a sandy-haired man in his forties, dressed in a tan trench coat and with a face like the hotel room. He started around to open Bill's door. "That's all right," Bill said. "I've got it. Let's move." The driver returned to his seat; Bill got into the back and closed the door. "Where?" he asked.

"The Old Executive Office Building, sir."

"Okay." The EOB . . . then who was this call from?

He had assumed it was in relation to the Fonsgraf response team. They had been meeting in the White House, though more sporadically as time had passed, the business traveling the normal Washington evolutionary path from crisis to ennui. Work was still being done on it, but he—and the others—had started getting bits of other enterprises to handle.

"Driver, who dispatched you?"

"Mr. Kuhn, sir. I believe he said he will meet you there."

So it was the response team. They had not met once in the EOB, and Bill had been in Washington a month now . . . so why this late-night meeting? Intelligence's original briefing had talked about a post-Christmas date for any possible events. Nothing had come through to override that.

He sat there, going over various possible meanings as the car sped down quiet streets that had a greasy look from a faint drizzle. It was quiet; the bustle of the Washington day had given up to the darkness.

The car turned off E Street, onto West Executive Drive, and drew up to the rear gate of the EOB, an ornate, wedding-cake pile that sat next to the White House on Pennsylvania Avenue. They quickly cleared through security and drove up to the side entrance. A figure waited there, standing behind the inner gate guards—Dale Kuhn from CIA. He stepped forward as Bill got out.

"Bill, sorry to wake you with that kind of call, but we're on a big, but very low-profile alert."

"What's up?"

Kuhn glanced around at the surrounding rooftops. "Let's get inside to a secure area first. Come on." He turned and walked quickly back into the building.

Bill followed him a short way down a corridor and into an empty secretarial room. Four desks with typewriters were arranged precisely in an even grid, the chairs placed just so, centered in their openings. Kuhn closed the door. Ceiling fluorescent lights lit the space as coldly as an operating room. It was very quiet.

"It happened. Someone snatched a set of weapons this morning."

Bill stared at him. Damn. "What? Who . . . where?" He thought for a moment. "Why are you telling me now, this late?"

"We don't know who took them, they hit a convoy in New Mexico. And the reason you're only finding out now is that our noble leader Charles Fonsgraf took you off his list."

"I don't understand."

"Neither do I, except maybe that you were the only one who argued with him about getting more security on the convoys. Fonsgraf is not one who likes to be reminded of his mistakes.

"Anyway, the Admiral came over a little while ago from the White House to sit in on a briefing session. I heard him ask Fonsgraf where you and Tina were. Fonsgraf gave him some crap that it was now a crisis and a military operation and blah blah. The Admiral told him to get you and Tina over here . . . set a rocket off up his ass."

"That's nice . . ."

"Sorry. Until the Admiral asked, I guess we all thought you were off on some project. So they sent a driver for you. Tina was still at her office; she's here now."

"What's the current status?" This is unreal, Bill thought. He had envisioned many crises—planned for some of them—but this was not one that he had thought could ever actually occur.

"Everyone from the convoy is dead. We have no idea who took the bombs, except for that warning a month ago about Ost-Sturm. The President is very concerned about national panic. He's ordered that we keep this very tightly buttoned up. I think that may compromise our ability to find these weapons if we can't work closely with local authorities, but no one outside is to know—max hush. That why we're meeting here at the EOB."

"So who's involved in figuring this out and finding them?"

"Basically the same team as a month ago. The President wants only the national services in on this—us, FBI, Secret Service, and the armed forces . . . no state or local people, which is going to really be a constraint. Fonsgraf is still in charge."

"Oh, come on! It's as if the President wants us to fail! Fonsgraf! Why him?"

"It seems that the President has chosen him."

"That's what comes from knowing whom to manage. You know what he's like: if you go into a revolving door with him behind you, you'll come out with him ahead of you . . . Any leads at all, any communiqués?"

"None." Dale looked at his watch. "It's almost two. I came down to brief you before you got into this, but there's another session set for now. I think we should get back up there."

Bill shook himself. What a mess. "Let's go."

As the CIA man turned to leave, Bill tapped him on the shoulder. "Thanks, Dale."

"Good to have you here."

The meeting room was located on the inside of the building—away from outside walls and windows. Twenty by thirty feet, with white-painted cork walls, it seemed crowded by the large rectangle of tables that had been placed together in the middle of the space. After twelve hours of meetings, it had a lived-in look: piles of briefing papers covered the tabletop, with the spaces in between crowded with Styrofoam coffee cups.

Most of the seats were taken when Bill and Dale entered. Bill recognized the rest of the Fonsgraf working group, with the addition of another twelve or so who seemed to be mostly staff, plus an Air Force and a Marine colonel, each with two aides.

"Is this all we have working on it?" Bill asked Dale.

"No, a lot of folks have been in and out, and the some of the staff people here are liaisons with departments who can manage better from their own facilities."

Bill looked around. Fonsgraf was conferring with a small group of Army men at one end of the table. At the other, Admiral Thomas was bent over some papers, talking into a telephone equipped with a hush cup. Tina Lucia was seated next to him, and on her other side was an empty chair. Bill motioned to it. "Dale, I want to find out what Tina knows."

"Sure. I've got to check in with my people."

As Bill edged around the chairs at the table, he noticed a faint, acrid scent in the air. It was something he hadn't smelled for a long time: the odor of fear.

Tina was reading from a sheaf of telexes as he sat, and she didn't look up until he touched her arm; she had great powers of concentration.

"Oh, hello, Bill. Good you're here."

"A fine mess," he whispered.

A large map of the western United States had been pinned to one wall opposite where he sat. A red line led from northern Texas west, and ended in a red dot just past the Texas–New Mexico border. "Is that where it happened?"

"Yes, on Interstate 40, about twenty miles into New Mexico. How do you think they knew what convoy to hit?"

"What do you mean?"

Before Tina could answer, a heavyset man in a gray suit entered the room and walked over to Colonel Fonsgraf. Fonsgraf rose to meet him and then banged a book on the table. "All right, quiet!" he said. "Let's get this session started."

The murmurs of conversation around the table lowered to silence. There was the squeak of chairs being pulled in and the rustle of papers being arranged.

"First, the FBI has reported in to me on the ground operations they've been running out on Interstate 40. They've had a roadblock and search operation up and running since thirteen-thirty central time under the guise of an antidrug operation. There has been no success on that.

"Next, this is Brian White from DOE. The department has come up with an accounting of what's been taken. Brian's going to explain that to us.

"Before I have Brian start, I want to tell those of you who have just arrived"—he glanced at Bill and Tina—"not to interrupt the proceedings with questions about what has happened so far. This short briefing session will fill in some of the events, and the rest you can ask about after the session is over." He motioned to the heavyset man. "Go ahead, Brian."

"Thank you, Colonel. At approximately nine A.M. central time, an unknown force attacked and successfully overpowered one of our weapons convoys in New Mexico on I-40. We have no witnesses; all of our personnel were killed. It was an ambush in a rest area by an attack in force that our security people estimate as at least twenty-five men.

"Somehow, they were able to breach the secondary defensive systems on the weapons truck itself and remove the cargo. We are working on how they managed to neutralize the guard force, and I'd like to outline what our security procedures were and how they should have been adequate."

"Son"—the Admiral stopped White—"I'm sure that is of great interest, but I think what's of importance to the folks here is what's been taken and how we're going to deal with it. I've got to get back and report to the President, so why don't you describe what they've got and leave details on the security lapse for later?"

The man from DOE wiped his forehead. "Yes, Admiral Thomas. Ah, well, it seems that we are somewhat in luck. The convoy that was hit was carrying some of our smallest nuclear weapons—model W33, eight-inch Nuclear Artillery Projectiles."—Lucky us, thought Bill—"These are shells designed for the M110 self-propelled howitzer. They had been serviced at Pantex in Amarillo, and were being sent to the coast for transport back to Korea. We've examined the site, and it appears that they took seven of them. These are some of the older weapons in our arsenal, with only a subkiloton to five kiloton yield, not the newer W79 Enhanced Radiation Warhead, which has a field-selectable yield of up to ten kilotons. You can be sure that the DOE's people are at your disposal in recovering them."

Tom Wald from State spoke up. "What do the FBI forensic people say about the snatch site? Are there any new leads on how the bombs were removed?"

"We're working on that. Since it was our own people who were hit, I think DOE will handle the initial investigation."

The Admiral bent over and conferred softly with Tina. Conversation in the room rose to a gentle hum. He straightened and looked again at White. "I'd like to keep things in perspective for the people here. You say that these warheads were some of our smallest weapons, only . . . ah, five kilotons or less. Am I correct?"

"That's right, sir. We would have been in real trouble if, say, a two-megaton baby had been taken."

"The term *small* seems to have changed since the last time I was involved in a shooting war. Tina reminds me that the bomb we used on Hiroshima was somewhere between twelve and fifteen kilotons. So . . . if whoever has taken these uses one in a major city, then the destruction might be up to forty percent of what happened in Hiroshima. Am I correct?"

The room was now very quiet. All eyes went to the DOE man.

Brian White wiped his forehead again. His voice was tiny. "That sounds about right."

"Do you know how many people died in Hiroshima?"

"Not offhand, sir."

"Tina tells me eighty thousand people died there—from a bomb that might have been just over twice as powerful as these 'small' ones you say have been taken . . . And we should remember," continued the Admiral relentlessly, "that whoever did this has seven of them."

The Admiral scanned slowly around the room, as if he were looking into the soul of each of the people seated at the table. "I think you all know that the stakes are very high in this matter—I pray to the good Lord that this is worse than anything else we'll ever have to deal with in our lives.

"I'm seeing some intraservice rivalry in how you are dealing with this. That must stop. Remember those numbers, ladies and gentlemen: seven warheads that each have up to forty percent of the power of the bomb that leveled Hiroshima.

"If I hear of any more of this turf-protection crap, I will personally destroy the person doing it. Is that understood?" His gaze went around the room again, then he continued. "Colonel Fonsgraf has put together a good team here. We all know we are operating under certain constraints imposed by the President: no state agencies must be involved, maximum security to prevent leaks, and no public knowledge to prevent panic.

"Those are difficult conditions, but this is a difficult situation.

Colonel Fonsgraf has suggested that our cover, if one becomes necessary, is that we are conducting a massive antidrug operation. That's a good idea. Now let's work together on this and get it solved.

"Now, Charles, why don't you tell us how this search operation is going to be organized?"

Bill looked at Fonsgraf. There was a pallor thinning his ruddy face; he was staring out at the middle distance, fingers fiddling with a pencil in front of him. My God, thought Bill, I bet the magnitude of what he's dealing with has finally hit him. No more status climbing, Fosdick; the bill has come due.

Fonsgraf shook his shoulders and looked back at the Admiral. "Yes, I think you're right, Admiral. The time has come to work together on this—we all have a stake in it." He turned to the heavy man. "Brian, as soon as this meeting breaks, I want you to get together with Peter Hanson, here, from the FBI. Coordinate getting his forensic people out to the site to examine it." He fiddled more with his pencil, and looked at his notes.

Don't fall apart on us, thought Bill. Keep making those decisions.

"Bunk," the Colonel continued, "I want you to find the best road expert the Army has and start figuring where it looks like they may have taken these things." He paused again.

"Are we sure it's Ost-Sturm who took the bombs?" asked Dale Kuhn. "Is there anything we can work on from that end?"

Fonsgraf looked confused for a moment and then brightened. "Tina," he said, "our leads a month ago said that Ost-Sturm might be planning something like this after Christmas. What information do you have? Could it have been anyone else?"

Tina looked up from her telexes. "I think it's got to be them. I've been communicating with my sources and gathering information, but nothing that is going to help us right now. East Storm—Ost-Sturm—has gotten a lot of publicity over the years, but for all that, they are a pretty shadowy organization. Their greatest strength seems to be the range of technical resources they can draw on, and their ability to make alliances of convenience with other terrorist organizations.

"Their most recent core leaders are Uli Rosstal, a former political science student, and Rudi Bruck, rumored to have been her lover. He's a killer who is reported to have been involved in a number of political assassinations on the Continent. As far as we know, neither of them—or any of Ost-Sturm, for that matter—has ever been involved with an operation in the United States.

"The Germans also had some leads on others who have been associated with the group, and looking them over, there's one guy that worries me—a camp follower by the name of Dieter Strasse. He was a student in physics at the Max Planck Institute in Heidelberg. Five years ago, he married a Japanese leftist student, quit the Institute, and seems to have hooked up with the radical fringe in Germany. She was later killed in a bombing attack on a U.S. multinational; he dropped out of sight."

"So why are you worried about him?" Jack Phillips asked. "We should be worried about the operational types, like the ones who attacked the convoy."

"Maybe, but once they've got the bombs, they've got to figure out how to use them. Dieter is a reader, a synthesizer. Do you know what that means?"

"No, Tina, why don't you enlighten us?" Fosdick's getting his old wind back, thought Bill.

"A reader can be dangerous. There're a lot of unclassified bits of information floating around out there in the public and technical press that put together would be top secret. Dieter Strasse had a lot of practical lab experience in the university. But he's also supposed to be a sponge for information, subscribing to everything, remembering hints and tidbits."

"Like that guy who wrote *The Hunt for Red October,*" said Dale Kuhn.

"Right."

"We don't have time to waste here; get to the point," said Fonsgraf.

Tina glanced at Bill and then continued, "Nuclear weapons are a little touchy to figure out and use. They've got security systems; they're complicated. Information about how to use them is, of course, classified."

"So, that's good for us, right?"

"But the right person, putting together the right bits of information, could figure out how to use them effectively. If Strasse is involved, then we have serious worries. My sources imply that if anyone out there can figure those bombs out and make them perform, he's the one."

"So how do we find him . . . and the bombs?" asked Bunk Cole.

"That's the question, isn't it?" Fonsgraf barked. "Let's drop this and get on to things that might actually help us find these bombs. Let's hear some suggestions from the military people here."

Before anyone could respond, there was a buzz from the phone in front of Fonsgraf. Bunk Cole answered it for him. Bunk whispered something in Fonsgraf's ear. "Bring him in," said the Colonel, and Bunk said something into the phone. The door to the corridor swung open. A young Army aide stepped in and handed a paper to the Colonel, then left the room.

Fonsgraf read the paper and looked up. "Ah, this evening, just off I-70 in eastern Colorado, police found a burning helicopter. They also found a shipping case near it, with DOE signage. DOE tells us that that case was on the convoy truck." His shoulders slumped. "It seems that we've been looking in the wrong place."

He slid the paper across the table to the FBI man. "Peter, get some of your boys out there as soon as possible. We can provide air transport if you need it. Jack, consult with Peter to see if anyone at Secret Service can be of help."

He looked around the room. "Things seem to be getting a bit more complicated. I suggest we break for an hour or two. Bunk's people will have briefing sheets with all the new and old info. Get in touch with your own organizations and see what you can come up with. Let's meet back here"—he looked at his watch—"at 0300. If you come up with anything important, then squawk my office and we can meet before then."

Fonsgraf looked at the Admiral. "Okay?"

The Admiral nodded.

"Well, let's break."

There was a sudden scraping of chairs and a burst of voices as the meeting broke up and the participants hurried off to their business.

The Admiral stood and straightened his uniform jacket. "Bill, Tina," he said, "wait here for a minute, will you?" He motioned to catch Bunk Cole's eye and summoned him over.

"Yes, Admiral?"

"Bunk, I have to get back to the White House to brief the President. Could you see to it that Tina and Bill are provided with an office here and some communication lines? They'll tell your people what they need."

"Yes, sir." He looked at Bill. "I have to finish getting this new information out. I'll be right back to see about setting you up with facilities." He moved off across the room.

Bill turned to the Admiral. "Sir, I don't like the feel of this: we're behind the curve, reacting rather than acting."

"I don't like it either, Bill, but we also don't have much real information yet. I want you and Tina to get on this. We know Colonel Fonsgraf's limitations; he has a certain kind of military mind—very linear, always a reactor rather than an anticipator. That's one reason I have the two of you on this team: Tina, we need your strength in remembering and pulling together little clues and facts. Bill, you've got a hunter's eyes. You two should be thinking of angles that everyone else may be missing. That's your job.

"If you have any trouble from Fonsgraf's people, let me know." He gave a tight smile. "Though I don't think there should be any more difficulty along those lines."

He picked up his papers and started out. "Keep in touch," he called over his shoulder.

The room was pretty much empty now. Just Bill and Tina at their end of the table and Major Cole and two of his aides at the other.

"I hope you can operate without sleep," Bill said.

"It's as good a time as ever to learn. Let's see . . . I have an assistant gathering information back at my old office. I'd better get over there and help. I should be back here in a half hour or forty minutes. I can get the rest of my stuff sent over in the morning." She tapped him on the chest. "The most important thing for you to do while I'm gone is to find the coffeepot."

"And steal it for our office, no doubt."

"I think I'm going to like working with you again."

Tina left as Bunk Cole came back. "Well, Bill, it was difficult, but I think I've found you and Tina an office. It's pretty small and it's in the basement, and some secretary is going to be surprised in the morning, but that's the best we can do."

The Major rested his rear on the edge of the table. "You know what burns me? This hijacking attempt wasn't supposed to happen until after Christmas. It's sort of hard to deal with so early."

Bill stared at him. "Life is tough."

"What do you mean?"

"This isn't some sports contest, Bunk, this is life: bad guys do bad things. You know . . . they lie, they cheat, they steal, they kill—they're bad guys. That's why we suggested you put on more security for the convoys. You wouldn't listen."

11

ROSS

The cockroach scrabbled across the brown Formica tabletop, trying to reach the edge and safety. It stopped as flame flared in front of it, then struggled to turn away, hampered because two legs had been torn from the left side of its body.

It got itself turned and started an awkward run in the opposite direction. The man moved the flame around in front of the bug, but closer now. It stopped, confused, and then tried to back up as its antennae detected the approaching heat. It has not been proven that cockroaches feel pain in the same sense that people do, but that did not lessen the man's pleasure.

"Rudi!" cursed Uli. "Just kill the damn bug and pay attention to what I'm saying!"

"Bug? Uli, this is a citizen of the wonderful safe house you've found us. I think it complements the decor!" Rudi gestured around the kitchen. "Puke yellow walls, kitchen machinery to match, a plastic floor with yellow glitter in it—this is the ultimate in domesticity!" He wagged his finger at her. "Uli, I always knew that, someday, your true bourgeois roots would show!"

Uli stared stonily at him as he laughed. He flicked his cigarette lighter once more and incinerated the tattered cockroach, waved his hands to dissipate the rank smoke. "Yes, I heard what you were saying—but don't treat me like some stupid drone. Yes, I will maintain our cover; yes, I will not get involved with any of the neighbors; and yes, I will remember to listen to my loud music with earphones and not the speakers . . . satisfied?"

"Thank you, Rudi," she rasped.

"Actually, I have a question for you: the walls in this paradise are thin plasterboard. Didn't you think about that?"

"Yes, and that's why I took these two units. We're on the top floor, with no one around us. The floor is concrete."

Felix stood in between the kitchen and dining room, leaning on the doorframe drinking a beer. "Ease up, Rudi. She did a fine job; it's a good place."

Uli seemed a bit surprised, and looked at him, waiting for a catch or some jibe.

Felix noticed her tension. "No, I'm serious. I went for a jog and checked out the neighborhood—this is a great location: the development is big enough to be anonymous, there are three entrances to the building from three separate sides, we're on the top floor. There are pipe runs connecting all the structures. This building is only three stories high, but it's the highest structure around." He raised his bottle and saluted her. "The only thing I might like in addition is parking under the building, but they don't build that way in Nebraska."

It was an eight-building, garden-apartment complex near Kearney State College in Kearney, Nebraska. Here, the group would be just another set of transient strangers: maybe students, maybe professors . . . maybe people who've just been transferred from out of town. They would not stick out.

The buildings were mostly two-story, rectangular, brick structures. Dwarfish, plastic shutters bracketed each set of windows. The glass entrances were capped by white, colonial door trim. Parking surrounded each building—rows of spaces, sheltered from the winter snow and the summer sun by long, steel-framed carports that looked like recycled drive-in restaurant shelters.

Rudi started fooling with his lighter again, flicking the flame on and off, aiming it at his palm as if playing a private game of chicken. "Well, cowboy, I'm glad you two agree."

"Place seems fine to me." Felix took another sip from his beer.

"When are Baalbek and Yataro getting back, and where's Dieter? We should be planning and executing, not hanging out . . . it's not like they're not looking for us."

Uli got up from the table. "Dieter's in the other unit, still working on the triggers. Baalbek went into town with Yataro to check out hardware stores. They should be here by six; we can eat, then talk. I'm going to do my exercises and take a bath." She walked out past Felix, brushing him with her hip as she passed. Rudi watched with a little smile on his face.

"Look out, cowboy," he said after she crossed the dining room and went down the hall to her bedroom. "Maybe she's got her eyes on your buns . . . likes rough men, don't you know . . . likes to break them in."

Felix snorted. "And you?"

"Oh, I'm a domesticated guy. Uli and I go way back . . . but she gets bored."

Felix finished his beer and tossed the bottle to Rudi. "You're spinning dreams. I'm going to talk with Dieter."

He turned and went through the dining room to the front door. Across their small landing at the top of the stairs was the tan, metal entrance door to the other apartment. He could hear the faint sound of music from the rooms beyond. Ah, our German artist, he thought.

Felix leaned over the railing and checked the stairway below; no one there. He took two keys from his pocket and opened the door; the music—something classical—got louder. Double locking the door behind him, he followed the music into the living room.

This apartment was on the south side of the building, and the clear, November sun streamed in to cover a worktable set up by the windows. The garish couch and chairs that had come with the furnished apartment were piled against one wall.

Dieter sat at the table, his head nodding to the music coming from a small CD player and speakers set up on the window ledge. The light turned his hair into a soft, blond cloud. He looked up as Felix sat next to him on a kitchen stool. "Oh, hello, Felix."

"How are things going?"

"Slowly, but well."

Felix had not been impressed with Dieter the first time they met, but Felix had seen him out of his element. Here was Dieter's world, created in the two months he and Hans had been here in the apartment: the tiny tools, soldering irons, testing apparatus, and quite a few boxes of periodicals, assorted manuals, and articles torn out of sundry technical magazines. Felix had spent the previous afternoon here, watching the German work. He was now impressed.

"The controls on these things are actually quite unsophisticated." The music paused, then surged again, repeating a theme. Dieter raised his chin and closed his eyes for a moment; he sighed. "Do you know this piece?"

"Can't say that I do . . . I'm not much on classical music."

"This is one of the most perfect pieces of chamber music ever written—Schubert's String Quintet in C Major." He bent back to his work, but continued talking in a somewhat dry, didactic manner. "Do you know what makes great music? When every note is both a surprise and inevitable. Now who said that?" He picked up a small pair of pliers with tiny jaws and made an adjustment in a wire arrangement. "But, in any case, that's how I got into revolutionary politics.

"I was a musician, composing and playing in small chamber groups while I was studying physics at the Institute; that is where I met my wife. She let me see that in music I'm not, and will never be, a Schubert.

"Ah, but there was still that desire to write a sequence of notes that's both a surprise and inevitable. She showed me that I was just trying in the wrong medium; I needed to work on a larger stage."

He turned and looked at Felix. "Done correctly, that's what a true revolutionary act should be to its target: both a surprise and inevitable." He bent back to his work. "Now I work for Uli and Baalbek. And do you think, Felix, that I am writing a masterwork, or just pasting together expected little pieces like a pop song hack? Eh?"

He pushed back his chair and smiled. "In any case, I know I can get these to work." He gestured to the cases on the other side of the room. "I've removed the warhead cages from the artillery shells, which saves us quite a bit of weight. These things on the table are the detonator mechanisms. Very simple, really, and very rugged, as you would expect. Yataro is bringing me certain parts, and I'll be able to rig them tomorrow to detonate by timer, trip wire *or* altitude sensor." He rubbed his face and then neck. "It's been a long night"—he looked at his watch—"and day . . . I'm hungry."

"Uli wants all of us to eat and talk when Yataro and Baalbek come back from town."

"Fine." He paused and seemed to check his internal calibration. "Then I will take a nap. Wake me a half hour before supper."

"A toast, a toast!" said Baalbek. He raised his glass of tea to the others sitting around the table, which was littered with empty dishes and wine bottles. "To Felix for getting us the weapons that will finally give our small band of soldiers the same strength as the major powers. To Uli, Rudi, and Hans for their cooperation and organization that helped lay the groundwork in Lebanon, Germany, and the United States. To Yataro, for his plan to cover our tracks. To Dieter, for— as he has told us—having figured out three ways to make our prizes work when we need them. Salut!"

He raised his cup and drank, and the others followed suit with their wineglasses.

"Also, Hans, a wonderful meal! After so long eating in restaurants and hotels, it is good to have a simple meal that has been prepared with care." Baalbek was weaving slightly, his face flushed—not from alcohol, for as a devout Muslim, Hussein did not drink—but from the intoxication of power and the thrill of a long-sought success now in sight.

"Now, Dieter, truly good news, wonderful news: three ways to use our little toys.

"We must decide tonight the final details of our first project. You have heard me speak many times of the deaths in the villages: nearly three hundred fifty killed by the Americans and their pawns, and most of our dead not fighters.

"We are united tonight in our wish to see this slaughter stopped, to have Lebanon reunited and governed by the majority.

To have the superpowers pay for the destruction that they have wreaked. Another toast to success!" He raised his glass again.

The others followed more slowly this time. "Hussein," said Uli, "let's get to the point of this meeting, get the details agreed to, and get to bed. Tomorrow will be a big day, our weapon will start its voyage; I doubt any of us will want to sleep tomorrow night."

Baalbek looked a little crestfallen, as if the payoff for his long years of anticipation was somehow being deflated. "Fine, let us proceed . . . I have found a place where we can kill four hundred of their soldiers. We will kill soldiers, not women and children: We are fighters, not murderers. We will never copy our American enemies. In two days, the communiqué will go out; until then, our silence will feed their fear."

"Yeah, but I want some sort of recognition. Why are we going to send it to Washington, and not to the press?"

"Fear, Rudi. We want to achieve our goals, not get press. I think doing it this way will have the greatest chance of success. They know the stakes. Give them a week to act on our demands, and if nothing happens, then we go public. In the meantime, we are hidden."

"Hear, hear," said Felix.

Uli sat playing with the remains of her meal. "You're letting them off too easily, Baalbek."

"We want a united Lebanon."

"What they have done to Lebanon is just *one* crime among many. Great crimes deserve strong remedies. You're thinking only of your own problems in Lebanon. We are thinking"—the royal *we?* thought Felix—"of the unavenged crimes of American imperialism."

"Uli, Uli. Don't start this now. In our negotiations, you agreed to this plan."

"Yes, but then I didn't think we would ever get seven warheads."

"Then let's wait and see what happens."

The next evening, two men left the apartment. A cold wind was blowing again, the stars hidden by high clouds. "Can you believe that Baalbek thought we were going to call from the apartment?"

"Felix, he tries, but he's an idealist, not an operative: just listen to him talk."

"What do you think of all this political crap? Do you agree with Uli?"

"I have my reasons, my friend."

"Well, I suppose we all do, you know. But for me, politics don't mean that much. What I mean is that it's the operation that counts. I decided when I was a kid that in whatever I did in life, I wanted to do the best I could.

"Maybe that's why Uli and her crew give me the willies—they may have passion, but God . . . expecting you'd phone from the apartment? What terrible tradecraft! I just hope that they haven't been doing that since they got here."

They walked along in the darkness until they got to Yataro's car. "Why did you get rid of the big Olds?"

"I thought a smaller Chevy seemed a bit more in keeping with the surroundings and my role here." They got in and headed toward town.

They rode for a while in companionable silence, Yataro driving sedately. Felix rolled down his window a bit as the heat in the car came on. "Were you ever in the military?"

"No, but I come from a military family. My father was in World War Two, of course, but the Japanese military today is obviously not what it once was. Why do you ask?"

"I wondered where you learned to carry yourself, where you learned strategy and tactics."

"Oh, I went to military schools, and I have studied kendo for many, many years."

"Is that some kind of karate or judo?"

"Kendo is much deeper, it trains your body—and mind—with swordsmanship."

Felix gave a wry laugh. "How often do you get to use your sword today?"

"Never outside the practice halls, of course, but training in the sword is really only a way to train the spirit . . . and for that kendo is much better than karate."

"Okay, why?"

"Look at their history: samurai had *daisho,* the long and short swords, which peasants were not allowed. So . . . the subjugated people developed a method of fighting using the empty hand. It is very effective, of course, but harmful for the spirit because the basis for the discipline is a state of inferiority: making do because you've not been given the right to carry a weapon. Kendo doesn't have that limit as its base—it starts from a position of power."

"Isn't that pretty arrogant?"

"No, you don't understand the Japanese mind. A samurai can serve, you know—serve his family, his lord. But it is the strong relationship between warrior and warlord—not of tiller of the earth and master.

"It is late in life to start, but you might look into this, Felix. I sense a quietness in you that might respond well to kendo training."

Felix laughed again. "Sure, right after I learn to play the cello. Where are you going to call from?"

"Just up here. There's a phone booth at the edge of this parking lot; we should have no company."

Yataro turned the car into the parking lot of a shoe store that was closed for the night. He stopped, then backed and turned the car a bit so that its headlights did not illuminate the booth. He picked up a heavy bag of coins from the floor of the car and walked over. Felix got out to join him.

Casually, Yataro scanned the surroundings for other people, then turned and lifted the receiver. He dialed a number, and then waited while the phone buzzed and clicked as it made the connection. "Please deposit"—pause—"three dollars and fifty-five cents"—pause—"for the first three minutes. Please dep—" Yataro cut off the voice as he started putting coins into the slot. "Thank you," said the phone, and then came the faint burr of the phone ringing at the other end.

There were ten rings, and still no answer. "He's out?" asked Felix.

Yataro raised his hand. "No, just hard to call into the present tense."

After another twelve rings, the phone was finally answered. "Hullo?" came the voice. "Who's this?"

"It's me, your friend with the fame."

"Oh, wow, Mr. Onryo. I wondered if you were going to call. Everything's set."

"Tonight is the first test; please proceed as we discussed. I would like you to cover the period from noon today until noon tomorrow."

"Sure, no problem, it's going to be fun. I wish I could see their faces."

"Not a wise thought. I will call tomorrow night. Good-bye and thank you."

"Hey, sure. This was easy. For the next test, see if you can come up with something difficult." He rang off.

Yataro hung up briefly and then lifted the receiver and put in another coin. He dialed seven digits. "All is well," he said when someone answered. He hung up and stepped out of the booth.

"That seemed straightforward," said Felix. "What next?"

"I checked the kitchen before we left—only wines. We will be up tonight, I suggest we find a bottle of very good scotch to spend the time with."

"Hear, hear."

They got back into the car and drove off into the night.

"That was our Japanese friend. 'All is well,' he says."

"Good. Uli, we are on our way," said Baalbek. "Are they headed back?" The two sat alone in the kitchen, drinking tea. Rudi and Hans read magazines in their room; Dieter was back to his continual tinkering at the workbench.

"He didn't say. We don't need them here until morning. I wouldn't be surprised if he and Felix didn't come back for a while . . . they're getting awfully chummy, those two."

"Oh, I'm not surprised that they get along so: they're both fighting men. It's good for them to form such bonds, it makes for a stronger team."

"I don't like them not acting like a part of my team. Why don't they hang out with Rudi?"

"Ah, Rudi . . . Rudi is not a warrior, he is a killer."

"He does what I ask him to do; don't insult my people!"

"No offense meant, Uli. He has proven that he is a very useful man of quite extraordinary talents. But always remember the difference between a warrior and killer—it might someday save your life."

12

HITCH

"Doughnuts? Do I smell doughnuts?" Tina bumped the door open and backed into the small, cramped room carrying an armful of folders. She dumped them onto one of the two desks.

"Yup. Cinnamon, powdered sugar, and for the true aesthete, chocolate honey-dipped."

She picked up the bag from the filing cabinet, opened it, and took a deep sniff. "Bill, I think I'm going to marry you; chocolate honey-dipped! Where did you find them in this place? You must be a magician!"

"Actually, I just picked them up on the way back from my hotel when I went to get fresh clothes."

"As simple as that, eh? Ah well, the marriage is off . . . speaking of which, Karen Hobbs dropped by to see you before I left."

"And what did you mean by that?"

"Didn't you two have a thing once?"

How could she know that? Bill thought. "I worked on a grab job with her once."

"Uh-huh . . . anyway, she's back in town from that security advance assignment she's been doing for the past three weeks.

Couldn't wait around; said she'd try again. You know, she's a good one."

Bill let it lie. Tina went over to her desk and collapsed into the chair. "What did we ever do to Fosdick and his sidekick to deserve this rat hole? Did you kill his firstborn or something?"

"Look, partner, we should sweat the important stuff. We got something—two staffers, on-net and civilian lines, comm facilities, and a computer tie-in. Let them think they won this one, and let's try to find those damn bombs."

"Righty-o." She leaned back in her chair and massaged her eyes and temples. "Awake, awake, awake," she mumbled to herself, then sat up. "I need a sugar fix . . . you?"

"Sure, give me another cinnamon."

She paused at the file cabinet and weighed the bag. "Another?"

"Well . . . see, this *really* big guy came in and *forced* me to eat it . . ."

"Right." She went back to her chair, bringing Bill his doughnut. "Then why don't you take this, in case he comes back. Anything else happen while I was gone?"

He picked up the doughnut and took a bite. Bliss. "They've found the seller of the helicopter."

"Great! Are we going to get anything useful from him?"

"I don't think so . . . They found him with his wrists and ankles tied, out in the middle of a field near Amarillo. Looks like he got there after exiting his helicopter a thousand feet up."

"Ack. You have a way with the facts." She put the remainder of her doughnut down on her desk. "Any other info?"

"Not much. Seems he was to meet a potential buyer—a Mr. R. Brown—at dawn for a test flight. No address, no phone number. End of story; dead end."

"I knew it couldn't be that simple. Anything new on these nuclear shells they took?"

Bill picked up the notebook he had been studying when Tina came in. "Nothing from upstairs, but let's see . . . I've been doing some reading about them, and despite what that DOE idiot said, I don't think we're lucky that these are what they got. The yield is relatively low, but the warheads are really small. They're a hell of a lot easier to hide, transport, and deliver than any of the bigger stuff, like a one megaton warhead that weighs a ton.

"These W33's are the older-model shells, back from when they designed for blast and didn't care that much about residual radiation. The newer ones are a lot cleaner . . . if you can speak that way about a nuclear weapon."

"It may even be worse than that. I did some checking, too. These things didn't have command disable."

"Which is?"

"A system that wrecks key components if someone tries to tamper with the warhead. Most of the new stuff has it, but these old shells just had mechanical combination locks."

"They can't have been that stupid."

"Oh, yes."

Bill dropped his notebook on the desk. "You can never underestimate the intelligence of the dimwits who hang around to make decisions in the peacetime military." He leaned back and bumped his head on the corner of the bookcase behind him. "Ouch! Damn you, Fonsgraf!"

"Sweat the important stuff, remember?"

"Right." He rubbed his head. "Tina, what do you think about this situation?"

"What do you mean? Our palatial quarters, Fosdick?"

"No, the bomb snatch—how they did it, why, who . . . things that don't fit. Something's bothering me, you know, nudging me, something that doesn't fit; I can't put my finger on it."

"Such as?"

"Maybe it's that we're getting mixed signals here." He took a long drink of coffee and then stared into the cup. "On the one hand, whoever took these weapons made a flawless execution of the attack—which implies superb intelligence, planning, and training. On the other hand, they had some stupid lapses, like leaving a shipping container with DOE markings near the torched helicopter, and the abandoned van, which gives us their escape route on Interstate 70. That seems out of character with the careful job that was done on the convoy.

"And then there are some little things. Why did they use that

Sikorsky for the operation? It was an S-76, Mk II, with auxiliary tanks—that's a fairly oddball ship, really a specialized, long-range job: it can do better than six hundred and fifty miles with eight passengers. Bell Jet Rangers and Hughes 500's are as common as fleas in Texas. Why search out an S-76 . . . coincidence? Planned?"

"Maybe because they had too far to go from the ambush site to I-70?"

"Nah, a Jet Ranger could've handled that easily . . . but that does give me a thought. We should get a reading from the hour meter on that burned chopper, and check it against the owner's base log. That'll tell us how long our friends were up in the air; might be something there."

"Sounds like we're grasping at very thin straws."

"But what else can we do? Fosdick's all ready to pull a raid, but there's no one to raid. There's been no joy from the various roadblocks, no communiqués from the bad guys; nothing beyond the dead end of a burned helicopter and an abandoned van on Interstate 70."

"I talked with Peter Hanson on the way down here. FBI's convinced that by searching west from that van, they'll be able to develop some leads. The current favorite for a location is Denver."

"Good luck to him . . ."

"That's what I say."

"Tina, no one's claimed credit yet; you still think it's Ost-Sturm we're dealing with?"

"Yes, I think so—it's a good fit. They're still the only nongovernment organization I know of who could have put this together: get our pilot out from under our noses in Lebanon, research the ambush, take the bomb, figure out how to get it to work. Unfortunately, judging from what they've done in the past, they also might have enough sociopathic weirdness to use it."

"So how do we find them? At this point, the roadblocks are long past doing any good. Whoever did it has gotten to some safe house and settled in. If it was Ost-Sturm, do any of their people have any quirks that might help us find them?"

Tina shuffled through her pile and selected a red notebook. She slowly turned the pages as she sipped her coffee. "The only one I see as a possibility is this Dieter Strasse, whom I mentioned last night in the meeting.

"The Germans had an interest in his wife, and when she was still alive, the BKA did a quiet search of their apartment. Nothing of interest on her was found, but the entry team did say Dieter was a real technical magazine freak: German, American, Japanese . . . lots and lots of subscriptions, lots and lots of files. Now, maybe he still does that—subscribe to a bunch—but I can't see how we'd find him through the magazines' customer lists, since he would undoubtedly be using a pseudonym. I think the French found the same thing on a search they once did. I'm checking."

"Right. Well, let's think about it, and have Robin get up a list of those publications. Maybe we'll figure a way to use it later."

The telephone gave a quiet buzz; Tina scooped it up. "Lucia here . . . Hello, sir . . . Yes, sir . . . Ah, nothing really new. Bill and I are just brainstorming. Sure, he's right here." Tina pushed the hold button. "It's the Admiral."

Bill picked up his receiver and pushed the flashing button. "Hello, sir."

"Bill, if you don't have anything hot going on, could you come over to my office?" said the voice on the line.

"Sure thing, sir. Tina and I can get back to this later. I'll be right up." He hung up the phone. "He sounds pretty worn."

"He should; dealing with the President is hard enough on its own. Add on the missing bombs, and . . . it's a pretty heavy load."

"He wants me to go over to the White House to see him. Don't eat all my doughnuts while I'm gone."

"Moi?" She looked at her watch. "While you're gone, I'm going to make some more calls . . . pump my contacts on Ost-Sturm people. I'll have Robin track down that hour meter for you, too. Who knows, we may get some leads."

"Have fun." He gave her a smile and left their basement room.

In the corridor, he could hear the buzz of activity from the other offices. Bill peered in as he passed by. Earnest young men in uniforms or white shirts and suspenders talked authoritatively into telephones, jabbing the air as they made their points, the atmosphere thick with cigar smoke. It looked good; it looked like not much was being accomplished.

He decided to walk outside and get some clean air, rather than take the tunnel. Bypassing the elevator, he took the stairs two at a time.

It was sunny as he walked through the security gate and across the roadway to the White House's west entrance. The noise of the traffic on Pennsylvania Avenue was just a faint backdrop. What a temptation to linger, he thought, but by the time he had reached the door the wind had cut through his shirt to chill him. In a tree near the entrance, a mockingbird was playing through his repertoire before putting it away for the winter.

The young guard at the desk checked his ID and then the list on his desk.

"Is Karen Hobbs on today?"

"Day off. You're on the Admiral's access list, sir. Please go on through."

Bill headed down the corridor. It was quiet here: a hush, as if all the world were at rest. The lack of activity was not reassuring . . .

He went up the half level to the Admiral's office. The same B school type was at the reception desk. "Please go right in, Mr. Hitch. Admiral Thomas is expecting you."

The door to the office was open. Bill paused at the entrance and looked in. The Admiral was leaning back in his chair, reading from a sheaf of cables. There were circles under his eyes that Bill did not remember seeing before. He knocked quietly on the doorframe and the Admiral looked up.

"Come on in, Bill. Shut the door." He dropped the papers on the table and gestured to one of the wooden chairs that faced the desk. "Have a seat. Any news since last night?"

"You heard about the helicopter salesman?"

"Yes."

"Then nothing else of substance. Tina and I are just trying to think of ways to track the Ost-Sturm people. She feels pretty strongly that they're the ones we're looking for. If they're the ones who did it, then maybe one of their people has some quirk or marker that can lead us to them. Tina's done some research, and is on the phone now doing more, trying to scare something up on people the Ost-Sturm core have worked with in the past. Pretty thin stuff to be sure, but . . ." He shrugged.

"Are you working with Fonsgraf's people?"

"The rest of the crowd over in EOB is trying brute force. They seem to be concentrating on searching at the roadblocks—that's what Peter Hanson has been pushing for. I think the time for that to be of any use is long gone. So, I guess we're keeping our own counsel on this, working our own leads."

"That may be the best." The Admiral pointed to his cables. "I've been informing the top military and consular people, but only a few, and that's with dire threats about not letting anything out. If the public gets wind of this, the panic will be terrible." He leaned back in his chair. "That is my biggest worry: panic. And Luke Wheeler is doing a civilian goo-goo. He's talking about having the President go public with this. Idiot. Come down the corridor with me while I twist his arm."

Luke Wheeler was the President's press secretary, a former student leader from his old Bible college. Bill knew most Presidents kept their press secretaries out of the information loop; then they would not be in the position of actually lying to the press; with lack of real knowledge, the Press Secretary could have plausible deniability. But this President felt he was talking God's Truth, and all a good press secretary had to be was a man who could pass that on. Wheeler was on the loop; his office was next to the President's in what used to be the Chief of Staff's quarters.

Bill trailed as the Admiral strode past the secretary and stopped in the open door of the office. "I hope to God that you've changed your mind."

Luke Wheeler had a plain office that looked as if he came from three generations of accountants. Everything was sparse and beige. All the papers on the desk were precisely aligned to an imaginary grid; all the books on the low shelves around the room arranged so that their spines were perfectly even. The only thing on the walls was one large, framed photograph of the President. It wasn't even signed. The Washington tribal rite of showing status by collections of signed photographs of those you were supposedly close to had been made unnecessary by the location of Wheeler's office.

Luke himself was not behind his desk, but sitting in one of four chairs drawn up to a round table that overlooked the Rose Garden, reading a book as the Admiral spoke. He gave a slight grimace at the use of the Lord's name, placed a bookmark to note his page, and set the book on the table. "Admiral Thomas, how can we not tell the American people? We are not a military government, but a republic, and the strength of a republic is an informed citizenry. When we tell them the truth, then the right course of action will be obvious."

"I don't think you're correct, there. Same knowledge does not mean the same acts: the Russians know the same facts we do—why don't they come over to our side?"

"Facts are not the same as the truth. They don't know the truth."

"Son, that's an argument I'm smart enough not to pursue, because I know it's one I'm never going to win with you. This is Bill Hitch. I don't know if you two have ever really met; Bill is one of my people working on this problem."

Son? thought Bill. He suddenly realized that the man sitting there was roughly his own age. But he looked like an adult, one of those mythic people you saw in your parents' old photos: sober and thick, lumpily dressed . . . not something Bill felt he would ever be before, say, seventy.

They nodded to each other and shook hands as Bill and the Admiral sat at the table. Bill sat so he could watch both the door and the window—old habits die hard.

"Let's talk about what the President is, or is not, going to tell the country." The Admiral leaned back in his chair and seemed to examine the other man.

"As I said, I feel that we are just stewards, not masters for the American people. They need to be told."

"Then what would you have the President say? 'My fellow citizens, some unknown group out there has seven of our nuclear warheads, which they may—or may not—plan to set off somewhere in the United States, sometime, we don't know when'?

"And what happens then? Millions flee every city and major town in the United States, heading for the countryside. What do they eat? What do they drink? Medical care, policing, shelter, clothing, latrines, washing, births. All of life of a whole nation lived on the road or in some field? How soon before order breaks down and people start stealing from each other, fighting, rioting, killing . . . What's the human cost? And it's a given that the economy is destroyed. And then imagine what's going on in the cities they've left. How do you maintain order and security there?"

Bill sat forward in his chair, mesmerized. He had been concentrating on finding the bombs: a nice contained problem. He hadn't had the time to raise his sights and consider the larger scene. He was too stunned to be scared.

"Yes," said Wheeler, "but what are the losses if they use the bombs?"

"That's a tough one. It all depends where and when they go off. Bill, do you remember what I said two nights ago about Hiroshima?"

"Eighty thousand lost from a bomb about twice the size of the ones they've got."

"That's right; and Luke, the math says seven times forty thousand is two hundred eighty thousand. Over a quarter of a million people; one percent of the population."

Wheeler watched him, unmoved by the statistics.

"I'm not trying to snow you." The Admiral rubbed his forehead and then continued, "That's a weak number. Cities are denser today. If they could set them all off in New York, losses could be higher. And I'm not in favor of a military government . . . There is something to what you say: who are we to keep this kind of information from American citizens, to make this kind of decision for them? Whether to stay in the cities or run to the countryside?"

He leaned forward and looked into Wheeler's eyes. "This is no easy decision. If we'd had any communication from the people who took the bombs—anything—then there'd be more to base a decision on. Maybe they want money. Maybe they want to get them out of the country to use somewhere else, though we do have the borders pretty tightly sealed up now. Maybe they hate us and want to kill as many Americans as they can. We just don't know. We don't have a hell of a lot of information, but we've got to help the President make a decision."

Bill had known intellectually that a big title could mean big decisions. But now he felt the truth of it: making decisions like the one the Admiral was struggling with was the other side of national leadership, the part one didn't think of. It was the counterbalance to the big office, the big limo, the title, the perks. You had the weight of huge decisions on your shoulders. Most of the bigwigs never had to confront it: nothing happened on their watch. But the Admiral was now in the chair and the weight was on him.

Luke sat with lowered eyes and said nothing.

"What's the best advice we can give the President, Luke? What's our recommended course of action; what's the lesser evil?"

Luke Wheeler placed his hand lightly on the book he had been reading. "It is not a question of what is the lesser evil, but the greater good."

Bill looked down; a gold cross embossed on the book's spine peeked through Wheeler's fingers.

"Say it any way you want, son, but we've got to recommend something to the President, and I come down on the side of the keeping the lid on this for the time being. I'd like your support in that."

Bill caught a shadow out of the corner of his eye and looked up. "Hello, sir," he said, and stood.

In the doorway was the President. The Admiral looked up and rose also. "Good day, President Western."

"It is a lovely day, isn't it? In spite of our travails. What are you three working on?" He stood framed in the doorway, profiling slightly. Tall, with great visual charisma, he had a magnificent mane of white hair and broad shoulders that were emphasized by the cut of the light-colored suits he was given to. The President had the teddy bear smile of men who know they wear the cloak of God. He walked into the room. "And I don't believe I know this young man." He stopped five feet away and looked at Bill, his eyes focused as if he were looking through him.

"This is William Hitch, Mr. President. He's a member of my staff."

The President's smile widened slightly, as if a switch labeled "warmer" had been thrown, but the eyes still didn't quite focus on Bill's face. It had the same effect as meeting someone who was listening to the news on a Walkman.

"I'm grateful that you are here, Bill. We need good men at this time. The theft of those bombs means that this is a time of great significance for our country; perhaps we should think on that. Why seven? That's a special number." The President's diffuse gaze turned to the Admiral. "What have you decided to recommend to me?"

"Well, sir, we may have a bit of a split here. I strongly suggest that we keep this under wraps for the time being. The alternative would be terrible panic and losses, perhaps even greater than from actual use of the bombs."

"And you, Luke? What does my press secretary have to say?"

"Sir, these are American citizens, and they deserve to hear the truth and be consulted by their leader."

President Western looked fondly at his secretary. "Luke, you should study that book a bit more." Wheeler flushed. "A leader of a nation is not like the leader of some civic group. He is a *shepherd,* a shepherd for the nation. A shepherd does not consult his sheep—he guides them, leads them. That is what the Lord teaches us . . . and that's what my daddy, the Senator, taught me, too. People want to be led, they want to *believe* in their leaders, they don't *want* to be consulted."

The President turned to look at the Admiral. "Chris, we'll keep this matter between ourselves, and not inform the public. That's the decision that makes the most political sense. You and I know that without a good political base, the best intentions in the world aren't worth a cup of spit . . . even the intention to do the Lord's will." He smiled at each of them, then turned to leave the room.

He stopped at the doorway and faced them again. "The American people are my flock. The Lord has entrusted *me* with their care. Just as the Lord is *my* shepherd. He knows best, and *all* is by his will. There's a passage I've been meditating on that I think you all should study. It is a joyful lesson for us to hear at this time. Come into my office and I'll share it with you."

The three men followed the President into the Oval Office and stood there like a trio of slightly apprehensive altar boys. The President walked over to a large Bible that lay on a pedestal stand to the left of the desk. He began to flip through the pages. The sun from the windows behind him haloed his body.

Bill looked around the room he had seen many times in the news, but never in person. The room looks the same, he thought, but I never imagined a scene like this.

A row of grandfather clocks along the wall worked a pattern of measured ticks—the only sound besides the rustle of the pages. "Here it is," said the President, "Revelations 21:8–12." He scanned the page as if to set his memory and then raised his eyes. There was a faint echo of the cadence that had brought thousands weeping to their feet, thousands proffering their contributions.

> *". . . But the fearful, and unbelieving, and the abominable, and murderers, and whoremongers, and sorcerers, and idolators, and all liars, shall have their part in the lake which burneth with fire and brimstone: which is the second death.*
>
> *"And there came unto me one of the seven angels which had the seven vials full of the seven last plagues, and talked with me, saying, Come hither, I will show thee the bride, the Lamb's wife. And he carried me away in the spirit to a great and high mountain, and showed me that great city, the holy Jerusalem . . ."*

13

FAYE

"This is the goddamned most boring job I've ever had! I hate it, I hate it! I'm going to tell that dirtbag sergeant that he can take this job and shove it where the sun don't shine!" Specialist Fourth Class Arthur Howard took a bag of mail and dropped it on the counter.

"Art, you've been saying that every morning for the past six months . . . don't you think I'm tired of hearing it?"

"Has it been six months? Seems like six years, and now we're shorthanded and there's even more of this shit to do. Jimmy, how did I end up sorting letters in fucking Utah? Fucking hicksville, one-road base. If I'd wanted to sort letters, I could have worked for the post office back home in Albany; at least I would have been home partying every night. When I get out, I'm going back and castrate that son of a bitch recruiting sergeant who conned me into signing up."

"Poor baby. But how about me? Every morning I got to come in and look at your ugly face. No one should have to do that sober." Jimmy Faye stood in front of his station, reading names on envelopes and flipping them into the dingy, sheet-metal postboxes that filled one wall of the low-ceilinged room. A small radio taped to an overhead pipe played songs of trucking, heartache, and pain.

It was stiflingly hot despite the cold air leaking through the rubber-skirted swinging doors that led in from the loading dock. Art stripped off his jacket and stood there in the slightly arms out stance that comes from too many hours of low-rep bench presses. "You'd think that with everyone out of here for those maneuvers we'd have less to do. But noooo . . ."

"Well, you're gonna have even more work to look forward to. My sergeant said I'm leaving here tonight. He says there's some kind of big drug-bust training operation going on, and they want more bodies. That means you're going to be here all by your lonesome."

"No fucking way!"

"That's right. While I'm out there freezing my ass off, you'll be here in steam-heated comfort."

"No fucking way! You like it here; how come I can't go?"

"Maybe they figured sending you on a drug bust was not the brightest idea. Must have heard about you in Washington—figured any evidence you found would never, ever make it to court."

"Drug busts, my ass. Since when has regular Army been used on drug operations?"

"I guess the President has plans." Jimmy took a letter and waved it in Art's face. "Anyway, you're the lucky bastard. Have you seen the new communications tech they moved in this morning?"

"No, what's he here for?"

"Something to do with his drug search, and no, Art. Not 'he' . . . 'she.' As in five four, dark hair, very nice tits, and an ass on her that will make you cry."

"Naww . . . where?"

"Just down the hall. In the staff room just before the supply closet. Where I guess you're going to be going twenty times a day now."

"Naww . . ."

"And she's got the look, Art. She's hot—someone to keep you warm over the winter, that's for fucking sure."

Art stuck his head out the door and looked down the corridor. "In that room there? Let's go check her out."

"She was there, but she left. She should be over at the mess hall at noon, though. If we can get this stuff sorted before then, I'll take you over and introduce you, you lucky bastard. If I wasn't shipping out tonight, you wouldn't stand a chance."

Art puffed out his chest. "You wouldn't stand a chance yourself, my man. When she sees my moves, it's all over for the competition." He gave his hips a pump. "Local talent . . . just what the doctor ordered."

"Get to work, idiot. If we don't get this stuff sorted, you're not going to make it over to the mess hall in time, and some other grunt will meet her first."

"Right, right." Art dumped his mail sack out onto the counter and started to sort the letters and packages. "Pretty mamas are getting scarce in this Army. When my brother was in four years ago, he said the bases were crawling with fine-looking ladies. But nooo, our President says that's 'a-mor-al.' "

"And what you have planned for her is moral?"

Art stopped to pose again. "No, my man, just natural, that's all . . . just what comes naturally. It's just with so few mamas around, even the sheep out there are starting to look cute. Are you sure that it was a woman you saw, not some kind of mirage?"

"Certainly wasn't no sheep. No fucking way. That was one fine-looking woman. Who some other soldier is going to end up banging if you don't get that sorting done."

Art started flipping letters into the boxes as fast as he could, not really worrying if they made the correct slot. "Tell me more about this drug bust you're going on."

"Not bust, dummy, just training. I talked with a guy who had been out, but came back with—get this—frostbite on his fucking toes. He said they were stopping cars and stuff on the roads and searching them with some high-tech sniffer they had brought in from Texas or someplace. Said there was real tight security on it all."

"Doesn't sound like a drug bust to me. Sounds like something else."

"What, aliens? Flying saucers?"

"That's right, sex-starved invading Amazons from Mars . . . no, I'm serious. It doesn't sound like drug-bust training to me."

"Art, it's no worry to me. Whatever the man says to do, that's what I guess I'm gonna end up doing."

"Yeah, but what if it isn't. Remember that reporter dude we met a couple of months ago? Maybe he'd be interested in this. I might make some change."

"Sounds to me like something they hang people for."

"No, man. He was network TV. I seen him on TV, he wasn't no commie dude. But they've got a lot of money to spend on stories and shit. And I'm going to need some extra money with that fine piece of ass you're telling me about." Art finished his sack and sat down on one of the drums that littered the mail room. "Let's go, man. It's almost noon."

"I got a few more to do. If these letters aren't finished for the lunchtime rush, there's going to be hell to pay. You figure out who that Federal Express package is for."

"Which one?"

"The one you're sitting on, dummy."

Art got off the cardboard shipping drum and looked at it. Two and a half feet high and two feet in diameter, it was plastered with Federal Express next day delivery labels. The metal top was secured by a bolted, band-clamp arrangement. "It's addressed to: 'Commander, motor pool.' What the fuck does that mean?"

"There's a maintenance depot, right? Must be someone there."

"There's no name on it."

"Well, open it and see what it is."

"Can we do that?"

"Art, you keep forgetting that lady that's waiting for you. Maybe I should offer her to someone else."

"Where's the fucking wrench?" Art banged open drawers under the counter until he found a screwdriver and adjustable wrench, then set to work on the drum's top, cursing all the while. "Goddamn Federal Express, getting in the way of my love life!" He undid the bolt holding on the band, and tried to tug off the lid. "Goddamn thing is stuck."

He looked at the clock—quarter to twelve. "Let's do this after lunch."

"Unh-unh. If the mail isn't out before lunch, it's my ass that's going to fry. Just pull on it."

"It's held down by some kind of wire."

"Here, you dumb shit, let me give you a hand."

GREG

It was cold out on the plain. The wind was rising and the sun had long ago been hidden by the heavy clouds. Jack Greg had been riding the hard hills since dawn, searching for coyote sign. It looked like an early winter, and he was worried about the predator losses to his adult sheep and early-spring losses to his lambs. Two years ago it had been really bad; it had set him back, wiped out his savings. He didn't plan for it to happen again. The paperwork to start a poisoning program was formidable, and if the truth be told, Jack had never been that good at reading and writing. He knew that if he didn't start the process early enough, he'd never get permission in time.

He turned the horse so that their backs were to the wind and scanned the rolling hilltops with his binoculars, looking for any kills. Nothing. The wind sang quietly around him—sighing choruses with the occasional dirge of a muted "baaa" from the sheep that moped along, backs to the wind. They stopped now and again to paw and scrape at the sparse grasses. Kicking his mare gently, he turned her east again and rode up the long slope. "Let's go, girl. The sooner we get this done, the sooner we'll get back to the cabin." His dog loped out ahead of him, stopping from time to time to sniff at animal burrows that went down into the hard, frozen earth.

He turned again out of the wind and paused. His dog stopped twenty-five yards ahead and turned back to watch him. Jack looked around. The sheep didn't seem upset; perhaps the coyotes hadn't moved in yet.

He stood up in his stirrups to ease his back. There was a sudden brightening of light, as if a sun, or twenty suns, had suddenly risen. His shadow stretched out in front of him, stark black against the white ground. His eyes were dazzled and he sat and squeezed them shut.

When he opened them, the awful light had faded. He turned in his saddle and looked behind him. There, a few miles away, where the small Army base had been, rose a tall pillar of smoke. The top of the pillar was a rolling, rising ball. "What the hell . . ." He sat there transfixed, finally hearing a sharp keening howl that caused him to look back up the rise.

There his dog circled, hopping on three legs while rubbing her face with one paw. She ran into a rock, fell, and lay there, frantically pawing at her face. "My God," Jack whispered, "that dog is blind!"

A gust of hot air blew past him.

14

HITCH

The book hit the desk with a crack. "Silence, damn it! Silence!" The noise lowered a notch as conversations ended, and then quiet descended. He surveyed the room; most present had been called to the meeting from their dinners. He continued with a low growl to his voice, "Okay, so they used one . . ."

The conference room was smaller; there were fewer aides in attendance; the chairs' cushions were not as deep. Charles Fonsgraf's uniform was just as sharply pressed, but there was a wildness at the edges of his eyes that had not been there before. "The President has asked that I lead this group while he is chairing the meeting upstairs. No one wants to get those bastards more than I do, so let's get to work! We need to find the rest of those bombs and organize the punishment for what they've done. That's what the President has asked me to concentrate on."

Fonsgraf gestured to the large map on the wall with its new red circle. "For those who just got here, there's where they hit, at Dugway, in Utah. It is"—was, thought Bill—"a small base at the north end of the proving grounds—small equipment depot and maintenance center. The normal complement is a little over four hundred officers and men, but we were a bit lucky—we had pulled out two hundred to staff the roadblocks and searches in Colorado." He leaned his fists on the edge of the table and stared around the room. "But that is still the loss of close to two hundred American boys to some terrorist scum. We want to find those bastards and make them pay!"

"When did it explode?" asked Jack Phillips.

"Just around noon today."

"What!" barked Tom Sinotti, a short and very pugnacious staffer for the Speaker of the House. "Then why did it take so long to notify us? The Speaker is going to be pretty ticked."

"We found out less than two hours ago," replied Bunk Cole. He knew the most important part of his job was the deflection of criticism of his boss. "The bomb got everyone on the base, and wiped out local communications. First reports came from a sheep rancher with a spread nearby. It took a while to get up the chain to us, then it had to be confirmed."

"How did they deliver the bomb?" asked Jack Phillips.

"We don't know yet, but we're working on it. From their communiqué, it seems that they had people drive it in. Or maybe fly it."

"What communiqué?" demanded Sinotti. "When did you get that, and why hasn't it been released to us yet?"

"Look," said Fonsgraf. He nodded at the ceiling. "This is now a military matter. The Speaker is getting the communiqué now. It's from Ost-Sturm, and they have certain demands about Lebanon. We can get into that, but I think first we need to formulate a recommendation to the President on who to hit over there."

"Bullshit!" said Sinotti. "You've been playing this pretty close to your chest . . ."

"On orders of the Commander in Chief."

". . . on whoever's orders, and you've made a mess of it. What we've got to do now is find the rest of the bombs and prevent them from being used, not act out some scene from *Rambo VII*." His face was flushed; red, mottled patches appeared over his cheekbones. "Our big problem is here, now, in the U.S."

"Why don't you just read the message?" said Dale Kuhn quietly. "Let's take first things first."

Fonsgraf looked around the table and got mostly stares that

agreed with Kuhn. "Read the damn thing," he said to Major Cole, and then sat down.

Cole opened his notebook and removed an 8½-by-11 sheet. "At seven P.M. this evening, the following was delivered by phone to a secretary in a Pentagon public-information office. There was no recording equipment in operation, but she could take shorthand. The call was untraceable. The person who phoned was male . . . no identifiable accent." Cole cleared his throat with a slightly embarrassed "um . . ."

This morning, our glorious, martyred fighters delivered a blow against the American war machine which has taken the blood of our people and attempted to divide our great nation.

Our women and children have been slaughtered by cowardly American soldiers who are afraid to meet our fighters face-to-face.

Over four hundred of our innocents have fallen. This is our answer: We have killed over four hundred of your soldiers.

We now warn you: stop bombing our people, stop dividing our country. Either reunite Lebanon under the power of the rightful rulers, the Muslim majority, or more of your soldiers will die in their dens.

You have one week to respond. The only acceptable response will be a worldwide declaration of your sins, a pledge to reunite Lebanon, and payment of just reparations. Any other response will mean that more Americans will die.

This is Ost-Sturm for the Action League for the Unification of Lebanon.

"Goddamned bunch of crazies," mumbled one of Fonsgraf's people. "What does Lebanon have to do with anything?"

"Is that it?" asked Dale.

"That's the entire message," said Bunk Cole. "We have nothing to trace, it seems, and the only thing to go on is this message."

"We've heard of Ost-Sturm, but what is this Action League?"

"Our people and contacts have never heard of it before. It may be just an event name for this operation. We're still checking."

Let's get some facts down in order, thought Bill. He took a pad of paper from his briefcase and laid it sideways on the table. "What time did that come in?"

"Seven o'clock, eastern time."

Bill drew a line across the paper and wrote *communiqué* halfway along it. "What was the time, as precisely as we can say, that the bomb went off?"

"Look, Hitch," said the Colonel as he rose again, "I already told you that. Let's move on."

"Colonel, I think it might make sense to start putting some facts down on paper."

"That's something for staff to do."

God, this guy is so dense. "Well, it seems we *are* staff for the people meeting upstairs." Maybe fear will bring him back to reality. "The President and the Speaker feel that way; the Admiral asked me to get the facts down and see if we can make any sense of them, catch any pattern. I can understand if you're going to be too busy to deal with that request . . . perhaps you can just give us the facts and then let Tom, Dale, Tina, and me work on them. We can report back to the Admiral." Keep it very sweet, Bill thought, don't attack him directly. Let him work it out for himself: he's no longer in charge of all aspects of this situation.

Fonsgraf stood still at his place at the table; he seemed to be consulting images inside his head. He twisted his hands; he didn't like what he saw. "Let me talk with Bunk for a moment." Major Cole bent over and the two men conferred in hushed tones.

"This guy is really an ass," Bill whispered to Tina. She sat next to him, intently watching the conversation between Fonsgraf and Cole at the other end of the table. "He still doesn't realize that his wings have been clipped."

"He hasn't the support of anyone except maybe the President," she whispered back.

"Especially since he botched his first assignment."

"Ever wonder if that's why the President still supports him?" she replied.

The thought hung there. That can't be true, Bill thought. I don't need that kind of paranoia.

Fonsgraf spoke up. "Look, ah, Bill. We will get to those time-sequence issues; I know the Admiral wants them. But first, ah, I want to go over a few items.

"The President is still demanding that at the present time this all be kept from the American people," the Colonel continued. "I want to impress on all of you here"—he looked especially hard at Tom Sinotti, whom many suspected to be an anonymous source for the *Washington Post*—"that there is a good reason behind that directive: stopping widespread panic. If this gets out, the whole country will be in chaos. The President has said that he will pursue any leaker to the fullest extent of his abilities. Anyone who does let this get out will be spending a large part of the rest of his life watching the world through a set of bars. Understood?"

There were a few low murmurs of assent around the table. His confidence returning, Fonsgraf's lecturing tone started to come back too, seemingly copied intact from Alec Guinness's Colonel Nicholson in *The Bridge on the River Kwai.*

"Okay, now, as I said, the President wants this to be a hush matter. That means that we are still going to deal with it using federal assets and not involve the states or the National Guard. This has been agreed to by the congressional leadership.

"The group upstairs will be handling national planning. The President"—he paused for a bit of drama—"has asked me to coordinate the groups represented in this room toward this goal: find the people who took the bombs.

"When we find them, the President"—he paused again—"has asked that I coordinate the various federal assets to be used in getting the rest of the bombs back. I have decided Secret Service through our contact Jack Phillips, and FBI, through Peter Hanson, will handle surveillance and intelligence. Army Special Forces through Bunk Cole and myself will run the strike force. Dale Kuhn will coordinate any foreign intelligence that we need through the CIA. If responsibilities are divided up in this manner, there should be no excuse for different agencies stepping on each other's toes. We need to work effectively." Fair enough, thought Bill.

"Okay, that's settled. Now Bill, let's get at your list."

Bill picked up his pad. "The time line . . . so the communiqué came in at seven P.M. When did the bomb go off?"

Bunk answered. "The best guess is about 11:50. That was the time found on the watches worn by a couple of bodies found near the perimeter of the base; they weren't completely destroyed by the blast. We found just two analog watches; the rest were digital ones and they just go blank on failure. So, we got no other readings."

Bill added that to his time line. "With the two-hour time difference, that means there was a five-hour lag between the bombing and the communiqué being issued . . . Why?"

"Could it be that it took that long for the bad guys to be sure that the attack had been successful?" asked Dale.

"And how would they be sure in five hours? It took us close to that, and we were called directly by the rancher. Bunk," asked Bill, "what would have been the nearest operating phone?"

"Well, the rancher's still worked, of course, but the nearest other place that would have had one would be a gas station about thirty miles away on the highway."

"We should check to see if any of those stations remember anyone coming in and using the phone after the time of the blast. Not a great possibility . . . If I were them, I would have used a radio from a car or from an observation plane ten or fifteen miles away."

"I agree, Bill," said Jack Phillips. "Bunk, is there any air-traffic data we can trace to see if they used a plane to deliver it?"

"That area really doesn't have coverage. We've queried any spy sats we may have had over the area, but cameras, as usual, were off on the U.S. transits . . . so, no luck there. Again, we are still trying to gather data. Don't hold out much hope for any help from that quarter."

"Could the bomb just have been driven up to the gates and set off?" asked Peter Hanson.

"No. At first information, it seems that ground zero was near the center of the base. Somehow, they got the bomb inside. Now all our bases are on full alert, with special attention being given to preventing a truck from crashing the gates or an aircraft delivery. By special directive, a three-mile air envelope has been declared around all our facilities. Surface-to-air missiles have been deployed and put on alert at all sites. Ost-Sturm would find it hard to get in a second time."

"It seems that the question of how they delivered the bomb is the area that might have the best chance of giving us some leads," said Hanson. "My people can start to question all stores, gas stations, and the like on the roads leading to the base; the FBI is good at that kind of detail work, and in any case, the military is tied up running those roadblocks."

"Peter's right," grunted Jack Phillips. "The rest of us who are nonmilitary should go back to our groups after this meeting and brainstorm ideas on how they got the bomb there to the base. Secret Service also has files on threat types here in the U.S. I've asked my people to start a search to see what we come up with on U.S. citizens in that area who might be capable of acting as liaisons or collaborators with Ost-Sturm. Colonel, do you still want all my people assisting on those roadblocks? I could use them on this search and the follow-up interviewing."

"I have decided to abandon the roadblock methodology and think that your people should leave here and work on suggested plans for alternate procedures for finding the bombs. I want a meeting back here at"—he consulted his watch—"zero hundred hours to discuss early options. Understood?" He leaned over and spoke to Bunk Cole in a voice that was a little too loud for privacy. "Take my things back to my office; I'm going up to see the President," and then marched out.

Others started to leave the room in small groups. Tina stood up. "I'm going to get back to our office to see if some data I've been waiting for has arrived from Europe." She gathered her papers and started out, then stopped and turned back. "I forgot, the information that you were looking for on the helicopter hour meter came in just before the meeting."

"And?"

"It seems that the helicopter was used for just about six hours after the salesman took off in the morning."

"That doesn't make sense." Bill did some quick calculations in his head. Cruise speed of 160 knots times six hours—say five and a half hours to give them some ground and idling time, say 125 knots to allow for averaging . . . that makes nearly 690 nautical miles. "Knots to statute miles?"

"1.15."

"So, 1.15 statute miles per nautical mile . . . hmmm, that means . . . right, that doesn't make sense. If they only went from Amarillo to the snatch site to the place they left the chopper, that would have been around 400 miles, as I remember. In the six hours it ran while the bad guys had it, that Sikorsky could easily have flown over 800 miles. I'll be down in a few minutes. This might be worth pursuing."

"Sure," said Tina. "It's going to be a long night. I'll start the coffee." She worked her way around the table and then out the door.

Bill turned to Dale, who he realized had been staring at Tina as she left.

"She really knows her stuff," said Dale. "Sharp mind . . . and body. Why does she dress so plainly?" He sighed. "Someone should tell her to wear something a little sexier."

"Ohhh, I wouldn't suggest you do that. Tina's a fierce lady about talk like that. Remember Frank Tanner?"

"I think so. He used to work for the Deputy Assistant."

"Right. The operative words are *used to.* He was one of those guys who was always making crude remarks when a woman was in the room. Told Tina once in a staff meeting that she should dress up, maybe show a little cleavage to lighten up the next meeting; embarrassed her."

"So what did she say to him?"

"Nothing."

"Well . . ."

"But Frank is no longer working for the Deputy Assistant."

"Yes . . ."

"She didn't say anything to *him.*"

"Ah . . . so what did she do?"

"No one's sure, but no more Frank Tanner. He's not even on staff anymore. Thing you've got to remember about Tina is that she knows things: facts, statistics, numbers, dirt . . . and how things work. Be careful around her."

"Well, maybe I'll keep my thoughts to myself." He turned and grinned at Bill. "But they are such *nice* thoughts."

"Be prudent," said Bill. "See you at midnight." He put his papers into his briefcase and snapped it shut. The conference room was now almost empty. He headed out into the corridor and down to his office.

Bill turned the knob and then pushed the door open with his foot. It crashed into an open file drawer. "Damn, sorry," he said, proceeded into the room, and was shushed by Tina's raised hand.

She was on the phone, evidently with a poor connection, for she brought her waving hand down to press at her free ear. "*Non, c'est rien. Répétez ça, s'il vous plâit . . . Oui, oui . . . bon . . . d'accord. Merci bien. Au revoir, Monsieur.*" She hung up the phone. "Gah! I thought phone technology was beyond the string-and-can stage. What a terrible line!"

"Who was that?"

"Night staff at the Sûreté, the French national police directorate; it's four P.M. here, ten P.M. there. They tracked down their report on a search of Dieter Strasse's luggage when he and his wife were stopped in transit there a few years ago. What I wanted was a list of the magazines he had with him to cross-check with the stuff the Germans found in their search. I'm trying to get a fix on a core list of technical publications that he seems to be a subscriber to."

"Any joy?"

"Yup. I've got twenty that showed up in both searches, a year apart . . . He's got an eclectic mind. But what to do with this is another matter."

"Here's an idea. I think that helicopter information is going to help. Watch this." He got up and took an atlas from the top of the filing cabinet. He pushed aside their papers and coffee cups and opened it on the desk. "Do you have a drafting compass in that junk box of yours?"

"I think so. What's up?"

"It's the extra mileage implied by the hour meter. I put it together with a couple of other details, and I come up with the suspicion that Ost-Sturm has been giving us a little misdirection."

"Well, there's no question that they did get and use a bomb."

"Yes, but our intelligence said they were going to do it after Christmas. They did it before Thanksgiving while we were still training. I still think that finding that shipping box by the helicopter was a little too convenient . . . things like that.

"And it's a total of only four hundred miles from Amarillo to the snatch site and then on to the supposed transfer place where we found the helicopter . . . but the hour meter implies that the chopper flew much farther than that. I think that the site on I-70 is just a plant."

"If that's true, it certainly got us to search in the wrong area."

"Let's take half the extra mileage and swing a radius around the location where we found the helicopter."

"Here's the compass."

Bill measured off two hundred miles from the scale on the edge of the map, and then drew a circle with that radius, centered on a spot on I-70. "Yeah, that could get them up to I-80, or over to I-25. I bet they're holed up somewhere within a hundred miles of this circle."

"Well, let's say you're right about the real transfer having taken place at a site other than near I-70. Why wouldn't they have just gotten to another highway and then driven the bombs five hundred miles or farther on?"

"Because of the helicopter they chose: it had a very long range. Why drive a long distance when you can do the distance faster and with less risk than driving? Remember, they would want to go to ground as soon as possible after taking them."

"Fair enough, at least for a talking point. So, so what? Excuse the rudeness."

"Let's put it together with your information on Strasse. If he looks like the asset that Ost-Sturm could be using to work on the bombs, and he is in the U.S., then past experience tells us that he is never without his beloved magazines. Right?"

"Sure, sure. Go on."

"So find out all the zip codes within a circle, say, one hundred miles larger than the one I've drawn, and query the magazines on the core list you've got about any subscriptions to those zip codes."

"Sounds like a lot of names."

"Maybe, maybe not. If the same name or address—other than a library—shows up on a lot of magazine subscription lists for the journals you have, then it might be that we have a match with Dieter."

Tina stared tiredly at him. "Might work . . . but don't get your hopes up." She picked up her notes from the phone conversation and considered them. She shrugged. "God knows we need every lead, idea, or clue; but I think we better find some ideas that are a little more substantial."

"Hey, trust me."

"Hah!"

"This is what they make staff for."

"Sure, sure. Well, I'll start Robin on it while you're up with the Admiral—you better get going or you'll be late."

"Up with the Admiral? Late?"

"Argh." She rubbed her forehead. "Sorry, I'm losing my mind . . . it's been a long day. Before you came in, the Admiral's secretary called to say he'd like you to come up to his office"—she consulted the wall clock—"in fifteen minutes. That was then . . . so now, it's in two minutes."

"Okay. I'll be back. Put on the coffee and have a cup."

"I think at this point, I need it intravenously."

15

HITCH

He exhaled. Smoke slowly wreathed his head as he leaned back in his chair. "... had thought this was a bad habit I'd left behind, but now . . ." He took another deliberate puff. "It's a good and welcome friend." The Admiral examined the long, silvery ash. "One sign of a good cigar—the length of the ash. Means a good, long-leaf—not chopped—filler has been used. Hard to find in the U.S."

Bill watched the older man's profile. Admiral Thomas had not looked at him since Bill had arrived in his office and he had gestured to him to sit with a wave of his hand.

"How did your meeting go with the Colonel?"

"Nothing accomplished yet. He wants to concentrate on retaliation; we got him—I think—to acknowledge the necessity of first finding the rest of the bombs."

"Good." Another puff, and then another slow exhale. "You and Tina working on anything?"

"Got some ideas . . . based on some information we developed from the wrecked helicopter: I think the place they left it was just a decoy site. Tina and I are pursuing it. We may know more tomorrow."

The Admiral still sat gazing off beyond the wall of his office.

"How did your meeting go, sir?"

Another puff; tension on his jawline. "It started well enough, while staff made their reports. Planning is moving along in a satisfactory fashion. Contingency evacuation routines are being set up. Serious damage estimates are being calculated for the decision makers to use. We all agreed on the need to maintain the hush on this: even the Speaker and the Majority and Minority Leaders . . . That surprised me, but they're three good, seasoned men.

"All went as smoothly as could be expected, though the President was acting as if . . . I'm not sure . . . as if he hadn't heard anything we'd said. Finally, someone—the Secretary of State, I think—asked him if we could bring in the Israeli intelligence groups to get some help.

"The President told him, 'No, we know they don't acknowledge true information.' The Secretary asked him what he meant, and the President told him, 'They've had the truth about our Lord Christ for two thousand years, and they still refuse to see. No, they will not be of any use to us in this.' "

He took another puff. "Then, we got a Bible class, a lecture on Revelations and the significance of the number seven. But then you were there with Luke Wheeler and me, weren't you?"

Bill was silent. What was going on? How could we be reduced to such a farce? You learned pretty soon after you got to Washington that this—and all governments—was a government of men, not superheroes, but if he hadn't been there when the President had done that Bible reading, Bill would have thought that the Admiral was the one who was going round the bend.

"Do you know the Vice-President, Bill?"

"How do you mean?"

"You traveled with him on the Pacific rim trip, didn't you?"

"Just to brief him on the situation we'd had with Sutan." The Admiral turned his head to look at Bill, then turned back to his cigar. "I flew with the Vice-President's party for a few of the legs. Worked on a UNCF scholarship fund-raiser with him, too. That was a while ago."

"But you did have some kind of personal contact with him at one point. What did you think of him?" The Admiral swiveled his chair to finally face Bill. "I am trying not to put you on the spot, but I haven't had much time with the man; I've been shepherding the President too closely. Also, the President refuses to have the Vice-President in on any meeting except those where ceremony demands it. I don't think it's race . . . maybe he found out the Vice-President is an agnostic. What I need now is a feel for Frank Bass: what's important to him, how he thinks."

Bill considered. "Well, from what I saw of him, he's a very tight, very controlled man. Very reserved with his opinions; when asked a question or when something comes up, he always seems to pause for half a beat to consider his response." Bill paused. "But not like someone who's out of his depth or trying to act profound—doing a Henry Kissinger with deep voice and accent—he really weighs all his responses and gives considered opinions."

"Overcautious?"

"Not at all. He's a strong man . . . self-assured and willing to make decisions. He just has a different style than most around here."

The Admiral again examined the ash on his cigar, then tapped it off in the ashtray. "Most of the other people I should be able to ask are the old-guard good old boys. They would never hang around with him, but you've at least traveled with him. . .

"I'm carrying water for the Speaker and the Majority Leader in this. I need someone to go with me in a few minutes to see the Vice-President—someone whom he knows and who is not in a position to benefit from what those two and the others they've consulted want him to consider. Things are getting to a point where he may have to step in."

"What do you mean, step in?"

The Admiral turned and fixed his gaze on Bill. "Take over for the President."

The two men walked down the corridors in silence. The rooms they passed were mostly quiet again. The institutional calm Bill had noticed on his last visit to the senior offices had returned. It was disquieting—as if someone were saying don't worry, the crisis of these missing bombs is happening someplace else, some other time.

The Admiral paused just short of the Vice-President's office and spoke to Bill. "You were with Luke Wheeler and me when we got that lecture on Revelations. Vice-President Bass is going to be a tough nut to crack on this issue of succession, but we think we're losing the President to his fantasy world. I hope you'll back me up in here." He turned and led the way into the Vice-President's office.

"Good afternoon, Admiral Thomas," said the receptionist. "Let me buzz the Vice-President, he's expecting you." She looked at Bill. "And this is . . ."

"William Hitch. He's on my staff."

"Very good, sir." She spoke quietly into her phone, then, "Please go in."

The Vice-President did not rise as they entered his office. He sat behind his desk, dressed in a dark brown suit and bow tie, a man of average height with a big chest. Not fat, not thin, he had a bookish look, accentuated by thinning hair and a pair of tortoiseshell, half-frame reading glasses that he removed and placed on the desk. Bill knew the cynics said he wore bow ties to imitate Archie Cox. Bass said he wore them because his father had . . . tradition was very important to him. "Good evening, Admiral. Good evening, Bill. How have you been?" His voice was unusually deep.

"Quite well, sir."

"What can I do for you . . . two this evening?" Frank Bass was a Southerner, but did not engage in the traditional, polite southern chitchat that comes before getting down to the real business of a conversation.

The Vice-President's desk was covered with thick legal volumes and a lined yellow legal pad that held notes written in a small, neat hand. So it's true, Bill thought, the President's given him so little to do that he's gone back to doing academic research.

"You know who sent me; they'd like me to talk with you about the President."

The Vice-President did not change expression, but sat with his hands resting on his desk watching the Admiral. "Yes?"

"The President's state of mind is our concern. What do you think of him?"

"That he is the President."

A subtle point, that, thought Bill.

"But he is not acting like one," continued the Admiral. "He gave us another Bible lecture at the meeting; no other comment on the loss of that base, no comments or reactions to the reports we received, no leadership or direction on what he wanted us to do . . . other than for us to consider Revelations."

"He is the President."

"I repeat, he is no longer acting like one! We are in the greatest internal crisis of our history, and we have a President who is refusing to deal with it, who seems to welcome the possibility of failure."

"And what do you want?"

The Admiral paused and said quietly, "We want you to consider taking over the Presidency."

"I won't ask you if by 'we' you mean more than the Speaker and the Majority Leader. That is not necessary. As I said, George Tipple Western is the President; that ends the conversation."

The Admiral's voice got tight and hard. "With all respect, sir, this is not an academic exercise. We have six more of those weapons out there, and no idea where they are. We could lose millions of citizens. President Western is refusing to deal with it. We need . . . we want you to consider taking over so that we will have a President who will deal with the crisis."

The Vice-President looked at Bill, then back at the Admiral. He leaned back in his chair. "I do not have the right to do that." The Admiral started to interrupt, but Bass continued to speak over him. "*If* President Western wants to send me a letter saying that he is unable to discharge the duties of his office, then the Twenty-fifth Amendment and U.S. law allow me to take over.

"His cabinet would never agree to write the Constitutionally required letter to remove him. You know that—or should. The Speaker and the Majority Leader may have talked with you, but I do not have the right to do *anything* with those two men; therefore, any action based on this conversation would be illegal."

"Then damn the law," barked the Admiral. "We need to deal with this problem!"

Bass watched in silence, and then said, "There's a quote on the law and a crisis from Sir Thomas More—as written by Robert Bolt in *A Man for All Seasons,* to be sure—but good words nonetheless: More says, 'And what would you do? Cut a great road through the law to get after the Devil?' Roper responds, 'I'd cut down every law in England to do that!'

"More's answer contains the important point," said the Vice-President, his voice deep and solemn. " 'And when the last law was down, and the Devil turned round on you—where would you hide, Roper, the laws all being flat? This country's planted thick with laws from coast to coast . . . and if you cut them down . . . d'you really think you could stand upright in the winds that would blow then?' "

The two older men sat and stared at each other. The Admiral finally spoke, this time without anger. "Again, with all respect, Mr. Vice-President, we have a very, very serious problem. There are six bombs left; we don't know where they are, where they are going, when—or if—they are going to be set off.

"Millions of Americans could be killed if we don't find those bombs, and the President is showing more and more evidence of some kind of religious dementia." The Admiral spat out these last words as if he had taken an unexpected bit of something foul. "This afternoon, he seemed not to listen to staff reports at all, and just gave us a Bible lecture on the significance of the number seven.

"We need him to take action, and he's passive. It almost seems that he welcomes these events. If he continues this way, then we will not find those bombs, and the result of that is too terrible to countenance. We would like you to *consider* stepping in if the President continues to refuse to deal with this, or gets worse."

" 'D'you really think you could stand upright in the winds that would blow then?' That is the situation here; the Constitution defines our country, Admiral. Our country has lasted for over two hundred years because of the strength of an unbreached Constitution. I will not be the one to undercut it."

"But we must act on these bombs!"

The Vice-President watched Thomas in silence for a bit, then said, "Admiral, you are a man of much experience in the *prac-*

tical ways of government. A President can lead, give direction, and deal with long-term strategy. He does not and cannot do all the detailed work for all of his people.

"*This* President wants to make certain fundamental changes in the way the federal government does business. He has not—so far—been able to do it. An institution has a strength that is independent of its leaders—'wiggle room,' if you will. So . . . if the President has not been able to get everything he *wants* done, why do you think he might be able to stop everything he *doesn't* want done? Has the President forbidden you to search for the bombs?"

"No . . . not directly."

"Then, if you want to find the rest of the bombs, I would imagine you should be able to do that without having to have me unconstitutionally take over from the President."

"But what if he gets worse?"

"George Tipple Western is presently the President of the United States of America."

A silence stretched for a bit. The Vice-President continued. "There are also the practical politics of the situation. You've done a good job of shielding the American people from the President's current state of mind; so as far as they are concerned, the man is fine.

"I am a black Vice-President swimming in a time of interesting political currents. Were I to somehow take over—illegally, in my view—the uproar that would follow could well do damage comparable to that of your bombs. If the President can be convinced to step down, or becomes obviously physically incapacitated, then the law prescribes a procedure. Otherwise, be organizationally creative, Admiral . . . but save the organization." He picked up his pen and, looking down, began to write again on his yellow pad. "Good afternoon."

Bill walked in silence with the Admiral back to his office. "Well, Bill, we gave it the old college try, didn't we? Perhaps Bass hasn't really seen how shaky the President is getting." He gave a quick, grim smile. "Maybe I'm doing too good a job on damage control. But by God, Bass is a tight bastard on the Constitution. Probably a good thing for me to hear at that . . . Help me remember what it is I am supposed to be sworn to defend.

"So for the time being, it's 'work within the system.' I guess I've got to dust off my old bureaucratic infighting techniques." He touched Bill on the arm. "I've got to report to the Speaker and the others. You'd best get back to work; call me if you come up with anything."

The Admiral's shoulders slumped the tiniest amount. He started to turn toward his door, then stopped. "Thanks for coming with me . . . It's a screwy world, isn't it?" He disappeared into his office.

Oh great, thought Bill, and headed back down to his own small office, lost in thought. As he turned the first corner, he sensed a shadow ahead of him, looked up as he started an automatic shift to the side, then stopped dead in his tracks. "Oh, hello, President Western."

"Hello"—the President paused for a second—"Bill." The smile came up again on his face, as if it was the normal resting position of his flesh. "A wonderful day, isn't it?"

"Ah, yes, sir."

There was still that slightly vacant quality to his regard of the younger man. "Are you married, son?"

What is this? thought Bill. What does this have to do with Dugway, the bombs, or anything? "No, sir."

"It's so good to see young people involved in government, but you know we shouldn't neglect the important things." He paused and continued to smile at Bill. "You and your family should surely come to the prayer services we have here on Saturday mornings. It would be good to have more young faces there. And it is so good for us to see the children there too, praising the Lord. How many children do you have?"

"I have none, sir; I'm not married."

The response seemed to mean nothing to the President, as if he had not actually asked the question. "Do bring them next Saturday. Talk to Luke Wheeler; he'll arrange for you to attend the service. People of all kinds and races, worshipping the Lord." His smile grew, and his gaze focused through Bill, then snapped back. "Oh, by the way, my office has been getting some calls about the bodies of the men killed when the bombs were taken."

"Sir?"

"The bodies are not being released to the next of kin for Christian burial. Please look into it for me, will you? It is causing some pain to their families."

"Yes, sir. There may be some difficulty in putting them together."

The President seemed to have misunderstood what he meant. His lips gave a kindly smile, and he said, " '*But some man will say, How are the dead raised up? and with what body do they come? . . . But God giveth it a body as it hath pleased Him, and to every seed his own body.*

" '*So also is the resurrection of the dead. It is sown in corruption, it is raised in glory . . . it is sown a natural body; it is raised a spiritual body. There is a natural body, and there is a spiritual body.*' "

The President continued looking at Bill, but his gaze focused back into the middle distance. " '*I am the Resurrection, and the Life, saith the Lord; he that believeth in Me, though he were dead, yet shall he live: and whoever liveth and believeth in Me shall never die.*' "

He turned and walked down the hall.

"You missed Karen Hobbs," said Tina. "She dropped by again but couldn't wait. Said you'd asked about her at the west entrance desk."

Shit. No time, thought Bill.

"You look beat, what's up?"

Bill sat and stared at the desk in front of him. It was the time of evening when he liked to take a drink or coffee over to a west-facing porch or window and watch the sky fade down through the blues to indigo and then blackness. Instead he was here in a small, close, basement room. "Chris wanted me to go with him while he relayed a message to Bass. The Speaker and Majority Leader—among others—want him to consider stepping in for the President."

"*That's* a big step. He show any interest?"
"No," he replied.
"But at least he'll think about it?"
"Not at all. He really refuses to even consider taking over from the President . . . even if the President seems to welcome the symbolism of seven bombs."
They sat in silence for a while. "Well," Tina offered, "there is the little matter of the Twenty-fifth Amendment to the Constitution."
"Sure. But there's also the little matter of the seven, now six, bombs. You haven't seen the President recently while he's on one of his Bible lecture jags . . . it makes the hairs on the back of your neck stand up straight."
"But even if Western is going off the deep end, no way?"
"Nope . . . and I quote, 'Our country has lasted for over two hundred years because of the strength of an unbreached Constitution. I *will not* be the one to undercut it.' "
"Well, you might expect that response from his writings, but this is serious shit. Why be so doctrinaire now?"
Bill leaned back and rubbed his neck. "What do you know about the Vice-President? Do you know what his college experience was like?"
"I know he went through a lot when he was a student in the early sixties."
"That's right. The first black student at a small state college of the old order."
"I know from my reading that things were rough there," said Tina.
"Rough . . . not the right word," said Bill. "Terrifying would be better. The point came when he was trapped in the science building, with a crowd outside wanting to kill him. The state was supposed to be protecting Bass, but the Governor—the devil take his immortal soul—pulled out the state troopers, saying that a *state's* forces should not and would not be used to enforce a *federal* directive. So . . . the troopers left, the crowd revved itself up to go in and get Bass . . . It would have happened, too, but the Justice Department got a court order and sent in federal marshals.

"It may seem I'm giving you a simplistic explanation for what has formed a complex man, but that experience must have made a big impression on him. If the President gets worse, or nonfunctional, Bass is going to be a tough nut to crack on this issue of succession; and I think we're losing the President to a fantasy world. I ran into him on the way down here just now. I've been invited to his Saturday prayer meetings."

"That's nice."

"My wife and children too."

"You don't have any."

"Yes, I told him that, but he said bring them anyway."

"Strange," Tina said, and softly hummed the theme from "Twilight Zone."

"Don't *do* that; it's bad enough without the soundtrack. The President also asked me to check into something about the bodies of those guys killed when they took the bombs; he's gotten some calls. Who's handling the site investigation?"

"FBI—Pete Hanson could give you the name of a contact."

"Right, thanks." Bill picked up the secure phone and punched in a four-digit code; he massaged his neck while the connection was being made. "Bill Hitch here. Is Peter available?" He paused while the aide checked. "I'll hold."

"What's the problem with the bodies?" Tina asked. "I thought they'd finished with that investigation and come up empty."

"Seems there's some holdup in releasing the remains to the next of kin . . . Peter, hi. The President asked me to check into something for him. It seems there's a delay in releasing the remains of the DOE guards to their families. Know who's handling that?" He listened for a bit, then grabbed a pen and scribbled a few notes on a small pad. "Thanks; have him call me. No, nothing new at our end, a few leads we're pursuing, but nothing yet. Take care."

Bill tossed his pen back on the desk. "Right again, Tina. Peter said he'd have the agent who's deputy coordinator call me. Should be a couple of minutes. Do we have a file on the DOE guards on the convoy?"

"We should. Check . . . ah"—she closed her eyes for a second, visualizing her filing system—"behind you in the second drawer down. It should be a green folder with the tab on the left."

Bill turned and opened the drawer. "Yup, here it is." He crossed his legs to support the file and started leafing through it. There was a series of sheets, Xerox copies of data forms: age, birthdate, address, family, years with force, specialty, training . . . a photo of each on the upper corner of the sheet. The copies had made the photos contrasty, but they were still clear: Ash, Tedeschi, Ross, Stanton, Kelly, Hilde. He studied their faces: six young men—strong, confident, even arrogant, one or two; always victors in their lives. Good at what they did, or so they thought . . . and death suddenly took them, Bill mused. Who did it? how? why? Dead men tell no tales.

He slowly closed the file. "Any word from the magazine people on the subscription-list search?"

"Robin should be finishing that up soon. She said it would take her until eight or so; it's quarter of now."

"Great."

"Slim hopes."

"Best I can do for now." The phone rang and he scooped it up. "Hitch here."

Tina drained her coffee and got up. She pointed to Bill's and raised her eyebrows in question. Getting a nod in response, she went over to the cabinet where the coffeepot was.

"That's right. The President has evidently been getting some calls. What do you know . . . ?

"Right . . . right." Bill listened as he accepted the cup Tina placed in front of him and took a sip. "What about his relatives? If they weren't the ones who called, send out the rest . . . I see." The man on the other end talked for a while. "Okay, well, do what you can to get some out; you understand the families' point of view. Thanks." Bill hung up and leaned back in his chair. "Well, that's a little strange."

"What?"

"Whoever took the warheads set off an explosive charge before they left; it pretty much tore apart the bodies of the DOE guards." He grimaced. Bill had once had the opportunity to see the results of a heavy explosive in an enclosed space. It was not like in the movies: no rows of bodies, lying quietly with eyes closed. Rather fingertips and ears, pools of blood, pink sponge of lungs, hair and bone splinters, all mixed together in a terrible stew. Returning the bodies to the families was not that simple: perhaps that's why we speak of "remains," he thought. "It's a difficult job to sort out all, or even some, of the pieces and match them to the right names, but the forensic people are having a real problem with one of the guards—a trainer actually, a Felix Ross. They can't find enough of the right blood type to be him."

"Was he there at all?"

"Oh, yes. Seems they have enough bits and pieces of vaguely the right size and hair color in another blood type to be him." Tina shuddered. "Sorry, but that's the way it is in that business. Anyway, they're checking now to see if their records for Ross were correct."

"Can't they release the others to their families?"

"You want to get it right the first time: don't want to go back to people and say, 'Gee, seems we sent you the wrong parts, could we have them back?' " Bill looked into his coffee cup and placed it down. "But some are obvious, and FBI will release those."

"What about this trainer? Are his relatives the ones who called?"

"No, that agent said as far as they knew this guy Ross didn't have any close kin, not even a girlfriend; just had a hotel room in Amarillo, and an apartment here in D.C." And who does that remind you of? he thought . . . no family, no ties. "No contacts, but he was a methodical guy: paid for his apartments a year in advance. Everything's still there, waiting for someone who's never coming back."

"Well, must be tough for the other families involved; though if FBI is not spending a lot of time on it compared to finding the bombs, that's to be expected."

"Let him be . . . he's gone."

The intercom buzzed and Bill picked up his phone. "Hitch . . . Hello, Robin . . . Great! Hold on. Uh-huh . . . good. Hold on." He picked up his pen and took notes while Robin explained at length. "Good work! Thank you, thank you. I owe you and your boyfriend a special dinner when this is over." He leaned back in his chair and looked at Tina. A lazy grin slowly spread on his face.

"Bill, what are you doing?"

His grin continued to grow until his eyes crinkled almost shut.

"Bill, what!"

"This, Tina," he squeaked, "is a shit-eating grin. A big shit-eating grin."

"About?"

"We know where they are!"

"No!"

"Yup. Robin found a correlation. Checked for subscriptions sent to an address within that radius we developed from the helicopter hour meter. Nineteen out of that list of twenty journals associated with Dieter in Europe are subscribed to by a Mr. D. Streete, General Delivery, Kearney, Nebraska."

Tina clapped her hands and jumped up. "Hot damn! We've got the bastards!"

16

ROSS

"Great crimes deserve strong remedies."

"Uli, all I want is a free Lebanon, not more deaths."

"Our lamb in the fields of history! We need to be wolves! We had a great opportunity thrust into our hands—we are finally strong enough to act in the arena of *Machtpolitik*—rise to the occasion! Think of the great, unavenged crimes of American imperialism; *we* are now strong, we can avenge them!"

"Uli . . ."

"You, Hussein, you would be the sheep, the coward who asks only for his own salvation, not to achieve the greatness that opportunity has thrust on him . . . you disgust me."

Rudi leaned against the wall, smiling as he watched Uli and Baalbek argue at the kitchen table. "Uli," he said, "Hussein thinks he's the big boss; listen to him."

Baalbek turned on the younger man and spoke angrily. "It's not a question of that! We made an agreement, we decided on a course of action. *I* am only holding out for what we agreed to. What would you have us do? Kill millions?"

"When you are given the opportunity, you must act," said Uli. "A strong remedy for those great crimes."

"They don't deserve greater crimes!"

"I think about our place in history."

"And I think about my countrymen. I am trying to gain the freedom of my country, to stop the deaths of the innocents among my people. *That* is why we sent the first bomb to the Army base. But to send the rest out around the United States would be a great, great crime. It would be a slaughter of innocents! Uli, we agreed to a certain path . . . Your group has a certain reputation of taking over in joint operations . . . be careful."

"You're a romantic, Hussein." Uli laughed bitterly. "The world has no room for romantics anymore. Now is the time for realists."

"Then be realistic! Give our first action time to ripen. They have two days left in which to respond; let them have that time. We may still achieve our goals with just that one bomb."

"*Your* goals." She scraped her chair back and stood up. "I think of my place in history, not just your goals." She pushed past Rudi and marched off to her room.

"Not a good person to get angry at you," Rudi said mildly to Baalbek. "It's not good for your health."

"Don't mock me, Rudi," said Baalbek. He didn't look at the German, but stared somewhat sulkily at the doorway through which Uli had left. "She calls me a romantic . . . *me.* Sometimes I wonder if you two, if anyone in Ost-Sturm, has any sense of reality, any sense of what is important to the people, the masses we are supposedly working for?"

Felix had heard all this from the living room where he was stretching after his morning run. He stood up. The sweat remaining on his skin under his light T-shirt chilled him in the cool apartment. He slipped into his heavier sweatshirt and quietly let himself out of the front door.

On the landing, he automatically checked the stairway below before he unlocked the other apartment and went in. The sound of classical music came from the living room, but he went instead down the short corridor and knocked on one of the closed bedroom doors.

"Yah?" came a voice from inside the room.

"Yataro, it's Felix." The door opened and the Japanese man stood in the opening, large and very quiet. "We need to talk."

"Here?"

"Fine. Dieter's the only one in this apartment and he's listening to his music."

"Then come in." He closed the door behind Felix and led the way to the far end of the bedroom where a low table had been placed under the window. A slim volume of what looked like poetry lay faceup, along with a small, black, handleless cup. "Tea?"

"No, thanks."

Yataro lowered himself gracefully to sit cross-legged on the floor next to the table. He closed the book and then sat quietly, hands resting on his knees. Felix paused for a second and then sat opposite him. "Our partners are falling apart," he said.

"There always was tension."

"But this is turning into something different. Uli and Hussein are at it again: 'You're an idealist.' 'I want my place in history.' 'You don't care for the masses.' A bunch of crap! I don't like doing a project for such a crew. I'm no longer even sure who's in charge. It's disorganized, unfocused; it's at a point where it could cause danger to us."

"You are not afraid of danger."

"You know what I mean."

Yataro took a sip of tea. "Why are you involved with this project?"

Felix drummed his fingers on the tabletop. He noticed his action and stopped, then put his hands in his lap. It actually was easy to talk with Yataro . . . easy to talk with him about things he could mention to no one else. "I think part of it was where I was coming from: working for a series of half-assed operations where no one was trying to do a good job, to achieve to potential."

"And this offered . . . ?"

"Difficulty, the chance to do what no one had ever achieved before: hitting DOE for weapons. A tough and interesting problem."

"Which you accomplished."

"And now what? I want goals. What do they want to do now? *They* don't have any goals—they argue. Hussein and Uli are both fools."

"I think you underestimate Uli. She has warrior instincts; she would take death before defeat."

"Sure, that's true, but that's not enough. If she wants to be a leader, she's got to pay more attention to goals, the team she puts together, and operational details, not acting as if she believed the politics."

"You don't like politics?"

Felix laughed. "Politics! That goes over my head. Politics are just different-colored uniforms. Left, right, Democrat, Republican, capitalist, communist. Those are just names thought up for the suckers while the big boys play their game, which is power, pure and simple. That's the way I see it: politics is just the uniforms you put on the teams: They're playing the same game: same rules—which is none—same field, same scoreboard.

"*I* don't care about politics, that's just for the fools in the crowd. And I don't mind that the game is played for the big boys: that's the way it's always been, in warfare, in sports . . . you know, in life. I'm just an operations man—one of the athletes. All I want to do is play the best game I possibly can. Only I don't play football, I don't play soccer, I don't play hockey. I play combat operations." He looked hard at the older man. "I've thought a lot about this, and that's what I come up with. What I do is a contact sport, and it's a team sport, and I don't like playing for a team with no goals and no leadership!"

Yataro gave him a slight nod.

They sat in silence for a while. Then Felix spoke again. "So, why are you involved?"

Yataro was quiet, with a great sense of power and reserve around him. Then, "For some of the same reasons as you: the challenge, the problem to solve, the battle. But for me there are also matters of family, honor . . . things I must avenge. This group seems . . . *seemed* . . . the best way of achieving that."

"Past tense?"

"Yes, there we may be in agreement. I think the arguments between Hussein and Uli are debilitating. I would prefer to work within their framework, but if their squabbles get worse, or start to endanger my own position or ambitions, I will have to reassess the relationship."

"Then keep me in mind. I'm a player, Yataro; and I like to play for the best team."

HITCH

"So it's a confirmed make?"

"By my best agent team. It's him all right—Dieter Strasse, alias Mr. Streete."

They were in a small, gray waiting room at Andrews AFB that was empty except for Bill and Peter Hanson. Outside the window, a generator truck hummed next to a Falcon jet. There was a faint smell of kerosene in the stuffy air.

"Photos, voice. We have a confirmed make on Dieter, but we don't know about the other guy. The team contrived to have him handle a piece of Plexy at the post-office counter when they went to pick up mail. We got some prints, but they were partials."

"So we won't get an ID on him?"

"I think we've got a chance. CIA's put their bogeyman print file onto AFIS; it's a computer fingerprint search system that can work with just a fraction of a print and find a few possible matches out of the hundreds of thousands in a file. Good stuff. If he's a European bogey, then it will take a bit longer, since they'll have to down load files from the Germans. The Kansas crew faxed the partials to Langley and Dale Kuhn's best boys are working on it now."

"How 'bout a hideout location?"

Hanson looked at his watch. "Should be soon. We have a five-car relay tail with a high plane backup. *My* best people. They'll get it, though we don't know how long these birds will wander before they roost. There's no guarantee that where they settle will be where they're storing the bombs."

Bill stifled the urge to get up and pace. Be calm, conserve your energies, he thought. It's still a long way to go; finding them is only the first step. He went to the window and watched the final preflight checks on the plane. The pilot was doing his walk-around, inspecting flight surfaces and controls. The sky was gray and low, as it had been for the past few days. Good hunting weather, Bill thought.

Peter Hanson joined him. "That ours? It's not a government ship—where'd it come from?"

"No, it's a Falcon 50, a nice, fast corporate boat. Dale borrowed it from a multinational they have some arrangements with . . . thought it might be better not to come in under government colors."

The door opened, and Dale Kuhn slipped in. "Speak of the devil," said Hanson. The CIA man nodded in reply. "Nice job your boys did on that ID of the German."

"Thanks. Hope you folks can do the same magic on the prints we sent you. Anyway, this is the guy who should get the kudos; he found them. Nice job, Hitch; you pulled our asses out of the fire."

"Couldn't have done it without Tina. And anyway, we don't know if we've found the bombs yet."

"Yeah, well, it's a start." He looked around. "You two alone?"

"Yes," Bill answered.

"Then where the hell is Fonsgraf and his shadow, Bunk Cole?"

"Still in conference with the President, one supposes."

"What the Christ for?"

Hanson pointed to Kuhn's nose. "Brownnose, son. What else gets you leadership in this administration? Certainly not competence. And these things take time."

"Well if he doesn't get here by the time that pilot finishes preflight, I'm hijacking that Falcon from under him. He bitched enough about not traveling in a big 'Air Force 707 with full comm facilities.' Don't they teach those military types anything about covert force entry?"

"Sure," answered the FBI man. "They have lots of classes . . . on polishing your medals, checking that the tanks are real loud, and making sure your unit flag is whipping nicely in the breeze."

"Christ," mumbled Kuhn. "He wants to go barging into Kearney in a fleet of government jets. 'Fast response team!' he says. My people have had this plane for hours now; and he's still in his meeting."

"He's seen too many Patton movies," Hanson said, laughing.

"Who does he think we're dealing with, the Bobbsey Twins? Those creeps are pros; they see five government jets fly into the local airport, and they're long gone with the bombs. Don't know what we would have done if Admiral Thomas hadn't stomped on him."

"Everyone else in place?" Bill asked.

"Yeah," said Kuhn. He rubbed his head and stifled a yawn. "No sleep last night, but we've got a pretty good base operation set up; all the preplanning we did helped a lot." He pointed to a corner where four, gray plastic chairs were grouped around a low table covered with chipped and cigarette-burned wood-grain plastic. "Let's sit down over here, and I'll brief you now . . . unless any messages come in, I plan to sleep on the flight. Pete, there's some new stuff you should hear, too."

"Here's the latest," he said as they sat. He took a sheaf of faxes from his briefcase. "Most of our crews are now in place in Kearney . . . we'll actually be the last ones to get there." He shook his head. "Assuming Fearless Fosdick does actually show up."

He laid one of the fax sheets down on the table. "This is a large-scale map of the town: the Platte River here borders the town to the south, just below Interstate 80. The airport is out here to the east; the college is here, just to the west. What industrial section the town has is here, toward the river. It's mainly farm machinery and service businesses, no real warehousing—we don't think that would be a place they'd choose to hide.

"On the opposite side of the river are a few sections of better single-family homes where your manager, business-owner types live. There's also a country club out there. The lower middle class homes are around the town center. The college forms its own little neighborhood, with some large old houses that have been converted to fraternity houses and a couple of newer, low-rise apartment complexes that house some students, faculty, and others connected with the school."

"Know if there is a radical element at the college that could be supporting these Ost-Sturm people?" asked Peter.

Dale grinned. "From what I hear, the most radical type you get there'd be a Democrat. No, this is a small, very conservative college: teaching, business, medical technology, and English. It *may* be possible that there is a support base there, but it's not as if this is Columbia or Berkeley."

"What about our facilities?" asked Bill.

"We're trying to remain flexible," answered Dale. "We've taken over a building in the industrial section as the command center; our people should be less obvious there. We're also scouting for other locations so when we find out where Ost-Sturm has holed up, we should be able to set up a base near them.

"The local people—police chief, city council, and manager—know we're there, but they don't know why." He nodded at Peter. "The FBI did the full-fanged scare call from the Director, telling them it was a matter of national security, and hinting that if any word got out, even to their spouses, then the FBI would see to it that they were ruined. All put in very patriotic terms, of course."

"Of course," said Hanson.

"Anyway, that's about it," said Kuhn. He leaned back and lit a cigarette. "Now it's just a matter of waiting until we find where they're holed up, and then making an assessment on how to proceed from there. We'll be staying at—"

The door to the corridor banged open; Colonel Fonsgraf stood there looking at the three men. "What are you just sitting around relaxing for? This is a crisis and we've got work to do. Let's go, the President is counting on us!" He strode across the room and out the other door to the waiting airplane. Bunk Cole followed an aide who carried their bags. He gave the seated men an opaque glance.

Dale Kuhn stubbed out his cigarette and stood. "I want to kill that bastard."

Bill rose. "You'd think that in the normal course of events, someone would have done it by now."

Two hours into the flight, Bill went to the rear of the cabin and sat on the arm of the chair opposite Dale Kuhn. "Dale," he said. "Dale, wake up." Bill knew better than to shake an ex–field man to waken him. He had seen two people make that mistake . . . fortunately neither had been killed.

The sleeping man opened his eyes. Bill saw the half-second pause for orientation, then Kuhn nodded. "What's up?" he said.

"A call for you on the scramble phone; it's from Langley . . . Tom Parelli."

"Right, thanks." He uncurled from the seat and followed Bill forward, flopping down at the communications table. A red phone sat there, connected to an olive drab scrambler box that had been attached to the tabletop with gray tape. He picked up the handset. "Dale Kuhn . . . hello, Tom. What have you got?"

The CIA man took notes for a few minutes while he listened without comment. Finally he lowered the phone mouthpiece and looked up at Bill. "Fax switch?"

Bill pointed to a small toggle switch. "Thanks . . . Okay, Tom, we'll be ready to receive; start in five seconds. I'll call you when I get to the command center." Kuhn flipped the switch and leaned back in his chair. "Some good news—we've got an ID on the other guy in the post office. We've also found out where they're staying, but that may not be such good news—it's going to be a difficult place to get adequate surveillance."

They walked back to the conference area in the middle of the plane. Colonel Fonsgraf was seated behind at the small oval table; Bunk Cole was in a swivel chair next to him. A semicircular bench was diagonally opposite them. "News," the CIA man said.

The others in the area sat up. Fonsgraf lowered his glasses and looked at them. "Well, come tell us," he said. Bill and Dale sat on the bench. Peter Hanson got up from his seat and walked over.

The plane was on max cruise at only fourteen thousand feet. Normally in flying, higher is faster: the higher you go, the thinner the air and the less air resistance. But the jet stream had dipped down to lower altitudes this fall, with a core speed of over two hundred knots. The computers said the fastest route would be at this altitude, four thousand feet below normally allowed jet corridors. All traffic had been cleared from their path. The rear engines were a steady, loud noise fighting the denser air. The vents overhead added their own roar. The airframe gave little creaks in the turbulence.

Dale cleared his throat and spoke loudly. "We've found out who the other guy is, and where they're staying."

Bunk uncrossed his legs and sat up. Fonsgraf put his papers

down. "Are any of our forces going to make a move before I get there?"

"Of course not," replied Kuhn. "They've just started the surveillance routine. We don't know if anyone else is staying there besides the two men, or if the bombs are there. As I said, surveillance is just starting."

"Who's the second man?" asked Cole.

"Hans Jüters, twenty-eight, last known as a free-lance enforcer for the German dock gangs in Hamburg and Bremerhaven. He also managed a couple of punk clubs and wholesaled bootleg tapes; some hint of cocaine trafficking, but that may have been only as muscle. The Germans have never been able to make any charges stick, except for a couple of simple assaults before he was twenty."

"No terrorist activities?" asked Bill.

"No, but this is interesting: he dropped out of sight eight months ago. Rumor around Hamburg was that he had been recruited for some Mideast project. At the time, the police assumed it was drugs."

Peter Hanson leaned over Dale and picked up the top fax, which had a small photo of Hans Jüters and an English summary of his German police records. "So if he was picked up by Ost-Sturm, what's his involvement?"

"Best guess is purely as muscle. He's got a reputation as a dangerous knife fighter and weapons man."

"And the location?" asked Fonsgraf.

"The two guys ended up near the college. They're on the top floor of one of three buildings in a mixed-use complex called Glencrest. It's mostly apartments with a few small office-type businesses in ground-floor units. We've checked with the rental agents, and the two top-floor apartments were rented in September by a Miss Lee Teller. She paid two months in advance and pays each month with a cashier's check, drawn on a variety of banks."

"Well," said Peter, "between your organization and the FBI, we should be able to put together some pretty good surveillance."

"Uh, my people say things are not going to be that simple,"

replied Dale. "We don't know how many others are in the two apartments. If we can't be sure that no one is there, we can't place inside bugs. We could try to put in contact mikes by drilling up from the floor below, but a floor mike in a carpeted concrete floor is a pretty bogus tool: results are bad to zero and it's noisy to install. Also, the way the stairway and apartment below are arranged, it would be difficult to make an undetected entry. My people recommend against it."

There was a moment of silence among the group. "What about a laser or microwave bounce?" offered Bill. "That could be done from another building."

"Sure," said Dale, "except that their apartments are higher than any other around. Angle of incident equals angle of reflection . . . we're stuck."

"Balloon pickup?"

"If we don't know who else is around, it might be seen by the wrong people; too great a risk that—"

Fonsgraf interrupted him. "Will you explain what the hell you're talking about?"

"Sure, Colonel," said Dale looking pleased that Fonsgraf had had to admit ignorance. "With a laser bounce, you aim a laser, generally an infrared one—or microwave beam—at a window of a room that you want to listen to. What we hear as sound is actually a series of pressure waves or vibrations in the air. Any sound produced inside a room will cause the window glass to vibrate sympathetically with those pressure waves. If you bounce a laser or tight microwave beam off that window, the vibration of the glass will cause slight frequency shifts in the beam that bounces back. If you can capture that reflected beam, you can reconvert the frequency shifts in the beam into vibrations—or sound. So, you can eavesdrop on a room from across the street, or even partway across town; we do it all the time to the Ruskies. They do it to us, too."

"So why can't we use it here?" demanded the Colonel.

"The bad guys have chosen the tallest building around. If we shoot the laser beam up at a window, we can't get high enough to capture the reflection."

"Oh . . . then what's this balloon crap?"

"Sometimes, if we can't get high enough to capture a reflection, we'll put a detector on a balloon. This town is too populated, and too well lit at night—too great a chance that it would be noticed."

"Any other listening toys?" asked Bill.

"Oh sure, we've got limpets, stickies, fléchette delivered, ones that look like a pile of dog turds . . . even one that we snake up a waste line to a bathroom or kitchen sink. They all work great, but right now we don't see a clear, low-risk way of delivering any of them. It's all under consideration now by our top teams."

"Well, I certainly need some intelligence," declared the Colonel.

"I'm sure of that, sir," said Kuhn, who bent over and studied his papers to hide a smile. "That's about all I've got at this time, ah . . . except that the ops crew is going to see if they can secure space in an unoccupied apartment in the Glencrest complex. That will be our close approach base for surveillance. They'll know by the time we get to Kearney."

The Colonel picked up his papers and put his reading glasses back on. "Just make sure that no one moves on them before I get there."

The airplane had taxied to the service area on the far side of the airport. Beyond a small gate in the perimeter fence, four cars were parked at the rear of the maintenance hangars. The plane's engines idled for a moment and then the pilot shut them down. In the following silence, the copilot came back and lowered the side door; as it opened, a cold gust blew through the cabin. The passengers stood and stretched their legs. "Time to make the doughnuts," said Peter Hanson. Fonsgraf gave him a sharp glance and then strode off down the aisle and descended the stairs. The others followed.

The Colonel stood on the tarmac, scarf whipping in the wind; his coat's collar had a perfect curve that framed his face. He waited until the others had joined him and then spoke. "Bunk, go find us a car. I want to be taken on a tour of this apartment complex." Cole took the two men's bags and left. Fonsgraf turned to the other men. "That's one of the lessons I learned from my study of General Patton: there is no substitute for seeing the field of battle for yourself."

"Uh, Colonel," ventured Dale Kuhn. "These Ost-Sturm people are real pros. Maybe it would be best to leave the surveillance to one of the trained teams."

Fonsgraf seemed surprised, then stuck his face close to Kuhn's and spoke with a harsh voice. "Son, I've been in battle with NVA regulars. Those were real pros, not this bunch of German punks led by some repressed feminist. I want to see the location. The President has put me in charge of this operation, and this is the way I'm going to run it. Patton was a great commander because he was not afraid of getting out there himself; that's my approach, too." He turned and walked through the gate to the waiting cars. Bunk Cole was holding open the left rear door to the largest one, a gray Ford sedan with blackwall tires and small hubcaps. Fonsgraf got in; Cole closed his door, walked around, and got into the right front seat.

Hitch, Kuhn, and Hanson stood in the cold and looked on in wonder as the driver backed it out and headed down the road. "Why didn't he just take one with a sign that said 'undercover'?" asked Bill.

"Christ," said Kuhn. He took a deep breath and then said, "Well, we deal with what we have to deal with. Let's get to the command post." They shouldered their bags and headed to the remaining cars.

17

ROSS

It was noon. The two had sat in the kitchen to their simple meal of rice and broiled fish, listening to the argument that went on in the living room.

"Uli, I won't hear it! I won't listen anymore. You'll make us the most infamous criminals in all of history!" His voice was hoarse, tired from the quarreling.

"Great crimes deserve strong remedies, Hussein. You act as if you still trust the Americans and their allies; I thought your injured leg would have taught you better." Uli's voice was icy now, bitter, hard; reasoning but never emotional. They had been arguing for over an hour, interrupted only by what Rudi thought of as his biting, sarcastic comments.

Uli continued, "Hussein, if one is given an opportunity like this, it must be used."

There was no response. "Hussein, come back and talk to me."

Nothing. "Answer me." The first hint of any emotion. "Damn you! Answer me!"

A delay, and then a muffled, "The time for talking is past."

"You don't know how right you are, Mr. Tenderness," sneered Rudi.

Yataro finished his tea and set down his cup. He looked at

Felix and then inclined his head toward the door. Felix nodded and took a last mouthful of rice. They rose together and started through the living room on their way to the front door. Baalbek was by the window; he had pulled back the curtain a bit, and leaned there, staring out, his back to the room. Uli was standing in front of the white sectional sofa, her arms crossed high in front of her chest. Rudi slouched in one of the armchairs; Hans was in the corner behind him, leaning against the wall.

Uli tore her glance from Baalbek to watch them traverse the room. "Where are you off to? I need you here to help me convince this man. We can't wait any longer; we must send all the bombs out. Tell him."

"Uli," said Yataro, "your argument is well reasoned. What could I add to it? I have something to show Felix. We will be next door."

They carefully let themselves out of the front door and stood on the landing. Felix checked the stairway down—empty—and started across the landing.

The door opened behind them. "Yataro, wait. I want to say something to you." She turned to call behind her. "You two leave him alone. I'll be right back." Joining Felix and Yataro on the landing, she closed the door behind her. She looked calm, with a strange air of resignation about her. She started to speak, but Yataro silenced her with a gesture and pointed toward the other apartment.

Quietly, he opened the door for them and they entered, leaving Felix behind on the landing. From the living room came the lonely sound of a cello.

Uli's voice was soft and calm in the semidarkness. "Yataro, I need your help with Hussein."

"I do not really think he will listen."

"He wants us to wait. We don't have the time to wait."

Yataro said nothing.

"Then do you understand why I say we must do what I propose?"

"I heard you arguing with Hussein."

"I tell him what I think he needs to hear . . . I talk of history. You . . . you I'll tell something I really believe: we will not be free forever. No one can do what we've done and not eventually be found. Then, to be found is to die."

Yataro gave a soft grunt with no inflection, then waited.

"Rudi doesn't think of this; of course, neither does Hans. Of the others . . . perhaps Dieter does; he keeps his own counsel. Felix? Felix is yours, but I think he is like an eighteen-year-old: he sees his own mortality only as an abstraction."

"That is why he can act so freely."

"Possibly. Myself, I know we live on borrowed time. We act *now,* or lose the chance. There is not enough time to do it Hussein's way."

"He worries about the people, there is something to what he says."

"And I worry about my legacy."

Yataro was quiet for a moment. "So what is your goal?"

"Goal? I have no goals, I only want to *strike*. That's what I have done my whole life—strike. I have been given a weapon, Yataro; I must use it! I want *you* to decide whom you're with, me or Hussein." She looked hard at him, then turned and left the apartment, passing Felix without looking at him.

He watched her pass, then joined the older man, closing the door behind himself. "We have to talk."

"Yes," Yataro replied. "Come to my room."

"Is Dieter almost finished?" asked Felix.

"No, he told me that he would not be done for at least another hour. We have time. Come." He led the way down the corridor to his room and opened the door. The vertical blinds were drawn, but not rotated completely closed; a row of sharp, white lines of sunlight patterned the table set under the window. Set on the table was a new compact stereo system. "Come, sit."

Felix lowered himself to the floor next to the table. He picked up a thick CD package from the table. It was still in its plastic wrap, unopened; the front bore a photograph of a young Japanese woman. Yataro sat opposite, waiting for the other man to begin.

Felix nodded at Yataro, and then returned the CD to the tabletop. "We have trouble . . . they may never get the bombs out. Uli has stopped paying attention to details—she started to talk on the landing. She's too concerned about Baalbek. Plus, what's Hans doing in the room with them? I thought he was supposed to be on outside watch now. It worries me. This is a big country, but it's not as if no one is looking for us."

Yataro sat for a moment, the light striping his head and body so he seemed even more like some large and quiet cat. "That is part of what Uli was saying, but she said it with an air of fatalism with which I am not sure I agree. However, there is something I saw yesterday afternoon—a car, driving through this complex. It had no insignia, but it seemed perhaps an official sort of car. Three men were in it, and two were . . . looking."

Felix stiffened slightly. "Why didn't you tell me?"

The older man inclined his head a bit. "Perhaps an error on my part. You were in town at the time, and the men in the car did not have the aspect of serious searching. They were more . . . surveying the scene. The texture of the town has not changed . . . but perhaps it is a warning.

"Baalbek does not realize how much danger he is in from that woman; she has no real reason to let him live, does she? *I* have my goals, I must insure that at least one is achieved. I think we should proceed."

"Well, I've got a place to stay there; it should be a good, safe hole if we need it."

"Safer than a hotel?"

"It's always a gamble, but I think they've forgotten me by now, and it's a much less public place."

Yataro considered this. "Fine, you are probably correct. Now . . . you were successful in town yesterday?"

"Not on lead shot, seems the store underestimated their last order. So I got fishing weights—even better, they come in one-ounce increments."

"Ah, good." He looked at his watch. "Let us go to Dieter. We both know our roles."

As they opened the bedroom door, music came in from the corridor. They trailed it into the living room, where Dieter was by the window, working at his cluttered worktable. Around him was a semicircle of brown cardboard drums, thirty inches tall and two feet in diameter. Two had been closed with metal lids, the other four were empty except for an internal framework of wooden struts. To one side of Dieter's table were four metal chassis, perhaps eighteen inches high, topped by small circuit boards that were connected by nests of multicolored wires. Two of the chassis had small, pocket-watch-like objects wired into their top boards: round brass cases, glass covers, but with only a single hand. Felix and Yataro walked up until they stood on either side of the German. Dieter raised his head. "Oh, hello, Felix, hello, Yataro. You're not with the others?"

"No," replied Felix, "the political air was getting heavy—Uli and Hussein were going at it hard. How is your work coming?"

"Quite well." He tightened a small screw. "It's a pleasure to work to this music." He looked at Felix. "Yataro bought me Fournier's Bach Suites for Solo Cello . . . very nice. Uli wanted these finished by two-thirty; I should be done well before then."

"She told you to go ahead?"

"Yes. Those two that are closed up are set and ready to go."

"Not on pull cords?"

"No, no. That was just for the first one. Remember, we weren't sure of the delivery time out there. The second set of parts you got for me worked out perfectly."

"So, the rest will be ready by two-thirty?"

"Sure. That's what Uli wanted."

Felix raised his eyebrows a bit. "Without final approval from our Lebanese friend?"

"I work for Uli."

"Then you've guessed what is in store for Baalbek."

"Doesn't concern me. I haven't been following things for a while, I have enough to keep me busy. This is just what I was asked to do."

"Just following orders . . . Now why does that sound familiar?" He grinned at Dieter.

"Uli is the political leader. I handle the technical side." He made an adjustment to a circuit board. "It's better for each of us to have our own job and responsibility."

"I vus just following orders," Felix repeated. This time with a German accent.

"You know, they condemned many Fascists after the war for

just that . . . after the war. But that's not what made Fascists Fascists." Felix took the board and carefully set it into the chassis in front of him. "The truth is, if you are going to have an efficient organization, then all must be willing to follow the orders of those in charge of the overall plan."

There was silence as Dieter connected the circuit board to the chassis's wiring harness. He snapped in a small battery pack, and a blank LED display set into the face of the circuit board came to life, flashing *12:00, 12:00, 12:00.* He checked his watch and then adjusted the LED. "There," he said, sitting back. He looked up at Felix and Yataro. "Hussein is Uli's area of responsibility, as are most areas in this operation. I deal with these"—he gestured to the table—"and she deals with the rest."

The two men watched the German for a moment and then Felix shrugged. He gestured to the two chassis with the brass cases. "Were these hard to set up?"

"No, the parts you found for me were excellent. I made hybrid triggers with a time lockout to safe them until they're on their last leg. These others are simple, straightforward clock mechanisms."

Yataro spoke. "Do they still work the way you showed me?"

"Sure. That's a good basic method; no need to change it."

Yataro was silent for a moment, then bent forward and picked up one of the chassis without the brass. He hefted it thoughtfully. "This feels to be about eight pounds."

"Seven pounds, six ounces."

"So what will it weigh when the warhead is affixed?"

"Just the chassis, or the whole drum?"

"Just this cage and warhead."

"One hundred thirty-nine pounds, eight ounces."

The Japanese man pursed his lips slightly and spoke quietly. "Such a wonderful job: such technology, so much in such a small package." He looked at Dieter. "You're sure you have plenty of time in which to finish?"

"Sure," said Dieter, puzzled. "Why?"

"I have a present for you. It took some work to find: I had to get it from Chicago, but I think it will be worth the wait . . . that suite of modern Japanese music."

"You told me about it!"

"Yes. It has a sense of focus, of stillness at the center that is quite profound. I am interested in hearing your reaction."

Dieter smiled at Yataro. "Well, put it on!" He started to reach for his own CD player.

Yataro placed a light restraining hand on his arm. "No, you said you have a little time to spare. Come down to my room. I also have a new small system to play it on. Its precision matches the music; hear it there first; it will only take five minutes or so."

Dieter looked at his watch. "Sure, I guess. I have plenty of time. I've lost touch with the Japanese music scene since my wife died, and that was something I enjoyed." He carefully took his soldering iron from its resting place on the crowded table and placed it in its protective holder. He rose from his seat. "Felix, are you coming with us?"

"No, not my scene. Yataro played it for me, and there doesn't seem much there to follow. You want to talk about steel guitar, then I'll listen."

"You miss so much," Dieter said, and followed Yataro out of the room.

Felix watched him leave, then whispered under his breath, "Right, let's see who's going to miss what."

He stood there until he heard the door to Yataro's room close, and then presently the start of a series of strange, discordant notes. Felix rose and set to work on one of the closed drums.

"Yataro, are you with me, or with him?" Three of them were there: Uli, Felix, and Yataro. The men stood on either side of the door. Uli sat cross-legged on her bed. The room was bare, without hint of anything personal.

"Uli," said Yataro, "this has been your operation. I am not one who tries to change the course of a river."

"Then you'll join me—you accede to the new plan?"

"You do not need me or my approval. Hussein has done me no harm, so I'll not raise my hand against him. However, what you do is not something I would interfere with. You know who my enemies are. I don't care if the bombs are used slowly or all at once, as long as one is used at one certain target—that is simply a matter of face. As far as Hussein is concerned, you don't need my direct aid, certainly as long as Rudi is with you."

"I don't mean about Hussein. I still need your computer genius to do his tricks."

"That is no problem. Merely tell me when."

"Just have him do it for the time I gave you."

"Fine. Now, if you will excuse us, Felix and I have some other things to attend to."

They stood well back from the window, though the blinds were still drawn. "We should consider our exit, Felix," said Yataro. "You see that helicopter traffic out there? And car traffic is a bit higher than it has been before; it may be that we are already in danger."

"I've gone over exit strategies again, and the first plan is still the best: the pipe run to the next building, and then leave from there."

"What about the car?"

"I have been leaving the white one parked in the carport of the next building. The trunk has our equipment and one change of clothing, the rest we can pick up on the road." He handed the keys to Yataro. "It won't take me long to strip my room of identifying details and wipe it down. I want to divide our profile—you take the suitcase to the car and exit the complex. I'll put on my running clothes and jog out. We'll meet at the small shopping center by the car dealership."

The older man considered for a moment and then nodded. "A good plan, though perhaps I will take a backpack that I bought—the weight is less apparent. Also, a box of laundry soap, in case there are any watchers."

Felix smiled. "It is always a pleasure working with another pro." He turned toward the door, and then stopped. "Are you going to call your computer friend?"

"I think yes. Not from here, of course, but who knows? We may be imagining monsters in the mist. There may be no watchers out there. Uli may pull her plan off. It is best to allow for that. I know *we* will succeed, Felix, and that would be enough."

■

"Where are Yataro and Felix?" Baalbek asked. "I haven't seen them for hours. They should be involved in this decision."

"Hussein, I think the decision has already been made."

"Nonsense. I haven't talked with them yet." He took a testing sip from his cup of tea. Satisfied, he pushed aside some of the papers and the forms that covered the kitchen table, placed the saucer down, and sat. "We have only a little while left to wait for the Americans' reply. You'll see, they'll come around."

Uli stood leaning against the kitchen counter, her arms crossed. She stared at the man in silence. Hussein sipped his tea, staring out into space in front of him. Presently, he lowered his gaze and idly noticed the papers on the table. He started to read them, then froze. He slowly lowered his cup and picked up one of the forms. "Weight . . . destination," he read to himself. "Uli, what is this?"

Her voice was tranquil. "What does it look like?"

Hussein read farther, then looked up. "These are Federal Express receipts." He picked up more and flipped through the sheets, counting and checking the dates. "There are six of them, all from today! What do you mean by this?"

"The time has come."

"No! I will not have it! We must stick to the original plan. Stop this foolishness and do what I say!"

Uli didn't move. "Hussein, we play the role that history gives us. This is the way it will be done."

Baalbek's sat and gawked at her, transfixed.

"I am the founder and leader of the Ost-Sturm; as always, what I say will go. I will use my opportunity."

Baalbek's face got very red. He started to speak, then thought better of it. He stood and stared at Uli. Without a word, he grabbed the receipts from the table, tore them in half, and then in half again. Squeezing them into a wad in his hand, he glared at her, then turned and marched out with his halting step. Uli followed him to the door and watched him retreat down the corridor toward his room. Rudi was sitting in the living room. She turned to him as Hussein passed from sight. "Now, Rudi," she said.

A slow smile spread over the man's face. "How do you want it done?"

She looked at him queerly. "Any way you want, but do it quickly. I don't want him trying to alert anyone."

"I'm a gentle man." He straightened his pants and then turned toward the corridor.

"Rudi." He stopped. "Just make it fast and quiet."

He didn't turn to face her, but slowly walked away to Hussein's room. He rapped his knuckles lightly on the door. No answer. "Hussein, let me in."

"Go away, I want to think." The voice was muffled.

"The time for thinking is past. Open the door."

"Go away, Rudi. I have nothing to say to you and that woman."

Rudi smiled to himself. "What makes you think Uli and I want the same things?"

There was silence from the other side of the door. "Why don't you listen to me? Maybe we can find something to do that will please us both?"

There was a pause, then the door opened a crack. "What do you mean?" There was a catch to Baalbek's voice, a note of hope breaking through. "Are you starting to come around to my view?"

"Open the door and find out."

One of Hussein's eyes was visible, watching from the narrow slot between door and frame. He regarded Rudi closely. Rudi's face was empty except for a slight smile and a soft look of need. Hussein pulled the door open all the way and stepped back. "Then come in. I hope we can convince Uli."

Rudi entered the room and closed the door behind himself. Hussein examined him in the light of the bright floor lamp that stood there by the door. "What are you so happy about, Rudi?"

"I think we can do something together."

"That is what puzzles me about Uli. How can she come from a country of such great philosophers and not understand what I am saying? Do you understand what I mean?"

Rudi smiled at Baalbek. "I understand."

The tension went from Hussein, and his shoulders relaxed. "Wonderful."

"Shake on it?"

Baalbek smiled again and extended his hand. Rudi took the

hand as if to shake it, but made no motion—he just held the other man's hand, looking into his eyes.

Small everyday gestures of social convention—like a handshake—have a correct timing: too short is rude; too long, overly familiar. Baalbek's broad smile deflated into a nervous line: he was suddenly aware that he was standing here, holding hands with another man. He tried to draw back, but Rudi's grip tightened.

"What I understand is that the German people have had too many philosophers, too much philosophical thought." Rudi stared softly into Hussein's eyes for a moment more, then sharply drew their clasped hands toward him as he brought up his knee into the other man's groin. Hussein doubled over with a wheezing cry. The German released his grip and took a half step back to adjust his distance, watching Hussein stumbling there, keening. Another slight distance adjustment, and then Rudi kicked the other man full in the face. Hussein jerked up and fell onto his back on the carpet, the pink scraps scattered around him.

As the older man lay there, Rudi turned and pulled the floor lamp's plug from the wall, took a large knife from his pocket, and opened its narrow blade. He bent and cut the cord where it exited the lamp's base, then straightened up, closed the knife, and returned it to his pocket. Hussein still lay there on the floor, rocking side to side, hands still at his groin. Rudi went over and dropped to straddle and pin the man's shoulders with his knees. He gently brushed a few strands of hair from the wounded man's face and patted his cheek. "Unfortunately, my friend, the time for philosophy is past." He slipped one hand under the back of Hussein's head, lifting it, then swiftly wrapped the severed electric cord around the neck.

In spite of Uli's request, it was not a quick death.

"A limp did it, what do you know!" Peter Hanson cradled the phone against his shoulder and started to take notes on the lined yellow pad in front of him. "We've got a make on another bad guy!" he called out.

Bill pushed his chair away from his desk and went over. "Who is it?"

Hanson covered the mouthpiece and explained in snatches as he listened, "Hussein Baalbek . . . the CIA made the ID. The guy's a Lebanese, a Sunni Muslim, so out of the Lebanese center of power . . . Not a fundamentalist . . . an elder-statesman type . . . a history and economics professor before the troubles. They think he's the link to Verre—he had some connections to the group that got control of the Lieutenant when he was shot down." He listened for a while longer, taking notes, then he hung up and grinned at Bill.

"The limp?" asked Bill.

"Ah"—Peter waved his finger at Bill—"that may be one reason he's involved with this: they say he got a leg full of shrapnel in an American shelling targeted for us by the Israelis—home village was messed up pretty bad at the same time. So . . . he's not one of our friends.

"B surveillance team saw him around Glenview; one of Dale's guys in Washington was on the loop to examine the tapes. The limp tickled his memory, he searched his files, and . . . bingo." He motioned to one of his agents with his notes. "Tony, take this info over to Fonsgraf's group and tell the fax operator a file on this guy should be coming in. Get 'em to make copies and distribute. The meeting's in ten minutes. I want all the participants to see it before then."

The agent took the yellow sheet and left the room without a word.

"So what's the count now?" Bill asked. "We've got Dieter Strasse, Hans Jüters, this guy Baalbek, and who else?"

"CIA also thinks they have a make on a fourth one, Rudi Bruck. The B team—again—got a photo of someone with white blond hair at a window, and that's who it looks like. If we've got him, then we've got Uli Rosstal: she's the brains behind Ost-Sturm."

"She been seen?"

"No, but the Germans tell us that if we've seen Rudi, then Uli is around. They don't think he's real deep; he's a killer, doesn't care about much else."

"Well, that's some progress, at least."

"Maybe not enough for our friend the Fosdick; he wants more information, more, more: 'Gather your intelligence, gather your forces, and then attack in strength.' Reminds me of Montgomery in Italy. I think we should put in some personnel, have them pose as cleaners or painters or something. At least replace one of the tenants in the other apartments."

"It seems strange for the Colonel, especially after his foray into Glenview in that Hollywood undercover car."

Peter slowly raised the tip of the paper tube he was holding, then let it flop down. "I think our hero is getting performance anxiety. If he makes a decision to go in now, and it goes wrong, then it's *his* decision that was in error. If he waits long enough, gathers enough facts, then maybe the decision will take care of itself. It's been, what, four days now?"

"Well, I was talking with Dale. NSA was going to try something early this afternoon; maybe they'll have results by the meeting. It's some sort of optically stabilized, ultra-high-magnification surveillance system they've been using for embassy spooking. They claim they can fly a fast helicopter past a window from an eighth of a mile away and read papers on a desk inside." Bill shrugged. "We'll see."

"Hmmm," Peter said, then grinned. "Makes you want to lead a cleaner life. Or at least be sure to draw the shades."

"Yeah, but it still burns me that we still don't have a clear count on everyone in that complex. We've got to move on them. I'm not convinced we have that much time to screw around."

18

The wind sighed softly in the pines above them—a rhythmic sound that had grown slowly louder in the forty minutes they had lain there, as if the wind were gathering confidence from the slow departure of the sun. The light was down at a golden, slanting angle, picking out the texture and pattern of things, but bringing no warmth . . . only the approaching cold of night.

"Hitch, why is it I always end up lying on my belly in the mud?"

"It's not mud; the dirt's frozen."

They lay on their stomachs under a small group of white pines at the edge of the apartment complex. The target building was 150 yards to the south of them, across a small access road and then the parking lot.

"I'm still on my belly, and I'm getting cold."

"Then Brother Hanson, get off yo belly! Believe! Rise! Walk!" Hitch's voice was muffled slightly by his gloves as he scanned the apartment complex above him with a pair of ten-power binoculars. The coordinating communicator whispered softly in his earphone.

Hanson grunted and shifted the strap on his Uzi so he was

more comfortable. "Nope, it didn't work; I'm still on my belly."

Two vans were parked among the tenant's cars in front of them—a new one from Jerry's Carpet Cleaning and the other, older and beat up, from Roto-Rooter. These were the forward observation, communication, and command points. Not the best, but the building they planned to hit was the tallest in the complex and separated from the others—a hard target to approach unobserved.

"Peter, admit it, you're having a great time. You're outdoors, with friends, doing interesting things . . ."

Hanson shivered and pulled his jacket cuffs down to cover his exposed wrists. The two men were both dressed in camouflage pants and light jackets over bulletproof vests; gear made for protection and quick movement, but not for warmth. "It's damn cold. You shouldn't have bothered bringing that useless goose gun and brought a portable heater instead."

Next to Bill's side lay an old Winchester Model 12 shotgun with a twenty-four-inch barrel, skeet bored and five shells in the tube. Good for close-in fighting, but pretty useless for anything over twenty yards. He had been offered a new Perazzi, but it had too many levers and bells to operate at speed. He'd decided on the old Winchester; many years ago his grandfather had taught him to shoot on one.

Bill had loaded it with three-inch mag buckshot. If you were hit by that load at close range, you went down. With a pistol, even a mortal shot could leave a foe operational for a minute or two; in that time you could die yourself. With a dense load of buckshot, the blow of a mass of pellets hitting over a wider area of the body could induce incapacitating shock. Such was the terrible calculation that went into planning an operation.

"Bill, do you see any movement up there?"

"Nothing yet."

"Tell them to hurry. I'm cold."

"We're still on plan."

"And it's still a shitty plan. Tell them that."

"Would you rather be here with the close-perimeter force or in the primary attack squads?"

Peter Hanson put his hand to his forehead in a mock *Thinker*'s pose. "Hmmm. No, I think I'd rather be most anywhere than with those unlucky bastards in the attack helicopters. Fonsgraf is about the worst planner I've ever seen—certainly the worst one who by some magic is still alive."

"True."

"I mean, to go from a 'hands-off, don't get close' posture to a full-entry attack, complete with balloons and streamers . . . this is not the smartest job I've ever seen. We've no intelligence. What are we going to meet in there? Who? what? when? . . . We just don't know without some recon. We need more facts, certainly more than a small pile of grainy photographs."

"Ah yes, the VIPSEI."

"What does VIPSEI stand for, anyway?"

"Virtual Image Platform, Stabilized Enhanced Image. You knew that, right? A nice toy; it definitely did work."

"Great, so all we know now is that they have, or had, the bombs in the apartment and have done some work to take at least some of them apart. Great. We had already assumed that, but who's in there and what are they armed with? We don't know that . . . why rush in?"

"Do you want the cynical answer, answer A, or the real answer, B?"

"Ah, Bill, why don't you give me A first."

"Well, as it turns out, answer A is the same as answer B: after the VIPSEI shots came in, Fearless Fosdick heard the Admiral was going to put pressure on the President to replace him, to get a real, experienced attack leader by tonight. With the photos, the need to go in and get the bombs is obvious to everyone."

"Even Fosdick."

"Right. And if Fosdick doesn't lead the attack, then Fosdick doesn't get any resulting glory . . . sooo, the attack has to go on right now, before he can be replaced."

"Say it ain't so, Joe."

"Wouldn't make any difference if I did." He raised his hand to halt a reply and listened to his earphone. "There's a delay, the choppers are holding their departure."

"Oh, great."

"Peter, what were the latest details of any activity here?"

"Well, we'd gotten Fonsgraf to pull his bozos back a bit from their close surveillance post; they were too exposed where they were."

"No surveillance?"

"Give me a break—we're not all fools. The road's been monitored since three-thirty. We put in a fake road crew and tore up part of the street. Cars going in and out had to slow down and we checked 'em out visually. None of the bad guys have shown . . . in fact, the only movement has been the normal delivery traffic: diaper trucks, mailman, Federal Express, and an ice-cream truck."

Bill lowered his binoculars and looked at Hanson. "Ice-cream truck? In this weather? Come on, that can't be real; you grab him?"

"Yup."

"And . . . ?"

"It was legit; guy checked out—we had him down to the office for a real friendly talk. He was just some poor bastard who'd had a bad summer and still needed to make payments on his note. We have him locked up so he can't talk to the media."

"So nice you folks are on our side."

"Protectors of the land of the free, home of—"

Bill cut Hanson off with a wave of his hand and pressed the small earphone tighter into his ear as a communication came in. "The helicopters have taken off."

Hanson looked at him, then shook his head. "You're going to have to relay me all the commands during this frolic? I can't believe we're doing this operation without enough radios."

"Oh, there were enough radios."

"On the same frequencies?"

"Ah well, you didn't *say* you wanted them on the same frequencies, did you? At least there's one for each group . . . Peter, you're really in a *foul* mood. Why are you so bitchy?"

"Only get this way when I'm very, very happy. And not enough radios on the right frequency just reinforces my opinion of the military . . . How many years has it been since the Grenada invasion, and they still haven't learned that lesson!"

"Fonsgraf wanted to go ahead, didn't want to wait for the new sets to arrive. They couldn't get here before tomorrow; he didn't think to ask for them sooner."

"If you had to think to shit, that bastard would have exploded long ago."

"True."

"We should wait."

"Maybe . . . but that's the perennial question in the hunt, take them now or later?"

"Shit. Fos-*dick* didn't do enough thinking so we could take them the right way—*now* . . ." Hanson muttered under his breath as he pulled down his sleeves again; the temperature was dropping. "So how soon does the party start?"

Bill checked his watch. "It's now seventeen-fifteen—"

"Bill, don't give me that military jargon, it confuses me. I'm just a poor FBI gumshoe. What's that in real time?"

"Five-fifteen. Their departure is ten minutes late. The fire will start in five minutes. That makes the helicopter arrival time ten minutes after that . . . which should be seventeen-thirty—sorry, five-thirty. I hope we have enough sunlight left."

"Why is the sun up so late anyway? What time *is* sundown?"

"We're at the western edge of the time zone. Five-forty."

"And they're still going forward with a diversionary fire? I thought Jack Phillips was trying to kill that idea—it's too tricky by half."

"Agreed, but Fonsgraf thinks he's the great general: quoted Clauswitz—badly—to justify it. Said it would allow us to get our forces in close enough to Glenview to 'bring a decisive thrust if necessary' . . . or some such crap. All his backup people are dressed as firemen and emergency personnel. They'll respond to the diversionary fire; the real firemen have been told not to respond to any call. They also couldn't find an appropriate abandoned building, so they evicted some family. Too tricky by half is right."

Peter glanced behind them. "Well, look at that." A thin stream of smoke rose into the air from the houses down the hill from Glenview. "Looks like the games have started." The thin stream thickened as they watched. A faint siren rose in the distance.

Bill checked his watch. "Three minutes." He went back to

watching the building. He thought it seemed suddenly colder, then realized it was the tension. It's about to start, he thought. Just like every other operation he'd been on: the jokes, the bitching, the forced relaxation before the event, all masking the tension, the chill, the tightness. But tightness meant slowness, and slowness could mean death. He tensed his muscles three times, then let them relax. Stay loose, not brittle. It was always the same. He took a deep breath, then held it. "Freeze, Peter. Motion at the window."

He saw the pale shape of a face, looking over and behind him down the hill. "Control," he said quietly into his throat mike. "Hitch here. I see a face at window three. Snipers see it? Good. Yeah, seems to be just watching the fire. Whup, he's gone now . . . No, not a positive, too faint an image, but it looked like the pale-haired one, Rudi Bruck. Okay, Hitch over and out.

"The clock is ticking, Peter."

"Tell me about it."

The wind had been noisy in the trees above them, but it subsided for a moment and they heard a faint whomp, whomp, whomp that faded out as the wind rose again. "Choppers," said Hanson.

"Army choppers—slicks," said Bill. You could tell the sound of a Huey a long way off; the blades had been optimized for load carrying, not quietness. His suggestion that the operation use Bell Rangers or other civilian ships had been ignored. This sound could give away the primary attack squads too soon, give the bad guys an early warning that it wasn't news or rescue helicopters coming in for the diversion fire below. Fonsgraf wouldn't listen.

He checked his watch and listened to the quiet voice in his ear. "Three minutes, Peter. They're loitering a mile south." The sirens were louder now behind them; the black smoke rose more thickly and was then blown away by the wind.

"Let's get this show on the road."

"If everything goes right, we're just gonna be observers." The primary attack squads were to land on the roof and make an entry via demolition charges to the apartments below.

"That'll be all right with me."

The back-up plan was entry by rappeling from the roof down

the face of the building and making entry into the north apartment. This would follow a concussion grenade attack to stun the occupants.

"Correct, Control. No further sightings."

"They getting nervous?"

"Just checking in."

"Time?"

"Two minutes." They caught further snatches of the helicopter's noise as the winds gusted and shifted.

"Those things are pretty noisy."

"The bad guys have their windows closed."

"Hope, hope . . ."

"Time one minute thirty; they're starting their run."

The fragments of helicopter noise pulled slowly together and their volume rose as the ships approached; first just the clomp, clomp, clomp of the blades, and then the rising hum of the turbines. A face appeared at the window. "Control, Hitch here. We've got a watcher again. Ups . . . he dropped out of sight again . . . Check.

"Peter, someone else is watching from the south window. The surprise may be blown."

"Great."

"Wind's from the southwest, the choppers will circle around our side to the landing." He listened. "Fifteen seconds."

The noise of the two helicopters suddenly burst louder and they rushed into sight above the apartment building, flying in a line, one behind the other. Bill followed them for a second with his eyes, then looked back to the building in time to see a small window on the top floor disappear.

"What was that?"

The choppers started their turn and slowed to their final approach. A thin, olive drab tube, perhaps three inches in diameter, appeared at the window.

"Damn it! Control, Hitch here. Patch me through to the choppers; they've got some kind of LAW up there!"

"What's going on?"

"Tell them to move it! The guy may be dumb enough to try it!"

"What's going on?"

"That bastard is too low for the snipers. Have them spray the room . . ."

A red point sped from the upper window to the belly of the lead chopper. Where it hit, yellow, then red flames bloomed. The aircraft shuddered in midair, then started to rotate slowly. The trailing helicopter jerked sideways in midair and dove down to the right to try to get behind the building again, out of the line of fire. "The stupid, filthy bastard!"

"Who?"

Bill pointed toward the building—a fireball was blowing out of the window, a figure with light hair hung over the lower edge of the frame. "You can't fire them from a room; the back blast killed him," he shouted. They watched the wounded helicopter. It was spinning faster and faster as it settled, the tail-rotor shaft damaged. It suddenly pitched on its side and exploded in an orange ball of flame, crashing to the parking lot.

Hanson started to rise to go toward it. "Come on!" he shouted.

Bill grabbed his leg and tripped him back down. "Leave it," he said.

Hanson kicked at the restraining hand, an incredulous look on his face. "We've got to help them."

Bill reached higher and grabbed the loose fabric of the other man's tunic. "Leave them, Peter. Leave them; they're dead."

"But . . ."

"Listen! They're dead! We have an operation to run!" The two men stared in each other's eyes, arms locked in tension. Hanson's eyes slid sideways and looked at the fallen helicopter. It was now a towering pyre of burning fuel. The metal of the rotors sagged, then fell in the heat. With them, his arms lost their tension. He looked back at Bill. "Okay."

"You all right?"

He shook himself. "Yeah. What happened?"

Bill gestured back toward the apartment building. Flames licked out of the window, a charred form hung halfway out over the flame. It had been a man. Now the back and hair burned with a smoky flame. "That idiot had a LAW, a Light Anti-armor

Weapon. It's a rocket in a tube; he fired it from the window. The back blast from the exhaust lit off everything in the room, including him; he died when he fired."

"Where's the other helicopter?"

Bill listened to his earpiece. "It's on the roof: came in from the other side. Let me check in.

"Control, Hitch here. Lead ship is down. All dead. Guy who fired the rocket is dead, too. A fire's been started. Advise."

He listened again, and after a pause said: "Roger. That's tough. Okay, we will move to help cover the west side."

"Well?"

"The second chopper is on the roof, but all of the explosives were on the downed bird. Including the concussion grenades. They want us to work our way over to the west side and help provide cover as they try a rappel entry."

"Let's go."

They backed down the rise and worked their way around the perimeter of the parking lot, dashing from planting group to planting group in short spurts. They finally threw themselves to the ground behind a four-foot-high boulder that marked the entrance to the apartment building behind them.

Bill hazarded a glance around its side at the building; not over the top, his head would be an easy target. He pulled back and rolled to sit with his back to the rock. The top floor on this side of the building had a row of quite small windows. There was one larger picture window in the northwest corner; that was the window to the master bedroom of the northern apartment. Most of the windows had been shot out from the inside to provide free fire lines.

Dale Kuhn was behind a white sedan parked at the edge of the lot. Bill gave him a short wave of greeting, then called in. "Control, Hitch here. We're in position. Roger, out."

"And?" said Hanson, slightly out of breath.

"The assault squad is ready to try the entry. Control wants the perimeter and sniper forces on the east, south, and west sides to provide suppressing fire."

"This is a lousy high angle of fire." He gestured at Bill's shotgun.

"Control just hopes to keep their heads down, but you'd better use that Uzi to do our firing. At this range, my shotgun'd hit our guys on the roof, too."

"How soon?"

"Counting . . . thirty . . . twenty . . . ten . . . five, four"—they gathered themselves on their knees—"three, two, one. Dance time!" They sprang up from behind the boulder and Hanson started shooting at the upper-floor windows in short bursts. From various places behind cover around them, twenty others followed suit.

"If anyone is at the back of these rooms, we can't touch them!" Hanson shouted.

The assault team on the roof snaked two lines down over the side and two men on each line started to rappel down the face of the building, head down in the style known as Australian rappeling. "Cease fire," Bill shouted, and Peter and the others around them quit. The firing on the south and east side continued unabated.

The two lower men on the lines paused just above the large window, sprayed the interior with their weapons, and then plunged downward. They jerked on their lines. Red blossomed on their backs and heads. "Oh, shit!" said Peter. The two bodies swung there, slow, black pendulums.

Bill forced himself to bring up his binoculars. "Control, Hitch here. Yes, they're dead. Someone's at the back of the rooms. We can't reach them from our angle."

The body of one of the troopers started to jerk. For an instant, Bill thought that the man might still be alive, and started to call out. But then he saw bloody, red pieces being picked off the top of the man's skull. Someone in the room was still firing. "Control, Hitch. Get them to hoist those bodies, someone's shooting them to pieces."

The rappelers just above the window were still alive. They had begun to unclip themselves and turn their heads up for the ascent when their lines started to be hoisted back up to the roof by the men above. Slowly the pairs on the rope, one alive, one dead, were brought up to the level of the roof and then back over the edge.

"Now what?" said Hanson.

"Stalemate. They can't make an entry without grenades to go in after. The grenades were in the first chopper."

"What a fuckup."

The voice whispered in his ear. "They're calling up the forces from the fire site."

"That'll take ten minutes."

"Too long—you know what they've got up there."

"Time's wasting . . ."

"Let's call Dale. Dale! Get over here! Cover him."

Hanson sprang up and sprayed a series of three short bursts at the building. At the first volley, Kuhn scrambled from behind his car and came fast and low over to the shelter of the rock. Peter finished firing and dropped back into a crouch again. "Hello, spook."

"Flatfoot, Bill, what's up?"

"All the explosives were in the first chopper . . ."

"Neat."

"Fonsgraf and Control want to wait until backups come up from the fire site."

"Super. Be dark by then."

"Or real bright," said Hanson.

"Dale, you know what they have up there . . ."

"Yep, Bill."

"And if we give them the time . . ."

"Bye-bye Kearney."

"So . . ."

"Time's wasting."

"You game?"

"Nothing better to do."

"Peter?"

"From the bottom up, just like in the comic books."

"Control . . . Hanson, Kuhn, and I are going in." There was a pause. "Well, your boys are stuck on the roof. Any better ideas?"

"Let's go; these other guys can cover our entry," Hanson whispered.

"What! Fonsgraf? Fuck him!"

"Temper, temper."

"Control, he's gotten fifteen men killed so far. He can follow us in! . . . Give 'em enough time, and they'll turn this into a very big hole in the ground. We're going in! Thirty seconds! Have the sniper teams give us cover fire. Hitch over and out."

"What's up?"

"Fonsgraf wants to stop and consider our options."

"Dickhead."

"He's in that Jerry's Carpet van. Screw him. He can follow us. We're going in."

"I hope those bombs are fireproof." Peter pointed to the black smoke rising above the roof from the window on the north side of the building.

The crack of small-arms fire started up again all around them.

"Let's boogie. Three, two, one . . ."

19

HITCH

It was quiet here. Glass shards crackled underfoot as they inched toward the stairway and the noise was surprisingly loud after the thunder of the guns outside.

"Peter, you know color-system hand signals?" came the whisper.

"Sure, but predator group might be better; it's all one handed."

"Show-off. Didn't know they taught you FBI turkeys the deep stuff."

"Lot you don't know."

A door up the stairwell banged open, and the three men flattened against a wall. A shout, *"Mach schnell!"* Footsteps running across a landing, then the bang of another door opening.

Silence.

This was not going to be an easy job. The stairwell was a shaft nine feet square, with walls of concrete blocks painted yellow-beige. The carpet-covered metal stairway went up around the perimeter, fastened to the wall. If you looked up from the center, you could see to the top through an eight-inch slot formed by the inner handrails. Bill did not want to look up the slot. Someone might be looking down; then the game would be over.

He checked the side straps on his armor vest, then idly pressed down the edges of the bright orange, adhesive circle he had placed over the lower edge of his sternum. He remembered what Peter had said when he put it on. "What's this, a target? You've got to be kidding! . . . Fosdick give that to you?"

Bill had been irritated at Hanson's sarcasm. "No, an old and good friend showed me this before a raid. Ex-DEA . . . had done thirty smash-and-enters for them. He said something that made sense to me: in a firefight, where your foe's eye goes, that's generally where he'll try to shoot. He'll tend to make eye contact with the person he's trying to kill: see where you're dodging, what your intentions are, if you're going to fire—all that stuff. If you've got your armor and the bad guy shoots you in the head, then you've wasted good money on the vest.

"This guy said give your opponent something bright to catch his eye and put it in a spot where you're protected by armor; it might help improve your odds." And here we are, Bill thought, with bad guys up there with guns . . . guns and atomic weapons.

No sounds from above, only echoes of the gunfire outside. The other two men looked at him. Bill folded down the fingers of his left hand sequentially, then held the thumb up: "Up the stairs"; palm down: "Slowly."

They nodded agreement.

Here was the game: if they stayed against the wall as they ascended, they could not be seen approaching from above. But the reverse was also true—they would not be able to see who or what was waiting for them until they turned the last corner.

Slow steps now. Quiet, get the rhythm; one, two . . . A sudden rush of footsteps behind them. The three men dove apart to spread their target area and crouched with weapons off safety. Fonsgraf—Bunk Cole with him—barged into the entryway, then froze as he saw the weapons pointed at their chests. Shit, Bill thought, he's had his camouflage uniform starched and pressed. "What are you doing?" the Colonel hissed.

Bill lowered his weapon; he noticed Hanson did not. "Quiet! We're going up."

"*My* forces will handle it!"

"They haven't so far," responded Bill. This is insubordination, isn't it? But he's military and we're civilian; tough for him. "Over half your forces are dead, the rest are trapped on the roof."

"Listen you two. I don't know what you think you're doing, but as far as I'm concerned, you're just bystanders. Keep out of it! The rest of my people will be here shortly, and we'll handle it. Butt out! That's an order, or I'll see to it your name is dog meat in Washington."

Bill saw that Hanson had still not lowered his weapon. Bunk had noticed that, too, and kept his hand away from the pistol in his waist holster.

"Colonel, it'll take at least five minutes longer for your reserves to get up here from the decoy site, and they'll be seen coming. There are six nuclear weapons up there. The more time we give them, the more time they'll have to arm and use them. We're going up now."

"Son"—Fonsgraf's eyes narrowed—"this is an Army matter. I know what I'm doing."

"No, Colonel," replied Hanson, "you *don't* know what the fuck you're doing. We do. If you want to follow us, fine. If not, stay back."

Dale Kuhn listened without moving, keeping his eyes and Uzi pointed up the stairwell.

The Colonel's chest expanded and he started to speak loudly. "Look here—"

Hanson shifted his Uzi from its aim point between Fonsgraf and Cole to point it at the senior man's face. "Quiet!" came his hoarse whisper. "Colonel, if we give them any more time, they'll be able to set off those bombs. So, there are three options: One—we stay here talking and then they kill us all with the bombs. Two—I kill you and Bunk, and then Bill, Dale, and I go up and try to stop them. Three—you agree to follow us up and I don't kill you. Your choice. You understand that?"

The Colonel watched him. Hanson's eyes were totally cold, his face a complete mask.

This Army goon's got too big an ego to back down, thought Bill. "Colonel, the whole point is to stop those people upstairs. You come along and it'll still be your credit."

The older man licked his lips. "Ah, I'm not looking for credit, but you put me in a position where I don't have much in my hand to bargain with . . ."

Bill motioned to Hanson to silence his rejoinder. "Then just follow along, one flight behind. Bunk, you agree?"

The Major looked sideways at his boss, to Hanson's gun, then back to Bill. He nodded yes.

"Well then," whispered Bill, "follow us up. No noise, stay to the sides. If we move fast, keep up, but give us room.

"Control, Hitch. We're starting up now. Slight delay, the Colonel is now with us. Unless it's critical, keep out of my ear; I want to concentrate on this." He repeated his earlier hand signal and started up the stairs past Dale: legs bent, shotgun butt tucked alongside the lower ribs, his weight on the balls of the feet.

Hanson kept his Uzi's barrel up until Bill had turned at the top of the flight and then he and the CIA man followed him up. "Close," he hand-signaled to Bill. He glanced back. Fonsgraf licked his lips, and slowly began to follow.

They went up the stairs, noiselessly, carefully; no signs of activity from above, the gunfire becoming more muffled as they rose higher.

Finally, they reached the last flight. Bill stopped just before he would come out of the cover of the last landing and into the sight of anyone who might be watching from above. "Wait," he signed.

This is crazy, he thought. What are we doing here? This is Delta Force country. You know, something for young, handsome guys who work out half the day and the other half do live-ammo entry drills. This is not for three thirty- or forty-somethings who don't have straight testosterone for brains. He took a deep breath. But this is what your daddy told you: deal with what you get.

"Me first," he signed. "Close up, ready, wait." Peter and Dale nodded their assent. Three, two, one—up the stairs backward, facing the doors at the top; very slow, crouch as you go up to keep your head out of sight until your gun can bear on anyone up there. Halfway up. Ready . . .

He popped to full height, swiveling to take in the whole landing . . . nothing. No one there.

Okay, breathe. Another signal: "Clear."

Slow steps backward up the stairs to the landing. Pause. Signal: "Follow to here." Dale and Peter came quickly up to the landing, maintaining target separation, Peter watching upward, Dale watching their back path.

There were two doors at the top. The one on the left, closed; the one on the right, open. Bill consulted the map in his head: The apartment to the left was where the LAW had been fired from. The apartment to the right was the one with windows on the south side. It was through those windows that the VIPSEI had seen the bomb chassis; that was the way to go. A simple, open-door entry . . . but did he need to leave someone here to guard their backs?

The smell of smoke had gotten stronger as they had come up the stairs, and Bill noticed a slight haze. He looked at the bottom of the closed door. Wisps of black smoke were puffing from the crack. Bad news/good news: bad that the fire in the other apartment was far enough along that the rooms were now filled down to floor level; good news in that there was no one left in there alive unless they had a breathing unit. He tapped Peter on the shoulder and pointed out the smoke. "We enter right," he signed.

Up the stairs to the edge of the doorway, gun barrel up, signal: "On three, me right, you left." Snap pivot, eyes forward, gun ready, acquire and identify before firing—nod, three, two, one . . . now!

Nothing. Okay, hallway's as in plan: living room to the right at the end of a long corridor; to the left, small kitchen and then bedrooms.

The sound of the gunfire from outside was louder here . . . good cover. Go left first so there'll be no surprises behind us when we do the living room.

Signal Dale: "Set up here; Peter, I check rooms this way." Agreed.

Signal Peter: "Entry: high and low. This one. Ready." Kitchen, on left—nod, three, two, one . . . now!

Nothing. Okay next. Bedroom on right. Signal: "Ready." Nod, three, two, one . . . now!

Legs sticking out from under table! Scan rest of room: nothing. Back to legs: no movement, stiff . . . face. Signal: "Dead, no threat. Guard here." Slow crouching approach. Older man, black hair. Black tongue, eyes dead. Kick, stiff. Survey room. Nothing. Why is he dead? Why is he stiff? Torn scraps of pink paper around him, with a few clutched in his left hand. No time. Back to corridor.

Signal: "Next." Nod, three, two, one . . . now!

Nothing! Last one. Don't like this, where are they? End of corridor. Signal: "Same again." Nod, three, two, one . . . now!

Nothing!

Peter signed, "Question? Don't like."

Think, damn it! Deep breath. Okay. Someone at least is in the living room. Something's wrong with these bedrooms, they can't be empty. Don't want to leave them behind our backs. Fonsgraf!

Bill signed: "Follow, cover." He ran quietly back down the door to the apartment, Peter covering his back. The Colonel and Bunk Cole were waiting there on the landing. Bill motioned them into the hallway and bent to whisper in the Colonel's ear. "Looks like there's no one in the kitchen and bedroom to the left, but I don't trust that and there's no time for a complete search. You and Cole go down there and check them out, cover our backs while we enter the living room. That's where we *know* some are."

He repeated the message in Bunk's ear and then pointed them down the corridor toward Hanson. They started away, then the Colonel turned to face Bill.

Oh goddamn it, don't—

"Bill," the Colonel said in a loud whisper, "remember—"

Gunfire erupted from the living room, crashing into the corridor wall opposite its door. Bill and Dale threw themselves flat against the inner wall, then back down into a ready crouch when they realized that the shots could not reach them here out of the line of sight.

Damn, damn, damn! "Colonel, thank you!" No need for silence now. "Get down there and do what I said. Peter! Up here!" Bill loosed two shotgun blasts down the hall toward the living room. "To keep them back," he said to Dale, and reloaded. He motioned them close for a whispered conference.

"Dale, Peter, what do you think?"

"Tough position," said Hanson. "How the fuck are we going to do this? They only have to aim at the door, we don't know where they are until we stand there."

Two more spaced shots came from the living room to smash into the wall. They all flinched.

"Dale?"

"Tough one. No grenades?"

"Nothing. Not until the back-up group gets here."

"Too long."

"Only thing I can think is if we hit the door at the same time the guys on the roof hit the window."

"We saw what happened to them last time . . . Hard to ask them to do it again."

"We've got the girl," shouted Fonsgraf from the second bedroom. Three more shots came from the living room, blasting chunks of plaster off the wall ten feet from them.

Hanson jerked his head toward the living room. "This guy'll keep for a moment," he said quietly. "Let's see what the Colonel's got. We need to try and take at least one of them alive."

"Right," said Bill quietly. "Dale, cover from here."

"You got it."

They backed down the hallway while Kuhn fired single shots to keep the man in the living room honest. They got to the bedroom door. Peter held up his hand for Bill to stop, then crouched down next to the doorframe, just shy of the opening. He set himself, braced his hands on the wall, and then darted his head into the opening for an instant's look and then back out of the line of fire. "It's cool," he said, then rose and entered the room. Bill moved down to look into the opening.

The room had a mattress on the floor inside the door, and a low, black table under the window. Its surface was covered with shards of glass from the broken window. Halfway along one wall was a large closet, and in its opening stood a thin brown-haired woman dressed in jeans and a black turtleneck shirt. Fonsgraf was covering her with his pistol, and his bulk partially hid her from view. She seemed to be standing among a pile of cardboard boxes that had spilled from the closet; her hands were raised. He had seen her face in the briefing notes; she had the totally empty expression of a gifted cardplayer.

"It's Uli Rosstal," Bunk Cole said. He stood beyond her, near the window. "She was trying to hide in the closet, but the Colonel saw a little movement of the door."

"I got her," said the Colonel. "Not bad for a military man, eh, civilians?"

"The Colonel's one of the best," said Cole. He examined the woman curiously, his arms crossed on his chest.

He's taking this kind of casually, thought Bill. "Great job," he said, "but we don't have much time; the fire's spreading, we've still got at least one more guy down in the living room firing at us, and we haven't found the bombs. Tie her up and let's get on with it."

"Look, son," the Colonel said as he turned to look at Bill. There was a sudden movement behind him as the woman dropped down to the boxes at her feet.

"Watch her!" yelled Hanson.

Something thumped onto the floor in front of the Major.

"We die!" cried the woman.

"Colonel!" shouted Cole, standing, just standing and pointing.

Hanson spun and dove back through the doorway, catching Bill under the ribs with his Uzi, knocking him toward the floor.

Bill's head banged into the wall just as the room exploded. Dust and smoke clogged his vision as he lay there with Hanson's weight across his legs.

"Peter . . ." He coughed; his head and ears rang from the shock of the explosion. He tried again, "Peter, what . . . ?"

The other man rolled off his legs and kneeled facing the doorway. He surged to his feet and stuck his head back into the room for a long look. Plaster dust covered his hair and shoulders. He turned and signaled "Safe" to Dale and then faced Bill and extended a hand to help him to his feet. "All dead. She had a grenade in those boxes . . . a ballsy lady."

Bill coughed again. Shit. "Never saw it. Thanks."

"No problemo." He jerked his head down the hallway. "Time's wasting. How do we take him?"

Bill considered. "Did she have any more?"

Hanson smiled at him. "Good thinking. I knew there was a reason I pushed you out of there. Watch the corridor." He disappeared into the room.

Bill faced down the corridor, gun ready. The shots from the living room started up again, then Kuhn answered, the muzzle blast reverberating in the small space.

"Bingo!" Hanson came up behind him. "She did indeed! They look like Soviet-block concussion grenades. I found two; here, take one." His hands were bloody. He grinned. "Seek and ye shall find."

"Okay," said Bill. His wind was coming back. He started to cough but was able to suppress it. "Finally, something simple and by the book, 'entry after grenade attack.' Let's do it."

They went back down the corridor to Dale Kuhn. The sun was now just down, and it was starting to get dark.

Time for quiet again, let's do this right. He tapped Dale on the arm. "Cover here," he signed to Hanson. "He, I enter."

Kuhn raised his eyebrow. "How?" he signed.

Peter held up his grenade and smiled. Kuhn nodded.

Bill pulled out his own grenade, and he and Hanson started to slowly inch their way up the corridor, backs pressed against the left wall, which held the door to the living room.

Just opposite that door a framed print hung on the corridor wall, miraculously untouched by the gunfire. It was a bad copy of a Leroy Neiman: dripped-white-paint sailboats swirling on a dark lake. Bill raised his gun and blew it to pieces.

Hanson stopped and gave him a glance.

"Reflection," Bill signed, and loaded a shell to replace the one he had fired.

Peter nodded.

Now, the first lessons-in-entry class: Pull the pin. Count off till two seconds are left. Throw the grenade and cover; enter the instant you can, guns in ready position. Don't anticipate what you'll see—that slows you down. Be empty, loose. React to what's there; do it fast.

How many seconds for the grenade? They looked like the ones he'd been trained on long ago. Which should mean they had seven-second fuses. What if they're shorter? He thought . . . the woman had tossed her grenade and it had gone off . . . Count in your mind, one—thump—two, three—"Colonel"—four, five—Peter hits me—six, seven—boom. So, assume seven seconds, same as the old days.

He signed to Peter: "Seven seconds. Pull pin, five seconds, throw. You left, me right. Enter: you left, me right."

Hanson nodded. Bill paused, then thought, waiting won't help this. He sidled up to the edge of the door, keeping as flat as he could. Slowly, carefully he lowered himself so Hanson could reach over his head. His gun held in his right hand, he pulled the grenade's pin with his teeth and heard the click above him as his partner did the same. Nod, three, two, one . . . release the bar. Count: two, three, four, five . . . toss! He stood and covered against the wall. The two seconds stretched and stretched . . .

Ba-blam! The explosions had a slight doubling. A "flam"—it came to him unbidden from his seventh-grade drum lessons.

Enter . . . now! Scan center to right. A man with brown hair sprawled on the floor under the window. An AK-47 assault rifle was on the floor next to him. Blood trickled from the edges of his eyes and mouth. Next to him was a folding table, covered with glass, tools, and electronics. Bill didn't see anything that looked like the bombs. Damn. The man on the floor's eyes were slowly starting to focus.

"Freeze!" Bill shouted. "Halt!" The man paused, his hand hovering over the weapon, then squeezed his eyes shut and opened them again.

There was no noise from Peter. Bill hazarded a quick glance left. That end of the room was a mound of cardboard boxes, and then a couch and chairs piled against the wall.

Back to the man on the floor; his eyes seemed to focus as he looked at Bill, then down at his own weapon.

"Freeze," repeated Bill.

The man looked up again and then very calmly started to move his right hand down to pick up the weapon. He grasped it, and just as slowly and deliberately started to raise its muzzle toward Bill.

"Don't . . ." The barrel continued its rise. Bill shot him twice in the chest. The man's body jerked, then the muzzle continued its rise. Shit, armor. Bill raised his barrel and shot the man in the face. Again, the body jerked, but this time it stayed still, propped upright, the face transformed into something raw, red.

Bill scanned right again—the room was empty there, just a few scattered small cardboard boxes of books—and then back left to Hanson's side. "Peter? Anything?" he said cautiously, and slowly sidled toward the window, increasing the target angle between the two men.

"Not sure . . . your guy?"

"Dead."

"Good."

"Careful, he had body armor." He reloaded by feel, carefully keeping his eyes scanning as he fed shells into the gun.

"Bill, I don't like this."

"Yeah?"

"Thought I saw movement when I came in, but nothing now." He gave a quick signal—"Stay. Cover."—and started moving to his left, around the first pile of boxes.

Where, where would I be if I were a bad guy here? thought Bill. The piled up couch, inside that tall box . . .

A gust of wind from the smashed window tumbled a small box of papers that stood at the top of a pile. Bill turned his head to track it and there was the explosion of a muzzle blast.

Scan back . . . Peter stood with his hands at his throat, blood leaking around his fingers, his Uzi swinging downward on its sling. No! The pile of furniture, it had to be. Bill fired three quick shots into the pile and it bulged outward, the figure of a man appearing as the pile of pillows fell apart. The man's gun swung toward him. Hold, Bill thought, only two shots left. Acquire your target. Time seemed to slow.

The pillows fell, and finally the man's blond head appeared. In the back of his mind, Bill noticed that the man's gun barrel was flashing yellow flames. Dieter Strasse, that's who he is . . . and he's shot Peter. Carefully, Bill's own barrel rose, and as he felt that he had his target, he fired, once, twice. The whole top of the man's head, wreathed in blond hair, disappeared into a red and gray sludge.

Bill turned back left again, and saw his friend falling, buckling at the knees, still clutching his throat. "Peter!" he called.

He managed to reach him, cradle his head before it hit the floor. But it was too late; he knew it was too late. The rough hole at the back of his neck, the tremors in the body as the dying nerves fired and twitched the frame . . . It was too late.

Dale Kuhn stood over him. "Bill," he repeated, "you've got to report in to Control."

"Right." Bill squatted there, holding Peter's head. Dale's right, he thought. This is what they pay you for, isn't it? To function under stress . . . Time to move. But it's always the same—there's never any special music, your friends just die, loose bodied and gone. Never any damn music. His eyes stung. And I'm going to have to call Becky . . .

"Right." Good-bye, old friend. "Control"—damn, my throat is tight—"Hitch here. Area is secured. Repeat, area is secured. Cease the cover fire. We see no warheads. Repeat, see no warheads. All the bad guys dead. We lost Hanson, . . . Fonsgraf, and Cole. Out."

"I'm going back down to look in those bedrooms, there's nothing in this room."

"Okay . . . Control, I repeat, Hanson, Fonsgraf, and Cole are all dead; all the bad guys dead. Get the fire fighters up here.

"No, Control, no bombs. We've done a quick search, so far can't find them anywhere in this apartment. The other apartment is too involved with fire to search. Get some men down from the roof, pronto. We need help on a better search. Yes, I'll hold. Out."

There was a short pause, then two lines snaked past the window and four men swarmed down them and into the room, weapons ready. Bill raised his hand in greeting. "Help Dale Kuhn search the rest of this apartment. He's down that corridor to the right. Call out and let him know you're coming." The leader of the group nodded his assent and went quickly to search, his men following.

Bill bent and straightened Hanson's body, folding the arms across the chest. He looked around him until he found a jacket, and draped that over the face.

Dale came in coughing, his face streaked with soot. "Nothing; not in the bedroom drawers or closets, not in the kitchen. They're going to have to do a radiation sweep up here, and the fire's starting to break through. Where're those fire trucks, anyway? I don't think they're going to be able to hold it, even if they do get up here. We've got to save some of this stuff for analysis.

"Right," said Bill. "Control, we're going to start dumping evidence out of the window—papers and equipment. Get some of the sniper teams to drag it away from the building. And get that helicopter ready to evacuate us, the fire is getting bad. Out. Dale, get those guys to give you a hand."

There was a faint roaring now from the hallway. Something crashed to the floor, then the roar was louder; suddenly, it was hot in the room. Bill went over and looked at Hanson's body. He squatted down and touched the shoulder. Why you, Peter? You'll never get an answer, his number just came up. Is that it? Is that all?

"Bill," said Dale, "we gotta go. The fire has broken through to this side. Get on your mike and tell them to lift us. Look, we gotta go."

Bill looked up at him. "We're going to take Peter's body."

"Just dump it out the window," said one of the soldiers.

Bill slowly rose and Dale Kuhn jumped to get between him and the man who had just spoken. "Bill, I'll handle this, just get him ready." He took the soldier by the arm and pulled him over to the window. "Look, funny man," he said near the man's ear, "that body's leaving with us."

The soldier tried to pull his arm away and then stopped when he saw the look in Kuhn's eyes.

"Agreed?"

The man nodded.

Bill spoke to his mike, "Control, get us out of here."

The return to Washington was smooth, not like the trip out. Only the noise was the same, the roar of engines at max cruise. The Admiral had called them back. "Let the experts search and sort out there. I need an eyewitness briefing here for the President and myself."

Bill sat there, thinking of many things, but mainly of Peter's eyes as he died, the feel of his strong grasp slowly loosening in his own hand. Leave it, he thought. You'll have time to mourn him later. Now you've got to think for those still alive . . . Where are the bombs?

They had not been in the building. In the quick search before the fire forced them out they had found no traces, only the empty shells and shipping cases and some electronic parts from the original triggers. Where were the warheads that came with them?

The plane banked left for a few seconds and then returned to level flight.

The fire had still been burning as they'd left, but from a distance, the radiation detectors hadn't sensed anything. He thought they wouldn't, even when the fire had died down . . . So where were they?

Goddamned Fonsgraf! Stupid, farcical, tricky plan. The fire had burned uncontrolled; most of the top floor and its physical evidence had been destroyed; the town's fire fighters had heard the calls, but no one in Control had thought to countermand their previous order given before the raid to ignore any call for help at Glenview. May he rot in hell!

Bill looked across the aisle to where Dale Kuhn was sleeping. A former field man: able to catch sleep when he could, despite everything, even the burns on his hand he had gotten as last man out, dragged from the apartment's window by the helicopter. True CIA: trying to get just one more piece of information, one more scrap to help in the deciphering of what had gone wrong, and what had happened to the warheads. He's right, catch a nap now . . . you won't be sleeping in Washington.

Bill knew he needed to rest, but there was something tugging at the back of his mind, a little voice calling out that he had seen something of importance, something that he was missing now. He knew that he should listen to that voice, track down the hint.

He tried to replay the raid in his mind, going slowly over each event, trying to look around each room and space, trying to pick up what his subconscious mind was trying to bring to his attention . . . The scene in the living room? The dead man on the floor, cold, stiff too soon? Nothing. The man on the floor had been

Hussein Baalbek, the Mideast connection to this whole mad bunch; the field staff had gotten Bill to identify him from photographs.

No, nothing; the thoughts would not come, it was a losing battle. He started to drift in and out of sleep, back and forth between the roar of the engines to the dream space where a fire roared through an apartment on a hill in Kearney, Nebraska.

The dreamworld enveloped him, and he was in the bedroom again, only this time it was Peter on the floor, throat torn; dead but still moving, hands signaling in a code Bill couldn't understand.

Peter's hands contorted. *What?* Bill wanted to shout, but his throat wouldn't work. Suddenly Baalbek started stamping on Peter, pushing him into the floor, shaking the scraps of pink paper down on him. Paper fell as a rain of petals. And the swaying terrorist moaning, moaning . . .

20

HITCH

He stood at the base of the stairs. A cold rain struck his face, but was slow to help him wake. Lifting his head into the dark sky, he took a deep breath.

Dale came down the stairs and paused beside him. Two government cars idled nearby, parking lights flashing cones of yellow streaks in the drizzle. "You can't save them all . . . That's the bitch, isn't it?" He gestured toward the cars. "Let's go give them the bad details."

Bill shivered slightly . . . from the cold, but also the letdown from action, his body sinking from the adrenaline rush . . . and a second friend lost in an operation. "Yes, let's go."

A young aide stepped out of the darkness. "Mr. Hitch?"

Bill turned. "Yes?"

"Mr. Kuhn and the others can take that car. This other one's for you; someone came out with it and is waiting."

Dale raised his eyebrows in question. Bill shrugged. "I don't know. See you there." Dale turned and walked away. Bill looked around for his bag, then realized he hadn't taken the time to fetch his before he'd left. Not important, he thought, and slowly went to his car. Now who was this? The young aide held open the door.

Bill ducked his head to enter, then stopped. "Why are *you* here?"

"Hello, Bill."

He entered and sat. The aide slammed the door behind him and the driver put the car in gear.

Karen Hobbs sat in the corner, looking small. "Tina told me what happened. She said you were coming in . . . she told me to come."

Shit, he thought, and tried to curl his pain around himself. He stared straight ahead. "Who's at the White House?"

"Everyone."

What a royal mess. "Is there any new word from Nebraska?"

"I'm not on that loop."

"Tina should be there; she'll have the latest."

"Bill . . . I'm sorry about Peter."

He had buried that for now; he made no reply. So the bastards got him. Deal with it *later,* he thought, and shivered; he was still wearing the camouflage assault suit, damp from rain and sweat. "I need to have someone pick up some clean clothes; it's going to be a long night. There must be some aide still on at EOB."

"I know where you were staying; I'll get them."

"No, never mind. That's an aide's job."

The two rode on in silence. She started to put her hand out to him in the darkness, then checked herself and pulled it back.

They waited for the President to answer. He stared off into the middle distance, face calm, perhaps a small smile at the edges of his mouth. It was in the cabinet room near the Oval Office: dark blue walls, white ceiling with ornate, molded plasterwork. The dark mahogany of the table spoke of two hundred years of history. The burgundy rug was deep and rich, seeming to capture all sound in the room except for the slow, deliberate cadence from a grandfather clock in the corner. Then the stately gong came, marking the half hour: two-thirty A.M.

"Sir . . ."

His eyes slowly came into focus on Admiral Thomas's face. "Yes, Chris?"

"Shall I start with the briefing?"

The President nodded. "Yes, please do."

The lights in the room were surprisingly dim. Eight people sat around the table. Western at the head with Luke Wheeler to his right. Next to Wheeler was Jack Phillips and then Dale Kuhn, his right arm bandaged—burns from the Nebraska fire. To the President's left sat Admiral Thomas, then Bill and Tina.

Alone at the other end of the table sat Frank Bass. The Admiral had insisted he be here—not for any input, for Thomas knew the President would never take Bass's advice, but rather so Bass could witness any problems with the President.

"As you may have heard, the attack on the terrorist's hideout was pretty much of a disaster." The Admiral's never been one to mince words, thought Bill. "They were more heavily armed than had been planned for, and they knocked down one of the attack helicopters with a small antitank weapon. The chopper hit the building . . . that, and the weapon itself started a fire which had not been allowed for in the assault plan. The resistance from the terrorists prevented bringing in fire apparatus . . .

"We lost sixteen men, between the helicopter crew and the assault squads. Bad planning." Through Fonsgraf's stupidity, thought Bill, but the Admiral can't make an issue of it without sounding like he's just covering his ass; Fonsgraf was the President's man. "More seriously," Thomas continued, "all the terrorists were killed and their apartment building destroyed: there's not a lot of physical evidence left. As the building cools, our teams are searching the wreckage. I had Bill and Dale fly back here to brief me personally.

"There's a good crew—everyone's best people—out there now doing analysis, trying to figure out what happened. What we *do* know is that the six remaining bombs were not in the building."

"Six bombs?" asked the President. He should know that, thought Bill.

"That's right, sir. Seven taken, one used on the Army base."

"Six times two is twelve."

"Pardon?"

"The number of Apostles," the President said in an aside to Luke Wheeler. Wheeler showed no reaction. "Go on . . . where do you think they are?"

"We don't know. We think all of the terrorists were killed in the attack or subsequent fire. The building was under tight surveillance starting late in the afternoon, and no one left it between then and the attack. As I said, there's not a lot of physical evidence to go on at the site." He checked his watch and made a little mental calculation. "The fire fighters said a careful search could start about now."

"Why wait so long?"

"It's a trade-off between breaking up and soaking the rubble—and possibly destroying evidence—and letting it cool naturally, which takes longer. We should be getting some reports from the analysis crew soon. In any case, the short answer is that we don't know where the rest of the bombs are. First-order assumption is that they are still in the Kearney area, since the terrorists were there and as far as we can tell, had been for quite a while. They would be the ones delivering the bombs, so we think that the bombs are in a hide someplace in the area."

"How are you searching?"

"On the pretext of a serious hazardous waste spill on the rail line, we have put a tight cordon around the whole town. All exit points are being checked with radiation scanners disguised as chemical detectors. We have also started a street-by-street search."

"What about the residents and their safety?"

"We're evacuating the town under the same toxic-spill rationale."

The President looked around the table. "I expected more from the Colonel. I grieve for his family; we shall all miss him." He looked down to examine the edge of one fingernail. "Admiral, do you think there is still a . . . danger . . . that the bombs will be used?"

The Admiral's voice was firm. "There is *no* way of telling. We don't know where the bombs are or who, if anyone, has them. Our obvious hope is that the search in town will turn up something. If not, perhaps our work with the residents will give us some leads. As of this moment, your question is unfortunately not one that has an obvious answer."

"Chris, Chris," said the President with a fatherly shake of his head. "This defeatist tone is not like you."

The Admiral sat very still, watching the President. "This is not defeatism, sir. This is realism. I do not like to speak ill of the late Colonel Fonsgraf, but excessive optimism has helped bring us to where we are today. We have consistently"—he hit the table with his palm—"*consistently* underestimated our foe in this matter, and we've paid for it. At the moment we do not know where the rest of the bombs are and who, if anyone, has them."

"Well, do you think there are any terrorists left? How many were killed in Kansas? Surely not all of them."

"We can't be sure. DOE said they thought a large force hit their convoy. I now have my doubts: I think DOE was trying to save face. Everything, especially the security that the terrorists have maintained, points to it having been a small force with good discipline. Were all of them killed at Glenview? Is there another group who now has the bombs?" He shrugged. "We're pretty sure Dieter Strasse, their technical genius, was among the dead. We should be able to confirm that from dental records. If the bombs were not armed before the raid, then there's a good chance the terrorists don't have anyone else now with the competence to arm them. They would have to find another technical wizard—that is, if there are any terrorists left."

The President picked up a small briefing notebook from the table and leafed through it. Most of the squibs were printed on light red "Priority Flash" forms. They reminded Bill of his odd dreams on the flight to Washington.

The President closed the notebook. "Well, Chris, then we must see if we can find those bombs. What forces are in place in Nebraska, and where do you recommend they search?"

As the Admiral started to detail the answer to the President, Bill let his mind go back to those dreams. He knew himself well enough to know his subconscious was trying to flag something for attention. What? No idea. Scraps, scraps of pink papers. The only thing it could be about was those scraps he had seen with the older man's body. So what?

"What are we going to tell the public, Mr. President?" asked

Luke Wheeler. "So much activity and shooting is going to be too hard to conceal now."

Is the important fact the colored papers, or is that just a marker for something else?

"Again, I counsel that we say nothing for now," interrupted Admiral Thomas. "I want the best chance we can get for searching the area. If any of the truth gets out, then panic is surely going to interfere with that search. I suggest, sir, that we stay with the story of a serious hazardous-waste leak."

Was it that the older man had no obvious gunshot wound, looked strangled? What, who had killed him . . . No, the dreams were about the papers. Something about them . . .

"Sir," Luke insisted, "we've got to deliver some kind of message to the media, or what they'll come up with will be worse. If . . ."

Deliver, thought Bill—then time seemed to expand: Wheeler, mouth frozen open, the President in the act of turning his head. The sound of the room silent between the ticks of the clock: it all came together.

". . . the bombs are hidden someplace in that town," continued Luke.

"I know where the bombs are now," said Bill quietly. His words were simple, but said with such conviction that Luke stopped. He turned to look at Bill; they all looked at him.

"Where?" asked Luke.

"Anywhere."

There was another moment of silence, then Wheeler spoke with anger. "Don't get cute. We don't need riddles here. What do you mean by anywhere?"

"Just what I said, anywhere. But we can find them." He turned to the Admiral. "Those paper fragments I saw in the dead man's fingers—the man found in a back room just before the fire forced me out. He had shreds of pink tissue paper around him and clenched in one hand. He had also been dead for a while, from before the raid." Bill paused for a second; that still made no sense . . . so worry about that later. "I just made the connection, they looked like—I think they *were*—shipping receipts.

"Peter said a Fed Ex truck had left the compound sometime in the afternoon. We found no bombs at the site because they were gone, all shipped out by Federal Express."

The President sat back and folded his hands.

"Stop wasting our time," snapped Luke Wheeler. "Federal Express delivers letters and small packages, not bombs." He made a move as if to stand.

"They could deliver these bombs," said Tina. It was the first time she had spoken during the meeting, and all eyes swung to her. "Federal Express will take large packages for next-day service and the weight limit is a hundred and fifty pounds."

"And the whole W33 shell weighs just over two hundred pounds. If the warhead birdcage were removed from the casing, it should make that one-hundred-fifty-pound limit easily," said Bill.

The President sat very still and calm at the head of the table. Luke looked back and forth between the President and Tina. The Admiral sat forward in his chair. "How do we check this out?" he asked. "You may be right, Bill, but it's just a theory. We don't have time now for just theories."

"That's right, Hitch. Why should we abandon the search in Kansas?"

"That's not what I'm proposing—"

"Let me call Federal Express," cut in Dale Kuhn. "The CIA is good at things like this." He went over to the phone on a corner table, picked up the receiver, and placed it on the table. With his uninjured hand he dialed, then picked up the receiver again. "What was the exact address of Glenview and their apartment?" he called over his shoulder.

"Four hundred Hilltop Drive, Kearney, Nebraska, zip 68847," Tina answered him.

Dale went to work and the rest in the room sat watching. Except the President; he sat looking into his private middle distance, no expression on his face. The large clock ticked slowly in the emptiness. Kuhn hung up the phone.

"What's wrong?" asked Luke. Kuhn held up his hand.

"Call back," said Tina. "Lets them confirm he is who he says he is . . . good procedure."

The grandfather clock began to toll out three o'clock, and then was overlaid by the higher tone of the phone ringing. Kuhn picked it up and started talking again. The conversation went on in fits and starts, then he hung up and returned to the table. He looks pale, thought Bill.

"What does Federal Express say? Did they pick any packages up?" asked Wheeler.

"They don't know."

"What do you mean? Everything they do is on computer; you just need to talk with someone more important. Use my name."

"No, Luke, even that won't help. As you say, everything is on computer . . . and they have a computer problem. They can't get anything up on their screens about where their pickups were today and where they're going. Not today actually, yesterday—we are into a new day. It doesn't affect the part of the computer system that does the routing, but they can't seem to query the computer and ask about a specific shipment."

"So when will their computers be up again?"

"They can't say, but the last time this happened, the problem cleared up by noon. They think it's some kind of virus, but—"

"Who would—" Wheeler started to cut him off, but he was interrupted in turn by the Admiral.

"Let him continue. Dale, you said 'the last time this happened . . .' What do you mean?"

"This problem happened once before."

"When?"

"November twenty-first and -second."

"That's when we lost the base," broke in Tina with her precise voice.

Silence.

"Oh shit, oh shit, oh shit," muttered Jack Phillips.

The President had sat there all this time, still, thinking or meditating. His voice rumbled out from the center of him. "So, it seems as if we now face the judgment. The bombs are out. How much time do we have?"

Tina spoke again quickly. "Well, sir, we may have a chance. I studied this once: the way Federal Express works is that they don't deliver directly from Nebraska to, say, New York. Shipments from all over the country go to a central hub—Memphis.

They're sorted among the assembled planes, which then head back to their home airports around the country. From there the packages are delivered by truck. This sorting happens around now, three to four o'clock. So we may still be able to find them all on the ground in Memphis, if we move quickly."

Others around the table started to speak all at once. The President's eyes focused back on them. He watched them for a few moments, brows knitted, puzzling something out. Then he sat taller, as if a decision had been made. He raised his hand. "Quiet please." The chatter around him stopped. "Dale, I want you to get the name of a contact high up in Federal Express. Someone who can take action at this hour of the morning. Luke, please get me the chairman of the Joint Chiefs of Staff." He stood. "I want General Ronson to direct this operation. He should be someplace around here in the White House or the EOB. Have him report to me in the Oval Office."

"But sir," ventured Tina, not put off by the President's seeming dismissal of them. "We should get on this right away. Those planes are not going to be on the ground much longer. We've got to stop them now!"

The President paused with one arm on the back of his chair. He held his head high, breathed in, and when his voice came it was as if from a pulpit: deep, resonant, commanding. The swing of his words found their revival-meeting stride. "Listen to me . . . all of you. Civilians have been in charge of this operation and you have failed me miserably"—*Fonsgraf* was in charge, thought Bill. Fonsgraf was *his* man—"failed the American people. You have had your chance, and now I want to go with my first instinct; I want the military to deal with this. They will be our defenders.

"Luke, I will be in my office. Have General Ronson come straight in when he arrives." The President turned and withdrew. Luke Wheeler followed, refusing to make eye contact with anyone.

The Vice-President cleared his throat. "I don't think there was any reason for me to be here this evening. The President seems to be handling this problem the way he would like to. I will be in my office, Admiral." He gathered his thin notebook and yellow oilskin bag of pipe tobacco and left the room.

"What's going on here?" asked Dale Kuhn of no one in particular. "Did I miss anything? Why aren't we dealing with Federal Express?"

"The President says we are now out of the loop," said Jack Phillips. "We are redundant, superfluous, extra, extraneous."

"Well why this Joint Chiefs gold shoulder? Why take the time to send for him? Every second counts! Is he another Charles Fonsgraf?"

"No," said the Admiral. "I've worked with him. Burt Ronson is a competent man, Air Force since Korea, a good soldier. He's direct and effective. You can trust him."

"Admiral," said Tina. "We only have less than a half hour before those Fed Ex planes should be starting to leave. What if this is a stall by the President?"

That should be an outrageous statement, thought Bill, but it isn't; we need to take some action. "Perhaps we should mosey on down to the President's anteroom and see what's going on," he said aloud.

The Admiral looked at him, then the others. "Unhappily, that's a good suggestion. Let's go."

They headed down the corridor and into the anteroom to the Oval Office. Another room furnished in tasteful elegance, it held four large desks for the senior secretaries and two shell-front, Chippendale lowboys along the inside walls. Luke Wheeler was on the phone at one of the corner desks. He looked up briefly as they came in, then went back to his conversation.

Double doors, now closed, led to the Oval Office itself. Next to them, a young Secret Service agent in a blue suit sat in one of a pair of straight-backed chairs. Jack Phillips nodded to the young man. "We're going to wait here until the President finishes his business." He then came over to where Bill was standing and pointed to the multiline phone that lay on the desk. "The upper three buttons are the lines from the President's desk." They were not lit.

Luke Wheeler finished his phone conversation and pushed a button on the intercom. To a muffled "Yes?" he replied, "I've got the contact's name, sir . . . Yes, sir, I'll be right in." He went over to the double doors, rapped once with his knuckles, then entered, closing the doors behind him.

"This is starting to scare me," said Dale Kuhn softly. "Where is the general?"

As if in answer, General Ronson came down the corridor and into the room. He paused for a second—a sparely built man, rail thin but much tougher looking than his sixty years would suggest. He had gray-blue eyes so pale they almost matched his short gray crew cut. "Hello, Chris. Bad business," he said.

"Hello, Burt. Yes it is."

The doors to the Oval Office opened and Luke Wheeler called out, "The President will see you now, General." Ronson entered. Wheeler closed the doors behind him, then faced the assembled group. "The President has ordered they not be disturbed"—he turned to the young Secret Service guard—"by *anyone*. I have other information to gather for him and should be back shortly." He marched out of the room and down the corridor.

"And good riddance," muttered Dale.

Bill kept his eye on the top three buttons. They were still dark.

"Admiral," said Phillips, "what if he doesn't move? How should we proceed?"

"A point of information," Tina broke in. "We don't need a contact at Fed Ex, we can just have the FAA hold them on the ground. It's part of the Executive Branch."

"Right. Good thinking, Tina." Admiral Thomas looked at his watch. "There are still fifteen minutes left. We will give him some time to act."

They all lapsed into silence. On one of the shelves, a small mantel clock ticked loudly, out of all proportion to its size.

"What is it with all these clocks? Every room here has these damned ticking clocks!" whispered Kuhn.

"Someone told me that he likes to be reminded that 'the time of the Lord is drawing near.' " Phillips's voice mimicked the President's stentorian tone.

"Oh, great."

The young Secret Service man pressed his finger to his ear, hearing a message on his earphone.

"We're getting close to departure time," announced Tina.
Bill started; the second button from the top burned ruby red. "Look!" he said.
Jack Phillips bent to look at the phone. "Thank God, he's taking action!"

DUQUINE

"So who do you have your money on? Roger tower. Eighty-five heavy holding short of Charlie."
"Green Bay."
"Green Bay? They're gonna get killed. How can you expect those guys to win if it isn't four below?"
"Talent."
"Hah! Roger, tower; wind shifted to three hundred fifty at eighteen, gusting twenty." In the cockpit of the DC-10 it was quiet except for the ATC chatter in their headsets; the big engines at idle were not even a background noise.
"Spoilers."
He touched the handle to check that they were retracted. "Spoilers. How 'bout you, Fran?" The pilot turned and looked at his flight engineer. "You got something on this weekend's games?"
"I'm not a gambling man, Tom."
"Oh, and why's that?"
" 'Cause flying with you is as much gambling as any man should do."
"Ow!"
There was a snort of laughter from the copilot. "You walked into that one, Duquine."
"Flaps," said the engineer.
"The plan calls for fifteen degrees; have fifteen on gauges, fifteen on handle."
"Plan calls for fifteen; fifteen on gauges, fifteen on handle," the copilot repeated.
"Verified."
"That, Carpenter, is 'cause I trusted my flight engineer. Roger,

tower. Eighty-five heavy turn left on Charlie, taxi to 36 Right. Fran, I'm going to see if I can get you a new assignment somewhere exciting, say in White Horse Bay." The sound of the starboard engine rose up to a quick roar as Duquine advanced the throttle, and then settled back almost to silence as they completed the turn.

"Flight controls," said the flight engineer.

Carpenter ran his control yoke through its range of movement. "Top's free."

Duquine checked his rudder pedals. "Bottom's free."

They bounced along the taxiway, little squeaks and groans coming from the panels around them.

"Hey, Tom, we first off tonight?" asked the copilot.

"Yep."

"How'd that happen?"

"Carl had a little trouble with his ground power unit."

"Well, well . . . we get a prize?"

"Sure, Mr. Carpenter," answered Fran, "you get to come back and do this again tomorrow night."

"Ah, the excitement of it all."

"Roger, tower." The big plane braked sharply to a stop just shy of a cross taxiway.

"Whoa!" said Carpenter.

Duquine brought the throttles back to idle. "Okay, tower, I'm holding short."

"Bastards."

"Why'd they stop us?" asked the flight engineer.

A red flashing light came up on their starboard side. "There's your answer," said Duquine.

Fran craned his head forward to look. "Oh, Christ," he swore. "It's Carl."

"You vil stick to za schedule," chanted Carpenter in his best "Hogan's Heroes" German accent. "The schedule is everythink: it is vvvery efficient."

They watched as another DC-10 crossed and then turned in front of them. There was a brief thunder of the other plane's exhaust as it accelerated down the taxiway.

It grew quiet again in the cockpit. "Goddamned pretty boy,"

mumbled the copilot. "Only reason they let him take off first. You watch, someday I'll get my hair bleached blond, and then they'll let *us* take off first."

"First you'd better get back some hair on top . . ."

The other DC-10 reached the end of the taxiway and started its turn onto the runway.

"Roger, tower. Fly runway heading to two thousand, then turn left to heading two-niner-zero maintain five thousand. Federal 85 heavy proceeding to apron Runway 36 Right and hold." He put his hand back on the throttles. "Gentlemen, are we ready?"

HITCH

The red light on the phone still glowed. It had been on for twenty minutes now, and in spite of the tension, Tina stifled a yawn. "Bill, this is crazy, I can't keep my eyes open. Can I get any coffee around here?"

"There must be a messman still on duty, but I don't know if we rank. Admiral?"

"They're here to serve." He spoke to the Secret Service agent who still sat almost motionless by the double doors. "Son, what number do I call to get coffee?"

The agent looked puzzled for a moment. "I'm sorry, sir, I don't believe I know. Perhaps the White House operator—"

"I'll try," said Tina. "It's me who needs it."

"What I need," said Dale Kuhn, "is to brief Langley. How can we find out what's going on?"

"Good point," said Phillips. "We've been here for a while, and after that speech of the President's, I'm not sure he's going to be in a mood to tell us what's going on when he finishes."

During the wait for Ronson to come back out of the Oval Office they had all gradually perched on the edges of the desks or settled into chairs around the room. Their tiredness had started to slip over them as the tension of the last few weeks started to release: the bombs are still out there, but we know where they are. The President is dealing with it.

Jack Phillips stood and rubbed his face. "There's no point in hanging out here. Admiral, is there a way we get some kind of briefing when they've finished?"

Admiral Thomas was leaning back in one of the secretaries' chairs, his arms crossed over his chest. He considered for a moment. "I seem to remember that Ken Butler is General Ronson's night-duty aide. I knew his father. Ken must be back at the office; let me talk with him."

"I'll dial it," said Phillips. He turned the phone on the Admiral's desk until it faced him and checked on a card attached to its side. He punched in the four-digit number, and then pressed the speakerphone switch. They all heard the soft buzz of the ring and Phillips swiveled the phone back to face the Admiral.

The speaker clicked as the call was answered. "Chairman's office," came the slightly tinny voice.

"Ken, this is Admiral Thomas."

"Good evening—ah, good morning, sir."

The others in the room started to rise and gather their papers and notes, half listening to the conversation, chatting among themselves.

"Ken, I'm over in the White House. I'll be back in my office in a few minutes. Could you have the General give me a call as soon as he gets back to that office or calls you? It's quite important."

Tina whispered to Bill, "What about my coffee?"

"Addicts, you both are drug addicts," commented Kuhn softly.

"I don't understand, sir," said the voice from the speaker.

"Drug? Hah! This is the very lifeblood of Washington!"

Their chatter was halted by the duty aide's next words. "Why don't you speak with him now? He's here in the office." Everyone in the room now stared at the little gray-grilled speaker. "Put me through to him!" the Admiral barked.

"Ronson," came a new voice, deeper but still flattened by the speaker.

"Burt, Chris. What's going on?"

"What do you mean?"

"What are your plans?"

"Don't know, Chris." The voice was casual and tired sounding. "I'm just studying a few papers; thought I might actually take a few minutes' nap and then get on over to the Pentagon."

"What do you mean?"

"Chris, I don't think I'm tracking you."

"What did you and the President plan?"

"Plan?"

"Oh shit," came a soft voice from someone in the room.

The Admiral leaned forward and gripped the edge of the desk. "Burt, I think we're playing two different games with the same deck of cards. I thought you were still in with the President, stopping those bombs in Memphis." He looked at the phone's second button down, still red. "I thought you were making the plans."

"The President told me *you* had handled that."

"Oh shit." The voice was Dale Kuhn's.

"Then, Burt, we've got a real problem here. Tell me exactly what happened with the President. I think we've been foxed."

The Air Force man cleared his throat. "Chris, this is a little painful to say, but the President really cleaned my clock. He told me the military had blown it in Nebraska, that he was putting the FBI and Secret Service in charge of the operation. Said you were going to run it for him, that any military liaison the civilian services needed would be done through you."

"Not true, the President told me *you* were in charge. How did you get out of that office? We've been sitting in the anteroom since you went in. Tina," he said in an aside, "use that intercom, tell—ah, *request* that the President see me."

Buzz. "Mr. President?" No answer.

"Chris, I was only in that office for two minutes! The President said I'd blown it and told me to leave. Said to leave by the French doors that lead to the path to the west guardhouse. Said I wouldn't have to be embarrassed going back out past you guys. He phoned a warning to the perimeter guards that I'd be leaving that way."

Buzz. "Mr. President?"

"Burt, get your butt over here, I think we've got bad problems.

"Hang up," he told Phillips.

Buzz. "Mr. President!"

"Tina, leave that. He's not going to answer . . . Damn it, I'm going in there!" The Admiral started to rise.

The young Secret Service man had risen and gone to stand with his back to the double doors whispering urgently into his comm mike. The Admiral took this in as four new agents suddenly came through the corridor door in threat stance. Everyone else in the room froze where they were.

"Jack," said the Admiral without moving, "tell them what is happening and that we want to see if the President is all right."

"Do you know me?" asked Jack Phillips of the four agents at the door.

"Yes, sir, Mr. Phillips," replied the agent farthest into the room. He let his hand fall away from where it had hovered near the lapel of his suit jacket.

"There may be a problem with the President," continued Phillips. "He does not respond to his intercom." He looked at the agent at the doors. "Open the doors, please."

The young man looked to the other agents. At their leader's nod, he turned and rapped once on the door. There was no answer.

"Open the door," said Phillips. His voice was forceful.

The young man looked to the other agents, then tried the handles; the doors rattled. "They're locked, sir."

Phillips strode to the French doors that led out onto the Rose Garden. "Follow me, we'll look in through the windows."

On hand signals, two of the agents at the door crossed the room to follow Phillips out the door. After a second's pause, Bill trailed after them.

The air outside was sharp and wintry. The group of agents stood outside one of the President's windows, their breath steaming in the cold. Bill joined them, looking over their shoulders into the light. There was the President, carriage firm, shoulders square . . . but head bowed, eyes closed as he knelt on the carpet next to his desk.

"Why, he's praying," said one of the agents.

Stunned, Bill stood and noticed the details: the phone off the hook, the receiver lying beside the desk blotter, the grandfather clock beyond the President, its big brass pendulum swinging slowly in the light of the room. It read five minutes after four.

"Jack," said Bill. "The planes have taken off."

21

KAKIMOTO

The car coasted to a stop in the cloak of a large pine tree's shadow. The engine died to silence and the two men in the vehicle sat there, quiet, listening, chilled by the air coming in their open windows. The driver adjusted the rearview mirror for a better view of the blind spot on the right side. "It seems clear."

"Yes."

"Shall I come up?"

"No, Felix, he will not be a problem."

"What if he's not there?"

"He rarely leaves. If he is not here now, he will soon return."

Yataro Kakimoto quietly slipped out of the car, holding a small but heavy canvas bag. He was wearing a long, dark gray wool coat. Closing the door with care, he set the bag down, wrapped a scarf around his neck, and pulled on a pair of thin leather gloves. He surveyed the street again and then bent to the car's window. "Do not be alarmed if it takes a while for him to let me in. This area is mainly university-student apartments, no families; there is not much chance anyone will question me, even at this hour." He picked up the bag and walked back past two small brick apartment houses and stopped at the third. Both apartments on the second floor showed lights at the windows—it looked as if exams were coming up. He walked up the path and entered through the glass door.

One wall of the foyer had a large, metal mailbox-intercom system. The inner doorway was locked. Yataro double-checked the little nameplate, then pushed the button for 3B. He waited. The entrance was quiet except for a faint buzz from the fluorescent light set into the ceiling; no response.

Yataro pressed the button again, this time for five seconds; no response. He casually turned and surveyed the street, moving his bulk close to the glass so as to cut the glare from the ceiling light. There was still no activity outside, other than the few dried leaves that scuttled across the grass.

He pressed the button again, this time keeping it down so the bell upstairs would ring continuously. After a minute, there came a scratchy voice from the small, aluminum-grilled speaker set into the wall in front of him. "Who is it?"

"It is the man who brings you fame," said Yataro.

"Oh, hi!"

There was silence. Yataro pressed the button again.

"What?"

"Mr. Cox, please open the door."

"Oh, right, sorry, sure." The inner door buzzed and Yataro pushed his way through and mounted the stairs in front of him. He went up quietly but surprisingly quickly, considering the weight of the bag.

Noise came from the apartments on the second floor as he passed: a television in one, an opera in the other. Yataro gave a faint nod of approval at how loudly they were being played, and continued up the stairs. As his eyes came level with the top floor, he slowed and checked the crack between the threshold and door to apartment 3A. Darkness, no one up. He continued up to the top of the stairs.

Yataro crossed the landing with a gliding step. The door to 3B was ajar. Loud rap music poured from the gap, along with a faint, gamy smell. Moving away from the frame edge, he unbuttoned his coat and pushed the door open with his toe.

The room inside was a crowded mess of boxes, files, clothes, fast-food containers, and soda cans. At the far wall, Kevin Cox sat with his back to the door, working on his computers. Yataro slipped quickly through the door, looked around, then closed the door behind him and set down his bag. With a flat, gliding step, he checked the other rooms in the small apartment: he was alone with Cox.

He wove his way around the various obstacles until he stood behind the other man. He placed his hand on Cox's shoulder. Kevin jumped. "Whoa! Oh, right . . . Mr. Onryo, it's you. That's right, you're here." He had to shout slightly above the noise; it was Fat Brat again.

Yataro gestured to the speakers. "The music," he said.

"Yeah, bad scene. They've been hassling me from downstairs to keep it down to six. Dweebs."

"Turn it down."

"What? That's vintage Fat Brat! It's the way I work."

Yataro leaned close to Cox's face so he did not have to shout. "Turn it down, not off. I want to talk with you."

Again the Japanese man's aura of power got through to Cox. "Okay, sure," said the young man, and he brought the volume down to somewhat of a background level.

Yataro ignored a nearby chair and stood close to Cox, looking down on him. Kevin edged back in his seat. "Well, what did you think? Neat, eh? Clean job."

Yataro stared at him in silence for a moment. "Yes, it did work, the first time. The Federal Express screens did refuse to call up the data. However, I checked from the road on the second test—"

"Even better. I told you *I* was the best. And soon they'll all know it again."

"But you did something the second time that was not in our bargain."

"What do you mean?"

"The screens do not go blank; there is a graphic."

"Yeah, great, huh? My logo; I've been working on it . . . of course, the resolution of those Fed-Ex monitors is pretty pissy, but you should see the version I'm going to use on cad-cam and publishing monitors! Snatched it off the database of some architect in Chicago. Really max!"

"Why did you do it?"

"To leave my mark, of course." Kevin looked hurt. "Look, you said you understood. You said you were going to make me famous again."

"But making you famous is not my main concern. What you have done may have jeopardized my operation. I do not like to be trifled with, Mr. Cox."

"What do you mean trifled with? This was *my* hack, I want the credit for it!"

Yataro looked at him. "Have you told anyone else about this project?"

"No."

"I want the truth!" he barked.

Kevin started to get up, but Yataro stood too close and he lowered himself back into his chair. "I didn't tell anyone, yet," he said sulkily.

"Not even on the net?"

"God, no, not anyone on the net, not them." He seemed outraged. "This was just a simple hack. I wanted to try my logo out on the Fed-Ex dweebs. Then, when I do the real job for you, and it's totally elegant, just like you said . . . that's when I'll put it on the net."

"Good," Yataro said quietly. He stepped back a bit and seemed to relax, taking a looser stance—his coat hanging slightly open, his hands a bit away from his sides. "Turn up the music, Mr. Cox."

"I thought you didn't like it."

Yataro smiled. "No, but it sums up many of my feelings about this country." Kevin reached over and brought up the volume.

Give it! Give . . . give! Give it t'us all
No work! Eat . . . skirt. Jerk'n a ball
Take it! Take . . . take! Take it all, what y' give us
Noon, get it up! Eat . . . corn flakes and Chivas
Das right, and heave! . . . Heave, heave, heave . . .

"Not too loud," said Yataro. "We don't want to upset your neighbors."

"Hell with them," said Kevin, but he turned the volume knob back down.

"Stand up, please."

"What?"

"Stand up, please, I want to show you something."

Kevin now had enough room to get up, so he stood slowly. Yataro faced him, two and a half feet away. "Hold your hands at your sides, please."

"Uh, sure," said Kevin, puzzled.

Yataro seemed to relax slightly more, and then there was a small flashing glint and a blur of movement. Kevin found himself raised up on his toes. "Gungh," he moaned. He looked confused—something seemed to be holding him up. He tried to raise his hands to feel, but they had no strength, no power; in massive shock, he felt nothing. Above the music there was a faint, wet, ripping sound. Yataro's face was close now, jaw tight with effort; then he stepped back quickly.

Kevin swayed there, still on his feet, with a hurt and bewildered expression on his face. He looked down briefly, to his intestines slipping slowly from a long slit that went from below his belt to the lower edge of his breastbone. He looked up at Yataro, still not understanding. He tried to raise his hands; his mouth worked as if he were trying to protest, but his diaphragm was cut; no sound came. He looked down again at the growing silvery white and red pile. His head raised once more, but as his face came up, there was no one behind the eyes. The head continued back and his body toppled onto the computer table, then to the floor. The rap music played loudly.

We're rude, das right! Eek! White boys . . . on the groove
We're crude, all night! Eek! Rich boys . . . in the mood
Got it! Hold it! Keep it! Use it!
Drink it! Screw it! Eat it! Lose it!
Fat boys! Rap boys! . . . Boozers
All toys! We're brat boys! . . . Users
Work? For jerks, losers

Play? That's a say, winners

Huh? Ya talkin' to me? Huh? Ya talkin' to us?
Huh? Ya talkin' to me? Huh? Ya talkin' to us?

Yataro watched this without expression, then went and picked up an old towel from on top of one of the boxes in the room. He found a clean spot on it and carefully wiped the knife he held in his hand. It had a fourteen-inch blade: a gentle arc of polished steel that ended in a bluntly angled tip—a samurai's *wakizashi,* or short sword. He examined the blade, and then slipped it back into the sheath at his waist, cutting edge up. He bent and cleaned a few spatters from his highly polished black shoes.

Ignoring the body, Yataro went to the door, took off his watch, and laid it on the floor. Taking his canvas bag, he returned to the computer table, pushed aside a pile of manuals, and set it down. From it, he brought out a large, black electromagnet and plugged its long, coiled cord into the plug mold that ran behind the computers. Methodically he set to work, a dark figure in the yellow pool of Cox's work light, passing the magnet over each of the floppy disks stored in boxes on the table, then taking the covers off the six hard disks that were stacked next to the monitors and passing the magnet over the components inside. He shut off all of the computers, then unplugged the magnet and put it away. The optical data disks were then collected and put into the bag along with the magnet. He retrieved his watch and put it on. The warm, fetid smell of opened intestines filled the room.

Going over to the stereo system, he switched the amplifier from CD input to radio, then adjusted the tuner until the university radio station's all-night rock show was clear. Giving one close, final inspection to the room, he picked up his bag and left the apartment.

"Smooth?" asked Felix.

Yataro settled himself in his seat and closed the car door. "There was no artistry, but it was quiet. Mr. Cox will not trouble us further."

Felix started the engine and pulled away from the curb. "They won't be able to backtrack us?"

"No. He keeps no paper records. I've destroyed all his magnetic data stores, and the optical ones I've brought with me. We can break them and bury the pieces a little farther along on our journey." He shrugged off his coat and placed it in the backseat over the canvas bag.

They drove carefully and sedately out of town. As they entered the highway, Yataro turned to Felix. "Have you heard of an American pop group called Fat Brat?"

"Hmm . . . maybe."

Yataro turned back and faced the road again, his face calm in the reflected headlights. He watched the road in silence for a while. "If I were you, I would worry for my country."

22

HITCH

"Damn it, he refused to take my call, but he has to see me!" Chris Thomas was angry.

The Vice-President's secretary looked calmly up at him. "Vice-President Bass has given me *strict* orders that he is *not* to be disturbed, for *any* reason." She was a stout woman in her fifties, neatly dressed in a blue sweater set and wool skirt. She looks like anyone's old fifth grade teacher, thought Bill. Anyone, that is, who attended fifth grade at Parris Island.

The Admiral saw that mere shouting was not going to do him any good. He bent down over the table. "Ma'am," he said in slow measured words, "I do not want to act rashly, but listen to me very carefully: this is a matter of the utmost gravity, and every moment counts. I would like to—make that absolutely have to see the Vice-President." He stared down at her.

If he ignores her and barges in, I suppose it will take even longer to sort out, thought Bill.

She returned his stare with a look of equal steeliness. Then, without dropping her eyes, she pressed the intercom's button.

"Yes?" came Bass's heavy voice.

"Sir, I am sorry to disturb you, but the National Security Advisor is here."

There was a moment of silence and then, "Tell him he has wasted enough of my time this evening."

The gaze of the Admiral and the secretary remained locked. "Sir, he says it is an issue of the utmost gravity, that he *must* see you."

Again the pause, then, "Send him in."

Admiral Thomas looked at Bill. "Stay here." He walked to the Vice-President's door and opened it.

The deep voice rolled from the room. "Thomas, this had better be good," then the Admiral closed the door behind him.

He's got the letters, Bill thought. The words of the Twenty-fifth Amendment that he had run through his mind over and over on this long night played again:

> *Whenever the Vice-President and a majority of either the principal officers of the executive departments or of such other body as Congress may by law provide, transmit to the President pro tempore of the Senate and the Speaker of the House of Representatives their written declaration that the President is unable to discharge the powers and duties of his office, the Vice-President shall immediately assume the powers and duties of the office as Acting President.*

We hope, he thought.

For five minutes he stood there waiting. At least Bass is still listening, he thought. Then the secretary's phone buzzed.

She held a short conversation and then hung up. A thin, young male aide in a gray suit entered the anteroom. "One moment, please." She disappeared into the Vice-President's office, shutting the door behind her, then returned with two envelopes in her hand.

The aide was clean shaven, even at this hour. His eyes were red-rimmed. He must be one of President Western's boys, Bill thought. Without a word, the young man took the envelopes and left.

The secretary returned to her chair and sat there, her hands folded on the red leather writing pad in front of her. She made no comment to Bill, and he was not about to ask her any questions.

After five minutes, the phone rang once more. "I'll put you through," she said, then pushed two buttons and hung up.

Finally the door to the inner office opened.

"Bill," said the Admiral, "the President pro tem and the Speaker have received their letters. President Bass wants to convene a meeting in the Oval Office immediately. All discipline areas on the planning council should be represented, with the addition of Moullins from BATF. There should be no cabinet officers present. Make the calls from here. He and I will be there in a few minutes."

Well, well, thought Bill, the Admiral succeeded. And I wonder whose idea it was to have the meeting in the Oval Office . . . his or Bass's? A smart move in any case . . . if you seek to rule, assume the trappings of power.

"Well, sir, as of five minutes ago, ah . . . 5:00 A.M. EST, the latest word was that nine planes had already taken off before our call to the tower—the rest were stopped at the Memphis hub. Those that were getting ready for takeoff are being taxied back to the sorting area to be searched."

It was crowded in the Oval Office, but surprisingly quiet: Bill and Dale had spent the last few hurried minutes before anyone arrived jamming the pendulums of the former President's collection of clocks.

"Matt, what about the planes that did get off?" asked the President; Matt Chesterton was Peter Hanson's replacement from FBI.

"For the moment, we thought it best to let them keep flying. We have enough to handle on the ground with the search of the planes that are still there."

"And what if those planes that are flying have any bombs in them?"

"Actually, considering the relatively—and I do mean relatively—small size of the warheads, they would do a lot less damage if they went off up there rather than on the ground at the airport."

"What about EMP?" said Dale.

"Don't go too technical on me," rumbled the President. "If I don't understand what you're talking about, then I'm not likely to make the right decision."

"Uh, EMP stands for electromagnetic pulse, sir," said Kuhn. "If you set off a nuclear weapon at a high altitude, the hard radiation from the explosion starts a downward cascade of very high energy electrons from the molecules in the atmosphere. This flood of electrons—the electromagnetic pulse—causes high voltage spikes that can destroy electronic devices. If you remember, sir, your briefings on war scenarios covered such a preliminary attack. With an attack like that, the Russians would seek to wipe out our communications, command, and control facilities."

"And we theirs, as I remember."

"Yes, sir."

"So why wouldn't we get a damaging, ah . . . EMP from these weapons, or am I missing something?"

"Perhaps I can answer, sir," said Ken Butler, General Ronson's aide. "There would be an EMP, sir, but the effect would be quite minimal. To get a big effect, the weapon would have to be a great deal larger and set off at a much higher altitude, say one hundred miles . . . not the five to seven at which commercial aircraft fly."

"I see . . . so, if there are bombs in some of those planes, and they are on their way to being delivered, how much time do I have to deal with them?"

"Well, you know what they say," piped up a young staffer to the President pro tem, " 'they absolutely, positively will be there by ten-thirty.' " He meant it as a joke.

The President did not laugh. He contemplated the last speaker for what seemed like a full thirty seconds, then turned his gaze back to Kuhn. "So you want to go on searching the planes on the ground before dealing with the ones that have taken off . . . why not start to bring them back now?"

"A lot of folks monitor the aviation channels, and we don't want a security breach that could cause panic."

Bass turned to Matt Chesterton. "Federal Express was having a computer problem earlier; has that been solved?"

"No sir, not yet."

"And do they have any idea when it will be solved?"

"They say shortly, but I wouldn't bet on it. Someone very good at computer hacking has gone to a lot of effort: I would assume that he would not have made the problem one that is easy to solve."

"What is the problem?"

"Whenever you ask the computer to report on what packages were picked up at a specific location, or where they are now, the screen goes blank."

"So the data has been destroyed?"

"Not really, because the automatic routing goes on without a hitch—at least it did the last time this happened. There's only a problem if you try to track the status of a *specific* package or location."

"Then the screen goes blank?"

"Well not blank, exactly. The Federal Express people said that a picture of a column of some kind is displayed on the screen, but nothing else."

Tina sat forward in her chair, suddenly very intent. "What did you say?"

"About what?"

"The display."

"That it had a column of some kind on it."

"What kind of column?"

"Tina, how the hell should I know? Am I an architecture student? Fed-Ex said a column, some Greek column; what does it matter?"

Tina sat there.

"Tina?"

She ignored him, staring into the air in front of her.

A phone on the side table buzzed. Jack Phillips went over and answered it. He conversed for a few moments and then hung up. Uh-oh, thought Bill. Secret Service guys aren't supposed to look upset.

Jack walked back to the group and stood there. "We have some bad news," he said. "That was a call from the Kearney site. The search teams have found remains that indicate the terrorists were working with altitude sensors."

"Oh, god*damn* it!" said Bill.

The President looked at him. "Explain yourself."

For a horrible moment, Bill thought the man was referring to his profanity. "That means the terrorists may have rewired the warheads with altimeter detonators. If that's so, then the warheads may be set to go off when the planes descend: we can't have the flying planes land to be searched."

There was a moment of stunned silence in the room. General Ronson was the first to speak. "This all sounds like the plot from some bad movie."

Tina gave a bitter smile. "*The Doomsday Flight*, 1966 . . . starred Jack Lord and Edmond O'Brien . . . actually not that bad a film—it was written by Rod Serling."

"You're kidding," said Ronson.

"I wouldn't bet against her," said the Admiral. "Bill, if they did use altitude sensors, why didn't the bombs explode when the plane from the Kearney area descended at the Memphis hub?"

Bill thought for a moment. "Good point . . . but maybe they used a time delay that would only arm an altitude sensor for the second leg of the delivery process . . . or more directly, they could have set up the trigger to go off on the second descent."

"Isn't that a little tricky?" said General Ronson.

"*Everything* these people have done has been tricky," replied Dale Kuhn. "The fact is, we've found evidence of altitude sensors at their hideout. We can't gamble that they didn't use them."

"Why would an altitude trigger make sense with such small bombs?" asked the General. "They're really too small to generate a good EMP."

"True," said Dale, "but there are a number of places where an altitude trigger might be quite effective—where the landing approach lets down near or over a city, for instance. Bombs of this size might be more effective in an air burst."

There was a pause in the comments, and President Bass spoke. "Gentlemen, and ladies, we seem to be losing the thread here." He had been lighting his pipe, and now took a series of deep puffs that added to the layer of smoke that hovered over the table. No one had smoked around Western, a very strict abstainer from tobacco or drink. Bill knew that there were a few other smokers in the room, but the disapproving stare of the Former President was still too strong in their minds. "Let's keep on the central issue and not get sidetracked."

He took another puff on his pipe, then continued. "There are still six nuclear warheads missing. They were not found at the site of the terrorists' hideout. There is some evidence, circumstantial evidence"—he looked at Bill—"consisting of pink paper, a truck leaving the apartment complex, and a coincidence in the timing of a Federal Express computer problem. The implication is that the bombs have been sent out via Federal Express.

"If the search turns up any bombs in the planes on the ground in Memphis, then the theory is confirmed. Let us assume for the moment that some bombs are found in Memphis. What do we then do about the planes in the air, considering that those bombs may have been fitted with altitude triggers? Admiral Thomas . . . ?" He went back to puffing on his pipe.

"Mr. President, General Ronson and I have discussed this together, and our feeling is that the planes will have to be shot down."

There were a few stifled gasps from around the table, Bill could not see from whom.

"Sir!" said Tom Sinotti, the Speaker's aide, "that seems pretty desperate. There must be alternative plans for this, something that will protect both the American public and the lives of the plane crews!"

"There are nine planes in the air," said the Admiral. "They each have a crew of three; that makes twenty-seven men."

"Yes, and—" Sinotti started to reply.

"Twenty-seven men," the Admiral continued relentlessly, overriding the aide, "and any *one* of those bombs could kill forty thousand people. *That* is the important point, that is what we must keep in mind. Any one of those bombs could kill forty thousand people."

"But only if they go off in the wrong place, no?" Sinotti continued. "And we are not *sure* that these bombs have been fitted with altitude triggers. Why not just have them land at some abandoned airport? There must be a lot of them around."

"It's dark," said Tina.

"What do you mean by that?" demanded Sinotti.

"Tom," said Bill, "it's still dark; there may even be cloud cover. Under those conditions, any of these big jets should have an airport instrument landing system in order to land—there's no more flying by the seat of your pants with a jet that big.

"An abandoned airport wouldn't have a functioning ILS; it wouldn't even have runway lights. So, if we were going to land them, we'd need an operating airport. What if there are bombs on most of those planes? Boom! Scratch the airport or whatever the plane was descending over! We'd need one airport for each plane . . . anyway, we'd have to explain what was going on. What if the pilots refused to cooperate? Remember, we would be communicating on an open channel. Someone would be sure to hear and all hell would break loose—a national panic could still be our worst scenario here. Would you want to chance it? Tough decision."

There was a moment of silence in the room, and then Sinotti sat forward in his chair. "Wait, there's something I don't understand. Why do we need to shoot them down? What does that gain us?"

"First, it makes sure that we don't have a problem with one of the Federal Express crews trying to make a break for it and attempting a landing in a populated area. Second, our people tell us that if we blow up the cargo plane with a sufficiently large explosive charge in the air-to-air missile warhead or shred it with cannon fire, and thereby damage the weapon mechanism, there is an excellent chance that the nuclear warhead will not detonate."

"Oh, come *on*! How can that be true? Those nukes were in artillery shells! They were built to take the force of being fired from a howitzer. How in hell do you expect that being shot at could possibly destroy them?"

"We are assuming that Strasse removed the warhead from the shell casing."

"We can't afford to assume that!"

Tina spoke. "You missed our earlier discussion. He had to have removed them; the W33 shell weighs over two hundred pounds. Federal Express's weight limit for overnight packages is one hundred and fifty pounds. Therefore, they have to have removed the casing and sent just the internal birdcage that holds the warhead components. That birdcage weighs under a hundred fifty pounds."

"Gentlemen, and ladies," announced the President. All eyes went to him. "I would like to keep my options open in case we do not find all the bombs in Memphis. Let's get some fighter planes up."

TAYLOR

"Damn it, Taylor, they should've let us use the soft truck!" The two men jogged across the ramp pavement toward the pair of F-16A's, flight suits jingling softly with their steps and soft puffs of breath trailing them in the cold, still air.

"You just don't get no respect, do you?"

"It's too late for respect, I just want some amenities."

"Kelly, if you wanted amenities, you should've stayed regular Air Force."

"Argh, you old-timers are just too thankful for the flight time they throw your way; it's pitiful to watch."

"Careful, sonny boy. Someday those words may come back to haunt you." Pat Taylor was old by fighter-pilot standards. He had been an F-4 driver in Vietnam—fifty missions north of the DMZ. He had come back with his soul intact, and his love for flying unquenched. He had kept up his Air National Guard rating long after most other pilots of his age had let it drop.

Ed Kelly was by comparison a young kid: twenty-six and one year out of the Air Force, he was back in school to get an MBA. They always seemed to be on each other's case, but in the year he had been Taylor's wingman they had developed a deep friendship.

The two men jogged on across the pavement in silence. They split as they arrived at the planes, Kelly climbing into his fighter, and Taylor stopping to talk with his crew chief.

"All ready to go, sir. Max load on twenty millimeter; checked everything personally."

"Thanks, Freddy," said Taylor as he returned the salute. "You think you've solved that overheat problem?"

"Hope so, sir. The day team couldn't find anything specific, but I think it might have been a bad fuel-metering valve. I replaced the whole UFC on your ship just to be sure."

"That's why I like you as crew chief, Freddy."

"Thanks, sir. That's what I'm here for.'"

Taylor clambered up his ladder and carefully settled into his seat. He strapped himself into his harness, then plugged in his oxygen and microphone lines into the crew 60 unit. After carefully surveying the cockpit, he looked over and noticed that Kelly had already closed his canopy. He snapped on his oxygen mask and keyed his mike button. "What's wrong, Kelly, don't like a bit of fresh air?"

"Are you crazy, Taylor? It's as cold as a witch's tit out there."

"Bitch, bitch, bitch." He activated the switch to lower his own canopy. "Let's get up there." At a signal from his crew chief, he engaged the starter, and his big Pratt and Whitney engine started its spin up to life.

"Taylor," called Kelly on the radio.

"Yes, kiddo."

"Do you think there's any chance the briefing officer's pulling our chain?"

Taylor thought a moment. The two of them had been pretty crude to the man a few weeks ago. "No, I don't think so."

"Shit. I don't like hunting someone who's not a warrior."

"Tallyho, I've got a visual," scratched Kelly's voice through the headphones. "Just on the horizon."

The cloud deck below them was bright from the moonlight. Younger eyes, Taylor thought as he scanned ahead, shifting his vision from side to side for maximum acuity. "Okay, I've got it," he replied to his wingman. There was a faint, stuttered double flash of the wingtip strobes, dead ahead where the clouds met the night sky.

"What are they doing way the hell up here at three-niner-zero?"

"This time of night, ATC doesn't have too many other customers to satisfy: Fed-Ex can go anywhere they want . . . Anyway, those DC-10's are happiest at forty-one thousand feet."

"No kidding?"

"You got their range?"

"Fifteen miles."

"Okay, we follow the briefing: close in, make a visual confirmation, then take up station a mile behind him. Kelly, let me handle the radio contact. Any conversation you want to have with me alone, use this frequency where they can't hear us. I'll monitor both."

"Roger."

He's doing 450 knots, Taylor thought, we're doing 70 better than that, so . . . "Just over twelve minutes to rendezvous."

"Okay."

They slowly drew up with the larger jet. When they were a mile away, Taylor called his wingman. "Kelly, let's drop our speed to four hundred eighty knots."

"Roger."

"I want to pass on his left side. Keep a thousand yards off. Making a left S-turn now; maintain station."

"Roger. Turning left." The two fighters moved to the left of the DC-10 and pulled even. Taylor could see the Federal Express graphics on the side; the purple looked almost black in the moonlight.

"Hello, Fed-Ex Heavy. This is Gold Flight, two F-16's from McConnell Air Force Base, passing you on your port side."

"Hello there, Gold Flight, what are you two doing up at this time of night? Thought only us Fed-Ex fools were out now."

"Training mission, Fed-Ex. Helps keep you sharp . . . they say."

"Hope they're paying you for it."

"I think they've figured out that just letting an old fart like me drive this sled should be pay enough."

"Roger, I hear you on that."

The two fighters had started to pull ahead of the DC-10, and Taylor made a slight adjustment in his throttles to keep even with the larger jet.

"Where you guys headed this fine evening?"

"The City of the Angels."

A chill went through Taylor.

"What about you, Gold Flight?"

"Ah, nearby," the fighter pilot lied. "We're headed into Edwards AFB. A little R and R in L.A., and then back to exciting Kansas."

"Hah, all we ever hope to do there is sleep. How do you find the time to party?"

"Long years of practice and self-denial. What you've got to do is—"

"Taylor . . . Kelly," came the interruption in his earphones. "Talk to me."

"Hold it, Fed-Ex, I got to talk to my wingman." He switched his radio to the shielded channel. "What is it, Kelly?"

"Ah, leader, I'm getting a little overheat notice here. Nothing serious, but it might make me nervous if I were that kind of guy."

"Where's the problem?"

"Tail pipe temperature is inching up. Fuel flow shows normal."

Damn. "Sounds like the problem I had. Your crew replace any of the fuel system on your plane?"

"Not to tell."

God bless Freddy. "You have any vibration?"

"Naw, nothing."

Taylor thought. If this is the same problem I had with the metering valves, if it goes on him, it'll go fast. "Kelly, I want you to scrub. Head back to McConnell, or better, divert to a closer one."

"Ah, leader, all I've got is an indication. I can ride it a bit longer."

"Kelly, get out of here. Either one of us could handle a couple of DC-10's. Inform base and get going."

There was a pause, and then, "Roger, leader. The temperature is rising again. Diverting to base. You take care of yourself."

"Right. Take it easy going back. Mine seemed happier below forty-percent throttle."

"Roger, leader. See you at base. Over and out."

The other fighter rose in a graceful curve and turned out into the darkness. Taylor cut his throttles a bit and pulled behind and above the Federal Express plane. He decided to drift back and hold station three-quarters of a mile behind.

"Gold Flight," came the scratchy voice in his earphones again. "I've been thinking. How are you going to make it to L.A.? I thought F-16's had a range of a thousand miles without the external tanks."

Taylor switched his radio back to the traffic frequency. "Got tankers meeting us," he lied again. What is this guy? "How's a truck driver like you know all the inner water mysteries of an F-16? Were you Air Force?"

"Nope: just a poor grunt in 'Nam. You?"

"Yeh, but I flew there. But you didn't answer. How do you know about fighters?"

"I was a wireman . . ."

Oh damn, oh damn, thought Taylor.

". . . and one of the reasons I used to have to pull you pretty boys out of the jungle was you'd get spooked by something, drop your external tanks too soon, and then run out of fuel. Should have made you walk out. I thought I could do it better, so I used my GI bennies to get flying tags. Ended up flying this truck instead of one of those sport sleds."

Oh damn, thought Taylor, a wireman. Of all the people I've got to hit . . .

Wiremen were the only people fighter jocks looked up to in Vietnam. Revered them, for the wiremen were the guys who pulled the pilots out of harm's way when they went down in the Vietnamese jungle. A rescue helicopter could home in on the downed pilot's emergency locator beacon, but the pilot would be down below the jungle canopy and the rescue chopper up above. A wireman was the guy who was lowered down on a cable, down through the treetops as the chopper hovered, down to where the pilot was . . . or down to where the Vietcong were with a dead pilot's beacon. You couldn't tell from above.

If the pilot was wounded, then the wireman would unclip himself and send the pilot up. And then wait down there in the jungle, all alone, until the chopper sent the cable down again.

So the pilots revered the wiremen. No one, *no one* messed with them in the Saigon bars without the pilots coming down hard.

No one messed with a wireman, thought Taylor, and now I may have to kill this one.

23

"I think we've found it!" Tina exulted from the corner. They all turned to look at her—hunched over her phone, as she had been for the last fifteen minutes, dialing through her mental list of computer-freak contacts on the East Coast.

"What have you got?" demanded Matt Chesterton.

Tina silenced him with a wave, listened for a few moments, then covered the phone's mouthpiece and called softly to them, "I'm on with Andy Couris at M.I.T.; he remembers the same thing I did, a bank hack with a column graphic . . ."

She waved her hand again and went back to her phone conversation. A few of the others in the room slowly moved over and gathered in a loose semicircle around her.

She talked rapidly in a low voice. Without a translator they had no hope of understanding more than a few scattered words of her conversation: she spoke the arcane argot of the computer freak.

Dale Kuhn walked over to Bill and whispered in his ear. "Chesterton is trying to get the Admiral to call in a military dude to take over from Tina . . . I think her being a woman is getting to him. Will the Admiral agree with him?"

"Never. She's his find, and she's the most efficient information/assessment person I've ever seen operate. This is the Vice-President's—I mean President's—show now; the Admiral's wearing his Executive Branch–National Security Advisor hat, not the military's."

"Good-oh."

They turned their attention back to Tina. "Use the code I gave you when you talk with the gatekeeper," she said. "That'll be the quickest entry . . . Sure, I'll be here; ring back when you get in." She covered the mouthpiece again and looked up at her audience. "Andy is logging on with the Fed-Ex computer, going to poke around and see if his suspicions are correct."

"The time is past for following up some computer freak's suspicions, we need to act."

"Look, Matt, it's more definite than that. A hack working against a bank eight years ago had the same effect on their computers as this one does on Fed-Ex's. No data was actually destroyed, but no one could get to it. All you got when you did an information call was a screen graphic of a Greek column—the same as we have here. Andy knew about this old hack because a roommate of his was hired by the bank to track down the bad code and kill it. He said it was a real quest; it was operating in their cash machines or something . . . Maybe it was the funds transfer programs, Andy wasn't sure."

"Tina," said the Admiral, "can we question Couris's roommate directly?"

"Former roommate, actually—he's overseas now, and I didn't think you'd want this to go over international lines."

The Admiral saluted her with a fingertip to his forehead. "Excuse my second-guessing; you're right." Nice play, thought Bill, that little comment was to show up Special Agent Matt Chesterton.

"Anyway," continued Tina, "Andy didn't know the name of the guy who did the bank hack, but he remembers his roommate saying that the guy had the board name The Greek . . . hence the graphic."

"Great," said Chesterton. "We don't need to screw around with your computer friend. Let's just get the court records of his trial, and we'll find the guy himself—that's something the FBI can do quickly. Then we can question him directly."

"That won't work, Matt; they never pressed charges or went to trial."

"Why not? You said the . . . ah, hack . . . did a lot of damage. They must have at least started the procedures, and those records will be all we need."

"The bank didn't prosecute, didn't even press charges . . . most corporations don't."

"Why ever not?"

"Publicity."

"Oh, come on, Tina, you don't know what you're talking about. This is bullshit."

"Easy, Matt," said Bill. The FBI man spun to look at him and started to speak, but Bill cut him off. "Tina's the expert here, and she's right. Companies that get hit like this don't prosecute."

"Because of a little publicity? Hardly likely!"

"Look," said Tina, "if they did prosecute, then their problem would become a matter of public record and therefore an embarrassment. They don't want others to know of their vulnerabilities. If you were a customer, would you want to give your business to a bank that had computer problems? If you were a banker, would you want the world to know that your computer system was so easily compromised? Remember, in a court of law, the method and technique of the attack would have to be detailed."

"So what do they do, take out hit contracts on these guys?"

"A contract, all right, but a different kind. Most cases of this sort are settled by giving a *consulting* contract to the hacker—the victims want him to tell them how they were hit and how to keep others from doing it to them again."

"I think I'd use muscle . . ."

Tina's phone rang and she scooped it up. "It's Andy," she said to the room at large and went back to her impenetrable phone conversation.

Presently she covered the mouthpiece again. "It was the same technique . . . when the Fed-Ex operators tried to pull up a screen of information, the little program this hacker installed ran a routine that's called a screen patch. The information was there, but they couldn't get it to the screen."

"And?" said General Ronson.

"Andy's writing a routine now that should . . ." She gave a wave and listened intently. She gave the crowd a thumbs-up sign then spoke again to the phone. "Okay, Andy, thanks. You're a real person . . . No, I *didn't* mean that as an insult! Thanks, I'll call you later." She hung up and turned to face the room; she sighed. Tina seemed somehow small in the pool of yellow light from her desk lamp; smaller, tired, but proud. Her quest was done. "He's cleared it. Fed-Ex is doing a search now to isolate the information on the pickups from the Glenview apartment complex. We should have it in a few minutes—they'll get right back to us here."

There was a soft chorus of cheers for Tina's work, and then a sharp rapping as the President knocked out his pipe into a large crystal ashtray that lay in front of him on the table. "Nice work, Ms. Lucia," he rumbled in his deep voice. "Stay on that phone, and give us the information as Federal Express relays it. Everyone else, please join us back here at the table."

"Should we alert the Memphis search crews, sir?" asked Ken Butler from his station at another phone.

The President paused and thought. "Let them keep searching, but get the group leader to sit right by the phone so you get him as soon as the information comes in.

"General Ronson, what is the status of your fighters?"

The General bent to confer with Butler. He frowned slightly and then straightened up. "Each Federal Express plane that is in the air is being shadowed by at least one armed fighter, Mr. President. They can fire on your order."

"I thought you said each plane had at least two fighters."

The General looked embarrassed. "Yes sir, but one of a pair following the Los Angeles plane had an overheat problem and had to return to base. It was an Air National Guard flight." Amazing, thought Bill, it's still regular service versus the weekend warriors. "Most of our regular Air Force fighters in the continental United States—those that are not up north on perimeter air defense—have been deployed to the Middle East."

That's okay, thought Bill. Some Air National Guard pilots did combat in Vietnam; most had more hours than the younger, regular Air Force jocks.

The President looked hard at Ronson. "General, I do not like surprises. Please inform me when you get information like that. Keep your assistant on the phone with Combat Command, and keep me informed. See if you can get backup for that one fighter."

He looked around the table. "You have convinced me that we need to shoot down any Federal Express plane that is carrying a bomb. If I need to order that, I want to be able to do it where we discussed, while they are over an unpopulated area. We do not have much margin for error here.

"I know that many of you have been up for a long time without sleep, but let us please keep as sharp as we can." He sat back in his chair and started to reload and light his pipe. "General, you have someone out in the other room charting the flight paths. Get him and his map in here where we can see it. I want information, good clear information. That is the most important thing."

Bill looked at Tina and raised his eyebrows. She started to say something, and then the phone in front of her rang.

"Lucia here . . . Great! Give me a dump." Tina started to write quickly on the lined pad in front of her in her precise, even hand.

Bill noticed most people in the room had jumped as Tina had grabbed for the receiver. The President had not . . . he had just kept filling his pipe. It reminded Bill of a scene in the Horatio Hornblower novels he had devoured as a boy: after seven months at sea on one of his first voyages as Captain, Hornblower had been below eating his breakfast when the lookout had spied the enemy's shore. Hornblower had barely restrained an impulse to rush topside to see for himself, taken another sip of coffee, and simply told his midshipman, "I shall come up when I have finished my breakfast."

Hornblower had been almost shaking in his eagerness to go up and see, but knew his act would convince his crew of their commander's coolness under pressure—and thus calm and steady them. Was that Bass's game here? wondered Bill. Was he really that cool? With great leaders, you never knew.

"Okay, got it!" Tina slammed down the receiver. "Six packages were picked up from Glenview. Destinations were New York, Washington, Los Angeles, San Francisco, Seattle and Langley, Virginia. Three packages in the air, three on the ground in Memphis. As you remember, only nine planes—the long-distance flights—had taken off."

Bill bent over and whispered to Dale. "Those guys at NSA are going to be miffed when they find out they didn't rate a bomb."

"Serves 'em right. Hope it helps us in the next budget battle."

"Thank you, Ms. Lucia," said the President. "Ladies and gentlemen, how to proceed? What are your suggestions? Admiral Thomas?"

"What, 'Buy CIA, the brand most feared by leading terrorists'?" Bill whispered.

"You betcha."

"Well, sir," said the Admiral, "I think we should concentrate on first finding the bombs on the ground. By now, there should be at least three weapon-tech teams at the airport. The bombs on the ground would seem to be a greater threat to civilian population and property than the bombs in the air. Tina, does Federal Express know which of the planes on the ground the bombs are in?"

"Yes, and exactly where they were loaded on each plane, too. I've the plane numbers right here, for both the ones on the ground and the ones already flying."

"Which planes are those?" asked Ken Butler. "Let's alert the fighters and pull the flights off the planes that have nothing on board. The fighters must be about to reach bingo fuel soon." He looked at the raised eyebrows that met his statement. "Bingo fuel is the amount of fuel that will just get a fighter back to base."

"General Ronson?" asked the President.

"That might be prudent," he replied.

Not a good idea, thought Bill. "Sir, I would suggest we hold off on taking that action."

"Any why would that be?" said Butler. He was a little flushed at being contradicted, especially after his boss had backed him. Everyone at the table looked at Bill. The President took another puff on his pipe and nodded at him. "Mr. Hitch?"

"We still only have the computer's word for it. And it is a

computer that has been tampered with. I suggest we wait a bit longer until we see if the bombs supposedly still on the ground are where the computer says they are." He glanced at the map which the Air Force people were bringing in. "Anyway, the planes that are flying are still over populated areas. We have a bit of time until they reach safe areas like the mountains and badlands."

There was a moment of silence and then the President spoke. "I think that is a valid point. General Ronson, have the fighters maintain station on all the flights."

"And the low-fuel situation?" asked Butler.

"Son," said the Admiral, "we're trying to save a lot of lives here. It may sound callous, but when they signed up for the military, they knew that their country might ask them to make some sacrifices . . . and I'm sure that's the way they'd see it themselves. If they flame out, they do have their parachutes."

"I have decided," said the President. "I want the fighters to continue following all Federal Express planes now flying. If we do *not* find the three bombs supposedly still in Memphis where the computer *says* they should be, then I want to take no chances; I want *all* the planes flying shot down." He pointed his pipe at them with each emphasis.

"If we find three bombs in the planes on the ground where the computer *said* they should have been, then I am willing to take a *small* chance. I will order you to shoot down *only* the three planes the computer says the bombs should be on, as soon as they are over unpopulated areas."

TAYLOR

The clouds had rolled away behind them, leaving only the darkness of the badlands below, the lights of the stars and moon above.

A hushed beep in his headphones and Combat Control came on the circuit. "Gold Flight, this is Dog Leader, come in."

"Gold Flight." He felt a heaviness in his chest.

"Gold Flight, your fuel must be getting critical, but we now have clearance. You've got one of them. Your target area is starboard side, upper level, ten feet aft of the wing root and four feet above. Execute, I repeat, execute. Code Bravo, Tango, Xray. Inform us on the results."

"Dog Leader, I copy. Starboard side, upper level, ten feet aft of the wing root and four feet above. Execute code Bravo, Tango, Xray." Taylor closed his eyes for a brief moment, and when he opened them, the muted instrument lights had faint halos.

"Gold Flight, you've been pretty quiet there, you fallen asleep?" It was the Fed-Ex plane.

Taylor swallowed. "No, guys, I'm still here."

"Tell us we look beautiful in this moonlight."

"That you do." Taylor flexed his right thumb. He scanned his dash. Fuel down. "You guys have family out in L.A.?" Why am I doing this? he thought.

"Negative, Gold Flight. This here is a southern crew. 'Cept for our poor, benighted copilot. He has the bad luck to hail from St. Paul."

"Terrible."

"Gold Flight, this is Dog Leader. What is your status?"

Taylor flexed his right thumb again.

"Say, Gold Flight, you ever been to Memphis?"

"Can't say I've had the pleasure."

"A good town. Good place to raise a family."

"Gold Flight, this is Dog Leader. What is your status? I repeat, what is your status? Have you executed?"

Taylor reached out and turned off his combat control channel. He looked at his fuel gauge. It was almost settled. "Fed-Ex, do you—"

He was interrupted by a loud alert. "WARNING, WARNING," flashed in his HUD—the clear plastic heads-up display that sat on top of the dash. The alert was repeated in his headset by a computerized woman's voice. He cleared the screen and silenced Bitching Betty. Was that another voice over the annunciator? "Sorry, I was interrupted. You say something?"

"Wasn't me. What interrupted you?"

"Oh nothing . . . this plane is so full of squawks, it's hard to get a good night's sleep."

The Fed-Ex pilot laughed.

"You know, wiremen were the only people we looked up to. You guys saved some very close friends."

"Aw, don't give me a swelled head."

He scanned his gauges. "Warning, warning!" said Bitching Betty again. The master caution warning and low-fuel lights came on: there were six to eight hundred pounds of fuel left—ten minutes max. That's the limit, he thought. "It's . . . ," he paused and swallowed, "it's been a real pleasure flying with you tonight."

"You off? Well, take care. Come visit us in Memphis sometime."

Taylor advanced the throttle in his left hand, bringing the fighter up until he was 2,500 feet behind the larger jet. He throttled back and with his left thumb threw the gun override switch outboard to call up the twenty-millimeter cannon and get a gun sight on the HUD. Bright cross hairs appeared in front of him. "Got the pipper," he whispered, trying to insulate himself by replaying his simulator training routines.

He put a slight pressure on the stick in his other hand and the fighter curved out to the right of the larger jet.

They were like this for a moment, floating over the dark earth below: the DC-10 a dark bulk, green and white navigation lights flashing, the F-16 a silver dart in the moonlight. Then the fighter curved back toward the left and red flames erupted from a teardrop shaped hole behind Taylor's left shoulder. The massive twenty-millimeter cannon began to fire its five hundred explosive shells in one ten-second burst.

A shredded hole appeared in the larger jet's fuselage just above and behind the wing. An instant later, the whole center section disintegrated as the airstream and structural damage tore the plane apart into a flower of rolling flames and twisting panels.

The fighter flew through the upper edges of the debris, then on alone in the moonlight.

The glow from the freighter faded behind it, and then, as if in answer, the light from the fighter's tail pipe faded, too. The F-16 curved slowly down to meet the desert.

There was no chute.

24

The room was quiet now; most of the smoke from the President's pipe had dissipated, except for a thin layer that hung placidly near the ceiling. The two men sat alone quietly, then one stirred.

"So, Bill, we got them all: three on the ground and three in the air."

"They pick up all the pieces yet?"

"No, might take some time—they're having trouble with a couple of sites. The planes broke up at high altitude, so they're spread out over several square miles; plus, one went down in a pretty rugged mountain area. There're cliffs and there's snow. They haven't *begun* to find all the pieces yet; they're going to have to outfit a bigger crew to get in there and search."

"And someone's going to have to call the families of those three Fed-Ex crews . . . Dale, they'll probably never know what their men died for. That's the way things usually work around here."

"Not even medals."

"Probably right."

"You want to join us for some breakfast at the commissary?"

"No." He yawned. "I think I'm going to head back to my hotel and catch a little sleep before the debrief at one. Maybe some of the others got to sleep in a real bed last night; I haven't done that in a while. Then, I want to get myself out of here and back to the Vineyard for a while to see to some things and figure some stuff out."

"I think I've got some bad news for you there . . ."

"What?"

"You must have been out in the can . . . President's decided he wants only a short, core staff meeting at one, and then a more complete debrief over the next two days, after the field staffs have had a chance to put their two cents' worth in on the other aspects of the operation . . . And he wants everyone on the core staff to be here for a short meeting Friday morning."

Bill stood there and closed his eyes. God, I'm so tired. He opened them again and looked at Dale. "Friday? He wouldn't miss me . . ."

"Bill, he thinks you're one of the shining lights of this whole operation. You damn well better be there."

"He wouldn't miss me . . ."

"Bill . . ."

"Dale, you CIA types are supposed to be real good at disinformation. How about practicing some of that black art for an old friend? Make him not miss me."

"Bill, you'd better be there." He searched around the tabletop and found a small rectangle of notepaper. "Anyway, there's this, too." He held it up to Bill.

Bill sighed and took it. " 'Bill,' " he read, " 'see me in my office Friday at four.' Shit! I just called old Burt and told him that I'd be there by tonight. I want to get out on the marsh—the season's almost over!"

"Bill, *this* is almost over, except for the paperwork. You'll get out there, just a few days later."

"Come on, it's late in the season, I have an old dog I've been away from for too many years. She doesn't have many hunting years left; I've missed too many already—she never leaves a trail."

"That sounds like you—they say people start to act like their dogs. Now go back to your hotel and get some sleep." He took an exaggerated sniff. "Maybe they start to smell like them, too. Better take a shower while you're there, too."

"Same to you, fella."

"Just trying to help. Get your nap. I'll see you back at thirteen hundred hours."

"Dale, if you liked me, you'd use some of that CIA magic—"

"You still here? I thought you'd be gone and asleep." Tina kicked the door to their office closed behind her.

"I just looked in to see if there were any messages before I went back to the hotel. What about you?"

"You know me, had to rescue my files from this rat hole. If I didn't get them packed and shipped back to my office, I knew I'd never relax." She dropped into her chair. "Christ, I'm beat."

"Take a car and driver. Pick your car up tomorrow."

"Maybe. I'm going to be moping around anyway."

"What do you mean?"

"The same as everyone—a big operation over; now comes the depression . . . I wonder if it's postpartum or postcoital?" She grinned. "Speaking of which, you seen Karen today?"

"No." I might as well ask, thought Bill. "Why did you send her out to the airport when I came back from Kearney? Did you think I needed some kind of help?"

She slowly turned in her chair and faced him. "No, you idiot. She did! *You* were in the action, you know how to handle that; she was waiting—it's harder. Bill, *she* needed it."

He stared back. "What do you mean?"

"You don't understand?" She shook her head. "You *are* dense! Look, we'd heard a lot of people were lost in the fighting out there. Karen came up, she was frantic; thought you might be one of those we'd lost. When we found out you were all right, she fell apart; she thought she'd lost you."

Bill sat, unmoving.

"What are you, a piece of ice? She cares about you! I can tell that, even if she won't say so. You could start up that relationship with her again, you know. I know she's willing; but what do *you* feel for *her?*"

I don't know, thought Bill. I'm just tired.

THOMAS

He sat alone in his office, holding the phone as if it were a great weight.

"Hello?" said a faint, firm voice in his ear.

"Simpson, this is Chris. I need some advice on personnel."

He looked around his desk distractedly, then lifted the edge of a tilted pile of papers and extracted a long cigar that had been hidden underneath.

"We're still trying to sort out what's happened to us," he continued, "but we may have leads on how certain things started in the Mideast. I cleared my picking your brains with Jerry. That okay with you?"

"Sure, folks here see it as a service they can provide. Of course, it does help them keep tabs on things—but I know you've figured that out . . ."

The Admiral unwrapped the cigar as he listened, started patting his pockets distractedly, then interrupted Simpson. "Hold it for a sec. Let me put on the speakerphone while I get this lit." He pushed a button on his telephone and replaced the receiver on its cradle. "I need someone to go out to the Mideast and do some exploring for us."

"And then take warranted action?" asked the scratchy voice from his speaker.

"If necessary." He found his clipper in the top drawer of his desk and removed the tip from the cigar.

"Independent action?"

"Within the usual guidelines."

There was a pause. "Chris, in terms of available personnel and time-to-start, your best guy would be Bill Hitch. He broke a lot of it, so the learning curve'd be shorter."

The Admiral lit the cigar and took a deep puff. "I don't think he's right . . . he's very good at reacting, seeing, synthesizing, but he's an action type, not cold-blooded. He needs hot pursuit to kill."

"Then flip him." The voice was quiet in the room. "Play on those he lost; I can turn him for what you need."

The Admiral sighed. "I don't know, he's performed well for me in the past; I'm not sure I want to tinker with that."

"Chris, are you turning into a liberal in your old age? Don't try to make him a friend; he's just a resource . . . an asset."

25

HITCH

On the other end, the phone rang once, twice, three times. "Hello?"

He hesitated. "Karen? . . . Bill."

She paused also, then, "Hello, Bill."

"Karen . . . this is, ah . . . an apology. I'm sorry about being short with you on the drive from the airport."

"Bill—"

"Listen, I—"

"Bill," she interrupted, "I shouldn't have come. It was business. I made it personal."

There was a silence between them; a faint echo on the line as if it were a long, long distance.

"No," Bill said. "I'm glad you came. I wish I'd handled it better." He swallowed. "I'd like to see you again."

There was another silence, then, "Me, too. Just say when."

He took a breath. "How about today? I'm leaving town tonight, just for a few days. I've a working lunch with some State Department staff in a couple of minutes, and at four I've got a meeting with the Admiral . . . how about in between?"

"I'm on duty then. What are you doing after six?"

"I've got to drop something off at an apartment in the north of the city, and my plane's at eight-thirty."

"Why don't I pick you up after I get off? I can give you a ride to your errand, then we can go somewhere and I can drop you at the airport later."

"Is this a date?"

"Oh, hush."

The Admiral had moved his office in the three days since the crisis. He was now in Luke Wheeler's old room. It seemed President Bass had decided to keep Thomas on, and there was a rumor he was going to be the new chief of staff, an indication of how highly the conventional wisdom valued that office's location.

The room was still large, beige, and essentially bare: just a desk and a bookcase. The Admiral's things had not been moved in yet, but the large desk already had his stamp; no longer the sparse, neat rows of papers as when it had been Wheeler's. Instead it was covered by a blizzard of memos, proceedings, and cables.

The Admiral was standing by the window, reading a staff report by the light of some last, golden rays of the sun that had been freed by the clouds near sunset. He turned as Bill entered the room and seemed about to speak, then paused. "Have a seat, Bill. I'll be with you in just a moment."

Bill placed his small suitcase and garment bag on the floor beside a chair and sat. He contemplated the pile of papers on the desk, then looked up.

Chris Thomas was no longer reading, but staring out into the fading sky. He took a breath, and returning to his desk, leaned on the top of his high-backed chair. "You did a good job on this, Bill."

"Thank you, sir."

"I . . . appreciate it. The President does, too."

They were silent for a moment. What does he want? Bill thought. I've never seen him so reticent. The silence stretched a bit more.

"Things pretty much finished up for you?"

"Think so, sir. The debriefs were quite thorough, though I'm sure when the dust settles a bit more, they'll want to go over things again."

"Any current duties?"

"Not really. I've moved out of my temporary office. Only thing left is minor: Jack Phillips asked me to help him out on something—looking around and maybe posting some notices up at an apartment in D.C. a bit north of here. It's where one of the DEA trainers used to live, one of the guys hit on the bomb convoy. We've never been able to find any relatives or friends; someone's saddled Jack with the job of tying up that loose end."

"And now?"

"I'm heading out tonight—out to the Vineyard. I've got some things to take care of there. I also want to talk some more with Becky Hanson, see if there's anything I can help them with."

The Admiral came around and sat at his desk. "Tough about Peter."

He's never talked with me about losses before, thought Bill. "Yes. A good friend. The second good friend I've lost . . ."

The older man looked at him sharply. "But *you* didn't lose him, Bill. It was war, it was battle, and you did your job. He did his."

"But he died."

"So the bad guys did theirs . . . you went in knowing you might not come out; so did Peter." He shook his head. "It's do that or never fight. We did our job better than the bad guys, but losses occur."

"Peter was a good friend."

The Admiral leaned back in his chair. "We have a small project you might be good for. There's a matter I want you to deal with for me."

"I've got a plane tonight, Admiral."

"No, I mean when you get back. It should only take a week or two to finish. It was brought up by one of our friends in the Persian Gulf. I need someone whom I can trust and who knows the way I operate. Henry Simpson thinks you need some . . . training for it; he'll see to that."

"Henry is getting a reputation as a strange bird."

"He's good at his job. Are you interested in taking on a project?"

"I think so. It depends on what happens this weekend. And I'd like to know more about it. Within security constraints, of course."

"How long are you gone for?"

"I was hoping for four or five days."

"I need to know sooner. Can you give me a decision Monday?"

There never was enough time. "Sure."

"Good."

At the window, the last of the sun had gone; the blue of night was creeping in and the city lights on the hill below them were starting to come on. The Admiral turned on his desk lamp. "What time is your plane? Ted Farragut said he wanted to take you to dinner."

"Tell him thanks, but no. I've got that errand to do. Someone's offered to give me a ride to do that and then on to the airport."

"Then I'll hear from you Monday. Have a good trip. Take care . . ."

"Here, take these. Throw your things in the trunk." She leaned across to the side window and handed him the keys.

It was an old, battered, two-door, red Toyota. "This city deserves nothing better," she'd said. Bill put his bags in the trunk, then went and settled into the right front seat. He closed the door. It didn't catch. He opened it again and slammed it shut. "Your keys, madam."

"Thank you, kind sir," Karen said. "Which way?"

"North. It's on Church Street, near Eighteenth."

She started the car and pulled out into traffic. "How did it go with the Admiral?"

"He's offered me something."

"So soon after all this?"

"That's the way it goes. It may be related to this stuff, anyway. I told him I'd like to think about it, though I'll probably take it on."

"What kind of project?"

"Don't know, precisely. He's acting a big strange about it. Anyway, I told him I'd let him know on Monday, so I've got to be back by then—a little sooner than I'd hoped for."

"You know, the more I see, the more I think Chris Thomas is something of a bastard."

"He's just doing his job, it's not personal."

"For sure—I don't really think he cares about anyone."

"That may be true, but where he's coming from, that's life."

She drove with calm abandon, reading snarls in the traffic ahead, slipping from lane to lane to avoid them. Bill watched her hands on the wheel, the line of her throat. She's too calm, he thought.

"So, you may not have that much time back in Washington, after all."

"Don't know, but it doesn't look like it."

A light turned red in front of them. Karen braked to a halt, then turned her head and looked at him. She put her hand on his knee for a moment, then returned it to the wheel and looked back out through the windshield again. "That's going to be the story of our lives, isn't it? Work, travel . . ." She sighed.

"I should be back soon," he replied.

"You have your job, I have mine; how often do you think we'll be matched up again? It's been what, four years since the last time, and since then we've been on opposite sides of the earth . . . that's not conducive to a stable relationship."

"You said the R word."

"Yeah, and I don't see how it could ever work." The light turned green and she accelerated away. "Let's get your errand done and go have a drink."

Sitting there beside her in the darkness, Bill had a sudden remembrance of the smooth touch of her thighs. This is foolish, he thought.

They stared up ahead at the building in the darkness. "That's one landlord who'll never know what happened to his tenant," said Karen.

Quiet night, chilly air. So normal after all that craziness. The flicker of TV screens lit scattered windows above them, others had the warm glow of a lamp lit for an evening's reading of a favorite book. They passed a streetlight and Bill watched how his shadow lengthened in front of him.

A quiet residential neighborhood: cars parked along the curb; people getting ready, soon, to sleep. A while ago, there had been those who planned a much longer night for this city.

Bill could feel her near him like a magnet.

He looked up; a cab roared past. In the quick flash of its headlights, he saw a face reflected in a side-view mirror, a man sitting in the passenger seat, watching him from the open window of a car parked two spaces ahead. The face had an intensity, a look of almost hunger . . . Must be jealous of me and Karen, Bill thought. She *is* nice.

Funny I should make eye contact with him, my head should be too high for that. He must have been tracking us with the mirror, quite the horny, hungry guy.

No, not hunger. He's watching me and Karen with . . . the look of a hunter.

All these thoughts cascaded quickly, then Bill's pace broke for a half step. He moved closer to Karen; his hand brushed her hip and then slid down to caress, then cup the swell of her buttock. She grew very still, taut. I can't afford to speak, he thought, he'll hear me. Keep on walking . . . But she started to slow. The man in the mirror watched. Can't use hand code; don't remember if she knows color code. Try it.

Bill pulled her closer. "I got a phone call from Mr. Brown." Her step faltered slightly. He lifted her along with his hand on her rear. "He said the red drapes were too much, he'd prefer something more gray." There: "Mr. Brown"—crisis; "red"—mortal danger; "gray"—continue present action. There was only a slight further pause, and she put her arm around his waist. The face in the window watched.

Bill leaned his head down to nibble at the back of Karen's neck, then nuzzled her ear. "Listen," he whispered softly, "I see a face; he sees us. Laugh, goose me, and hope to God we make it to the corner."

She turned her head to him, gave a giggling laugh, and then slid her hand down to give a quick, hard pinch to his ass. Bill jumped and then laughed back.

Another car passed and from the corner of his eye he saw—almost felt—the eyes still on him. He lifted his hand off Karen's hip and reached around to cradle her chest just under the breast, then slowly walked his hand upward. "Push it down," he whispered. She gently pushed his hand down to her waist. Bill made his steps weave slightly.

The car was now six, now five feet away. They passed and he risked a glance sideways into the car, his eyes now shielded by the car's roof from the watcher's gaze. There was only the shadowed bulk of legs in dark pants and a torso in dark sweater. A shadow on the seat cushion told him that there was a driver, too. The passenger's right hand was hidden, hanging down near the door. Armed, thought Bill. Gun out, cocked. I've passed in front of him, can't draw myself before he can take me out; we have to continue the walk. There were faint noises of city life around them—the rustle of distant traffic, snatches of TV and music, the scratch of bits of trash blowing in the street—but the compelling noise was the sound of their feet on the pavement. Five feet past.

Another car went by. Good. Keep the witnesses coming, please; raise the cost of his doing a preventive hit. Bill strained to hear any metallic noise behind him. Would he be able to hear the click of the car door opening if the guy decided to move? Ten feet past. Think! Are they the only ones? Did we pass any other shadows in cars? Fifteen feet.

He and Karen walked on, as close as lovers, bodies vibrating with something stronger than sex: the fear of death . . . the fear of it all ending here, on this dark and peaceful street.

Trip your toe slightly, recover, and use that to hide a glance around. Nothing? Replay the scene of the car. What else did you notice? Two-door sedan; Nebraska plates; dirty car with new tires. Twenty feet on; sixty feet to the corner. Bill's hand slid down to caress Karen's rear again. She hooked her fingers into his rear pocket. Take it step by step. Bill thought of stopping to kiss: no, too arty, keep it simple and get to that corner. This walk is like a decoy set: everything has to be perfect, with one difference—if this set works, they *don't* come in. Forty feet to go. No noise behind him. One foot in front of another.

The street was quiet, no cars, no traffic. Come on! Bill thought, if they are going to try to take us, they'll do it now. Let's have some traffic. Thirty feet.

A motorcycle on the cross road slowed and then turned onto their street. It accelerated past. Good, Bill thought, then heard the sound of a car starting behind them. Shit. Something's wrong with the set; I need something more here. Then he had it. From the watcher's point of view, why had Bill and Karen been in the apartment building, then stood out front looking at it? Only bad reasons. They'd have to stop in front of another, become apartment hunters. Only twenty-five feet. Bill stopped and swiveled Karen toward the building to their right. "Look at the building," he whispered. "Covering our tracks." The two stared upward. "Now that's a nice place," Bill said out loud. "Look at the large windows." He gestured to the other side of the street. "Just as nice on that side, but they don't get the morning sun." He swung Karen around again and gave her shoulders a squeeze. She squeezed his rear. They leaned their heads together and continued on. Fifteen feet. The car behind them still idled, but had not been put into gear. Bill exhaled, but kept his pace the same. Ten feet to go.

They got to the corner. Bill looked at his watch: 7:10. A car came toward them on the cross street and he saw it was a cab. He stepped out and waved. It slowed quickly and came to rest in front of them, an old and dirty-looking Ford Granada. "I love Washington cabs," Bill said. He opened the door and guided Karen in. "Don't look around." He got in and slammed the door.

"Where to, mon?" called the driver in an island accent.

"Keep going north." The cab started up and Bill watched the reflection of the road behind in the plastic security screen. A car had moved out into the intersection and stopped there.

"What was—," Karen started to say.

Bill cut her off. "We're still on. Rest your head on my shoulder." Karen did as he said. Bill watched the reflection as the car dwindled behind them. They were not being followed. "Driver," he called, "go up five or so blocks and then cross over one to the right and come back south again."

"Why don't I just take a right on New Hampshire? That cuts across, would be faster, Brother."

"I know where I'm going. Humor me."

Bill sat back in the seat and moved slightly away from Karen.

"Ah, Bill," she said. "Do you have a reason for that performance, or am I just that irresistible?"

He gestured toward the driver. "One second."

The driver made the two turns and when they were a block north of Church on Seventeenth Street, Bill had him stop. He handed the driver a ten. "Keep it."

"You're the boss."

Bill and Karen got out onto the sidewalk and the cab drove away. "Come," he said, and retreated off into the shadows of a corner doorway. Out of easy view, but still with good sight lines up and down the street.

"Who did you see? Why the performance?"

"Felix Ross."

"But he's dead . . ."

"Not anymore. And that means it wasn't Felix Ross who got killed with the convoy and that means . . ." He let the thought hang there. They both knew what it meant: they may not have gotten all the bombs. "I caught his face in the side-view mirror of a parked car we passed."

"How does he know you?"

"He couldn't, but he saw us checking out his old apartment; I think he almost took us out . . . acted as if he was armed. There was someone else with him. I didn't see his face, just his legs.

"It was their car that started up behind us. They watched us from the corner after we got into the cab, but didn't follow us farther—must have bought the story that we were just lovers, apartment hunting. Good acting."

She looked at him. "Bill, I don't act with you." He could sense the fighting tension in her.

"Was that a gun I felt?"

"Or am I just glad to see you? Yeah, I'm carrying." She pulled a 9mm automatic from a holster on her waist; it had been hidden by her jacket. "I felt yours. So now what?"

Bill let his breath out. He realized he had hardly been breathing. "I think we find a phone and alert someone, then sneak back and see what Ross and his friend are up to."

"Who do we call?"

"The response team's been disbanded . . . I guess the White

House. The Admiral should still be in his office. Whoever we call will have to check with them anyway: starting at the top will save some time . . . Now where's a phone?"

Karen pointed to a pay phone a half block away. "You call; I'll stay in the shadows and guard your back."

"Right."

He checked the street for Ross's car and hurried to the phone. Change, do I have change? Yes.

He dialed an unlisted, inside line. The soft ring, and then, "Good evening, may I help you?" came the neutral answer.

What was current code? Ah, "A cat lover here. Could I speak to the doctor, please?"

"Yes, sir. Please hold."

There was only a short wait, and then, "Yes." It was the Admiral.

Good, they'd gone direct to him. "Sir, Bill Hitch."

"Bill—"

He cut him off. "Admiral, I know this is not a secure line, but I have to speak in clear: this is important and we haven't got time. There's a problem. I'm up near Seventeenth and Q streets. I just saw Felix Ross near his old apartment."

"Ross?"

"He was the trainer on that DOE convoy. He was supposed to have been killed in the attack. He wasn't. He's here in Washington, with another man, in a car with Nebraska plates."

There was a pause on the other end of the line. "You're sure?"

"Yes, sir. I'm very sure. He almost took out Karen and me, but I think he decided we were just harmless civilians: he has no reason to know who we are."

"This is coming at me a bit fast, Bill."

"I think we didn't get all the bombs. Ross's body is the one they had trouble identifying in the mess they found at the snatch site: wrong blood type. That's because it wasn't his body; it was some stand-in's. If that's so, then he was in on the snatch, the inside member. And if he's here in Washington, with a car with Nebraska plates, then he was out there at the site where the bombs were worked on. And—"

"Maybe we haven't yet found the bomb in the mountains

where one Fed-Ex plane crashed because it's not *there,*" the Admiral finished for him. "We may have a bomb here in D.C. . . . You're on site. How do you suggest we proceed?"

"Get a plainclothes team up here right away. You can probably strip one from the President's guard. I'll go back and see if their car is still on Church Street—last we saw, they were up near Eighteenth. How long should it take to get that team here?"

"Fifteen minutes."

"That's what I'd guess. Then meet us on, ahh"—he looked up the street and read the signs—"Q Street, between Sixteenth and Seventeenth. That's a block away from Ross's apartment. I'll have Karen tail me a half block back while I check out Church Street. She'll meet you if I get into any trouble going in."

"Okay, Bill, we'll meet you fifteen minutes from now at the designated spot. What kind of description do you have on their car?"

"Right, sorry. It was a white two-door—Ford Cougar, I think. Nebraska plates, first digits were six-four-seven or six-four-nine. Dirty bodywork."

"Okay. You be careful going in. I don't want to spook our quarry."

"All right. And sir . . . I'd consider getting people into the shelter."

"I've already thought of that."

Bill replaced the receiver and jogged back to Karen. "They're sending a team. Let's go back and see if our friends are still there. And let's take it easy. I have no idea what their game is."

"Nothing?" asked the Admiral.

"Nothing," said Bill. "We've searched in the apartment . . . no obvious clues, though it looks like someone had been there. We didn't touch anything; FBI should be here soon to do a high-tech search. No sighting of the car?"

"No." The Admiral shivered and pulled up his collar. A chill wind had risen; it had been warmer inside the dark blue minivan with the blacked-out windows—one of the Secret Service vehicles that were normally part of the White House squad. He had been using the communication facilities to confer with his staff back at the White House. "This crew will mount a guard until the FBI arrives to search the apartment. I'm going to keep everyone else out and searching for that car. All the roads should be covered by now."

"What about air?"

"We've put an umbrella over the whole metro area. Airports are shut down and helicopter services have been warned not to pick up any fares."

"What about the President?"

"He refuses to leave town with his family. There's no way we can evacuate D.C., and he says he'll live with that decision along with the rest of the city . . . which may be noble, but is not that smart from a government continuity point of view—which is my view now."

"You going to stay here?"

"No, they should have a pro from NSA in to run this any minute now. I want to get back to the White House and try to convince the President to get down into the shelter. Can you and Karen give me a ride? I don't want to pull out a car just to drive me down there."

"Sure," said Karen. "It's just a little Toyota, but we should all fit. It's down this way, around the corner."

"Okay. Bill, you might as well come back to the White House with me. I don't know what else you can accomplish up here." He started off at his usual brisk pace toward where Karen had parked, and then stopped and faced them again. "Good work, you two. I don't know what this means yet, but recognizing Ross was a helluva good catch."

It was a tight squeeze to get them all into Karen's car. The Admiral insisted on sitting in the back and Bill moved the front seat as far forward as it would go. They rode south for a while in silence.

"So where would they set it off?" asked Karen.

"That's the question, isn't it?" said the Admiral.

"You've got to ask yourself, what do they want to do?" mused Bill. "Embarrass us?"

"That's a pretty mild term for destroying Washington, isn't it?"

"Could they do that?" asked Karen. "Is that bomb big enough?"

"I was being somewhat melodramatic," said the Admiral. "What do you think they could do with it, Bill?"

"Well, it wouldn't destroy the city, but if they could maximize the damage by setting it off in the right place, they could pretty much finish D.C. off as a place to run a government. We've got to assume that these people know what they're doing. We made the mistake of underestimating them before, and look where it got us. So . . ."

"What do you do to maximize the damage from a small nuclear weapon?"

"What do you want to do, Admiral, kill a lot of people or destroy a lot of buildings?"

"Let's say the maximum shame—damage our honor."

"Then they go for the destruction of the buildings, because then they destroy the image of the U.S. Then *height,* they're going to need height. An airburst; from what I've read, best burst height is somewhat of a guessing game. A lot depends on terrain and weather conditions. You sure that all possible airports are shut down?"

"Yes."

"Overpressure can be maximized by an airburst—you can get local winds of over a thousand miles an hour. That knocks down *everything*. Even farther away, the winds are still high enough to clean out between the floors of high-rise buildings."

"What about radiation?" asked Karen in a small voice.

"It isn't really the direct radiation that kills right away, it's the overpressure caused by the explosion. For maximum fallout damage, they might try a ground burst, though in any case, an explosion in central D.C. would make most of the metro area unsafe for a year. But to knock down the greatest number of buildings, and for maximum fires, I think an airburst, not too high, because with a bomb this size you can start to lose punch. Say over two hundred feet but less than a thousand."

"Well, we have all the airports shut down. We also have the congressional and military leaders headed out of town at this moment."

"What about the executive branch?" asked Karen. That, after all, was her area of responsibility.

"We've got some of the cabinet members out, including the Secretary of State, but with the President refusing to leave, there's some kind of stupid macho contest going on . . . I just hope I can get him into the shelter."

They lapsed back into silence again, each in his own thoughts. Bill looked out ahead, lights of the various monuments winking into view as they passed open spots in the skyline. One set of lights slowly rose in the sky as they traveled south. Bill finally had to bend his head down a bit to keep them in sight. Damn, he thought and straightened up, hitting his head on the windshield frame. "Damn!"

"Watch yourself," said Karen.

"I've got it! . . . That's where they must be!"

"Where?"

"Five hundred and something feet . . . the perfect height for an airburst; the tallest place around, and centrally located . . . The Washington Monument."

26

HITCH

Karen Hobbs pulled into the parking lot on Constitution Avenue and set the brake. "You can take this back to the White House. Bill and I can hoof it from here."

"Karen," said the Admiral.

"Sir, this is what I'm trained for."

"I guess that's right," he said, and clambered out of the rear seat on the driver's side. "Is this a wild-goose chase?"

Bill pointed to the monument. "Isn't there normally a light that illuminates the base?'"

The Admiral looked. "Damn it, you could be onto something." He climbed into the car and started to close the door. "I'll see what forces I can get down here. Do you want to wait for them?"

"Don't know if we have the time; Karen and I'd better start. Just make sure your guys don't come in shooting, we'll be up there . . . Wish we had some radios."

"Okay, good luck . . . good hunting." He clashed the engine into gear and accelerated across Constitution onto Sixteenth Street and then back around the Ellipse toward the White House.

Karen and Bill turned and faced the monument. "The entrance is on the east side, facing the Capitol," he said. "We should probably get off the path and into the darkness while we figure out what to do."

"Your kind of operation, so you're the leader. Wait a second, though." She took off her light tan trench coat, revealing a dark blue Secret Service blazer underneath. "This should help a bit."

"Good thinking."

They jogged off onto the damp grass and stopped twenty yards from the path. The surrounding field looked empty; the cold wind had driven away the scattered bunches of tourists that usually wandered around the base. "Now," said Bill, "it looks like they've knocked out the lights that illuminate the base. There's a small theater on the other side, and a grove of trees that might give us more cover." He thought a bit. "Nah, take too much time. It's pretty dark; let's go straight up this way."

"You're the boss."

"You ever been up the monument?"

"You kidding? I grew up in Washington; that's for tourists. You?"

"Yeah, maybe five years ago. As I remember, there's an elevator to the top and a set of stairs that runs up around the inside."

"If they've already gotten in, shouldn't there be some kind of alarm going off?"

"Probably bypassed it. They certainly have the talent to do it."

There was a sudden series of gunshots off to the south, perhaps a half mile away. They both dropped to one knee.

Gunfire? Bill listened to the rhythm and echo of the sounds. No. "That may be their diversion; does it sound like gunfire to you?"

Karen considered. "I think you're right. The sound's not sharp enough, might be firecrackers. Where's it coming from?"

"I think from near the Mint buildings, beyond Independence and Fourteenth." Bill stood up and searched ahead. "If we keep to this side, and approach the monument from the northwest corner, we should get some shielding from the door side. We can circle the walls from there." He looked around. "First let's check and see if any of our friends are out here in the darkness."

They searched in silence for a moment, then Karen said, "I see something on the ground up there. One hundred and fifty yards out; a little to the right, say at two o'clock."

Bill looked where she was pointing. There was a dark shape lying on the grass, just off the pavement that surrounded the upper plaza. He watched it for a while. "I don't see any movement."

"Me neither, but it looks human-sized."

Bill pulled out his gun. "Let's check it out. I'll head in first, you keep twenty yards behind me and off to the left."

"Got it."

They separated and Bill took off in a darting run toward the top of the hill. Fifty feet from the figure he stopped and dropped to a kneeling position. He looked hard ahead of him. It was dark up here, but he could see the silhouette of the figure against the base of the monument. It looked like a man . . . lying on his back . . . no movement. He signaled Karen to stay where she was and continued up the slope until he reached the still form. It was a park ranger, lying on his back on the grass, green nylon parka unzipped slightly to where a dark, wet stain soaked it. He motioned to Karen to join him.

"Oh damn," she said.

"Well, we know they're here." He looked around them again. "I still think this is the best approach angle. Let's get up there."

"Poor bastard," Karen said, and followed Bill up to the plaza.

They skirted the edge of the pavement in a crouch, sidling around toward the east face where the door was. All the lights were out on the plaza. Only the distant spotlights that illuminated the upper part of the shaft were still on, and the top of the tower hung there above them, ghostlike.

"Karen, stay back here where you can cover me. I'm going to edge along the front wall and check out the entrance."

"Got it."

He tucked his gun under his armpit and wiped his palms on his pants legs. He shifted the gun back, took a little breath, then sprinted across the pavement, vaulting the row of benches and flattening himself against the tower's wall.

Silence.

Slowly edging his way to his right he came to a low metal fence that bordered the entrance. He listened carefully. Nothing, only the faint sounds of traffic and the explosions by the Mint.

He checked the fence's gate. Locked. A little jump over it and he was against the wall, next to the door. The outer, night door of ornate metal bars seemed intact, then he noticed that it was slightly ajar. They're here. Now what?

He shifted his gun to his left hand and set his feet slightly apart. A little breath, and then a quick duck of his head to look down the entrance corridor. No one there.

Breathe again and consider what he had seen: no one in the entrance, twelve feet in, the glass inner doors broken. They may already be on their way up, he thought. He signaled Karen.

"What is it?" she whispered as she joined him.

"Outer metal door's been forced, inner door's been breached."

"Plan?"

"I'm going to open this outer door. You step back a bit and cover me. Keep a lookout left and right."

Karen stepped back a few paces and started scanning, gun at ready.

Bill took a quick glance down the entrance again. Still empty. He pushed against the metal door with his foot. It wouldn't move. He braced his shoulder against it and it slowly gave, swinging open with a slight creak.

Ahead of him were the double glass doors to the inner room. The glass on the right-hand door had been smashed out of the frame. Facing him were the white metal doors of the elevator. He knew a corridor went around to the left, circling the central elevator structure. There should be a door to the right, leading to the stairway up. He carefully stepped through the broken door, feet crunching on the broken glass. He stopped and listened: no sound beyond the mechanical noises of the heating system. Again: breathe, quick duck of head around the corner, and back. Empty.

He motioned Karen up to the second doorway and then made a quick search of the rest of the lower floor. Empty, too.

"No one down here," he said. "The elevator doors around the other side are open and the car is there . . . shut down for the night. They must have taken the stairs."

"Won't that take them forever?"

"I seem to remember that the record for a run up *and* down is something like fifteen minutes. The bomb cage isn't that heavy—should be easy with a backpack."

"So we follow them up?"

"Looks it. I don't want to wait for a response crew to get here. We may not have the time."

"Okay." She slipped her gun into her pocket and bent to remove her shoes. "If we're going to climb it, let me get these off."

"I wonder how much time we have."

"Less than you think," said a tight voice behind them. "*Don't* move, pal. Place your gun down. Now, both of you, arms out to the side. Turn slowly."

They did as he said, and slowly turned to face the voice. They saw the pistol first: a Browning automatic with a long, black silencer. They looked at the man.

Felix Ross. Where did he come from? thought Bill. Outside? . . . Must have.

"I thought so. Keep those hands up!" He looked closely at Bill. "You're the guy who was up on Church Street. Now, who the hell are you and who are you with?"

Bill said nothing.

"Buddy. I think you just made a little mistake."

"Who are you?" asked Karen.

Ross ignored her and kept staring at Bill.

"Look, mister, who are you?" Her voice was no longer firm, but held a slight quaver.

"Doesn't matter who I am—you aren't going to be alive long enough for it to mean anything. We're just going to wait here until my partner comes down from upstairs."

"Look," she wailed. "I don't know what this is all about. This guy told me he had to see someone about a debt. He didn't say *anything* about people with guns. Leave me out of this, *please* leave me out of this. I won't tell anyone *anything*." She was almost sobbing.

What the hell's she talking about? thought Bill.

Karen had her hands out, palms up, beseeching. There were tears on her face as she slowly inched forward. "Look, *please* leave me out of this, I give you my word, I won't tell anyone anything. You won't hurt me, will you?"

She was three feet from him. "Please! Here, I'll turn around, you can tie me up."

Two feet away, she slowly started to turn, then accelerated. Suddenly, she had her back against his stomach, and his gun arm trapped over her shoulder in the crook of her right arm.

The swirl of motion continued as she fell forward. With the snap of breaking bones and the muffled ponk of a silenced gunshot, Ross arched up and over to slam into the floor. Karen came up on one knee, swept back his chin, and chopped at his neck with her other hand. He arched and slumped back, his body twitching. His gun arm had developed an extra elbow.

Karen rested on her hands and looked up at Bill. "I wouldn't have given an *ippon* for that throw, but we won't have him behind our backs."

Bill stared at her in wonder. "When you said—"

"So I lied to him, right? Don't look so shocked. You men go crazy for that helpless-woman act. What an idiot," she grumbled.

Bill shook his head. "Let's go on up, tiger."

Karen started to rise to her feet, then collapsed back to her knees. "Oh, damn!" she swore. "It's my ankle."

Bill bent and looked. There was a deep, torn gouge just below the bump of her ankle; he could see the whiteness of bone. He lifted her foot and she gave a stifled cry of pain. "Looks like Ross's gun went off as you threw him; you caught a glancing shot."

"Oh, damn." She leaned over to examine her foot. "Doesn't seem to be bleeding too badly." She tried again to get up, and gave another cry. "Ow, damn it!"

She sat back. "Looks like I'm stuck here. Damn, damn, damn!"

"Karen . . ."

"You go on up."

"Karen . . ."

"Oh, don't give me that crap, Bill; we don't have the time. I still have my gun." She pulled it from her pocket. "I'll be all right. Get up there."

He nodded and put his hand on the door. "Thanks."

"That's what dear friends are for, right? Good luck."

He paused in the gloom at the bottom of the stairs. "My partner," Ross had said. Singular. So maybe there was only one person up there, Bill thought. Just the owner of those legs that I saw in the car on Church Street. So what do I know about him? Nothing. Time to climb.

The stairway stretched upward. The monument was hollow inside, a square space, twenty-five feet on a side at the base. The elevator went up the middle, and the stairs went up around the outside. He could see across and upward eight flights or so in the dim, bluish light, but the metal mesh that enclosed the elevator works prevented him from leaning out into the shaftway to look up farther. Also keeps anyone from looking down, he thought.

There was a loud rumble from the heating system next to the elevator. An air plenum—a white, metal tube four feet in diameter—rose up and out of sight. The noise should mask my footsteps, he thought. It will also mask the bad guy's.

Assume he's made it to the top, Bill thought, and he's setting up the bomb. Get there as fast as you can. Five hundred and fifty feet; he started his run up.

The metal doorway at the top was slightly open. Bill backed against the outside wall and paused, trying to catch his breath. Quiet, listening . . . nothing. Only the sound of his breath and the rumble of the heating system, muted by the height.

He inched slowly closer to the doorway as his breath became quieter, until his ear was near the opening. Nothing; no clink of tools, no scuffing of feet.

He carefully pulled the door open with his foot.

Still no sound.

So what was the layout? Bill searched his memory. There were two levels up here. A lower one where the elevator loaded for the trip down. He seemed to remember a C-shaped corridor that ran around the solid metal elevator enclosure. Then narrow stairways at two corners that led upward to the upper observation level where the elevator deposited the arriving tourists.

So, how to enter? By the book. Breathe . . . one, two, three.

He slid through the doorway, down low, legs bent, gun clasped in two hands.

Nothing. He was in a narrow corridor, six feet wide, that went around the elevator core. Dim light from fluorescent tubes in the ceiling reflected from glass panels that protected the walls from graffiti.

He carefully checked the rest of the floor; no one there. So . . . he must be up on the next level, if he's here.

Two metal stairways led upward from the corner. Which one to take? Eeny, meeney . . . right.

He slowly mounted the stairs, crouching lower and lower as he went up to keep his head below the top of the stairs.

He paused just short of the top. A stone plaque was mounted into the wall there, one of a series of tributes that had lined the way up. It was from David Porter Heep, MD, 1853.

Doc, wish me luck.

He popped up so his eyes were above the floor level. No one in sight. He slowly, quietly climbed to the top of the stairs. The lamps up here were off; it was dark except for the spill from the flashing, red airplane clearance lights that shone out through holes in the tower tip ten feet up and the little bit of spotlight that came in through the narrow windows.

Bill stilled his breath and listened. He thought he heard a slight scrape of metal, but then there was quiet except for the slow heartbeat click of the airplane lights. Which way to go? The observation deck up here was partially obstructed by six-foot-wide buttresses—again covered with protective glass—stuck out from the outer walls.

He tried to think. Where were the elevator doors? Around the next corner. Slowly he inched ahead, straining to see in the darkness. Quiet, quiet, quiet. He tried to remember to breathe.

The other narrow stairway between the levels was to his right. That should mean the elevator exit is around the next corner.

Slowly, slowly he approached the corner. Breathe, he thought, and popped around the turn.

Nothing.

The elevator doors were open, the open shaft yawning wide, lined inside with faint traces of the blue light from the shaft below. In the flashing red light from above he saw an empty canvas backpack on the floor in the middle of the corridor. Maybe he's behind the next buttress, Bill thought. He moved over toward the outside wall and inched ahead. Quietly, quietly.

He approached the next buttress and paused. As he started to creep forward again he caught the faint reflection of movement in the glass in front of him and heard the faint whisper of wind from something traveling fast.

He's behind me! Bill threw himself to the left, but not fast enough. Something aiming for his head smashed into his wrist, knocking his gun from his grasp.

He rolled as he landed, then swiveled and came up on his feet, bracing himself on the ground with his good hand. A man stood there, five feet away, holding a long metal bar. There was a low chuckle.

"So, dark one, you're quick, but not quick enough. Who are you?"

Bill slowly stood. His gun hand was numb. He tried to flex it; nothing seemed broken. In the slow, flashing light he could start to see the details: strongly built, Asian, looks fifty or so . . . but very tough. Tough enough to laugh.

"Not a talker, eh? Americans are such talkers, acting like big bosses." The man reached out with his foot and kicked Bill's gun behind him into the corner. "Now you are in your proper place"—there was a glint as the man drew something from his waist—"and I am the master."

Who *is* this guy? thought Bill.

"Somehow, you have gotten past my guard downstairs. That must have taken some talent. But you show surprising lapses: never leave an unchecked stairway behind you." The man threw away the metal bar and raised the shining object in his other hand. "Come, butter breath. I plan to avenge my family, and you, certainly, are not one to stand in my way." A long, curving blade glittered there in the red light from above. "Let me teach you a lesson."

A sword, Bill thought, he's got a goddamned sword. He slowly backed up as the Asian man advanced.

"There is the elevator shaft behind you. You can jump, or

resist. Either way, you die, and block my task no longer." Despite his words, there was a sense of reserve and power about the man.

What to do, what to do? That quietness, Bill thought, he's a trained fighter, but he's arrogant. His arrogance shows he scorns me, he assumes I'm not trained; I may have one chance.

Bill moved back slowly, remembered Karen, and gave his right leg a slight stiffness, dragging it a bit.

"A cripple, it seems; not a proper challenge; but you are not worthy anyway." The man raised his sword sharply and Bill jumped back.

Look scared, he thought—hah, tough job. Make this guy think I'm always going to retreat. He backed slowly, letting his knee buckle a bit.

"You are close to your choice," said the man. "To jump and die, or stand and give me the pleasure of killing you."

Bill slowed. It's time. He let his right knee quiver.

The man brought his sword hand back and started it forward.

Now! thought Bill, and leapt toward rather than away from the blow. Inside the arc, he grabbed the man's right sleeve, blocking the blade's path.

Surprised, the man grasped Bill's jacket, trying to pull him to the side and clear his sword. They circled, struggling as Bill strained, trying to keep his grip on the man's sword arm.

They completed a half turn. Never become weapon dependent, Bill thought, and pushed hard against the man's chest.

It was not expected and the man resisted, pulling Bill toward him. Bill dropped, then went sharply upward with that pull, butting the top of his forehead against the man's nose.

It was an effective blow; stunned, he loosened his grip. Bill dropped down and grasped behind the man's ankles and pulled sharply. "Yaaah!" he yelled as he stood, flipping the man backward and out.

There was no answering cry. The body fell, disappearing into the void of the open shaftway.

Bill stood, shaking, breathing hard. And he tried to count to himself, ". . . two, three, four . . ." There was a faint crash from the darkness in front of him, then only the quiet rumble of the heating system.

"Never get weapon-dependent," Bill whispered softly. "I was close enough to get you, and you were only thinking of your stupid sword."

He turned. The bomb was there, sitting in the corner between the buttress and the wall: a small cage with metal shapes and wiring. Bill approached it cautiously. A red LED blinked slowly, counting out the time.

He picked up the flashlight that lay next to it. Do you remember the briefing? he thought. "Don't be a fool," he mumbled. "All it can do is kill you."

"Sweat the important stuff," he murmured to himself. "That's what I told Tina, isn't it?"

The wind picked up a bit and rustled a few stray papers on the street. The red lights of the FBI's cover vehicles flashed and reflected from the buildings around him. It was quiet again.

There were steps behind him. "They'll handle it from here," said the Admiral. "How are you feeling?"

Bill looked at his watch. Only two hours had passed. He shook his head;, is this finally over? "Fine."

He flexed his shoulders, then rubbed his neck. "I'm going to need more time than till Monday morning to give you an answer on that job. I want to rethink a lot of things."

"I want to get someone else for that assignment anyway, Bill."

"If it can wait, I might be able to do it for you."

"No . . ." The older man looked off into the flashing lights. "I'm not sure I'd want you for it in any case. I have to talk to Henry Simpson. I . . . want to use you for other things." He turned back and faced the younger man. "Take some time off; you've earned it. I can get someone else, someone else who's better suited for the task."

"If that's the way you want it."

"Come on back to my office; I think we both could do some damage to a fine, old bottle of bourbon I've been saving."

"No . . . I want to go over to the hospital and see Karen. They should be discharging her tonight or tomorrow morning. I'm going to get her to come up to the Vineyard with me; I think we've got some things to talk about. She's a good partner—

someone maybe I should have stuck with the first time around."

"When are you going to try to leave?"

"In a couple of days, as soon as she's mobile enough to deal with commercial air travel."

"That doesn't make much sense to me," said the Admiral; Bill gave him a sharp look: this was not an expected response and there was the ring of command in the older man's voice. "I'll have my driver take you up to the hospital to see Karen now," he continued, "and then tomorrow morning, you two will go on out to National. My plane will be there; you'll be on the Vineyard in an hour. Call your caretaker and tell him you're coming."

"Thanks." He looked up at the monument, its red lights pulsing slowly at the top, and then back at the Admiral. "Things got a little close there . . . for everyone. If we stay here in Washington, it'll be all congratulations, conferences, and postmortems . . . and the important thing for me *now* is to have some time alone with her. They won't need us here, at least not for a while. Karen and I could use the time."

The Admiral regarded him quietly. "Are you coming back?"

"I—"

"We could use you." He spoke softly. "I'd like you back. But you decide."

"We'll see." Bill smiled at him. "It's a job."